GEORGIA HILL

I used to live in London, where I worked in the theatre. Then I got the bizarre job of teaching road safety to the U.S. navy – in Marble Arch! A few years ago, I did an 'Escape to the Country'. I now live in a tiny Herefordshire village, where I scandalise the neighbours by not keeping 'country hours' and being unable to make a decent pot of plum jam. Home is a converted oast house, which I share with my two beloved spaniels, husband (also beloved) and a ghost called Zoe. I've been lucky enough to travel widely, though prefer to set my novels closer to home. Perhaps more research is needed? I've always wanted to base a book in the Caribbean! I am addicted to Belgian chocolate, Jane Austen and, most of all, Strictly Come Dancing. Keep dancing, everyone!

www.georgiahill.co.uk

@georgiawrites

While I Was Waiting

GEORGIA HILL

Harper*Impulse* an imprint of
HarperCollins*Publishers* Ltd
1 London Bridge Street
London SE1 9GF

www.harpercollins.co.uk

A Paperback Original 2015

First published in Great Britain in ebook format by Harper*Impulse* 2015

A catalogue record for this book is
available from the British Library

ISBN: 9780008123260

This novel is entirely a work of fiction.
The names, characters and incidents portrayed in it are
the work of the author's imagination. Any resemblance to
actual persons, living or dead, events or localities is
entirely coincidental.

Automatically produced by Atomik ePublisher from Easypress

Printed and bound in Great Britain

For Geoff. I'm so glad I waited.

Prologue

June 1963, Clematis Cottage, Stoke St Mary, Herefordshire

I am really not sure why I am writing this. A foolish whim by a foolish old lady and it will probably sit in a box unread and decay much like its writer when Death makes his careless decision. But perhaps someone will find it. Someone will care enough to read it and somehow I know this is what will happen.

Hetty snorted and slammed down her fountain pen. Pompous stuff! She could hear Richard saying the very same thing. He had always hated any whiff of pretension. She smiled. Richard and Edward. The aunts. Papa. Dear Peter. She hadn't allowed herself to think of them all for such a long time – had been too busy tagging on to other people's lives. She sat back to ease her stiff shoulders. Gazing at the view from the window in the sitting room, where she had placed her desk, she realised she had always been squeezed into other people's lives.

'A veritable cuckoo,' she said out loud to the emptiness. 'I've never, until now, had the luxury of being myself, of having my own life, as I want it.' She glanced around the sitting room of her little cottage. 'And I've never had a home of my own until I moved here.'

It was all the fault of that pesky young curate at the village church. He was the one who had suggested that she write up her life. He seemed to think she'd had an eventful one – she'd certainly lived through a time of great change, of great tragedy.

She picked up the pen again.

I was a young girl when I went to the big house ...

Chapter 1

She was mad, they'd said. Utterly mad.

Rachel stood with her hands on her hips and surveyed her new home. Buying this little house was the only truly impulsive thing she had ever done. She swallowed; there was no going back. It was all hers now. Clematis Cottage belonged to her.

The house in question was tiny: little more than a two-up, two-down but pleasingly symmetrical, with windows flanking a satisfyingly solid red front door. A straight path led up through what must have once been an old-fashioned garden.

That was the good news.

It had been six months since Rachel had seen it last. She'd forgotten the ivy growing up the walls and across the windows – choking the brickwork and stealing the light. She'd forgotten the crazily dangling guttering. She'd forgotten the five-foot-high weeds obliterating the front garden.

She was mad, they'd said. Perhaps she was.

Rachel turned her back on the house and faced its view instead. This was what had sold it. The cottage stood on rising land, some way from the rest of the village of Stoke St Mary and could be reached only by a rutted track. The farmland behind sloped gently upwards, but in front of the house there was nothing but glorious open countryside.

The estate agent had said that spring was when Herefordshire was at its finest. Mr Foster had been a nice old boy, very different from the gelled-up-haired and shiny-suited types in London and she'd dismissed him as eccentric. She'd been wrong. She'd first seen the cottage in October and thought the landscape beautiful then, clothed in crimson and brown. But now, in early April, it was magnificent.

To her right she could see the baldy-smooth Brecon Beacons and beyond the jagged mountains of Wales loomed. Her eyes followed a sweep of hill to where the river valley sank and then rose again towards the east. Isolated houses were dotted about burnt-sienna fields, vast patches of a yellow so vivid it hurt her eyes interspersed ploughed fields and the apple orchards yet to blaze with blossom.

The furniture removers had finally gone. They'd backed the van, in a haze of dust and diesel fumes, down the track that led to the village and the outside world. Rachel felt her shoulders drop and exhaustion creep in. She turned back to scrutinise her new home once again. Behind it, the curving slopes of farmland seduced. Each field, green or red, was shining with fertile promise. Rachel tried not to look at the roof of the cottage; the choking moss and missing tiles were a symphony of neglect and future expense.

Was she mad? Her friends might yet be right. When she'd announced her decision to leave London and set up home in this tiny village in an isolated part of an isolated county they had forecast doom, gloom and a hasty retreat back to 'civilisation'. No matter how much she tried to persuade them, they all thought it was a mistake.

A cottage?

In where?

On your own?

But Rachel was to be thirty soon. That's when people made changes, she'd told them, made big, life-changing decisions. That

4

her parents had announced their imminent departure to spend their retirement in the Algarve and had given her a lump sum in advance of her inheritance, had seemed like fate dealing her a hand. It had been the catalyst for change. She'd grown weary of London, anyway, and of the men who just wanted to play games and hurt her in the process. She wanted a simpler life; somewhere she could work uninterrupted. And maybe, just maybe, she would get the chance to become a new person – reinvent herself.

'But won't you miss all this?' Best friend, Jyoti, gestured to the packed cocktail bar they were in. Rachel scanned the crowd. To her it looked full of men on the pull for another empty conquest. It made her queasy. She'd met Charles in a bar like this – and he'd screwed with her head and then cheated on her. If he was typical of London men, she was in no hurry to meet another.

She smiled at Jyoti over her margarita and thought hard before answering. When she'd moved to London as a student, she'd seen every play and gone to every exhibition and museum she could afford. Now she lived in a flat in the dusty suburbs of south-east London and rarely went to the West End. This was the first trip for ages. She simply didn't feel the need any more.

'I won't be that far from Birmingham and I think there's an arts centre in Ludlow – that's only half an hour away and Malvern has some good pre-West End things on.'

'But won't you be lonely, sweet-pea? You'll not even be in the actual village itself, will you?' Kind-eyed Tim was concerned. Secretly so was Rachel, but with her small circle of friends coupling, moving abroad, having babies, Rachel was lonely now and too proud to admit it. She thought she might as well be lonely somewhere beautiful.

So she had sold her little London flat and bought Clematis Cottage. She had been shocked by what little her money would buy, even when it had been swollen by her parents' gift. She was self-employed too, meaning that a bigger mortgage was difficult. Last year, she had been bumped up the steep track by a Mr Foster of Grant, Foster and Fitch Estate Agents to be shown Clematis Cottage. And she had fallen instantly, irrevocably in love. It had been the biggest decision she had ever made and it might be the biggest mistake. But she was determined to prove everyone wrong, including herself. With hands back on hips in a defiant gesture, she abandoned thinking and looked to the view that had been the deal-maker. She would make a success of this – she knew she would.

She thought back to kindly old Mr Foster's words. When it had become apparent that she was seriously intent on buying the cottage, the comfortably rotund estate agent had seemed worried.

'It's an awful lot of work to be taking on, dear girl.' He looked doubtfully at her high-heeled suede boots and thin jacket. 'And with you being on your own. You'll have a survey done, I expect?'

'Erm, I don't know,' Rachel had said, feeling foolish, 'It might put me off.'

Mr Foster gave her a steely look and sighed. 'Here,' he scribbled something on the back of his business card. 'It's the number of Mike Llewellyn. He's a builder, but he'll turn his hand to most things. He lives in the village and he knows the house. He's not the cheapest, but he's reliable and he does a good job.'

Rachel had thanked him and stored the card away in her bag. In the months since she'd last seen it, the cottage had taken on an unrealistically romantic air in her mind and she had forgotten just how much work it needed. She was glad she'd kept the number.

Brought back to the present by some crows flying overhead, cawing as they went, she closed her eyes and listened for a moment. Those who claimed that the countryside was silent were lying, but it was certainly peaceful. The air was full of sound. She could hear birds; she recognised a blackbird's melodious tune, somewhere in the distance there was a tractor gearing up and nearer, the noisy lowing of cows. The wind got up and she could hear it making the trees on the hill behind the cottage shiver. It made a change from emergency sirens and the incessantly thumping bass from her London neighbour. The breeze lifted her hair and cooled her neck. She was glad; it had been a warm day to be moving house. All in all it had gone smoothly. True, she hadn't got her washing machine plumbed in, she was without a landline and couldn't coax the boiler into life, but the removal men had been hard-working, cheerful and nothing had been broken.

That she knew of.

They had been surprisingly good company, but she had wanted them gone long before the day was out. She flexed her tense shoulders, glad to be, at last, completely on her own.

Rachel tore herself away from the view and turned to explore her new home. As she did, she caught sight of a man striding up the rough track. To her intense irritation he stopped when he got to her and joined in her examination of the cottage.

'You do need me. Mr Foster was right.'

Rachel stared at him. Her first impression was of gold and brown. He had longish hair, burnished treacle by the sun and tied back in an untidy ponytail. He was tall and lean with smoothly tanned skin and looked to be in his early twenties.

The man smiled and showed even white teeth. 'Always said this place had the best view in the village. You could put up with a lot for that.' He held out a long-fingered, capable-looking hand. 'I'm Gabe Llewellyn. Mr Foster said you might be needing my services.' His voice was deep and humorous and only slightly softened by a rural accent.

Rachel shook his hand warily. She was surprised to find it cool and dry and very firm. It was at odds with his grubby and sweaty-looking orange t-shirt. The name Llewellyn was familiar, though. 'If I was expecting anyone, it would be a Mike Llewellyn.' She was tired and it was an effort to speak. Wincing, she realised how rude she sounded.

Her tone didn't seem to faze him. 'That's my Dad. He's just finishing a job over Hereford way. Thought I'd come and take a quick look round, see what needs doing. Easier to see before you unpack your stuff.' To her surprise, he seemed to pick up on her mood. 'Sorry. Were you looking for a bit of peace and quiet? Long day when you're moving, I reckon.'

Even though he was being surprisingly sensitive, Rachel couldn't shift into politeness. 'Yes it has been,' she said stiffly. 'What did you say your name was?'

'Gabe.' He suddenly looked defensive. 'Short for Gabriel.' When Rachel looked blank he explained further. 'Mum had a bit of a Thomas Hardy thing going on, when she was pregnant. Just as well I was a boy. Would get a bit of stick down The Plough if I was called Bathsheba!'

Ridiculously, his knowledge of one of England's greatest writers had the effect of reassuring Rachel. She relented – he probably wouldn't take long after all. 'I suppose you can come in,' she said, aware that she still sounded churlish. Gabe looked at her hopefully. After a day spent with the removal men she knew the ropes. 'I'll put the kettle on, shall I?'

His grin widened and his brown eyes crinkled attractively. 'Sweet. If I don't have a look now, don't know when I'll get round to it. Busy time. Been working all day.' He gestured to the sky. 'Been making the most of the weather.'

It explained his scruffy appearance. And the faint whiff of masculine sweat.

'I'll just get the truck; I left it at the bottom of the track out of the way of Dave Firmin's blokes. Dave's been known to run into things.' Gabe laughed. 'I'll have a look at that old boiler first. Been empty a while, this place. Pressure will have gone, I bet. You'll need to get some oil delivered as well. Got some in the truck, though, which might see you through for the time being.'

Oh God, another thing to think about, but if he got the boiler working she could have a hot bath tonight. The idea of a long bubble bath made Rachel smile with relief. Gabe grinned again. He held her eyes for a moment and then swung round and, with an easy stride, loped back down the track to get his truck.

Gabe proved to be both thorough and relentless in his inspection of the cottage; another surprise, she had expected him to be neither. Two hours later he had got the boiler going and had disappeared into the attic to have a look at the inside of the roof.

Rachel made them both yet more tea and then, leaving him to it, unearthed a sweater and took her drink to sit out on the front step. She seemed to have been drinking tea all day and was sick of it, but it was a comfort of a sort.

Gabe eventually joined her. She'd left him investigating some possible damp. He sat beside her companionably and began totting up the estimate of work on the back of a tatty envelope.

'I'll get Dad to give you a proper costing in a few days, but this'll give you an idea.' When he handed it over she blanched.

'Tell you what,' Gabe said, when he saw her expression, 'Some things don't need doing straight away.'

Again, he seemed to have a knack of tapping into what she was thinking. It made her curious about him and she wondered what had caused him to be so sensitive to people's moods.

'The roof'll need fixing, though,' he went on, 'that corner's been letting in water for a good while, I reckon. But you don't need to do everything at once and it'll give you a chance to pay for things gradually too.' He shrugged. 'Dad and I can't do most of the work immediately anyway, we're booked up, so it'll give you a chance to think it over. Oh,' he said, as an afterthought, 'I found this.' He reached around behind him and handed her a large tin. 'Found it in the attic, tucked behind the water tank and covered with a wasps' nest.'

Rachel took the box from him. Once upon a time it must have held biscuits; she could just make out the name Huntley and Palmer underneath the rust. 'What is it?'

'I didn't look inside.' He drained his mug and began to gather his pen, tape measure and tools together.

It was getting late and Rachel shivered. The evening spring light had fooled her into thinking it was much earlier. Perversely, now Gabe was about to go, she wanted him to stay around. Stranger that he was, she was afraid of having to face up to her responsibilities alone. Wrestling her thoughts away from an expensive new roof, she turned all her attention to the tin in her lap. She smoothed a hand over its side – it felt cool and rough and snagged at her soft fingertips. With a struggle, she wrenched the lid off, cutting her thumb on a sharp edge in the process. 'Damn,' she cursed. She always took special care of her hands; they were her precious commodity.

To her surprise, Gabe took her hand in his and examined the wound. 'You want to clean that up. You can get some nasty infections from rusty old metal, take it from me.'

He bent over her thumb. 'Doesn't look too bad, but make sure you treat it as soon as you can.'

She could feel his breath warm on her wrist. He was very near and an urge to run her fingers through his silky hair overcame her. Disconcerted, she snatched her hand out of his and then regretted it. Blaming it on tiredness, she pulled herself together and moved fractionally away from him.

'So, is there anything in the tin?' he asked cheerfully, shoving his stuff into his work belt. 'Jewellery? Gold? Or just spiders?' He laughed.

Rachel shuddered. 'Don't joke, I've got a thing about spiders.'

'Would you like me to have a look first? I don't mind them.'

'Thank you,' she smiled, 'that's really kind of you but it's okay.' She peered inside, almost afraid of what she might find. Taking a deep breath and sucking her injured thumb, she gingerly lifted out a package. It was heavy and wrapped in some dull, greasy material. She unpeeled a corner and something fell out. A postcard. 'I think it's a book and papers of some sort, postcards and things. Old, though. This one's dated 1965.' She held it to the light and read out the message: 'Weather delightful, food excellent. Hotel pictured on front. All my love, P.' Rachel flipped the postcard over and laughed. 'Oh, it's Brighton sea front. It hasn't changed much.'

'Wouldn't know, never been,' Gabe said absently, but his interest had obviously been sparked. 'Who's it to?'

'Mrs H. Lewis, Clematis Cottage.' Rachel looked at Gabe. 'Oh it's to here! To someone who lived here!'

Gabe smiled at her delight. 'Yes, suppose it would be. There was a woman who lived here once. Think she was called Mrs Lewis. Lived here for years.' He smoothed a lock of hair behind his ears. 'Looks like you've found some of her stuff.' He peered over her shoulder. 'It's fascinating, isn't it? What else is in there?'

Rachel removed the rest of the fabric, the old smell making her nose prickle. She wasn't sure she wanted to touch it but she wanted to get at what it was protecting.

'It *is* a book,' she cried and laid it in her lap. Opening the first few pages she saw it was a collection of writings, a few photographs, drawings, a few of which had been carefully stuck into the pages of the book. Rachel turned to the front page:

'Henrietta Trenchard-Lewis, Her Life.'

she read off the frontispiece.

She looked thoughtfully at the postcard. 'I ought to give it all back to her.'

'Can't, lovely, she died a few years back. She lived to a ripe old age, though.'

'Oh, that's sad.'

'Sad? Oh I don't know. I think she had a pretty long and full life. She was a right character, by all accounts. Used to give them what for at the home she ended up in. Had two husbands, bit of an old dragon I've been told. Terrorised the neighbourhood.'

Rachel looked at him curiously. 'Did you know her?'

'I vaguely remember a really old woman on a bicycle – that must have been her. Always wore black. I kept well clear of her.' He grinned, boyishly. 'I was scared of her, to be honest.'

'Were there any children? Perhaps they'd like to have it. I know

I would if it were my mother's.' Rachel began to leaf through the papers again. It seemed to be a barely begun scrapbook of sorts, with a mixture of an odd assortment of documents: pages cut from an exercise book, some closely covered with tiny handwriting, more postcards, a few faded sepia-tinted photographs. Then she found, slipped to the bottom of the tin, a bundle of letters tied with a faded velvet ribbon.

'Don't know. Mr Foster'll know about that, probably. Who did you buy the place off, then?' He rubbed a hand over his face in a weary gesture and stifled a yawn. 'Sorry, it's been a long day.'

'A firm of solicitors. Brigsty and Smith.'

'I know them. In Ludlow?' He raised his brow at Rachel in enquiry and she nodded. 'Well, they'll know what you do with it.' He glanced at his watch – an expensive one, glistening on a very suntanned arm. As he raised his hand the golden hairs on his sinewy forearm caught the light from the late-evening sun. 'Better be off. Way past opening time and the first pint isn't gonna touch the sides. I'll be round next week with the job spec and I'll fix up a date to see to the roof.' He rose to his feet to go, but hesitated and looked down at her. Perhaps he sensed her loneliness. 'Do you, erm, do you want to come down the pub? It's a nice friendly crowd. Meet some of your new neighbours.'

Rachel shook her head. 'No, too tired. Off to have a long soak in some very hot water, thanks to you. Thank you so much for all you've done, Gabe.' She smiled up at him with genuine gratitude for the first time. Their eyes met and a frisson of something, some expectation, passed between them.

He gave her an odd look. 'No probs. Are you going to be, you know, alright on your own?'

She nodded. 'I'll be fine. Thank you.'

'See you, then. Oh, and don't forget to see to that cut.' With that, he swung himself into his pick-up, this year's registration, she noticed. He and his father must be doing well. And with a wave and a cloud of dust he skidded down the track.

Rachel stared after the Toyota for some time. An intriguing man. And kind. Even though he'd had a long day and was obviously tired, he'd gone out of his way to help. Unsophisticated, yes, but incredibly sensitive and thoughtful. Honest too. No game-playing there. She'd never met anyone quite like him before.

She blew out a long breath. At last she was on her own. But, somehow, now she had what she thought she wanted, the weight of her alone-ness was oppressive. Rising stiffly, she turned her back on the promise of a glorious sunset to go into the house.

'You'll be happy here. I was.'

The voice had her whirling around again, heart thumping. No one there. Standing frozen, Rachel listened. Nothing. She shook her head. Must have been the wind in the trees. On edge and blaming tiredness, she went into the house.

She put the tin in the kitchen. She didn't want to look through the contents tonight. It didn't feel right somehow, not when it might belong to someone else. And besides, she had other more pressing things to do.

Chapter 2

In the village's only pub, The Plough, Gabe's late arrival was met with raucous cheers. The gang had been there for well over an hour and were onto their fourth round. Gabe's first two pints of Stella were downed in swift succession, until he felt he was beginning to catch up.

'So where've you been, then, our Gabriel?' Kevin, his best mate since school, put an arm around Gabe's shoulders and peered into his empty pint pot. 'Oi, Paul,' he yelled at the man, standing at the bar, trying to chat up Dawn the barmaid. 'Stop pissin' about and get us another round in. Boy's dyin' of thirst over yere.'

Paul gestured what he thought of Kevin and returned to Dawn.

'Wanker,' Kevin said affectionately. 'He's got no chance there. She fancies you, though.'

'Shut up, Kev.' Gabe shrugged off Kevin's arm and tore open a bag of crisps with his teeth. It had been a long day and he was starving.

'No, it's the truth. Her sister told me. Dawn fancies the pants off yer.' Kevin grinned myopically. He never wore his glasses for a Friday-night drinking session on account of the times he'd fallen over on the way home from the pub and smashed them. 'Mind, never met a bird with a heartbeat who didn't fancy you.' Kevin's good mood left him abruptly. 'Could do with spreading some of that Llewellyn charm around boy, to those of us who ain't got none.'

Gabe shrank from his mate's beer breath. God, he hated it when Kev got maudlin like this – a sure sign of too much beer drunk too quickly. He wished, not for the first time, that Kevin would learn to pace himself. For some time he'd felt he was outgrowing his old school friend. They had little in common nowadays. Gabe wanted more than just a pint on a Friday in the local. He wanted some of the big wide world that had blown in with Rachel. He loved his family and the village, but it was beginning to stifle him. If he stayed working for his father much longer, he'd end up stuck here. He frowned. Not much chance of chasing his dreams at the moment, though.

'So where've you been, then?' Kevin persisted. 'I rang your old woman and she said you was up at that empty cottage on the ridge.'

'Yeah, I was.'

'Doing what, then?'

'Getting a job costed.' Gabe wished Paul would hurry up with the drinks. Another pint would keep Kev quiet for the next ten minutes and he was seriously getting on Gabe's nerves. For some reason he wasn't ready to talk about Rachel to him. To anyone. Not just yet.

'I heard as some woman's moved in. Some toffee-nosed tart from London. Bloody incomers.'

Gabe nodded in agreement. This was an old hobby horse of Kevin's and the easiest thing to do with him in this mood was to go along with it. 'Might be a bit of work coming your way though, mate. The place is in hell of a state.' Kev's prejudices didn't extend to him turning down casual labouring when offered.

'What's she like, then?'

'Who?'

Kevin gave a melodramatic sigh. 'The woman what's moved in, that's who.'

Gabe thought back to his first sight of Rachel. He could see her so clearly that, for one mad moment, he thought she'd taken up

15

his invitation after all and joined them in the pub. He remembered how her hair swung over her face and hid those extraordinary grey eyes, the way she hardly ever smiled, but when she did it was worth waiting for, her height and slenderness, her elegance even in dusty jeans and a baggy sweater. She'd felt exotic. There was no one around here quite like her.

She was like a long, cool glass of water, he decided, or more like an icy one, for she hadn't been that friendly. Far too self-contained. Shame. Still, he could work on that. Kevin had been right about the Llewellyn charm. Girls liked something about him and, although he'd never fathomed out quite what, it had never failed him yet. He gave Kevin a quick glance. 'Oh she was alright. Bit toffee-nosed, like.'

'Bet she fancied you.'

'Oh, shut up, Kev.'

Chapter 3

The following Monday morning, Rachel rang Mr Foster, who explained that Mrs Trenchard-Lewis had died several years ago in a local nursing home and that Rachel would need to contact the solicitors about her find. He also said that the house had been cleared and, as it was unlikely the tin contained anything valuable, she could probably keep it.

'The house was sold complete with chattels, wasn't it?' He didn't sound as interested as she thought he might be, but she could hear voices in the background and several phones ringing, so maybe he was having a busy day. She thought back to the worm-infested kitchen table and the two bookshelves that constituted 'the chattels'. 'Erm, yes.'

'Well, especially as there seem to be no descendants to make a claim, I would have thought the box is rightfully yours. Do let me know if there's anything of interest in there, I'm quite keen on local history. I do apologise, Miss Makepeace, but I must go, the office is getting rather hectic.'

Rachel thanked him and a further call to the solicitors confirmed that the tin was, indeed, her legal possession.

Over the next few days it lay on the kitchen table, hidden by the mess that had accompanied the house move. Stuff that, try hard as she might, she couldn't find a home for. The tin and its intriguing contents remained undisturbed; she had other things to do. Rachel was desperate to get organised. She liked order and she liked everything in its place. No, she admitted to herself with a smile, she *craved* order and until she had everything sorted there was no hope of doing any work. And if she didn't work, she may as well give up on the idea of living in the cottage completely; she'd never make the mortgage.

So for the next three days she toiled long hours into the night to replace the chaos and unpacked boxes with calm and organisation. On the third attempt to scrub the sitting-room floor, the first two efforts being not to her satisfaction, she sat back and grinned. She remembered, long ago, Tim claiming she was getting far too much like her mother. That her perfectionism would risk her ending up alone, with only cats for company. She didn't need a psychoanalyst to tell her it was an attempt to live up to her mother's intolerance to mess or dirt of any kind. Paula Makepeace was fanatical. She'd gone through dozens of cleaners, as none of them did the job to her exacting standards. No one came up to Paula's standards – in any way – and that included Rachel. She didn't know how her father coped.

She gave a shrug, pausing only long enough to turn up the radio, and scrubbed even harder.

Thanks to Gabe, the boiler continued to produce copious amounts of scalding hot water and, after a day's cleaning and sorting, Rachel was only too glad of a long soak in the bath. As she lay there, listening to Radio Three and the sounds of the cottage settling quietly for the night, she mulled over what she was going to do with her new home.

The kitchen she was going to leave more or less as it was, once she'd brightened it with paint. She liked its old-fashioned, unfitted quality and the quarry tiles and wooden plate rack, which she suspected were original. She would get the old table mended; she guessed it was oak and too good to simply throw out. Her own electric cooker looked out of place, but the long-desired Aga would have to wait.

She looked around the bathroom as she idly blew soap bubbles. The tiles were pale green – not very exciting, but liveable with. The suite was old-fashioned but thankfully white and the bath was deep, with enormous taps. She lacked the power shower that had got her through so many sticky days in the city but, again, that would have to wait.

The rest of the house was, thanks to her hard work, becoming grime-free and small though the rooms might be, some good-looking floorboards had been revealed. A sander would do the trick, she thought dreamily, and then it would be the home of her dreams.

Eventually.

She put Gabe Llewellyn and his long list of expensive repairs firmly to the back of her mind and blew another bubble.

Below her, the old house shifted in agreement.

Chapter 4

In the end, it was almost two weeks later when the Toyota came revving up the track. It was another yellow spring day full of the unadulterated light that Rachel was slowly getting used to. She'd been working in the sitting room, which had a commanding view from the front of the cottage. It received good, useful light for most of the day.

She watched as Gabe and another man got out of the truck and held an animated conversation. There was much pointing at the roof, which Rachel felt was ominous. With a frown, she left her drawing board and went to greet her visitors. She opened the front door just as Gabe went to lift the rusty old knocker.

For a second his hand hung comically in mid air, then he grinned. 'Hi. Erm, this is my dad. Dad, this is Rachel.'

The older man nodded his head in a quick greeting. 'Mike Llewellyn. Pleased to meet you.' They shook hands briefly. He looked from Rachel to his son and then back again. He smiled, making his eyes crinkle like his son's. 'Gabe said there was quite a lot of work to be done on the old place, so I've come to have a look myself.'

He was a shorter, wirier version of Gabe, but lacked his son's laid-back charm.

'Sorry we couldn't get to you earlier,' with this he gave Gabe a meaningful look. 'Another job went on a bit, like.'

Ever since moving in, Rachel had done little else but clean, scrub, unpack and sort her belongings, not to mention wait around for the phone to be connected, the oil delivery to be made and for the sander she'd hired to be delivered. This was the very first morning she had felt able to sit down and do some work, real paying work, not the sketching and watercolours she found herself lured into doing by the seductive view. The last thing she wanted to do today was play host to builders. The roof would probably be fine. It hadn't leaked once since she'd moved in, conveniently forgetting it hadn't rained either. Rachel looked at their expectant faces, so alike in expression, and sighed inwardly. They were here now and her concentration was already interrupted. If they were quick, she could get back to her work by lunchtime. 'You'd better come in, then, I suppose,' she said and led them into the cottage's sitting room.

'This has changed a bit!' Gabe looked around, admiringly. 'You've been busy.'

Rachel followed his gaze around the room. She had worked her hardest in here, keen to get her working area organised. A rug lay over the newly scrubbed and sanded floorboards. She'd even got around to painting them – a pale yellowy cream. She'd set up her bookshelves in the alcoves on either side of the fireplace and they were overflowing with her beloved art books. She'd even had time to hang her favourite prints. A Georgia O' Keeffe still life looked down from over the mantelpiece – the best sort of company. The room was restful, colourful – just how she liked it.

Gabe walked to her drawing board, positioned neatly in front of the uncurtained sash window and fingered her pencils. 'What do you do?'

Rachel hurried over and nudged him out of the way. She shut her sketchbook and flipped the cloth over her drawing board. She hated people seeing her work until she felt it was finished, perfect. Or as perfect as she could make it.

'I'm an illustrator. Freelance. I do drawings for magazines, books. That sort of thing.' In a nervous gesture she put her pencils back into their size order and turned her back on the window, her hands resting defensively on the now safely covered drawing board.

Gabe looked at her intently. 'Never would have guessed.'

'What?'

'That you were the creative sort.'

Not many people did, thought Rachel. She often wondered what it was about her that made them think she wasn't artistic.

'So where would I see your work?'

Rachel was beginning to feel hounded. Christ, would he let go? To fend him off she resorted to the truth. 'Well,' she admitted through clenched teeth, 'Most of my bread-and- butter work is greetings cards.'

'Is that so?' Mike came to join them and picked up a pile of drawings due to be sent off for approval. 'These are nice. Your mum would like these,' he said to Gabe as he studied the watercolours of poppies and irises. 'You're good.'

Gabe peered at the drawings. He took one from Mike and examined it. 'You're *really* good. These are fantastic. Realistic, but you've made the flowers look almost like people reaching up to the sun. Yearning for it. For its life force.'

Mike harrumphed, obviously embarrassed. 'Don't take any notice of Gabriel, Rachel. He talks like this on occasion.'

Rachel was taken aback at Gabe's perceptiveness. He was right; that was exactly the effect she'd been after. Another side to this intriguing man. However, she now felt thoroughly invaded.

'Thank you,' she managed as she snatched them back. 'Come into the kitchen and I'll put the kettle on. I was just about to make myself some tea.'

'Well, if it's all the same with you, me and Gabe's got to get over to Ludlow later on today so we'd like a look round now. The tea can wait, lovely.' Mike grinned his son's smile.

She felt a knot of panic form and frowned. 'But Gabe's already

22

done a quote.'

Mike held up his hand. 'I know, but we were thinking. Place has been empty for a good few years now. Good chance the wiring'll need doing and you might want central heating put in.'

'I thought I'd just make do with a real fire in here.' She looked to where her saggy old sofa, with its deep-red throws, was placed optimistically in front of the open fireplace.

Mike snorted. 'Might change your mind come winter. Windy old spot up on the ridge, this is.' Then he saw her anxious expression and relented. 'Well, if you want a fire best to get that chimney swept and get that done in the summer.'

'Oh.' Yet another job to add to her list. It was all too much. Rachel felt her knees weaken and she sat down on the arm of a chair. It groaned in sympathy.

Gabe tugged at a long lock of hair that had escaped his pony-tail. 'Don't scare her, Dad. Look, Rachel, as I said the other day, you can get things done in stages. Don't have to do it all at once. I brought Dad up so as he could sort a timetable for you. He's better at that than me.'

'What, working to a deadline? Never been your strong point, has it Gabriel?' Mike laughed.

Rachel saw Gabe blow out a breath. He looked tense. She wondered if father and son had problems working together. She suddenly felt sorry for him. He'd had his bubbly and genuine enthusiasm quashed and he looked defeated. Rachel knew about lack of confidence – she knew all about how hard it was to try to be the son or daughter your parent really wanted. It was something she'd spent most of her life attempting – and at which she had spectacularly failed. In their brief acquaintance, Gabe had been nothing but kindness itself and, although she suspected that the kindness was going to cost her a fortune, she found she wanted to reciprocate.

'You'd better follow me, then,' she said, resigned to her fate and rose to lead them upstairs.

23

Two hours later they were sitting at the kitchen table, drinking the inevitable tea. Rachel had never felt so stripped or so exposed. It was one thing to have Gabe look over her house when there were only packing cases in it; it was another when most of her belongings were out on show.

The two men had inspected every inch of the house. They had spent twenty minutes inspecting the wall in the back bedroom, with much tutting and discussion, and had proclaimed damp. To her dismay, they had even poked about in the bathroom, as Gabe had thought he'd seen a silverfish invasion. She bit her lip. From the way they were talking, she would have their company for some considerable time. She wondered if she was being taken for a ride but had no prior experience to go on. Her London flat had never needed any work so she hadn't a clue if the men were talking sense or inventing jobs for themselves.

Uncannily, Gabe again seemed to sense her mood. He turned from his father and said, 'You can ask around, for references and the like. The Garths up at the farm had us in to do a fair bit of work last year; they'll tell you if we're ripping you off.'

Rachel smiled at him, embarrassed at being so transparent but grateful. 'I – ' she began.

Mike had been poring over scribbles in a notebook and interrupted, ''Bout four months' work here, more if you wants heating put in.'

'Four months!' Rachel sat back in disbelief. She saw her independent and solitary life leaking away.

'Well, might take less if we do it all at once, but you say you don't want that?'

Rachel shook her head at Mike. 'No, and to be honest, I can't afford to have it all done at once.'

Mike smiled. 'Well, we don't expect payment straight away. Trust works both ways in this game. You trust us to do a good job and we have to trust you to pay us eventually, like. We'll better get off then, our Gabe.' He stood and then looked down at her. 'We'll leave you to think it over.'

Rachel nodded. 'I'll get back to you. I'll need to get a few more quotes, you know.' God, this was so embarrassing, but this is what you did, wasn't it? You didn't just take on a firm of builders without checking out the competition?

Mike looked from his son to Rachel and gave a cryptic smile. He nodded.

Gabe spoke. 'Yes, well of course you need to do that. Ask the Garths as well, number's in the book. Get back to us when you can.'

'By the end of next week would be better,' Mike interjected. 'Otherwise we might not be able to fit her in along with the Halliday job.'

Rachel had had enough. She rose decisively. 'I'll ring you on Friday, then. And now I think we've all got things to do?'

She saw them out and, before the Toyota could be heard grinding down the track, was hunting through the Yellow Pages.

Later that week Rachel took a pot of mint tea into the sitting room and collapsed on the sofa in front of the fireplace. The weather had turned cloudy and it was a clammy but chilly sort of an evening. If she could trust the chimney, she'd risk lighting a fire, but remembered Mike Llewellyn's words that it would need sweeping first. She made do with her little electric radiator and wrinkled her nose against the dusty smell as it heated up.

The cottage had a strange atmosphere this evening and she needed comfort. Last night, her heart thumping, she'd woken up to sounds outside – some kind of screeching. Common sense told her it was probably an owl or something, but it had sounded disconcertingly like a person in pain. It had taken hours to get back to sleep and she'd become very aware of being alone in a remote place. Today she had wanted to continually look over her shoulder, certain someone was there. She wasn't entirely sure she believed in ghosts, but there was definitely a weird atmosphere in the cottage sometimes. Putting it down to tiredness, she tried to shrug off her mood and took a sip of tea. She shivered. Perhaps it would be nice to have central heating after all.

After thinking through what Mike and Gabe had said, she was resigned to the inevitable; that the house needed work. A lot of work. So she had applied herself in her usual methodical and thorough way and had tried to get some comparable quotations for the job. But her search for other builders had proved fruitless. Two firms were unable to visit for another month; another local one had managed to come and had then quoted a price far higher than the Llewellyns'; one said they were fully booked for the next three months and yet another hadn't even bothered to reply to the messages she'd left on their answering service.

'Looks like it'll be the Llewellyn boys, then,' she said to no one in particular and tried to warm her hands around her mug. 'It shouldn't be too bad,' she went on, forcing herself to be optimistic, 'as long as I can find a way of working around them.'

She already had some work overdue, inevitably delayed by moving house. She was also getting far too distracted by the sumptuous countryside around the cottage. 'I wonder if I could combine the two,' she murmured. 'Who would like some stunning landscapes?'

Rachel shook her head and laughed. It felt like madness talking to an empty room but, in some peculiar way, it really felt as though there was someone listening. Someone not completely unfriendly, more curious.

Her mother had always poured scorn on the thought of ghostly presences. 'I leave the arty-farty nonsense to you, darling,' she'd giggled, already on her second gin and tonic. 'After all, you're the one who claims to be artistic. That's just the sort of rubbish you lot believe in, isn't it?'

Rachel knew it had been the gin talking. When sober, her mother excelled in the odd, sly, caustic comment. She declared wide-eyed innocence if anyone took offence. She only really loosened up with alcohol. Rachel hated seeing her mother so out of control. She almost preferred the closed-up, sarcastic version.

She shook herself, trying to instil some sense into her head. It helped make up her mind; she'd ring Mike first thing in the morning. She lay back on the cushions, more relaxed now that she'd come to a decision, albeit an expensive one, and her eye was caught by the Huntley and Palmer biscuit tin. She'd shoved it out of the way when clearing the kitchen to paint and it was wedged between Sister Wendy Beckett and a book on Kandinsky. She'd forgotten all about it. Putting her mug down carefully, not wanting to stain the floor, she took the tin down and settled back on the sofa.

'So, little tin, what secrets are you hiding?' Part of her was aware of the air shifting around her as she unwrapped the book. There were the eclectic mixture of papers again, a few neatly stuck in. Some looked as if they had been cut from a diary and were covered in densely written handwriting. The photographs caught her eye. One, a wedding photograph, featured a tall man in uniform with a vibrant-looking woman at his side. They were both holding themselves very erect, looking tense. Another was of a very dashing dark-haired man on horseback, a whip in his hand and a grin splitting his face. Both photographs looked old; they were sepia-tinted and spotted with age.

As she sifted through the loose pages, Rachel noticed that each was neatly numbered at the top right-hand side.

'Someone after my own heart,' she said with a smile.

She flipped back to the very beginning until she found the frontispiece again. 'Henrietta Trenchard-Lewis,' it proclaimed in an elegant and imperious hand. 'Her Life.'

Henrietta? Lewis? Rachel found the postcard from Brighton and again looked at the address. Mrs H. Lewis. There was no doubt about it; it must be the same Mrs Lewis who had lived in the cottage.

At the bottom of the tin lay the letters, tenderly tied with their faded-pink velvet ribbon. Rachel laid them to one side; it felt far too much of an intrusion to read them now. She checked the tin for any more loose pages and, satisfied that there were none, pulled the throw around her, snuggled into the sofa and started to read.

Chapter 5

I began to be who I am when I went to the big house for the very first time. This is my story.

Hetty readied herself. She re-filled her pen with indigo ink, took a sip of tea and grimaced. It had cooled since she'd sat down at the little table in the window and had become distracted by the view, as always. She gave herself a mental shake and began. If she didn't start this now, in her seventieth year, it would be too late. She forced herself back into the past, the distant past, and began to write.

I was a young girl when I went to Delamere House. Now, I am an old lady seeing in a year I may not see out and surrounded by the detritus of a long life lived in many parts. I live in this cottage, with a blue clematis growing around the front door and am bothered by few. It is how I like it. For too long I have been at the mercy of others. I now intend to see out my days in a pure and blissful self-ishness. The big house has long since been sold. The family has not, after all, managed to keep it. Perhaps if I'd had children? But I digress. I jump forward when really I should start at the beginning. The beginning of my life. I began to be who I am when I went to the big house for the first time.

It's been over sixty years. Hard to believe that all those years have passed, but I can remember it better than yesterday. It was a fine spring day in 1903.

Papa delivered me, thrust a package at me and then, almost immediately, went away again. As a small child I never did hold the same fascination as his spiders and insects.

I was to stay with my very distant relatives Aunts Hester and Leonora whilst he travelled on an expedition with the then Royal National Geographic and Scientific Institute. I loved Aunt Hester from the very beginning. She was all lavender scent and soft skirts. I detested Aunt Leonora almost as quickly. And I believe the feeling was entirely mutual. She never failed to point out my lack of manners and decorum. I asked for cake before sandwiches once and it was never forgotten or forgiven.

There were two boys in their charge, motherless as was I. Edward tall and slightly pompous, but kind also, and Richard. Ah, Richard! As handsome as the day, with the cheek of the devil. He got me into many a scrape as a child. And I was only too willing to follow his mischievous lead. Wicked, charming, irresistible Richard.

On that first day, I failed to notice the decrepit nature of the house, the gentility that papered over the lack of income.

As Richard often teased me, the hope of all was for me to marry Edward and therefore save the great house with my money. It did not quite work out that way.

Rachel woke with a start to find herself still on the sofa. She looked down at the biscuit tin in her lap and smiled. She could still hear the woman's voice in her head. Slightly priggish and as imperious as her handwriting. She must have been a handful when she was a little girl. Rachel caught sight of the clock and groaned. Two o'clock in the morning and she had to go to London tomorrow.

'No, Henrietta, no matter how fascinating you are, I have to go to bed.' With a yawn, Rachel tucked the pages into their tin, replaced it on the shelf and went upstairs, smiling as she did so, her head still full of an Edwardian childhood.

Chapter 6

June 1963, Clematis Cottage

Hetty sat in her usual place by the window in the sitting room and looked out at the view. An unseasonal rain fell and, with it, she sank into a gloom. Old age loomed on the horizon; she even had to push her bicycle up the track to the cottage nowadays.

She laid her elbows on the small table she used as a desk – it had been Hester's from her dressing room at Delamere – and cupped her chin in her hand. She thought back to the tea parties, the dances – before it all changed so horribly, horrifically, and not just for those at the Front. Hetty frowned. Could she do justice to this task? There were too many gaps, too many lost memories. Too many regrets. She watched, amused, as a blackbird flew down into the garden and began to groom his damp feathers. Straightening her shoulders, she reminded herself that she had never undertaken a challenge without facing it square-on. After all she had lived through this really ought to be easy. She picked up her pen, dipped it into the ink and with it dipped into the past.

The bond between Richard and I was quick to form, thrown as we were into each other's company. We had few other companions to dilute our friendship. I quickly regarded him as my best friend, although he irritated me more like a teasing brother.

It was a glorious summer afternoon in July 1907. I had been at Delamere for nearly four years and considered it my home. Richard was on holiday from school and had been taunting me from the door of the schoolroom while I did my lessons. In exasperation, Miss Taylor dismissed me. We found ourselves in the summer house again. It had quickly become our sanctuary, the place we came to when we wanted to escape the adults. Not that the aunts paid us a great deal of attention. As long as we did not cause any obvious mischief, they left us alone.

But we were no longer small children. We were growing up. A strange tension sprang up between us, making us unsure as to how to behave with each other. It was all terribly confusing.

Richard was in a strange mood that day. He often was. His mood would change in mercurial fashion from petulance to wild enthusiasm to an almost cruel delight in practical jokes. He had so much energy. He was easily bored and his mind danced like quicksilver onto the next enthusiasm before I had barely begun to grasp what it was. It was as if Delamere was too constricting, too limiting for him and he was bursting for more than anyone could offer. Today, he was almost febrile.

He sat me down on the flaking wooden seat and then looked about him furtively. There was no need. I'd spied the gardener over in the kitchen garden picking peas. I hoped they would appear at supper and my stomach rumbled in anticipation. Food, however, was all forgotten, when I saw what Richard drew from his pocket.

'Look what I have!' His eyes were enormous. 'Isn't it spiffing?'

'A knife! Richard, wherever did you get it?'

I regarded it, in its leather scabbard, with fascination. We were barred from the kitchens, so my experience of such items was limited. Richard held it out to me and allowed me to take it. My hands shook with excitement. I repeated, 'Where did it come from?'

Richard merely shook his head. 'It doesn't matter.' He took it from me and slid the blade out of the scabbard. He held it up to the light and we watched in awe as it caught the hot sun and cascaded light around the shabby summer house. It made the place magical.

'I have an idea,' he said. 'Would you like to be bound to Delamere and Edward and me forever?'

I nodded. Of course I would. After a dull childhood spent in a small villa in Kent, the Trenchard-Lewises seemed impossibly glamorous.

Richard's eyes shone. 'Then we can be bound together.'

'How?'

He slid closer. 'We can be blood brothers!'

I laughed. 'But I am a girl, Richard! How can I be your brother?'

He looked affronted at my pedantry. 'Blood brother and sister, then.' He held up the knife again. The light caught the edge of the blade and it looked brutal.

I gasped. 'Do you mean to cut me?'

Richard nodded. 'It won't hurt, Hetty, the knife is sharp. It will go through your skin like butter.'

'No!' I shrank back. 'I do not like it.'

'Are you scared?'

I nodded.

'Feel the tip, Hetty. It's sharp.'

I was terribly afraid, but Richard, even then, had a way of making me do things. He made me feel so dull, so unadventurous when I demurred. I reached out a shaking finger to the blade and tapped it, ever so slightly, on the

34

tip. 'Ow!' I snatched my hand back.

He grinned. 'Shall I go first?'

I watched, with a morbid fascination, as he pulled back his sleeve and pressed the blade to the white skin on his wrist. At the last moment, he stopped. Looking at me, with a mischievous glint in his blue eyes, he said, 'You have to promise to do it too, otherwise I will bleed and it will go nowhere.'

'Stop!' An idea had occurred to me. 'If you bloody your suit there will be an awfully nasty row. The aunts would not like it.

Richard shrugged.

'They will not let you in here again,' I warned. 'You will have to do extra school work, even if you are on vac.'

He put the knife down and looked so disconsolate, I wracked my brain for an alternative plan. 'What if we only prick our finger?' I suggested.

'Like the princess?' he said, scornfully.

I grinned. 'A finger will not bleed as much as a wrist. No one will know if we have cut our finger tip.'

Richard looked somewhat mollified. 'Only if you do it too.'

I took in a great breath. 'Very well,' and then, with a quick look at the knife, I added, 'you first.'

Richard nodded, held up his forefinger on his left hand and stabbed. Blood welled immediately. I could not tell if he was in pain as he grabbed hold of my hand and did the same before I had second thoughts.

'Ow!' It was done.

The knife clattered to the floor as Richard pressed our fingers together. Perhaps he had pricked my finger harder because a thin trickle of blood ran down my hand and dripped onto my pinafore. It made a tiny but unmistakable stain, just below the ruffle on my shoulder. I had to lie to Nanny afterwards and claim a nosebleed.

Richard's eyes gleamed. 'It's done. Now we are bound together, you and me, Hetty, forever.' He tugged out his handkerchief to dry our wounds. It was so filthy already that no one would notice one more brown blot.

I sucked my finger. It throbbed. I could not quite believe what he had made me do. He had half-charmed, half-dared me and I could never resist him. He could be quite cruel sometimes, I thought – nothing like Edward.

'Now we must dance in a circle and recite the Lord's Prayer backwards.' Richard put the knife back into its scabbard and stood up.

This was one step too far, even for me. 'Oh no, Richard,' I said, firmly. 'That will send us to Hell. I know that for a fact.' The other fact being, if Aunt Leonora heard of this, we would be thoroughly thrashed.

'A game of tag and then I must lie down before tea. All this blood is making me quite faint. Remember, I am only a girl.'

Before he could disagree, I'd run out of the summer house. Sometimes, being a mere girl had its advantages!

Christmas of that year brought great excitement to the occupants of Delamere House. My father had, at long last, returned from his travels, albeit temporarily.

He had come to stay at the big house, our more modest house being shut up whilst he had been away. He entertained us all with his stories of exotic people and places and only Aunt Leonora tired of hearing him speak.

One evening, we gathered, very unusually, in the drawing room after dinner. The room had been opened up just for Father's visit. By now, I knew enough of the workings of this enormous house to understand that only a few rooms ever had a fire. I never had one lit in my bedroom. We existed in a scant few rooms and shivered even in those.

36

Money was scarce but no one would ever admit as much. Richard and I had been allowed to stay up late, as a special treat.

'Oh I wish I could go back with you. To see those things – the mangrove swamps and the waterfalls!' Richard, now a lanky, restless boy of fourteen, was hanging upon Father's every word, egging him on, continually asking questions. 'The tribes and the animals! Did you really see elephants? And lions? And zebras? And crocodiles?' Richard babbled on, 'if only Ed were here!'

'Richard, do calm yourself. You have been allowed to sit up to talk to your Uncle Henry, but do let him get a word in edgeways!' Aunt Hester, as always, was laughing indulgently at Richard's enthusiasm. Aunt Leonora simply tutted her disgust and turned away to her sewing. Not for the first time did I wonder at how two sisters could be so different.

Father, too, laughed at his newest admirer. Here was a boy after his own heart. Nothing like the untidy, lumpish daughter he had sired. I was finding it rather more difficult to engage in the conversation. Four years had passed and Father, I could no longer give him the more familiar moniker of Papa, was a stranger to me. I had, long ago, lost my fascination with his travels and only wanted to talk to him about the information Richard had intimated at when I first came to Delamere. Father had resolutely ignored the questions with which I filled my letters. Did I really have money? If so, where was it? Why could I not have it? Was I really to marry Edward, currently at university and expected to enter the army?

I was fourteen, too, and nearly at my next birthday. Strange things had been happening to me over the last few months; things I could not bring myself to broach with a father now unknown and distant to me. Nanny knew, but even telling her had been painfully embarrassing. She had explained that I was a woman now and could no longer, at certain times of the month, play as I was used to with Richard. Gone were the games of chase around the gardens, the meetings in the summer house to pore over a battered atlas, the endless adventure stories made up by us both and continued week after week. I no longer slept in the night nursery and had my own room. Part of me felt important at entering this new stage in my life, but a greater part felt desolate at leaving my childhood behind. I did not feel ready to face the adult world, particularly if it involved marrying Edward, more or less as much a stranger to me as Father, having been away for most of my time here. Now Richard had followed his brother to school and I did not even have his enlivening presence at our lessons with Miss Taylor to look forward to.

 If this was adulthood, I thought it very dull.

My one consolation was retrieving the journal Papa had given me on my very first day at Delamere.

'We live through great times,' he had said then. 'You must chronicle them, child. One day you may be great too. You must get into the habit of writing everything down.'

To my shame, I had hardly written anything at all. I had been too busy running around the grounds with Richard – and getting into trouble with Aunt Leonora. Now, with the boys away, I fell on my own company a great deal more. I am sure Papa had in mind my recording scientific fact. With these strange new happenings in my body, I was far more interested in exploring my emotions. I had taken to recording my thoughts and feelings as much as I had time for.

I looked at Richard, still deep in conversation with Father. He was as tall as me now, still energetic, still getting into scrapes. Only this term the aunts had received a written warning from his school. According to the letter, Richard had sneaked out of his dormitory one night and tried to buy beer at the local public house.

He was home for the holidays and had been refused permission to visit our neighbours, the Parkers, whose horses always proved irresistible to him, as a punishment. School had changed him, had made him scornful of the limitations put on him by the aunts. They, in turn, having only had to deal with placid Edward in the past, struggled with this new, wayward Richard.

He had chafed at his imprisonment and had taken it out on me. Puzzled by my reluctance to engage in our childish games he had taken to spying on me, pulling my hair or my pinafore tails. Once he had put a worm in the neck of my blouse and watched with glee as I danced and shrieked and scrabbled to get it out. Vile boy. As bored as I, his natural sense of fun and mischief found expression in vindictiveness and spite. Our love-hate relationship was even stronger.

Only once had I glimpsed an even stranger Richard. We had gone exploring, as we used to and strictly against the dictates of the aunts. We had found our way up into the old attics. I did not like the attics; they were gloomy and the dust made me sneeze. As usual, Richard goaded me, claiming I was unadventurous and dull and, as usual, I responded by being even bolder than he.

In one of the rooms were stored some old tailors' dummies, from goodness knows where and when. I hated them with a passion. They stood, headless but watching, silent in a corner. One or two were cloaked with dust-sheets and that made them even more terrifying.

I ran ahead, wanting to put them behind me and furious that Richard had called me chicken for being scared. In

39

the furthest-most attic, the roof had partially fallen in and pigeons were nesting and cooing on the rotten beams. It was lighter and colder here, the winter air whistling through the gaps. As I ran in, the pigeons took flight and disappeared, leaving a choking mess of feathers and swirling up the dust and their droppings. Shaking it out of my hair, I turned to where I thought Richard was behind me. And screamed.

I thought one of the Trenchard-Lewis ancestors had come to haunt me – a white-robed figure danced in front of me. I put my hand to my heart; it was beating so. I feared I should drop down dead. About to scream for help from Richard the 'ghost' let out a familiar giggle and dropped down to reveal the boy behind the dust-sheeted dummy.

'Richard, you perfect beast!'

'Jolly good wheeze, Freckle-Face.'

Looking about me, I spied a piece of rafter. Grabbing it, I attacked Richard. I was furious. But, even then, Richard was stronger than me. Easily overpowering me, he held me fast, managing to wrap the filthy dustsheet around me, trapping my arms against my body.

He held me to him, his blue eyes vivid and a little wild. 'A kiss as a forfeit for your release.'

Struggling and calling 'pax' I began to giggle. 'Richard, you are a shocking boy. How can I kiss you when I cannot move my head.' He loosened his hold a little and I took advantage. Stamping on his toe with as much force as I could muster, I ran off as he let go. Shrieking, as he chased me, I ran.

Now, in a clean dress, I watched as Father and Richard began to trace Father's most recent journey through West Africa in the atlas. My thoughts turned to Edward. He was a mysterious figure, only at home for holidays and currently in his second year at Cambridge. He was due home soon. Edward had inherited the family tendency to be tall; he was well over six feet now. Thankfully, to his relief, his hair had darkened to a quite nice dark brown, with reddish glints, rather like Aunt Hester's. His eyes, not as vivid as Richard's, were a gentle shade of grey. We had never really grown to know one another and he still treated me in a stiff and formal manner, as if I were a creature as exotic as one from my father's collection. Was it still expected that I should marry him? Richard always averred that it was so. How did I feel about marrying Edward? What did I know of men and marriage? What did I know of anything? I sighed.

Richard, hearing me, looked up from the atlas. 'I say, old thing, come and have a look at this. It's where your father was last month and it's the most spiffing-looking place. Look at the river, it goes the whole length of the country. Can you imagine?'

Aunt Leonora's mouth thinned at Richard's use of boarding-school slang.

I smiled at him. His enthusiasm was, as always, appealing. Perhaps he wasn't being so awful after all. I joined them at the table and sensed Father's warmth at my interest.

Chapter 7

Edward arrived the next day, just in time for afternoon tea. Tall and adult, with stubble on his cheek and smelling of the outside world. Beside him Richard looked like the little boy he was desperate to grow out of being. Tea in the drawing room reminded me of the tea parties when I first arrived. We hadn't had many recently; little point with the boys away most of the time. Much was the same, except that it was even shabbier and the fire a paltry affair. He and Father were getting on famously, another reason to put Richard's nose out of joint and the aunts beamed with pride at the splendid young man they had raised. Aunt Leonora was especially ecstatic at his return, for he was always her favourite. He didn't cause the trouble that Richard and I did. He was holding court, with Richard on one side of the couch and Father on the other. The admiring females, including Nanny, gazed on.

'So, Edward, tell me what you are reading and what is your college again?' said Father, beaming at a fellow scholar.

'Natural Sciences, sir, at Trinity.' replied Edward, with his usual politeness.

My father's eyes lit up. 'Splendid, oh how splendid! I must

tell you of the moth I have discovered – as big as a saucer and twice as ugly. You must see it. Come, I have brought it with me. Come,' he said more impatiently, 'let us find it. I have it in my room.'

The two men left in a flurry of scientific excitement and I felt a sneaking sympathy for Richard, who was left out. He huffed and threw himself back on the couch.

'Sit up, Richard,' murmured Aunt Leonora automatically.

'But I'm bored. Can I have another piece of seed cake?' Richard's lower lip jutted in a sulk.

'It is "may I" and no, you mayn't, you have had two pieces already,' responded Leonora, frowning and about to launch into one of her tirades.

'Why don't you take Hetty to the library, Richard?' As ever, Aunt Hester stepped in as peacemaker. 'We have it open for your Uncle Henry and Edward. Take her to look at the history books. I don't believe she has seen them.'

This was not strictly true. One of the things Richard and I had always enjoyed was exploring the house, delighting in the many closed-up rooms, playing hide and seek amongst the dust sheets. The library had been a regular haunt and we had discovered many hidden gems: maps of Asia, stories of far-off and long-ago Greece.

I looked across at him; he was sitting up, his blue eyes gleaming. I knew that look. It meant trouble was afoot.

'What a super idea Aunt Hester, please may we be excused?' That settled it, such elaborate politeness from Richard could mean only one thing; he was up to something.

The door to the library opened with difficulty, stiff with lack of use. I loved this room; it was one of my favourites. Bookcases lined the walls, double height so that library steps were needed to reach the more remote volumes. Chairs and a chaise longue crowded around the space but were arranged in a careless manner, hinting at the room's long abandonment. Today, however, the dustsheets were gone. Dorcas, who glorified in the title of housekeeper, when really she was the solitary upstairs maid, had obviously been busy polishing the mahogany bookcases. The woodwork gleamed and the aroma of lavender hung in the air, testament to her hard work. Richard, with an enigmatic look at me, pushed the library steps over to the furthest-most bookcase, climbed up and fiddled with the lock on the top glass door.

'Richard, you mustn't. We're not supposed to look at those books. It is forbidden.' But I said it half-heartedly and followed him, avidly curious as to what lay behind the protective glass. I stood at the bottom of the steps, looking up. He opened the door and, looking behind us to check for adults, passed down to me a large leather-bound volume. I struggled over to the table with it.

Richard hopped down and pushed in front of me. Saying nothing, he proceeded to open the book at pages obviously well known to him. I stared over his shoulder until I saw what he was laughing at. Then I caught my breath. The images seemed to me, at that time, grotesque. They were engravings of human forms entwined in unspeakable acts. The men and women seemed intent on doing violence to one another. The men, with bared teeth, fastened on throats thrown back. Hands were clutching parts of the anatomy I did not – had not – known exist. Richard saw my reaction of horrified fascination and sniggered.

'This one is the best.' He pointed to a picture of a man mounting a woman in the way I had seen the bull do to a cow at the Parkers' farm, until Nanny had pulled me away. She had responded to questions with tight-lipped silence. 'What do you think?' Richard asked, watching my face intently. 'If you marry Ed, that is what he will do to you on your wedding night.'

I backed away, shaking my head violently, clutching my heaving stomach. No man was ever to do to me what I had seen in those disgusting pictures. But even then, part of me was acknowledging the truth of what was being shown to me. Forgotten images were remembered: Elsie the kitchen maid and Robert the under-gardener looking red-faced and untidy when I walked in on them in the empty stables, Edward being teased over Flora Parker until he blushed crimson and hurried from the room, Nanny hushing my questions about the bull.

Information was sliding greasily into place and locking together to make a truth.

'No ...' I looked at Richard.

He grinned back, 'Oh, yes. And then your stomach will grow and grow and one day a baby will come out. The chaps at school told me.' He spoke conversationally and completely without malice.

My eyes filled with tears and I felt sandwiches and cake threatening to return.

'I say, Hetty, old girl. I didn't mean to upset you.' He made a move towards me, concern on his face.

I turned and ran from the library, the scent of lavender polish sticking in my throat.

'Wait Hetty! Hetty I'm sorry! I just thought it would be a wheeze.'

I found myself in the summer house, the old refuge. It was intensely cold and I could see my breath making clouds in the frigid air. I wrapped my arms around myself and began to rock to and fro.

What was the connection between what had been happening to me and those pictures? At some deep level the links were forcing themselves to be made; there had to

45

be a connection. Was that what it meant to be a woman?
If so, I wanted no more of this adulthood. I yearned to be
a child. I yearned for my long-lost mother. Tears began to
drip down my face and I hid it in my pinafore.

After a time, and when my tears had dried, I heard a
sound outside. The sound of footsteps. I froze, willing
them to go away.

'Henrietta – Hetty – are you in there?'

It was Edward. Of all people, I could face him the least.
I stayed still, my face hidden in my skirts, like an animal
gone to ground.

'Hetty, there you are! Richard said you had been taken ill.'
A relieved-sounding Edward came into the summer house.
'We've all been looking for you. Come back to the house,
you'll catch your death of cold out here.' He sat down on
the crumbling bench beside me. 'Hetty, are you unwell?'
I remained silent, but my shoulders began to heave again.
I felt a tentative hand on my arm and shrank away.

I heard Edward sigh. 'Look, if you won't come back into
the house, shall I fetch the aunts, or your father? Only,' he
paused and then went miserably on, 'Richard said something about a book? Some pictures? He said they frightened you? If it is what I think it is, I think it better the
aunts don't know.'

I heard no little anger in his voice and raised my wretch-
edly tear-stained face to look at him for the first time. 'I
saw –' and then had to stop.

Edward's face tightened with anger and he nodded. 'I
thought as much. When I get my hands on that little
so-and-so I'll thrash him until he can't sit down. The little
–' he bit off what he was about to say with another look
at me.

I found my voice at last. 'Richard didn't mean to upset
me. He thought it was a joke.' I wiped my damp face with

my pinafore and shivered.

'When will that boy ever learn to think before he acts?'
Edward said it softly. He shrugged off his jacket and laid it
gently over my shoulders. It was heavy and made of rough
tweed, but warm from his body. He cleared his throat.

'Erm, so, what do you know?'
I looked at him in panic. He blushed and became very
busy lighting a cigarette.

'You know, it really ought to be your father or Nanny or
Aunt Hester talking to you.'
I shook my head and hid it back in my skirts.

Edward sighed again, even more loudly. 'But, as it seems
to be me in the wrong place at the wrong time, perhaps I
ought to tell you.'
I sneaked a look at him. He was concentrating fiercely on
his cigarette. His nose turning pink with cold.

'I should quite like it to be you.' I said in a tiny voice,
hardly believing my own daring.

He coughed slightly and put a hand through his hair,
making it stand up in comic fashion. 'Oh Lord,' he
groaned.

'Please tell me Edward,' I said, 'I think it might be better
to know it all than some of it. It might make it seem less
frightening.'
Edward shook his head.

'Father always says if one wants to know something one
should ask questions.' I straightened my back and took
comfort that Edward's discomfort seemed even greater
than mine.

He gave a little nod, as if a decision had been made and
smiled at me through the blue tobacco smoke. 'And your
father is a great scientist, a very learned man. Well, shall
we be scientists? Shall you begin with a question, little
Hetty?'

And so I did. And Edward, in halting fashion and with many blushes, told me of what to expect on my wedding night. He told me the simple biological facts at first, but then, as he elaborated, I became more and more fascinated, my natural curiosity taking over.

'But it looked so, so violent in those pictures. As if they were killing one another, not loving one another!' I thought back to the images with this new information whirling around my brain. It was at once repellent and fascinating.

Edward shifted on the bench and there was a long pause. 'Well, I understand it can take one like that.' He looked at the gathering darkness outside. 'But remember, Hetty, it is for people who love one another very much. And sometimes love takes many forms, sometimes it is passionate. And that passion can seem like violence.'

I looked at him, sitting in the cold, shivering openly and being so brave for my sake. I wondered, perhaps, if he were thinking of the beautiful Flora Parker. 'Have you, have you ever –' I began.

'Good Lord, Hetty, the questions you do ask.' He lit another cigarette with trembling fingers and made much of flicking away the match. I had my answer. It satisfied me.

'Richard says I am to marry you and you will take my money to rebuild the house.'

Edward turned, a startled look on his homely face.

'Richard is a –.' Here he said a filthy word and the oath came out violently. He sucked deeply on his cigarette and there was a long pause. 'Sorry, Hetty. Forgot myself. You know our family has little money.' He gazed around at the shabby summer house, full of hints of lost glory. 'And it would take a great fortune to restore Delamere. More than you have, I am sure.' He smiled. 'If you would like to marry me, then so be it. But that is for many years from now. And we have all the time in the world to decide. Come along, we must go back to the house, they will be wondering where we are and it is bitter in here!'

He held out his hand to me and I stared up at his face in a daze. I had hardly known Edward before today. This strange little interlude in the summer house had convinced me of one thing: he might not be as much devilish fun as Richard, but he was an infinitely kinder person.

I took his hand, not sure if I had just received my very first proposal – and even less sure how I felt about it.

Chapter 8

It was the first day the Llewellyns were expected to start work and Rachel sat at her drawing board, too wound up to do anything other than stare at the view.

She felt half resentful, half relieved. Although pleased that work was to begin on the house, she was reluctant to give up sole possession of it. Knowing it was pointless to paint or do any more work until Mike and Gabe had finished, she had limited her refurbishment to the sitting room.

Reluctantly.

The room had become ever more her refuge. She'd had to grit her teeth not to put the rest of the house in the same order. However, bringing a temporary halt to any DIY had freed up time for her to sit at the window, gaze enraptured at the view and begin, at last, some serious drawing work.

Until this morning.

She expected her builders any minute and it made her too on edge to even pick up a pencil. She was worried about so many things: how she was to get any work done with muddy-shod builders stomping through the house, the noise, the mess, most of all the disorder. Not to mention the expense.

She'd got used to the tranquillity in the house. She liked the solitude, the freedom to talk to the walls if she chose, and to ignore anybody she didn't wish to talk to. She'd even cut back on phone calls to Tim and Jyoti. Tim was too loud, too demanding, somehow, for her current mood and Jyoti had seemed preoccupied and uncommunicative.

Looking at the clock for the fifteenth time that morning Rachel began to draw randomly. Sometimes the very act of having a pencil in her hand, making marks, could calm her, lead her into doing something more useful or productive.

She braced herself, pencil poised in mid-air. She could hear a vehicle advancing up the track. She watched as Gabe and his father unpacked an alarming amount of tools and materials. Her knuckles clenched to white on the drawing board. It felt like another Llewellyn invasion. Behind her, the room seemed to prickle and a wave of apprehension rippled around her. The house seemed to disapprove of the interruption too. Rachel liked a place for everything and everything in its place. Several builders roaming around – and their accompanying mess; it would be enough to drive her insane. God, she was turning into her mother.

Gabe spotted her at the window, said something to Mike and came along the path to the house. He rapped on the front door.

Rachel, taking a deep breath, and with a feeling that life was never going to be quite the same again, rose to open it.

'Hi Rachel,' Gabe said cheerfully. 'We're just unloading the stuff. Dad's got to go on to the Halliday job, so I'll wait here to supervise the scaffolding lads. There might be a bit of noise, bit of to-ing and fro-ing today, but after that we shouldn't have to disturb you too much until the radiators arrive. You won't know I'm here, I reckon.'

'Oh,' said Rachel, taken aback at how easy he made it sound. 'Fine. Shall I, erm, put the kettle on?'

Gabe shrugged. 'I've got a flask with me, so don't worry.'

'Right,' said Rachel, now thoroughly deflated but feeling some of her tension easing. 'I'll just go back to – I'll get on with some work, then.' She was disappointed she wouldn't be seeing more of him.

'You do that. I'll knock if I need anything, but apart from that, you won't see me.'

After that anti-climactic start, it was exactly as Gabe said. The scaffolders were a noisy, cheerfully coarse bunch, who swore freely but who were only there for a couple of hours on the first day. Rachel guessed they'd been chivvied along by Gabe and her gratitude and liking for the man increased. After the scaffolders disappeared, apart from the odd thump and the sense that there was someone else around, it was relatively quiet, even peaceful.

The days settled into a rhythm. Gabe arrived early in the morning, sometimes with Mike but more often on his own and, without ceremony, got on with the job. After waving to Rachel as she sat at her desk in the window, he disappeared around the back of the house. Unless she made an effort to do so, Rachel hardly saw him.

On lunchtime of the third day, Rachel's curiosity got the better of her and she went to find Gabe to ask about progress.

Her beautiful red-brick cottage had been encased, almost in its entirety, in ugly scaffolding. She found Gabe perched halfway up the back of the house re-pointing the wall. She peered up, shielding her eyes from the glare of the sun. He was dressed in his customary jeans and scruffy t-shirt. From her position on the ground, she couldn't help but admire the view of his beautifully shaped rear and long, well-muscled thighs.

'Hi,' he said, without turning from his work. 'Surprised the damp hasn't penetrated that back wall more. This mortar's shot to bits.'

'Would you – would you like a tea, or coffee or something?' Rachel said hesitantly. 'I was just going to make myself one.'

At this, Gabe did turn round. He looked down at her and blew his hair out of his eyes. 'That would be great. Could do with a break. This job gets really tedious after a while.'

'I'll be on the front step, then.'

'Sweet. I'll be there in five.' He gave her a charming grin, which made Rachel's heart skip to a girlish beat.

And so, a pattern for the days was set. Most lunchtimes Rachel and Gabe met on the front step of the old house, just as they had on that first evening, and sat, drinking tea. Rachel began making sandwiches too, which Gabe ate like a man starving. She thought it might be awkward, but strangely it wasn't. It was companionable, even. He was the exact opposite of someone she expected to get along with, but even when they had nothing to say to one another, the silence was comfortable. It was all very odd.

Once or twice she'd shared an ongoing piece of art and, again, he'd shown that surprising sensitivity.

'The views from here must be inspiring. Maybe you could do something based on a landscape,' he suggested. It echoed an earlier idea she'd had.

'The views are stunning and they are inspiring,' she admitted. Then she'd turned to him and laughed. 'They're also really, really distracting. I had no idea watching a flock of sheep chase a farmer on his quad bike could be quite so fascinating.'

Gabe had grinned and told her it was Terry Garth. He'd shaken his head. 'He's completely addicted to his new toy, but claims it speeds up feeding time.'

'When are you coming down The Plough?' he asked one day, having demolished the doorstop cheese sandwiches Rachel had provided. 'There's a good crowd on a Friday night.' He turned his face up to the sun with evident pleasure. 'Oh boy, we're lucky with this weather. Makes the job so much easier. We can get on far more quickly.'

Rachel could feel the heat radiate from Gabe. Could smell him; soap and something expensive. His smooth skin seemed even browner today. She looked away, anxious not to be caught staring. He disconcerted her. Something about his animal presence attracted her deeply. But it was that very quality which disturbed her too. None of the men she'd known had that almost primeval, base quality that emanated from Gabe. And her first impression had been right. He was resolutely straightforward and honest. It was very refreshing.

With difficulty, she focused on his question. Part of her knew she ought to try out the local pub; it would be a good way to get to know some of her new neighbours. 'Oh, maybe sometime,' she said, deliberately vague. 'Thank you for the invitation, though.'

Gabe was not to be deterred. 'I'm usually in there. I'll introduce you to one or two people, if you like. Kev can be a pain, but Paul and Dawn are okay and Stan Penry's started to come in again now. He's a character, lovely bloke, though.' He twisted around and pulled a newspaper out of his back pocket.

She put him off, saying she'd think about it. It wasn't that she wanted to seem aloof, but she didn't think she felt quite ready to go into the village local on her own, however friendly the crowd and with the promise of Gabe's presence. Or maybe it was the possibility of Gabe's presence that made her so wary.

Rachel risked a glance at him, as he bent over the battered copy of his tabloid. He was a revelation. His sensitivity was all-encompassing. If he sensed she was working, he left her completely alone. It still surprised her how easy it was to have him around. The solitude she usually craved when working didn't seem as important now. In fact, she was getting more done by having him there. She found having Gabe in the background easy company and relaxing. In one way. In another, she found him very disturbing indeed. The thought made her smile.

Gabe snorted at something he was reading, threw down the paper and picked up Rachel's copy of the *Hereford Times*. Turning to the back, he was instantly engrossed in the sports pages.

Without really knowing why, Rachel found herself wanting to make contact with him. Wanted him to talk to her.

'I've been reading through some of the contents of that tin you found,' she said, 'you know, the one in the attic? Hetty, Mrs Lewis, that is, once lived in a big house in Upper Tadshell. It was called Delamere House. That's not far from here is it?'

Gabe glanced up.

'And she had two relatives. Well, very distant relatives. And two aunts, one called Hester and –'

'What?' Gabe looked at her, patently not having heard a word. 'Sorry, just checking on how Hereford got on.'

'Hereford?' asked Rachel blankly.

'United. They were away on Saturday. Won, though, three nil.'

'Oh football.' Football had never featured in Rachel's world. Before now.

Gabe misunderstood her tone, thinking she was being dismissive. 'Yes, football,' he said, amused. Some of us lesser mortals like to watch it.'

Rachel had the feeling she was being teased.

'Aren't you interested? In Mrs Lewis I mean. I thought you might be, seeing as you were the one who found the tin.' Having read the next few pages of Hetty's journal on her long train journey to London, Rachel was bursting to discuss it with someone. Jyoti was again being peculiarly distant and Tim was in the middle of another break-up with boyfriend Justin. That only left Gabe.

'Sorry. Just had to check up on how the boys were doing.' Gabe folded the newspaper away, leaned back against the front door and looked at Rachel from underneath long, dark lashes. 'I'm all yours now.'

'Erm, I, erm –.' There was suddenly something about him that made her lose all interest in Hetty. Her throat constricted and Rachel couldn't have spoken had her life depended on it.

A silence built between them, unusual in that it was awkward.

'Could look at this all day and still see something different,' Gabe said. Then, finally taking pity on her, he looked away. He smiled and nodded at the prospect before them. 'This view, I mean.'

'I know, I still think it's gorgeous. It's why I bought the cottage,' Rachel said in a rush, feeling heat flush her cheeks. For a minute, she wasn't sure just what Gabe was referring to.

He laughed. 'Would you have changed your mind if you'd known how much work there was to do?'

She gave him a quick sideways glance. 'You know, I'm not sure I would.'

'So, you're settling in? No regrets, then?'

Rachel thought about what she had left. Rows of once-proud houses converted into flats, their front gardens concreted over, on which to shove cars, no sense of community, alarms sounding out in the night, the scream of sirens wailing past. The shallow men she'd always seemed to attract.

'Not one,' she said firmly and meant it. And then pulled a face. 'Although it's a shock having to go and get your papers from the shop. There's something so nice about having them put through the letter box on a Sunday morning.'

'I know, Dad's always moaning on about it. Lucky we've still got a shop, though, the one in Stoke Bliss closed down. Reckon ours will at some point, when Rita retires.'

'Stoke Bliss,' murmured Rachel. 'Upper Tadshell, Nether Tedbury, Stoke St Mary.' She rolled the words around her tongue, enjoying the sounds. She loved the place names in the area. 'Why doesn't she do a delivery service?'

Gabe shrugged. 'Says it's too scattered a population to do it. Would cost her too much. You can see her point, though. It'd take ages. Mind, I reckon it's because she can't get any paper boys. No one'll work for her.' He pulled a face. 'Not the easiest woman in the world.'

Rachel laughed. Having come across Rita, who ran the shop and post office, she knew exactly what Gabe meant. She lifted her hair from her neck in an effort to cool down, her face still felt hot. 'In London, I used to pick up the early editions on a Saturday night on the way home from a night out. Then they'd be there, ready to read on Sunday morning. With good coffee and a pastry making crumbs in the bed.' Still holding her hair aloft she nodded her head from side to side to ease out the kinks from a morning at the drawing board.

As an unconscious gesture, it gave off a wholly and peculiarly erotic charge.

Gabe couldn't look away. Didn't want to. A picture was forming in his head. Rachel: her long, dark hair tousled, wearing a silk robe – no, better still, a silk negligée, Sunday papers scattered as they abandoned them. He shut his mind off and concentrated on the view, watching as a tractor on the Garths' farm ploughed an immaculate furrow. Did she have a clue about what she was doing to him? To distract himself he asked: 'So what's this about Hetty, then?'

'You *were* listening!' Rachel, delighted that she had an audience, gave Gabe a beatific smile. She began to tell him all about Hetty's traumatic experience at Christmas. 'So, I can only assume Richard showed Hetty some kind of Victorian –'. She stopped, embarrassed.

'Porn?' Gabe questioned and guffawed. 'Now that'd be worth looking at. Don't suppose there's any in that tin of yours?'

'No laughing matter,' Rachel said, trying not to sound like her mother, 'it must have come as a hell of a shock to poor Hetty. She wouldn't have known anything.'

'What, nothing at all?' Gabe was scandalised.

'Nothing. I remember my grandmother telling me she knew absolutely nothing until the wedding night. And that was only fifty or so years ago.' Rachel felt the treacherous heat rise in her face again. She wasn't sure it was quite the thing to talk about sex with Gabe.

'Jeez,' Gabe said. 'Makes you wonder how folks managed. It's hard enough the first time when you know what you're supposed to do!'

Rachel studied him. Despite what he'd said, she imagined Gabe having no problems in that department. He seemed very at home in his skin. 'Erm, yes. Edward must have been an unusual man to have that conversation with her. I just can't picture a repressed

Edwardian telling a young girl the facts of life like that.'

Gabe scratched his head with the pencil that seemed to be permanently stored behind his ear. 'Don't know how repressed they were. You say this Edward was some sort of scientist?'

Rachel nodded. 'He went off to university, apparently.'

'Well, maybe he took a scientific approach. Just told her the bare facts, like. Probably the best way. Better than being all coy.'

Rachel nodded. 'Possibly.'

'Kind thing to do, though. Think I like Edward. So, do you reckon she'd been hauled in to marry him, then?'

'Well, Hetty certainly had that impression. It sounded as if they needed her money to keep the house going. It had fallen on hard times.' Rachel paused. 'She sounds torn, though, between the two brothers. As you say, Edward is kind, but Richard sounds far more fun.' She turned to Gabe. 'Do you know anything about the old house?'

Gabe shifted, as if uncomfortable on the step. 'What, this Delamere House?' Gabe shoved the pencil back behind his ear and shrugged. 'Don't know, I've never heard of it. Likely it's been pulled down. Especially if you said it was in a pretty poor state.'

'It was, at least Hetty gives that impression. What a shame. I was hoping I could go and see it.'

Gabe couldn't bear the disappointment evident in her expression, so he added, 'Tell you what, I'll ask Mum. She's lived round here all her life and she's interested in old houses. She might know something.'

'Oh, thanks Gabe, that would be wonderful. And thanks for all you're doing, by the way. I really appreciate it.' He always went that one step further, like today; she was sure he wasn't supposed to be clearing gutters as well as re-pointing.

'Not getting in your way too much, then?'

Rachel shook her head. 'Not one bit. In fact, I really like having you around. I hadn't predicted how isolated I'd feel up here sometimes. It's lovely knowing you're here.'

Gabe coughed to hide his pleasure. Rachel hadn't said anything as nice to him before. Most of their conversations centred around jobs in the house or this Hetty woman. He smiled. 'What you going to do about the garden?'

Rachel looked about her. If anything, the neglected weeds had grown even higher since she'd moved in. She'd been concentrating on getting the house sorted. Thank goodness it had been dry; a damp spell would have made the garden even more rampant. The back of the house was better, it was shadier there, in the lee of the hill, but out here she had to concede that it really did look a mess.

'I don't know,' she admitted. 'I've just been commissioned a job, quite a big one. That's why I had to go to London.'

Gabe nodded. Ridiculously, he'd missed her. It had meant he got on with the guttering twice as fast, but he'd missed her presence. He gave himself a mental shake. He was getting in way too deep here. 'What's the job?'

'A series of flower drawings for a nature magazine. They want some seasonal paintings, twelve in all, to go with an article about identifying wild flowers.' Rachel bit her lip. 'It's a huge job, the biggest I've been offered in ages, but it's not going to leave much time for gardening. Such a shame,' she added, almost to herself, 'I'd seen myself sitting out here enjoying the garden, a glass of wine in my hand. Oh well, maybe next year.'

Gabe could see her sitting there too, in a big hat and flowery dress. He'd like to sit beside her. He sat up, as a thought occurred. 'I might know someone who could help!'

'Oh Gabe, you are kind.' Impulsively, Rachel put her hand on his arm. 'But I can hardly afford to pay you and your dad, let alone hire a gardener.'

Gabe couldn't tear his eyes away, dazzled by the warmth in her voice. He could feel his skin humming at her touch. 'I don't think there'd be any money involved,' he began at last. 'There's a friend of mum's. Stan Penry. I mentioned him before. He's not long lost his wife and he's looking for something to do. He likes his gardening. I could get him to come up and see you if you want.'

He coughed again, to cover his pleasure at being touched. If he reacted like this to one innocent touch on the arm, what the hell would it be like to kiss her? Or do more? He cleared his throat again and shifted away.

'Well, maybe that would be an idea,' Rachel said, not entirely enthusiastic to have yet more people disrupting her life. She looked at Gabe in concern. 'Are you all right? You're not getting a cold or anything?'

It was too much. Not only had she been nice to him, she was now worrying over his health. 'Fine, I'm fine.' He stood up quickly. 'Better get on. Want an early finish today. I'll get Stan to give you a ring.'

He began to walk away, but then changed his mind. 'You know,' he said, slowly, as he turned back to her. 'You could write this up, couldn't you? Hetty's story, I mean.'

'I'm an illustrator, not a writer.' Rachel shook her head. 'Never written a thing in my life. It's not a skill I possess.'

'But the writing's been done, hasn't it?' Gabe added, thinking through the idea as he spoke. 'All you've got to do is add the pictures. The illustrations.' He spread a hand to the view. 'And you've got most of the material here.'

Rachel stared at him, mouth open. 'What you mean? Like a sort of –' she wracked her brain to remember the name of the book that had taken the publishing world by storm, years before.

'*The Diary of an Edwardian Country Lady!*' Gabe supplied triumphantly, slapping his thigh and making brick dust fly. 'It could be something like that. Mum loved that book. It's still on the shelf in the kitchen somewhere. She'd buy another like it.'

Rachel felt excitement rising. Could she produce the drawings and paintings that would fit with the strange mix of writings Hetty had left? It might just be something she could do. And it would sell. She knew enough of the market to know that. It would be a charming book if she edited out some of the more personal stuff; she didn't think she could allow Hetty's intimate details to be known. Then her cautious nature kicked in. 'It's a bit early to be thinking of things like that, though, isn't it? I've only read a few pages.'

He gave her a long, measuring look. 'You underestimate yourself a lot, don't you? Of course you could do it. Have confidence in what you do! From what I've seen of your work, you'd have no problems.' The easy smile appeared and she realised how much she looked forward to seeing it every day. 'I really think there's mileage in it. Never say never, Rachel. I bet Hetty never did.'

And with that, he strode away, leaving Rachel staring, unseeing at the view.

Chapter 9

On the following Thursday, Rachel went into nearby Fordham. It was a little market town, full of traditional half-timbered, black-and-white houses, with a library and a reasonable range of shops. Most importantly, for Rachel, it had a main branch post office not manned by the inquisitive and bad-tempered Rita. The place was heaving with what seemed the entire county's over-sixties. She assumed it was pension day. Joining the queue and enjoying ear-wigging the cheerful conversations they were all having, she finally managed to send off some examples of her work to a prospective client.

It was a soft sort of a day and Rachel was reluctant to return home immediately. Strolling along the town's main street, she found herself outside the windows of Grant, Foster and Fitch, the estate agents. Out of habit, she glanced at the houses for sale. There was a chocolate-box thatched cottage not far from Stoke St Mary on offer. In the usual estate agents' parlance, it claimed it was immaculately presented and deceptively spacious. 'No work required, move in condition,' Rachel read. She couldn't help a sigh escape and then gave a twisted grin as she saw the asking price. Far more than she'd paid for Clematis Cottage and far more than she could ever hope to afford. It looked as though Clematis Cottage and she were destined to have a scruffy and dusty relationship for a bit longer.

She was just turning away, intent on investigating the irresistible smell of freshly baked bread wafting from the baker's next door, when she saw Mr Foster smiling and waving at her through the window.

He came out into the sunshine. 'Miss Makepeace. How lovely to see you! Come on in, have a coffee with us. Do.'

Rachel hesitated.

'I've got raisin croissants, they're my weakness, I'm afraid.' Mr Foster patted his impressive stomach ruefully. 'Shouldn't eat them at all and if Mrs F finds out, she'll have my considerable guts for garters. Come and eat the third one I shouldn't have bought.' He made a face. 'Save me!'

Rachel grinned and nodded. She followed him into the office, familiar from her weekend property-hunting trips, and which now seemed to belong to another lifetime and lifestyle. As her eyes adjusted to the comparative gloom she saw another man rise from behind a desk.

'How nice to meet you at last,' he said and held out a hand.

He was startlingly good-looking. So much so that Rachel took his hand in silence and only mustered up a smile as a first response.

'Miss Makepeace,' said Mr Foster, 'allow me to introduce you to my partner, Neil Fitch.'

'Hello.' She took in the man's height, blue-black hair and vivid, blue eyes. 'It's Rachel,' she said, a little shy, and then pulled herself together. 'If I'm about to share your food, perhaps we ought to be on first names at least.'

'Delighted to be so,' said Neil Fitch formally and gave a dazzling smile.

'Splendid, how simply splendid,' said Mr Foster. 'And I'd better be Roger, then. I'll just see to the coffee. How do you like it, Rachel?'

'Just milk, please.' She tried to say his name, but just couldn't call him Roger, somehow. It didn't seem right. She looked to where he had disappeared through a door at the back of the office. To the kitchen, she presumed.

'Where are my manners? Neil leaped into action. 'Please take a seat.' He dragged out an office chair and gestured for her to sit down. Resuming his position at his desk, he leaned back, idly twirling a fountain pen between long fingers. 'And, how are you getting on with Clematis Cottage? Such a beautiful location but a lot of work I imagine?'

Rachel nodded. 'I do love it, but you're right, it is a lot of work.' She'd never met such a stunning-looking man. He quite took her breath away.

'You've got the Llewellyns working on it, I believe?'

Rachel forced herself to concentrate. 'Yes, although they haven't done all that much yet. The roof is in need of serious repair and I'm having them install central heating, too.' She pulled a face. 'I think the wiring may need re-doing, as well.'

Neil nodded. 'Only to be expected, with an old house like that. But Mike Llewellyn's a hard worker and reliable. He'll do a good job.' He treated Rachel to another attractive smile. 'And some heating is an excellent idea. It can only add value to the property, should you wish to sell, that is. Yes, Mike's a good worker. It's just such a shame about his wife.'

He was interrupted by Roger bringing through a tray loaded with a cafetière, cups and saucers and a plate piled high with pastries.

'It really is a scandal having an office so close to Mervyn's bakery,' he said, as he put down his load on Neil's desk and began to arrange cups, saucers and plates.

Rachel smiled. 'I was just on my way to it. I simply couldn't resist the smell.'

Roger tutted and raised his eyes to the ceiling in comic fashion. 'It's death to the diet, I'm afraid.' He pouted. 'On a daily basis. Not that my young friend here has to worry about these things.'

Neil laughed and reached for the plate of cakes. 'I'm one of those insufferable people who never puts on any weight, I'm afraid.' He offered Rachel first choice and, after deliberating, she took the smallest.

'It's all the running he does,' Roger's tone was gloomy. 'Can't join him, not at my age and with my knees.' He began to pour coffee. 'Neil has run three marathons,' he added, with pride.

'Roger!' Neil began to protest.

'Nonsense, my boy, if you've got the energy to run twenty-six-odd miles you should make more of it. I'd have a job to walk that far!'

Rachel took the cup of coffee Roger offered, sipped and relaxed. It was pleasant to witness the men's banter. They were obviously great friends as well as work colleagues. Working from home as she did, she'd never had the chance to develop office friendships.

Roger, after fussing with the crockery and making sure everyone had everything, sank down onto a chair. He took an enormous bite of croissant and closed his eyes in bliss. 'Perfection. But the last one I'll ever have,' he said, still with his eyes shut.

'He says that every Thursday,' Neil said and winked at Rachel. 'Thursday is a croissant day. On Mondays he has a doughnut, Tuesdays a Danish, Wednesday's a Belgian bun day and on Friday Roger treats himself to a fresh fruit tart. You must try one of those, they are really delicious.'

She laughed and, at the sound, Roger opened his eyes. 'It's the tiny pleasures in life that makes it more bearable, I've often found.' He sat up. 'Now Rachel, tell me how you are getting on with old Mrs Lewis's cottage.'

Rachel hesitated. She thought of the Huntley and Palmer's biscuit tin still containing the secrets of Hetty's life. That the memoir had been so candid had surprised and shocked her. She had expected something duller; a dry account of an Edwardian miss, perhaps.

After the initial excitement, she'd avoided reading any of it recently, having become uneasy at delving so deeply into the woman's life. When she was on her own in the evenings and it was quiet, it was all too easy to imagine the tangible presence of Henrietta Trenchard-Lewis in her home. Sometimes there was an echo of the woman so strong that Rachel could almost conjure up her image. She thought of Friday night when she'd suddenly become very aware of the dense blackness of the country night beyond her sitting-room window and how she'd jumped when a plump moth had beaten against the glass. Although she didn't feel scared exactly, she still didn't know how she felt about sharing her new home with what might possibly be Hetty's ghost. She shuddered slightly. 'Mr Foster, I mean Roger, she didn't die there, did she?'

'Oh no, my dear. She became very frail at the end. She was extremely old, you know, when she died. She had to be taken into a care home, when it became obvious she wasn't coping on her own any more. That's why the cottage was sold, to pay the fees. It's why it got into a bit of a state too.' He shook his head, making his jowls wobble. 'Poor woman, after all those years on the planet and she died all alone. No relatives at all, as far as we know. Now, why should you ask about where the dear lady died?' He took a sip of coffee. 'Not worried about the place being haunted, are you?'

'No,' Rachel answered, taken aback at his casual assumption. She repeated it a little more firmly. 'No. I don't feel it's *haunted* exactly, but there's a very strong ...' she stopped, too embarrassed to continue.

'Well, she was a very characterful woman, in many senses of the word. So I believe, I never had the pleasure of meeting her, to my regret. Those who did say she grasped any opportunity that came her way, even when she was very old. Such a vibrant woman, by all accounts. So eager to taste all that life offered. Such a positive attitude. I wouldn't be at all surprised if a little something of her lingered, shall we say? An essence, perhaps?'

'You don't think I'm completely mad, then?'

Roger patted her hand in avuncular fashion and then rose to pour more coffee. 'Not at all, dear girl. And I'm sure, if it is her, she means you no harm. I don't think she was like that in life, so there's no reason to assume she would be vindictive in death.' He turned to Neil. 'We've heard of much stranger things happening in houses, haven't we?'

'Indeed we have.' Neil smiled at Rachel. 'I hear you found something in the house? Some papers or letters? No wonder you have the lady on your mind.' He held out his cup for a refill.

Rachel looked at the two men. They were being so kind, so understanding.

'Oh yes,' Roger rubbed his hands together in glee and sat back down. 'Do tell. I was so sorry I couldn't give you more time when you rang up the other day. We had a rush on. Most unlike us.' With this he gestured to the empty office. 'Have you managed to read much of the contents?'

Rachel gave a brief version of what she'd read so far. They were a good audience and hung on every word with apparent fascination. She warmed to her theme. 'So it's the story of her life, as far as I can tell. There are bits of her diary, letters and postcards and, most exciting of all, what looks to be an attempt at a memoir.'

Neil leaned forward, his blue eyes aglow. 'What a thing to find. If it was me, I wouldn't be able to resist reading the whole thing through in one fell swoop!'

Rachel gave him a rueful look. 'If I had the time, I don't suppose I'd be able to either, but there have been other things for me to do at Clematis Cottage. And I have to work too.'

'Well, of course. Silly of me to suggest otherwise. But it's a discovery and a half, isn't it? That's for sure. What are you going to do with it?'

'Yes, my dear,' Roger echoed. 'What are planning on doing with it? It must have some wonderful stuff in it. Think of what she lived through. She was over a hundred when she died, you know. She lived through two world wars, the invention of the motor car and the aeroplane, the atom bomb and the computer.'

'Oh no, you've got him started now,' Neil said but fondly.

Roger chuckled. He seemed a chuckling sort of a man. 'Be a shame to let it go unrecorded somehow. Now, what could you do with it, I wonder?'

'Aren't you some sort of writer?' Neil interrupted the older man.

'No, illustrator.' Rachel shook her head.

'Shame.'

'There is an idea ...' she began, as if to voice it aloud would make her do it. 'Someone suggested I try to put something together of Hetty's writing and illustrate it.' There, it was out in the open now. She might well have to give it serious thought. And Gabe was right, Hetty would have jumped at the chance.

'Oh, I say!' Roger said. 'Sounds marvellous.'

'Sounds eminently workable.' Neil said. 'Might well be mileage in it.'

She looked at them in gratitude and gave up a little prayer for Gabe's suggestion.

'And, if you want any help putting it together, then I'd be only too happy to oblige,' Neil added.

'That's really kind of you.' Rachel said, unwilling to be rushed. 'I'll need to think it through a bit first, though. Oh, look at the time!' She glanced at the office clock and drained her cup. 'I must go, I've someone coming to see me at two.'

Thanking them for their hospitality, she promised she'd visit again soon. She half ran to where she'd parked her car, her mind on fire with possibilities. The idea of the book could work ... it just could.

'You never know, Hetty,' she said, as she turned the key in the ignition, 'we could be on to something with this. Here's to a long, and hopefully, fruitful relationship!'

Chapter 10

Rachel willed her groaning car up the steep track to the cottage and parked it in a swirl of dust. Her visitor was already there, waiting.

Stan Penry was leaning against the horse chestnut tree, which dominated the parking space in front of Clematis Cottage. He was enjoying some shade and a cigarette.

Rachel stared at him for a moment, preparing what she wanted to say to him. She'd found it surprisingly easy having Gabe around, which was just as well as he often was. To have yet another stranger invading her privacy might be a step too far. She wanted to be alone, so she could be the person she really wanted to be, not beholden to whatever others forced her into being.

On the other hand, she thought, ruefully, looking at the over-grown front garden, she could really do with the help.

She pondered on what Gabe had told her about the old man. Stan was seventy-three and recently widowed. He lived with his son and daughter-in-law in one of the new 'executive' houses, which flanked the church, in the village proper. Ripped away from his beloved ramshackle cottage and smallholding by well-meaning relatives, who worried he wouldn't cope on his own, he'd been given a home in their magnolia-painted modern house. Stan hated it, according to Gabe, and was keen to find somewhere he could grow his fruit and vegetables while he waited for an allotment to become available. In return, Gabe had assured Rachel, Stan would be happy to do some general gardening for her.

Rachel looked at the man, drawing him with her eye. He had on a pair of those trousers of indeterminate colour and shiny fabric that elderly men adopt and a short-sleeved white shirt. He was very thin with a slight stoop and a sour expression on his face, made more so as he sucked on a roll-up.

She got out of the car and made her way over to him. 'Hello,' she said, cautiously, 'you must be Mr Penry.'

Stan came away from the tree almost grudgingly. 'Miss Makepeace?'

Rachel held out her hand and found it enveloped in a calloused and nicotine-stained grip. 'Rachel, please.'

'Ar. That'd be Stan, then. You got a bit o' work for me then, like?'

'A bit of work?' Rachel smiled at the understatement. 'Well, yes. If you're interested, that is.' Rachel pointed to the front garden, knowing perfectly well that Stan had given the place the once-over before she'd arrived. She half-hoped he'd say it was too much for him and leave her in peace. After her conversation with Roger and Neil she couldn't wait to get back to Hetty's story again.

'You know what you want doing with it?' Stan squished his cigarette between finger and thumb, fished out an old tobacco tin from his trouser pocket, placed the butt inside and immediately began to roll another.

'Erm, no, not really,' Rachel said, a little helplessly. This hadn't begun well. She couldn't ever see herself warming to this man and certainly didn't want him prowling around her garden.

'Mrs Lewis used to have a fine old clematis growin' up that wall.' Stan gestured to the side of the front door. And she had hollyhocks and suchlike growing up in front. It were a rare old sight. She liked her gardening, did old Hetty.'

Rachel stared at him in astonishment. 'You knew her?'

Stan met her look. His eyes were full of a wicked humour. It was in direct contrast to his pinched and thin mouth.

'Knew her a bit, like. When I was living in the village afore. Before I got married to my Eunice, that is. Never had much to do with Hetty. Bit of a loner, bit scary, like.' Stan leaned over to Rachel and winked. 'But me and Eunice, we used to come up here to do a bit o' courting. We'd have a good old look at the garden before she'd come out and shoo us off. Reckon she had a fancy man up here, I do. Made Eunice giggle, it did.'

For a second, Stan's face clouded.

'I'm sorry for your ...' God, how was one supposed to say these things and why was it so hard? 'I'm sorry to hear about your wife.'

Stan took a deep pull on his cigarette and looked away. He cleared his throat. 'Ar. Never enough time with the ones you love, is there?'

Thinking back later, Rachel realised it was that moment which made her decide to take Stan on. That he'd known Hetty, even at a distance, was a draw, of course, but it was that statement which did it. Unsentimentally said, but with such feeling. Such love. She was getting quite good at making snap decisions!

Instinct told her Stan would be unwilling to accept any gesture that smacked of charity. She adopted a bracing tone. 'So, it's a lot of work. The garden, that is. Have you – have you got any ideas about what I could do with it?'

'Might have.'

He was obviously a man of few words. 'Look, Stan, why don't you come in and have a cup of tea?' She smiled at him.

'Don't mind if I do. Coffee, though.'

'Sorry?'

'Don't drink tea. I likes me a coffee. Milky, three sugars.'

'Coffee, then,' Rachel said slowly and wondered if he was making this deliberately difficult. Then she saw the expression in his strange yellowy-green eyes. He was teasing her. Well, in that case, she could get her own back. 'Oh but –' she stared pointedly at the cigarette.

Stan scowled at her. 'You another one o' them anti smokers? Just like my Sharon. Me daughter-in-law. She can't abide it neither.'

'Well, if you wouldn't mind not smoking in the house, I'd be grateful. Come on, let's get the kettle on and we can get going with some plans for the garden.'

And so it had been decided. Quite easily in the end. Stan would begin by clearing part of the garden for his vegetable beds; he'd share some of the produce with Rachel. In return, he was willing to get the rest of the garden into shape.

'Might take a deal o' time, though,' he warned her.

Rachel didn't mind and assured him so. It occurred to her that she was adapting to the slow pace of the way things happened around here. And what's more, was happy about it.

'Thank you, Gabe,' she whispered, as she lay in bed that night. It was one more favour to chalk up to him. 'And thank you, Hetty,' she tried out, tentatively. There was no answer, but Rachel heard what might have been a giggle. Content that, if Hetty's ghost was haunting the cottage, she meant no harm, she turned over to face the sigh of breeze that floated in through the open window. She heard the house settle around her and fell asleep, feeling blessed.

Chapter 11

It was one of those gifts of a summer morning, when it was a privilege to be awake with the dawn chorus.

Rachel had been woken at five by Indignant the Sparrow. The bird had got into the habit of sitting on the roof above her bedroom, cheeping loudly and, well, *indignantly,* until the moment she leaned out of her window and he took fright.

As she did so this morning, the view took her breath away and stole time. After heavy rainfall in the night, the sun shone, jewelling the landscape. It was a morning washed clean. After two months of living in the cottage, the trees had greened up even more, making the bucolic scene teem with life. The sky was still pale and cold, but even Rachel, with her rudimentary knowledge of weather, could tell it was going to be a wonderful day. It was shaping up to be a fantastic summer.

She pulled on her newly purchased Wellingtons and her fleece and slipped out into the magic. Making her way down the track from the cottage, she turned right down the narrow lane that led away from the rest of the village. She was surrounded by apple orchards, which enveloped her in a scent so sweet it nearly made her weep. Stopping for a moment to enjoy the sweet melancholy she leaned on a gate and stared into the field. The blossom fuzzed around the branches like so much pinky-white candy-floss. In contrast, in the next field, there was a decrepit building housing a tractor. The unploughed field was furrowed deep in red clay mud and, above, the sky had deepened to an azure blue, warm with promise. Beauty and dereliction side by side. Swallows dive-bombed flies and then swooped under the beams of the building, popping neatly into their mud nests. It was as far removed from city life as could be imagined.

Rachel heard a light and fast tapping on the tarmac behind her and turned, expecting to see a small dog. Instead of which, she came face to face with a hare. It had an alert, inquiring expression. She and the hare stared at one another for some moments, its large, pale eyes contemplating her without fear. Then it trotted off, squeezed under the hedge on the opposite side of the road and disappeared. Rachel released the breath she hadn't known she'd been holding.

She walked on, further down the lane, past a field of sheep. She paused again to enjoy the sight. The lambs were beyond the tiny cute stage but were still suckling, every now and again, in between grazing. Rachel could hear their teeth tearing the grass and watched as a mother bucked off a lamb attempting a cheeky suckle.

In the opposite field were some enormous cows, even Rachel recognised them as the distinctive breed that had marked Herefordshire on the world agricultural map. Big and lumbering, with red flanks that echoed the colour of the soil, their cream faces bore a sweetly vacant expression. To Rachel's delight, they had calves with them. They trembled on unsteady legs, far too insubstantial to bear their weight. She leaned on the gate, entranced. Some of the cows spotted her and plodded over, their offspring doing a wobbling dance behind. One cow mooed ominously. Rachel backed away, suddenly very aware of their size and protective mothering instinct.

She moved on, wondering if Hetty had enjoyed walking the same lanes. It was no wonder the woman was lingering in such a beautiful place, even after death. Rachel felt even more sure Roger

Foster's words held true. It just didn't feel right that Hetty would wish her harm. The vibes she got from the atmosphere that occasionally sprang up in the cottage were girlish, mischievous even. If Hetty wanted to stay in her old home, she supposed it was fine with her. As long as the ghost or spirit or essence, or whatever it was, didn't mind sharing with a load of builders too.

The lane wound round in a long, slow loop and Rachel found herself back on the edge of the village coming up behind a rambling house, bearing a sign proclaiming 'Michael Llewellyn and Son, Builders.' She checked her watch; she'd been out longer than she thought and it was getting on for nine. Gabe had offered an open invitation to visit whenever she had time. Country people got up early, didn't they? Perhaps it was time to test the theory.

It was a large and solid-looking house, painted white, with small-paned windows set at odd intervals across the walls. It looked as if bits had been added on over the years and wasn't the smart, done-up building she had expected. From what Gabe had told her, the family never used the front door, so Rachel ignored it and made her way down a narrow, rutted drive to the side of the house. She squeezed past Gabe's Toyota and a hatchback, feeling like an interloper. As she did so, a door in the house flew open and a middle-aged woman sprang out, a large bundle of letters pressed against her. She stopped and appraised Rachel, with a broad smile.

'You must be Rachel, from old Hetty's cottage. How do you do?' The older woman held out her free hand and smiled. 'Gabe and Mike have told me so much about you. It's good to meet you at last.'

Rachel went shy. 'Hello,' she managed. She wondered exactly what had been said and how she had been recognised so immediately.

'Sheila Llewellyn,' the woman explained, although it was hardly necessary; the resemblance to her son was unmistakable. The same golden-brown hair, the same sherry-coloured eyes. 'Now, I'm so sorry to dash off, but I must get these to the post and, if I don't go now, I'll miss it. Be back in a mo', though, and I'll get the kettle on. Mike's out, but Gabriel's in his shed if you want to go on through.' Sheila nodded her head to the back of the house, raised her hand as a goodbye and hurried off.

Rachel stared after her for a second and then made her way further along the drive to the back of the house, following the sounds of a tool being applied to wood. Some pale-brown chickens scattered before her, scolding her for the intrusion. The outbuildings rambled on in an untidy way, but the door to the one nearest the house was open. She stepped over a ginger-and-white cat lazing fatly in the doorway and stopped short as she caught sight of Gabe.

He had paused in whatever he'd been doing and was instead staring intently at a large piece of wood held in a clamp. He had his back to her, so she couldn't see his expression, but she had a feeling an important decision was being made.

He was dressed casually, as usual, in disreputable jeans and a ragged green t-shirt, with a logo now so faded it was indecipherable. Rachel enjoyed the view for a moment. Gabe's back was strong and well muscled, but in the way created by physical labour rather than hours put in at a gym. He had long muscles, well defined but not huge and bunchy in an off-puttingly he-man way.

Her eyes were drawn to his arms. She always liked looking at them. Sinewy and tough, the bulge of his triceps was revealed under the fraying sleeve of his t-shirt. She longed to draw him like this.

Gabe picked up a chisel and lightly tapped it on the wood. There was some pop music playing on an old Bakelite radio wedged on a dusty shelf. Dust motes spun in the sunlit air and the place hummed with the smell of sawdust.

It was wonderful.

Gabe, still unaware of his audience, tucked a length of hair behind his ear and reached sideways, bending over as he did so. He ran a long, brown thumb along the length of the wood, feeling the grain. It was a tender caress, as if he was touching a woman in that first questioning contact before making love. It made Rachel go liquid inside. She wanted to call out but couldn't speak. She refused to break the mood. And then, just as she was beginning to feel like a voyeur, the cat got up and, after stretching, wove its way between Gabe's legs, making him jump.

'Christ, Ned, you nearly gave me a heart attack.' Gabe picked up the cat and turned to the door, scratching it under its ears. Then he saw Rachel.

'Fuck!'

At the oath, the cat protested loudly and jumped out of Gabe's arms, sliding past Rachel and making good its escape. Rachel wished she could follow.

'I'm sorry. I didn't mean to startle you. Your mum said –'

Gabe crossed his arms, defensively. 'It's okay. You just gave me a bit of a fright. Didn't hear you come in.'

'No, the, erm, the music.' Rachel gestured to the radio, from which still blared pop.

Gabe rubbed a hand over his face, leaving a sawdust trail. 'No, it's tiredness really. Been up most of the night on a job, trying to get it finished. Dad's just gone over now to fit the last bit.' He crossed the workshop to the radio and turned it off.

'A job?'

'Oh a kitchen. On the house we've been working on. Owner changed her mind at the last minute and then wanted it done by yesterday.' Gabe shrugged and Rachel could see how weary the gesture was.

'I'm sorry, I didn't mean –' Now she really felt like an intruder.

'No worries, it's okay.' Gabe appeared to be recovering himself. His shoulders relaxed. 'I was just having a look at this.' He ran a hand lightly over the piece of wood. 'Can't beat a bit of English oak and this is a beaut. Was just having a look to see what to do with it.'

Rachel's curiosity piqued. 'What do you mean? For part of a kitchen?'

Gabe grinned broadly, his eyes shining through his tiredness. 'Wouldn't waste it on something practical, not this.' He leaned against the workbench, obviously amused. 'Don't you ever get that feeling with a blank piece of paper? When it speaks to you. Wants you to do something really special with it?'

Rachel did. Often. She was amazed that Gabe felt the same about a piece of timber. She nodded.

'Well, it's exactly the same here. Only better, because with wood there's already something there. Pattern, grain, shape, colour. A suggestion of something inside waiting for you to release it.'

Rachel couldn't speak. A whole new Gabriel was opening out to her.

'Sometimes I look at wood and see a piece of furniture, you know a chair, table. Sometimes, though, it wants me to make something more, something less useful, more ... ' he shrugged as he struggled for the right word.

'More purely aesthetic?' Rachel whispered.

Gabe grimaced. 'If you say so. I have to stop and take a good look. See what I can make of it. See what it promises, what it's asking of me.' He stopped, embarrassed. 'God, that's the sleepless night talking, I reckon. I'm bloody knackered.' He grinned again, this time sheepishly and ran a hand through his hair, making it untidier than ever. 'Good to have someone to rabbit on about these things to, though. No one else round here really gets it. But I knew you would. Thank you for listening.'

There was a beat. A complete understanding between them. A connection.

'I do. I absolutely get it.' Rachel said, eventually. A thought occurred and she stopped, embarrassed, not knowing how to phrase it. 'But I thought you were just a –'

Gabe raised his eyebrows and let her suffer for a minute. 'You thought I was just what?'

'Erm ...' How could she tell him she'd had no idea he was this much of a craftsman, that he was so passionate about it. That she was so turned-on by the sight of the muscles in his back working that she felt faint? No, she couldn't tell him that. She couldn't even go there.

'I thought you were just –'

'A labourer?' Gabe laughed. 'Bit more to it all than that. Learned most of it on the job, and from Dad. I've qualifications too. But I'd love to do more of this sculptural sort of stuff,' he gestured to the block of oak in the clamp, 'but there's never enough time. Too much paying work going on.'

'Do you exhibit anywhere?' Rachel's heart was pounding. It was almost as if Gabe's potential had yet to be unlocked, like his sculptures from the oak.

Gabe pursed his lips. 'Just not the right time at the moment. I can't dedicate enough hours to get the pieces together.' He looked down and scuffed his already disreputable trainers. 'Besides, Dad doesn't think much of it all and while I'm living under his roof, it's all a bit awkward.'

Rachel wondered why he didn't follow his dream. It was a crime for him not to. What was stopping him? Fear? Idleness? She didn't know how to respond, so remained silent, her mind racing in its search for some way to help.

He took pity on her and grinned, the smile chasing its way up to his eyes. 'Come on, enough arty stuff. Mum's promised coffee and bacon sandwiches when she gets back.'

Rachel followed his lead into the house, her perception of Gabe sliding all over the place, as were her feelings for him.

In contrast to the heady atmosphere that had built up in Gabe's workshop, the kitchen was warm, light and full of Radio Two. Sheila stood at the Aga frying bacon and the smell reminded Rachel how long she'd been awake. Her mouth watered.

'Go and get washed. Gabriel and I'll get these on the table.' Sheila turned and smiled at Rachel and pointed to a chair pulled up to the kitchen table. 'Just move some of that junk aside and make room. If I've told Mike once about doing his paperwork in the kitchen, I've told him a million times.'

Rachel sat down and moved a pile of papers to one side. She could see the appeal of working here. She would want to as well;

it was an inviting space. It was a big room, with a sofa covered in faded chintz at one end. Ned, the ginger cat, was now washing his paws and sitting in state on it.

The table dominated the space and was cluttered with the detritus of family life: envelopes, a letter with the local hospital's logo on it, coffee cups, a plate with toast crumbs, car keys. It was very different to her parents' stainless-steel and manicured beech kitchen. Rachel loved it – and itched to tidy it in equal measure.

'I hope you don't think I'm –' she began to say to Sheila.

''Course not, lovely. It's really nice to meet you. I told Mike and Gabriel to ask you down one day. You're welcome any time. We don't stand on ceremony, here. Didn't like to think of you all on your own up there, either.'

And you were dying of curiosity to meet me, thought Rachel and, as the older woman looked at her, she had the strangest feeling Sheila knew exactly what she was thinking.

Gabe swept back into the room. He had brushed his hair and tied it back more neatly and had washed his face free of the sawdust. He went up behind his mother and put his arms around her waist. 'God, I'm starving, Mum. Where's my food?'

Sheila laughed. 'If you'll leave me be, Gabriel, it'll be on the table. Sit down and stop making a fool of yourself.'

Gabe kissed his mother's cheek, making exaggerated smacking noises and then pulled up a chair opposite Rachel. 'Mum makes the best bacon sandwiches in the world.' He picked up the letter with the hospital heading on it, frowned and tucked it under the pile of envelopes.

'I didn't mean for you to make … I didn't expect ...' Rachel floundered. It was one thing to burst into someone's home unannounced, but another thing entirely to expect them to cook her breakfast. Her own mother did not approve of unexpected guests. Paula's mouth would thin at the very thought. Any visitor needed at least two weeks' notice to ensure a full and proper preparation. She had never done spontaneous.

Gabe shrugged. 'It's no bother. We don't mind one extra at breakfast do we, Ma?'

His mother smiled at her son and put down a plate with the biggest bacon sandwiches Rachel had ever seen. 'Of course not. You tuck in, love. Looks like you could do with something inside you.'

Gabe bit into his sandwich, chewed with obvious pleasure and then asked, 'So, what are you doing round here so early in the morning? Nothing wrong in the house? That rain didn't cause you any problems. Roof okay, is it?'

With a struggle Rachel concentrated her mind back onto Gabe the builder. She hadn't given a thought to the still-to-be-repaired roof, so seduced was she by the stunning morning. 'No, don't think so. I didn't look actually,' she admitted, as she sipped at the mug of coffee put in front of her. She eyed the enormous sandwich, made from what looked to be homemade bread and oozing brown sauce and wondered how she was going to eat it without making a mess. 'I've been for a walk. I went down the lane at the back of here. Racecourse Lane, is it? I saw a hare!'

Sheila joined them at the table and nodded. She wasn't eating, Rachel noticed, but drank her coffee. 'Always been hares there, that's how it got its name. I saw a couple dancing round one another last week. So, Rachel, what have you done with the old place? And has Stan started work yet? Be the saving of him, that will be.'

Rachel paused in the act of cutting her sandwich in half to fit it into her mouth and explained.

'Sounds like you've got big plans for the place, then. So you'll keep that old kitchen, then, not put in new? And you're getting central heating in? That's wise, we've had some rare old winters lately. You'll keep my boys busy, I'm sure.' Sheila looked at her son with a smile. 'It'll do Mike good.'

Gabe snorted. 'He's never not busy, Mum.'

'I know, but ...'

Whatever she was about to say was drowned out by Mike himself bursting into the kitchen. He was swearing quietly and constantly under his breath. 'Ruddy woman's only gone and changed her mind again.'

'Oh, that can't be the delightful Mrs Sutherland-Harvey you're talking about?' Gabe winked at Rachel and mouthed, 'Last night's job,' as his father swung himself down into a chair.

'You know we moved them sockets for her?'

Gabe nodded, a little warily, Rachel thought.

'The silly cow now wants 'em back where we put 'em in last week! That's another week's work. And she wants it done afore she moves in. We should have finished this job last month. The Hallidays'll wonder what's going on, they will.'

Sheila rose silently and went to pour another coffee. She put it in front of her husband and he caught her hand to his shoulder. 'It's her stupid money she's wasting,' she said. 'The Hallidays will wait. No need to be getting het up. Bit of bacon, love?'

Mike nodded and leaned into her. There was silence for a moment, then he became aware of their guest. 'Oh, hello, Rachel. What brings you here? Roof causing some bother?'

Rachel shook her head and felt in the way. The family dynamic was so very different to the one she had been brought up in. Both she and Gabe were only children, but his upbringing obviously had a warmth and a close companionship hers had lacked for too long. Perhaps had never been there. Never had she experienced the casual fooling around she'd witnessed happening between Gabe and his mother. Never had she seen her mother and father express their love and understanding in the way Sheila and Mike had just done. She suddenly felt very much alone and needed to escape.

She pushed her chair back and it screeched on the quarry tiles, the sound making her wince. 'I really need to go.'

'Oh, stay a while longer! You've hardly touched your butty.' Sheila turned from the stove, where she was frying more bacon.

Rachel managed a smile. 'Let Gabe have it. He looks more in need.'

'You really don't need to go so soon,' Gabe added.

'No, I really have to go. I don't want to impose any more.'

Sheila came to her, a concerned look in her eyes. 'It's no imposition, lovely.'

'Thank you, but I've really got lots of work to do.' Rachel looked around at them, 'Thank you again.' And then, uncomfortable at being the centre of so much attention, fled.

How could she explain to them how empty their happy family made her feel? How could they possibly understand the sterility of her childhood, shunted off to boarding school as soon as she was old enough? That her parents had never once said how much they loved her, how proud they were? That instead, her mother never lost an opportunity to belittle 'Rachel's little arty hobby.' She'd never been good enough for either of them. She was not the daughter they wanted. And never would be.

She took the direct route back, marching up the track as fast as she could, as punishment for indulging in the negative cycle of thoughts coming here was supposed to banish. She had to stop halfway up and made a promise, between gritted teeth, to get fitter.

As she leaned forward, hands on knees, trying to get her breath back, she forced herself to think of something else. Something other than being an unworthy offspring.

It was no less disquieting. How had she misjudged Gabe? She'd thought him little more than a casual labourer, someone who worked for his father because he had fallen easily into it and it saved having to think about what else to do. But, she could see from the way he'd handled the piece of wood in the workshop and from the way he talked, he was far more of a craftsman, a true artist. And they had so much in common! Rachel giggled in disbelief and then, just as quickly sobered, as the memory of him caressing the wood flickered across her vision. She wished it was just the steep climb that made her suddenly feel so warm.

Once back at the cottage, she tried to settle to some work. After a fruitless hour of twirling pencils between her fingers and staring blankly out at the view, she gave up. The only thing that was making her fingers twitch was the back view of Gabe. She made a few rudimentary sketches of his muscles, creating sexy lines under his t-shirt, and then stopped.

Irritated with herself, she threw the cover over her drawing board and went to make a pot of coffee. Banishing all thoughts of Gabe's faded jeans stretched tightly over his behind, she reached for the old biscuit tin and, once more, sought refuge in Hetty's life. Somehow, reading about her soothed and inspired in equal measure. To her delight, the little book she picked out of the tin turned out to be a diary.

Chapter 12

December 1907, Delamere House

So, Diary, I am to despoil your lovely white pages with my copperplate. Good, then, that it is exciting news. So exciting I can hardly breathe underneath my new, and very restrictive, corset.

We are to attend tea with the Parkers! Aunt Hester is to chaperone. How utterly glamorous it will be! The boys have been to the house many times, of course. Edward was at school with David and Richard often rides with Lawrie and Flora.

Ah, Flora Parker.

How I try to not dislike her, dear Diary, and how I fail! She says all the right things, does not broach the subject of the scandalous old king, holds her teacup just so – and is utterly boring. I shall report in full, as requested by Papa. No detail shall escape!

Well, Diary, it was thus:

I wore my only best dress, a tired blue serge, which has become rather tight underneath the arms, but Aunt Hester put up my hair. I felt very grown up and really quite la-di-da. Sadly, this only lasted until I saw Breckington

House. The house is a monster and really quite vulgar, but grand. The portico is a ridiculous size. I willed my courage to stand stern at the sight. I think I rather prefer dear old Delamere, even if one wing is falling to ruin.

Mrs Parker greeted us in the music room. There was a huge fire burning (I have never seen such an amount of coal at Delamere) and it was very hot. 'It gets the afternoon light,' she trilled. She has a serene countenance, alas not shared by her daughter. Mrs Parker had on a shimmery dress of some kind, festooned with lace at her neck and sleeves. Aunt Leonora would tut at the sight of silk so early in the day, but it must be the new fashion. I thanked the Lord for the lack of lace on the sleeves of my blue serge. Dangling into the teacup would not be countenanced. I ensured I sat next to Aunt Hester, as she has saved me from many such social grievances.

David and Lawrie Parker are handsome, but nothing to compare with Richard. Flora wore pink and simpered.

I have never before seen such food. Dear Diary, I tried not to be greedy, but there were three kinds of cake and scones too. Richard sat in between Flora and Lawrie. He flirted with everyone. He even flirted with Mrs Parker! The boy is a disgrace. I spied Flora making eyes at Edward. My Edward!

After tea it was suggested we might like to dance. Aunt H took to the piano, Edward and David rolled back the rug. We had room enough to waltz. It was divine. I danced with each boy in turn, but they had to wait in between partners as they were outnumbered. I feared for their toes as my steps were not neatly executed. Then Mrs Parker took over at the piano and Aunt Hester danced. And, dear Diary, there was mistletoe! All the boys kissed me on the cheek. They had to kiss Flora too.

It was a gilded, golden time. A very happy afternoon, only

spoiled by Richard muttering to me, while we danced
together, that he intends to make Flora his sweetheart.
Silly boy.
Dear Diary, how should I feel about this? I know everyone
hopes for Edward and I to marry but, in truth, although
he is very kind and solicitous (he made sure Aunt and I
were wrapped in rugs in the Parkers' carriage home) he is
so much older. And I do not know him. Perhaps I should
marry Richard instead? I wonder what Flora would make
of that!

Rachel, reading the account with glee, laughed. Hetty was
getting even more irrepressible. She continued to read.

December 1907, Delamere House

Dear Diary, I am in a state of confusion. I do not seem
able to be comfortable within my own skin; I feel scratchy
and raw, as if every emotion were on the outside and clear
to everyone. It is perfectly horrid.
I find I can suddenly not bear to be with Edward. All the
things he told me in the summer house keep returning. I
make every effort not to be in a room with him. This is
made easier as he is often ensconced with Father, investigating some horrid old insect or some such. I do not
know how to be around him any more.
Richard, I ignore as best I can.
To prevent myself from dwelling, I have become extremely
busy and helpful. It has not quite gone to plan.
Today, Dorcas complained I was getting under her feet. I
scandalised Cook by offering to help and she shooed me
out of the kitchen and even Leonora became irritated with
my attempts to read out the newspaper to her.
'Child, if you really want something to do,' she hissed, 'go

and decorate the tree. Sam has brought it in now. Go. The devil makes work for idle hands. No! Walk, Henrietta. WALK!'

A Christmas tree. I love Christmas trees! I shot out of the drawing room and slid on the polished hall floor. As I turned the corner, I saw an enormous tree being put in its place by Sam from the stables. In all my time at Delamere, Christmas has never warranted such magnificence. I could only presume it was in honour of my father.

'Oh, it's so, so lovely.' I clasped my hands together in, for me, an unusually demure fashion. Then I spoiled everything by hopping excitedly from foot to foot.

Sam blushed. 'Thank you, Miss Henrietta. Got it up by Stoke Bliss woods, miss. It's a fine looking one an' all.'

'It's perfect, Sam. It's the best tree we've ever had in the house.' So wrapped up by its splendour and by my unusually emotional response (I had been veering wildly between emotions all winter and had given up trying to understand myself) I missed Richard creeping up behind me.

'Now, that can't be Hetty going all gooey over a Christmas tree. I say, old girl, would you like to borrow my handkerchief to mop up your soppy tears?' He reached from behind me and put his arms tight around my waist. He lifted me up and twirled me around. He was astonishingly strong.

As Richard held me in his vice-like grip, I cursed him. I have learned a deal of school language from him this vac! I certainly wasn't going to let him get the better of me. I still had not forgiven the trick he'd played on me in the library. Or what he had said at the Parkers' tea party. It had been so nice until he had spoiled things.

'You perfect beast.' My voice became shrill and distinctly unladylike as I tried to struggle free. If I had a girlfriend like the ones in my favourite stories, then she would surely have come to my rescue. 'Put me down at once. Put me down!'

As this had no effect, I screamed and kicked his shins. Hard.

'Ow! You little –'

'Stop it at once, Richard. Let her go, for goodness sake.' Edward's calm and authoritative voice was welcome. 'Put her down!'

He strode into the hall like an avenging angel and took hold of Richard's collar. Richard became all at once still and subdued. Whatever punishment Edward had meted out in lieu of the 'book incident' had worked.

'Now, little brother, as penance I suggest you help Cousin Hetty make some new decorations for the tree. Some of last year's are a bit beyond the pale.' At Richard's protest he added: 'Yes, I insist. Flora is visiting later and she can help too. You'd best use the school room. It will contain some of the mess. And it will be a pleasure, Richard, do you understand? A pleasure!'

And it was. For a while.

Despite the cold in the school room, we were soon engrossed in making all kinds of decorations. We sat, side by side, at the old scrubbed pine table, breathing out misty clouds of air as we worked.

Of course, Richard muttered oaths and profanities under his breath for the first five minutes – truly shocking – and fascinating. Listening avidly, I stored some of the worst ones away for future reference. But he soon got busy. I was halfway through crayoning the paper boxes in which to put the toffees Cook always made, when he spoke to me.

'I say, Hetty old girl. I'm awfully sorry about the book, you know.' His voice was squeaky and embarrassed, but I could tell he was sincere.

I sighed, knowing I was about to capitulate. I always found it hard to hold a grudge against Richard. Somehow, he charmed his way out of all mischief he created. Besides, after my startling talk with Edward, I was feeling rather superior.

'It doesn't matter a bit,' I interrupted him. 'Edward has told me all I need to know,' I added, airily. 'So you can never play that trick on me again.'

He stared at me wide-eyed.

'In fact, I think I may now know more than even you, Richard!'

His eyes widened even further.

'And, if I am to marry Edward, perhaps it is just as well I do know these things, for I am a woman now.'

Clearly, he had no idea to what I was referring, for he remained silent and flushed and returned to the task in hand, which was repairing the angel.

I looked at the angel with fondness; it had graced every tree at Christmas since I had come to the house. She was looking distinctly worn around the edges now, but Richard was tidying her up beautifully.

'She will look lovely, Richard.' I put my hand out to his in an impulsive gesture. 'Don't let us quarrel when we have been such friends. Let us make up.'

He looked up at that, with an angry flush still staining his face. He looked all at once older, almost more of a man.

'What is the point of us being friends when you are to marry Edward?'

I did not reply to this comment, which I thought remarkably silly. Instead, I pulled my sleeves further over my hands, which were, by now, freezing, and reapplied myself to my own undertaking.

The frigid silence was only interrupted by Flora Parker

coming into the school room.

From the moment she sat down, Richard focused all his attention on her. His comment that he intended to make her his sweetheart came back to me.

I knew what he was about. Despite being banned, he was trying to bag a ride on one of the Parkers' hunters over the Christmas holidays. He had developed an unhealthy passion for the creatures.

Needless to say, the Trenchard-Lewis household could only afford an old nag to pull the little dog cart that was Sam's responsibility. Snowy was so aged that no one could ride her and certainly not Richard; he already had a reputation for riding his mounts hard.

I gazed surreptitiously at Flora Parker, safe in the knowledge that she was so enraptured by Richard to not notice my rude staring.

She was slightly older than I, perhaps by two years or so, and had blonde curls and a round face, which was always a delicate shade of rose-pink. I still suffered from freckles on account of my always forgetting to wear my hat, and the snub nose remained defiantly turned up.

But, dear Diary, it is more than Flora's wealth and good looks that irritate me, although that is enough surely? It is her perfect social composure. I have never seen her drop crumbs on the rug, she never has ink-stained fingers after having to write the lines: "I will not be cheeky to Dorcas," a hundred times. She never becomes hot and sweaty as I do after playing French cricket. And she has a strange way of twisting everyone around her dainty little finger. She and Richard sweethearts? Actually, they make the perfect pairing!

But back to the school room of earlier today. I was pouting and gilding walnuts and ruminating on how life was simply not fair.

Flora was now talking to Richard and captivating him in a way I rarely did. Even her voice was pretty: soft, with a tinkling little laugh. It was very unlike my raucous bellow or endless giggles.

I wondered why she came to Delamere. She took every opportunity. I could not see why she found a crumbling, half-closed-up house with no land so fascinating. It certainly did not compare to Breckington.

Leonora had once intimated that Flora's father was in trade; she'd said the words in scandalised tones, which had made Richard and I giggle, Mr Parker's business being something to do with cloth. They were very up to the minute, going so far as installing electrical light down-stairs, with a generator to provide the power! Now, this was something I found very exciting. At Delamere, we were still managing with the old oil lamps and candles for upstairs.

Richard and Flora were having an animated and whis-pered conversation and I thought it rather a poor show. Richard was lapping up the attention, however.

I scowled to myself and added the last nut to the others, laying them in a neat row to dry. Then I slipped out and went to the library to speak to Papa. I was cross and scratchy and seeing Flora and Richard flirt made me worse. Was it possible I had become violently in love with Richard?

As I entered the room, the smell of lavender and beeswax assailed my nostrils again and I was transported back to when Richard had brought me in here. Something had changed since that day and I could not analyse quite what. Richard was playing games with me. Jealous that I may marry Edward, but taunting me with Flora.

Diary, I have to marry someone. There is no other path for me. The aunts are unable to launch me into Society, so it is unlikely I will meet someone other than Edward and Richard. I fear Mrs Parker would not deem me suitable for her sons. The alternative is to stay at Delamere and grow older and more decrepit with the house. I wish it could go back to when we were all younger, when Richard and I shared the nursery and ran wild in the gardens. It all seems far too complicated now.

However Diary, I digress. Back to the library.

The men did not see me as I approached. They had their backs to me and were bending over a case of specimens. I heard my father say: 'So, Edward, old chap, do you understand how the hissing cockroach makes its sound? It is the air being forced through its respiratory openings, here on its abdomen, d'you see? Quite remarkable, quite remarkable. They are quite splendid to hear but are fearsome beasts to behold, truly fearsome.'

'And you say you collected these in Madagascar? One day, sir, I hope to make the same journey as you have done.'

'I think, perhaps, you should go further.' My father sighed with longing. 'There is so much of this world to see. So many of its wonders to experience.'

'I should dearly like to visit the great pyramids.' Edward was being polite. I knew nothing of this longing to visit Egypt. I, however, yearn to see them.

'The world has much to offer, dear boy. And I have no doubt you will see some of it, at least!'

I coughed and both men turned. Father looked thoroughly disgruntled at being disturbed.

'Henrietta, so there you are,' said my father, as if he had been looking for me. I knew nothing was further from his thoughts. I had never really existed for him as a child, or indeed now, when I was on the brink of adulthood. Not for the first time did I thank the heavens for Aunt Hester and Nanny. They were more family to me than this bearded stranger peering myopically at me now.

'Yes, Father, here I am. I wish to speak to you.'

With an embarrassed glance at my father, Edward slipped past, murmuring something about seeing how the decorations were coming along. Jealously, I wondered if what he really wanted to do was see Flora.

I shut the door behind him and went to sit at the table containing the specimen case and averted my eyes. I did not want to look at giant hissing cockroaches.

'Father, a long time ago you told me if I needed to know an answer, then I should ask the question.'

Father sat down opposite me, took off his spectacles and polished them in nervous fashion. 'Indeed. And what do you have to ask, little one?'

I took a deep breath. 'I have two questions,' I began. 'Firstly, am I rich and where does my money come from? And two, am I really to marry Edward?'

Father replaced his spectacles and stared at me owlishly. He looked relieved and I wondered what he thought I wanted to ask. He smiled. 'Dear child, who has been filling your head with such tittle tattle? The servants no doubt!'

I shook my head. 'It matters not where I heard it. What I want to know is, is it true?'

Father smiled. 'Well, if I must answer you, yes, you have a little money, not a great deal, but some. It comes from your mother's side of the family. As you know, I have none to speak of. You will inherit it when you come of age. It is not for me to touch. That, I promised your dear Mama.'

I was excited and dismayed, all at once. 'Not until I am twenty-one?' It seemed a lifetime away.

'Indeed.'

'And am I to marry Edward?'

Father gave a little cough. 'Well, Henrietta, I cannot

answer that question.' He shook his head, amused. 'It is surely for you and Edward to discuss and I'm not at all sure he thinks of you in quite that, erm, way. If he does, then he must come to me, of course.' Father sat back and beamed, indulging me. 'But you are very young to be thinking of a husband. Surely there will be all the time in the world to decide on that when you're older. You're just a child!'

'I am nearly fifteen, Father,' I said, somewhat tartly.

'Good Heavens, are you really? How the time does fly. Fifteen. Nearly grown up, then.' He smiled again. 'My little girl, almost fifteen, how extraordinary!' He shook his head in amazement, then glanced, longingly, at his specimen cases.

I thought then, if I were a peculiar-looking bug with a pin stuck through it and presented on silk, that I would hold more fascination for my father. It was at that moment I realised he had neatly deposited me, at an age where I was to prove most expensive, with nannies and governesses and so on, in my distant relatives' home, therein causing the rumour and speculation, which had no doubt fuelled Richard's wild imaginings.

Diary, rarely have I been so enraged!

The gong sounded for tea and I had an excuse to rise. Father had already turned his concentration back to his horrid creatures, so I slipped away. Furious and again on the verge of tears, this time angry ones, I had the misfortune to bump into Richard coming in the opposite direction.

'Hetty? I say, what's the matter, Hetty?'

He came to me and held my shoulders. Gone was the annoying schoolboy. There was genuine concern in his eyes. 'Hetty, I hate to see you upset.'

He folded me in his arms and I took comfort from his

strong embrace. He could be irritating and wild sometimes, but the bond between us was unbreakable. We had sealed it in blood, after all. If only he could be like this all the time, then I would certainly marry him. Flora or no! But there was Edward. I did not know his expectations. I broke away from Richard's embrace.

His face clouded. In an instant his mood changed. 'Do you need my handkerchief again? Are those yet more soppy girl tears?'

I stamped my foot. 'You always make things worse, Richard. You are impossible.' With that remarkably silly speech, I ran off.

Rachel put the diary down and rubbed at her eyes. Poor Hetty! She was so confused.

'Who did you end up marrying, Hetty? I hope it was someone who was kind and who loved you for who you were.'

A ripple of amusement ran around the little sitting room. 'Wait and see,' it seemed to suggest. 'Wait and see!'

Rachel picked up the dairy again, although she knew she ought to be getting on with some work. A thought occurred to her. She and Hetty were similar in many ways. Rachel's parents made no secret of their disappointment with their daughter and Hetty was hardly a daughter at all to her Papa. But Hetty got angry and stamped her foot, whereas she just became more and more subdued, living life timidly, terrified of opening up to anyone or anything.

'Hetty, sweetie, you're a bit before his time, but you'd've loved what Philip Larkin had to say.'

Again, there was approval and amusement rolling round the room. 'Learn from me,' it said this time. 'Learn from my experiences.'

Rachel read on.

I have been in no mood for more teasing from Richard. I am in no mood fit for any company! I skulk and scowl and am very cross indeed. And so confused. This morning simply made things worse.

Despite his ban, Richard went riding with the Parkers. He even inveigled an invitation to join them for, of all things, his very first hunt.

The northeast Herefordshire meets, as tradition has always dictated, on the front drive of Delamere, every New Year's Day morning. It is one time when I think the old house echoes with hints of its glorious past.

There was a hard frost this morning and I hopped from one foot to the other, toes cold in my boots. I shoved my hands in my armpits in an attempt to keep them warm and stared at Richard and Edward, mounted and ready. The air was full of the stench of horses and the sound of their snorting breath against the cold.

Edward, I could tell, did not have his heart in it. He was going at Flora's special request and had been loaned Major, a solid chestnut hunter, who was beginning to slow with old age. Richard, however, was mounted on one of the Parkers' new geldings. It was an enormous black beast with flaring nostrils and I disliked it on the spot. It rejoiced in the name of Lucifer.

As Richard fought to control the straining horse, its hooves made a skittering sound as it slipped on the ice. In contrast, Flora, David and Lawrie, dressed in all their finery, sat unmoving on far more patient mounts.

The Parkers put Richard's shabby riding clothes to shame, but he did not seem to notice. He looked the far better rider, controlling the wild horse as he was, with aplomb. He drew the horse, even now frothing up with excitement, alongside the main group, where he chatted animatedly to Flora. She, in her black riding coat, top hat and veil, looked ravishing. For the first time, I felt a pang of longing to ride.

'Such a splendid sight,' Aunt Hester said. She stood at my side and pulled a shawl more closely round her, against the chill. The aunts, as predicted, had relented when Flora pleaded Richard's case.

'He won't have another chance to do any riding this holiday and you know how he loves it. It will be his very first hunt,' she had wheedled. 'And besides, he's the only person who can master Lucifer. Please let Richard ride, otherwise the horse won't get a chance to take part and Father says it so needs the experience.'

The aunts had crumpled in the face of such persuasion. Flora was the only person to whom Leonora ever gave way. It infuriated me.

'My, Richard looks magnificent, does he not, Hetty?'

I stared at Hester open-mouthed and then looked at Richard. How did he do it? Just how did he manage to worm his way out of anything and get precisely what he wanted?

Richard caught my eye and touched his whip to his top hat with a wicked grin. His face was flushed with cold and, even from this distance, I could see his eyes glint vividly blue in the January air. This morning he had a hint of the man he would grow into: good-looking, energetic, lethally charming and reckless.

Something stirred deep within me, a mysterious and unknown force. I knew it had to do with the changes overtaking me. A feeling of uneasiness overwhelmed me and it wasn't simply because Lucifer was skittish and skidding slightly, his legs trembling with the need for speed. Richard had the same need – and an iron will. Horse and rider were perfectly matched.

I did not say this to Hester, however. 'Aunt, should he really be riding that horse? It looks awfully lively.'

Richard reigned in the gelding hard and smoothed a hand down the animal's neck. He sent another wicked look my way and the odd feeling inside spread and warmed me. It flushed a heat throughout my stomach and down to between my legs.

'I am sure he will be perfectly fine.' Aunt Hester gave me a sideways look and whispered, 'And it might run off some of that dreadful energy Richard has. I'm sure that is why he gets into these awful scrapes; he simply hasn't enough to do, cooped up with us.' She put an arm through mine. 'Come along, Hetty, shall we find your Papa and have breakfast? Cook has made kedgeree as a special treat.'

I gave one last, longing, look at the gathered hunt, now being served their stirrup cup by a nimble-footed Sam and turned to follow my aunt.

Diary, I had no real desire to join them. Horses hold no fascination for me – smelly, recalcitrant beasts that they are – but how I longed to be Flora Parker. Just for an hour or so. To be looked at like that, by Richard. To be flirted with. As I entered the house, I heard her tinkling, pretty laugh ring out. She would be at the centre of attention, as always.

Breakfast was a somewhat dull and stilted affair. With no Richard to enliven proceedings and my father and I hardly conversing. We ate without interest, each sunk in our own thoughts.

I left the table as soon as it was possible. I wanted to get away from the stultifying atmosphere and, besides, I needed time to think about Richard and the peculiar way he had made me feel and to record it all in here. Diary, I sometimes feel that you are my only true friend.

Chapter 13

'Sweet pea?'

Rachel answered the phone and immediately recognised Tim's voice.

'Tim, how lovely to hear from you! You haven't rung for ages. How are you?' She hadn't spoken to Tim or Jyoti for weeks and was afraid they'd lost touch.

'Darling heart! Been in New York. Having a fantastic time. The men, wonderling, the men are to die for!'

'What, working?' Rachel frowned. Tim was a lecturer in English at an HE college. She couldn't see how he'd wangled a work trip to New York.

'I wish.' The sigh coming down the line was heartfelt. 'I'd work there like a shot. I loved it. No, it was just shopping and some shows, bit of clubbing. Justin took me.'

'Oh, so it's back on with Justin again, is it?' Tim's relationship with his on-off boyfriend was very much more off than on. They were a volatile couple. Rachel suspected they both liked it that way.

'Well, you know how it is. We muddle along, like an old married couple.' He gave a short laugh. 'Not that anyone'll let us actually get married, of course.'

Rachel thought of her parents, who never argued but then rarely spoke enough to each other to do so. Her father seemed happy at his golf club and her mother made a career out of sunbathing and going out to lunch. And nagging the latest cleaner. They lived very separate lives while maintaining the illusion of a perfectly happily married couple. It was a cold existence, though, and not one Rachel wanted to replicate.

The cosy domestic scene she'd witnessed in Gabe's kitchen came back to her. That was more the sort of marriage she'd like. The solid companionship and affection evident between Mike and Sheila. Not that she was thinking of marriage, of course, she added, hastily.

'Rach? You still there? Don't the phones work out there in that god-forsaken corner of the unknown universe?'

Rachel giggled. 'Yes, they work. Sorry, I was miles away.'

'Aha! Already losing your edge, that's what it'll be. Stuck in that rural backwater, braiding your hair and wearing smocks.'

Rachel laughed again. 'You've got a perverse and very peculiar idea of what goes on in the country, Tim.'

'Take my word for it, you'll be knitting yoghurt any day now.'

Before he got distracted, Rachel butted in, 'Lovely though it is to swap insults, did you ring for a reason? Some of us have work to do, you know.'

'Ooh, excuse me. I had no idea life was so terribly *hectic*. Flowery watercolours begging for your attention?'

Rachel settled on the arm of the sofa and stared out at the view. As ever, it drew her gaze. 'Actually, I've had an idea, or rather someone else gave me the idea. Although I think it might have been in my mind before he mentioned it and I've been thinking about it, sort of, ever since. A book, maybe, of illustrations. You see I've found this …'

'Told you, you're losing your edge,' Tim interrupted. 'A book indeed! Wonderling, you're waffling in a way I've never known you to. Think I need to get myself down there and sort you out. Been meaning to visit for ages, but you keep putting me off.'

'Tim, the house is hardly fit to live in!' Rachel exclaimed, thinking of the extra scaffolding about to go up so that Gabe could really get cracking on the roof. The rain had, after all, caused more damage and it had become a priority. Mike had also mentioned someone called Kevin to her, to help install the central heating. He still hadn't begun the work; the Halliday job having been delayed by the redoubtable Mrs Sutherland-Harvey. What with Stan too, the place would be overrun with workmen. She said as much to Tim.

'I can't think of anything I'd like more,' he declared. 'I'll sort out trains – you do have public transport in the sticks, don't you?'

Rachel ignored his sarcasm. 'Yes, Tim, we're not completely uncivilised.' Resigned to her fate she added, 'I'll pick you up from the station, then. Let me know which train you're on.' She knew, once Tim had made up his mind, that there was no changing it. His stubbornness was legendary, one of the many flashpoints between him and Justin.

Her heart sank. She loved Tim, she really did, but she worried about him in her little village. He was outrageously camp and he'd often gone out of his way to shock people. Rachel had stepped in time and again to smooth things over and steer her friend away from situations that threatened to get violent. Tim never learned. And – *her* village? Since when had she begun to think like that? Catching sight of the thick layer of dust on the windowsill she realised there was another problem. It was impossible to keep the house clean while all the work went on. She had so wanted the cottage to be at its best for her first visitor. Or, for the building work to be finished, at least.

With an effort, she tuned back in to what Tim was saying.

'I'll have to pop into Selfridges to get myself all togged out. Ooh, I just don't know what to bring. I mean, what does one wear in Hertfordshire?'

'I've no idea, I live in Herefordshire,' she corrected. It wasn't the first time Tim had mixed up the two counties. 'And, if you can survive the New York gay social scene without any problems,

102

I don't think Stoke St Mary will faze you.'

'Mee-ow! Claws out, pussycat. Perhaps I was wrong about you losing your edge! Can't wait, darling heart. I'll let you know when I'm free.'

'But what about when I'm free?' Rachel began to protest, but got the blank dialling tone. Tim had put the phone down.

'Well, he'll just have to lump it.' Rachel looked around the sitting room. 'At least this room's not too bad, apart from the dust.'

Her eyes were drawn again to the view beyond her worktable; it was yet another lovely day. 'And, if I've begun talking to myself, perhaps it's about time I had company.'

Gazing up at the tin holding Hetty's life story, sitting on its shelf, she said, 'Did you start talking to yourself, Hetty? Is that why you began the journal?'

Rachel was getting used to Hetty's presence. She found herself talking more and more to her, even sometimes asking advice. Occasionally, if she was really lost in Hetty's world, as she had been the other day, she would sense meaning coming through the strange atmosphere that swirled and misted around the room. Today, however, the sitting room remained silent. Shaking her head and forcing a laugh, she jumped a foot into the air as the phone began to ring again.

Thinking it was Tim calling back, she was startled to find it was Neil Fitch, from the estate agents. She was even more taken aback when she found herself accepting his invitation to dinner that night.

Neil took her to the Pheasant in Flight, a gastro pub on the top of a hill overlooking the village. He'd picked her up in his Freelander and was looking smart in a dark suit. Rachel was glad she'd fished out a half-decent skirt and silk shirt. She sensed the pub wouldn't be the sticky-carpeted type.

It wasn't.

Traditional on the outside, it was all leather seats and scrubbed pine tables inside. There were no locals having a drink at the bar and all the tables were set for dining. It was far more restaurant than pub. Rachel wasn't sure she liked it. Then, remembering Hetty's lust for life and her enjoyment of a small tea party, she forced herself to be more open-minded. Don't be like your mother, she vowed to herself, do not get into the habit of pre-judging everything and finding it at fault.

A young blonde girl greeted Neil enthusiastically and showed them to a table in the window. It was a lovely evening, but not quite warm enough to eat outside. Rachel loved this time of year when there was still light in the sky until late. She gazed, enraptured, at the setting sun.

'There are the most wonderful evening skies in this part of the world, don't you think? So open and vast. And the colours of the sunsets are incredible,' she murmured, almost to herself.

Neil had been busy studying his menu. He looked up and smiled, but she could see he didn't really understand what she meant and felt foolish. With a pang, she realised Gabe would have known instantly.

'That must be the artist in you, Rachel. I'm afraid I've never really noticed. Now what would you like to drink? Wine?'

'Thank you,' Rachel murmured and shifted her concentration back to the menu. It was a brief list, but everything was described in florid detail, with many mentions of 'jus' and 'pan-fried'. There was a lot of offal on it, at which she repressed a shudder. She decided on the sea bass.

The waitress returned and had a lively conversation with Neil; they obviously knew each other.

'Stacey,' he explained, once she'd gone with their order. 'I sold her parents' house.' He smiled. 'The curse of the estate agent in a rural area. You get to know everyone!' He didn't quite keep the smugness out of his voice.

And she likes you a lot, Rachel thought. Looking at Neil, she could see why; he was an astonishingly good-looking man. Her mother would love him. Attractive, well-mannered, promising career; he had all the attributes she had always wanted for her daughter. She didn't approve of Tim and had made clear her opinion of Rachel's boyfriends. None of them had passed muster. Neil would – and with flying colours.

He had all the makings of a perfect man. So why was being with him proving so awkward? When the wine had been opened, with Neil making a show of tasting it before it was poured, a silence descended.

'Do you …?'

'Have you …?'

They spoke at the same time and both laughed nervously. Another silence landed, during which they watched as other diners began to come in.

Neil took a sip of wine and sighed.

'I thought you liked it?' Rachel asked.

'Oh yes, it's wonderful, but I'll have to make the one glass last.'

'Of course, you're driving.'

Neil nodded. 'There is that. I'm also training for a triathlon. Alcohol plays havoc with the training schedule.'

'A triathlon! What does that involve?'

While they waited for their food to arrive, Neil filled Rachel in on what was expected. He went into so much detail about the three events: the cycling, the swimming and the ten-kilometre run, that Rachel wished their food would arrive. She'd tried to be interested, but had heard enough about the differences between on-and off-road running and the trials of open-water swimming to last a lifetime. Neil was obviously a very keen athlete.

Stacey returned to unfold the napkins and place them on their laps – Rachel was amused to see she took a long time to get Neil's just right – and then served their starters.

It had seemed a long wait and Rachel was starving. Ashamed at herself for not enjoying the evening more, she vowed to be more positive. 'This is delicious,' she said, forking up her cheese soufflé.

Neil nodded. 'I've heard the food is good here but haven't really

105

had the excuse to try it out. My soup's good too.' He broke some bread, then changed his mind and put it back onto his plate. 'You know, I'm really glad you agreed to come out. I've wanted to ask you out for a while … well, to be honest, ever since you came into the office, but Roger can be a bit old-fashioned about staff dating clients.'

Rachel didn't really know how to respond. She'd been single for so long she'd got out of the habit of this kind of conversation.

'Well, thank you.' Embarrassed, she stared out at the now-dark sky. 'Roger must be good to work for,' she settled on eventually, after another long pause. Roger seemed a safer topic.

Neil sat back and smiled. 'He is. Not sure how long I'll stay there, though. I want to broaden my horizons a bit.'

'What, go to a city branch? Hereford?' She'd been right, then, he was ambitious. Another point in his favour, in her mother's eyes at least.

'Maybe, or maybe get into land management. There are quite a few large estates round here. I like being outdoors and it seems a good life to me.' Without finishing, he set his soup bowl aside.

Rachel had no idea what land management would entail, but she had no doubts that Neil, if asked, would tell her. He was the sort of man who liked the sound of his own voice. Their starters had been cleared and there was the danger of another awkward gap in the conversation, so Rachel asked the question, 'What does a land manager do?'

'Well, it's quite complex. It can involve property law, valuing, selling and managing rural assets. You know, machinery, crops and livestock.' And Neil was off again, seemingly not requiring any answer other than the occasional nod from his dining companion.

Rachel took refuge in finishing the bottle of wine.

Having shown no interest in asking Rachel anything about herself and hogging the conversation entirely, when their puddings came Neil asked her about Hetty's journal. Although Rachel was keen to discuss it, at this stage in the meal she was exhausted from the effort of appearing interested in subjects she knew little of and cared even less about. Neil seemed to pick up on this but it meant that the meal ended in another series of awkward silences.

The Freelander made it up the track to the cottage without any of the wheezing and rattling that Rachel's Fiat usually made. 'That's why Roger insists we all have four-by-fours,' Neil said, a little pompously. 'You really need four-wheel drive to get to some of the properties we have to visit.' Having gained his second wind, he began to elaborate, telling her all about the hair-raising places he'd nearly got stuck in, the perils of snow and mud and landslides. 'It can be a tricky county to navigate in the winter. You'll find out all about that later in the year, though, of course,' he finished, with an unspoken criticism of her choice of vehicle.

With an old-fashioned courtesy, he came round to open the passenger door and walked Rachel up the path. He stood with her while she unlocked the front door, but didn't seem to expect to go in.

'I'll be off now, then. We athletes need our beauty sleep.'

'Well, thank you for a lovely evening, Neil.' Rachel pushed open the door, desperate to get inside.

'No, thank *you*, Rachel. I've really enjoyed talking to you.' He took her hand and bent closer.

Don't kiss me. Don't kiss me! Worried she'd said it out loud, Rachel backed away against the door jamb.

But Neil was merely demonstrating his impeccable manners. 'I've thoroughly enjoyed this evening,' he said. 'You're such a good listener. Can we repeat it sometime? And of course, I'd love to see Hetty's journal one day. I really would.'

Relieved she hadn't had to rebuff an advance, Rachel smiled and said, a little more warmly than she meant to, 'Come and see it anytime. And yes, thank you, I've enjoyed tonight too.'

She waved as he strode back to the car. Neil sounded the horn once, then reversed the car neatly and disappeared down the track.

Shutting the door against the night, she let out a long breath.

He *was* nice, she tried to convince herself. Attentive, with excellent manners, not at all pushy, a gentleman and, of course, very good-looking. And he seemed to like her. Her mother would be ecstatic. In fact, she'd start planning the wedding straight away. She'd always been critical of her daughter's steadfast singledom.

But something was missing. Rachel frowned. Apart from Neil's tendency to talk too much – it wasn't that he was boring, exactly, he just went into too much detail and didn't expect a reply – he was perfect. Wasn't he?

So, why was she not standing in the hall with her heart pumping, hormones fizzing? And why, though she wouldn't mind if she saw him again, was she not that bothered if it didn't happen too soon?

'Must be something wrong with me,' she announced to the silent and listening house. 'Oh, well, I've got too much work to do, anyway. Can't take time out to be wined and dined by good-looking men, however eligible they are. Did you have these problems, Hetty?' she whispered as a relaxing floorboard creaked upstairs. 'Did you have to endure men going on at great length about things you had no interest in whatsoever?' The house refused to answer. Somehow, Rachel didn't think Hetty did suffer in silence, despite the mores of the time.

Aware she was more than a little drunk, she yawned. 'You got through two husbands as well. Wonder what your secret was? Way to go, Henrietta!' Rachel said and staggered up to bed.

Chapter 14

'Well, colour me rural and call me Felicity Kendal! She's gone all Good Life on us!' Tim leaped out of the car obviously impressed. 'Hello Clematis Cottage.'

Rachel snorted with laughter and went to get Tim's bags from the boot. She'd picked him up from the London train forty minutes ago and had been giggling ever since. Now, though, his camp voice seemed to ring too loudly around the hills. She glanced about nervously, worried that Stan might have changed the habit of a lifetime and come to garden on a Friday. Somehow, she didn't think the two men would see eye to eye. 'Come on in, let's break out the corkscrew.'

But Tim stood for a moment, enjoying the view. 'Oh darling heart, it's enchanting, simply enchanting. I can *so* see why you did it.' He watched as swallows swooped and dived across the sky and then lifted his face to the warm June sun. He took a theatrical breath in, 'I love it here!'

Rachel frowned. She was still feeling defensive about the state of the cottage. 'I'd reserve judgement until you've see inside, Tim. I haven't been able to do much with it yet, what with all the building work going on. The sitting room's okay, but the rest of the house is in a bit of a mess. I wish you'd waited and seen the house when it was finished, when it was all perfect. Not that you're not very welcome, of course,' she added hastily, realising how ungracious she sounded.

Tim followed her into the hall and raised his eyes to the, still unpainted, ceiling. 'You haven't changed,' he said drily, 'still obsessing over perfection. Relax.' Then he giggled, 'Just wait until you see my wellies, sweet pea. They've got diamante strips down the side! Besides, I wasn't going to wait another second before seeing my best bud, no matter how horrible a state her little house was in. I've come to see you – oh God!' He stopped abruptly.

'I did warn you, Tim! It's a bit primitive still.' She looked around through his eyes. Mike had finally begun to install the central heating, having persuaded her that summer was the best time to get it put in. He and Gabe had begun to rip up the floorboards to lay pipes. In most rooms, at the moment, there were gaping holes in the floor and the tiny hall was being used as a store for the radiators yet to be fitted. The walls still had to be re-plastered, now the damp had been fixed and Rachel had given up keeping the dust at bay. It was pointless and even she was beginning to learn to live with the mess.

Tim let his bag drop with a thump. 'How the hell do you get any work done?'

'I just try and ignore it all.' Rachel shrugged. 'And I manage to most of the time. The workmen aren't here all the time anyway, so I squeeze in some work when they're not around. Actually, Gabe's very good. He makes sure they don't disturb me unless it's absolutely necessary. Kev's a bit of a nuisance, though. He's a friend of Gabe's and helps out a bit. And I never get much done when Stan's here.'

'Kev, Stan … *Gabe?*' Tim chuckled. 'Well, I know we haven't seen each other for a while, sweetie, but you have *got* to fill me in. Are they all gorgeous rural types with muscles like tractor tyres?'

Rachel thought about Stan's skinny torso revealed through his string vest and laughed. 'Not quite. Come into the kitchen. The holes in the floor aren't quite so life-endangering in there.'

'Oh,' said Tim, clapping his hands together as he followed her across the hall. 'I can just see it. An Aga to toast my tootsies on, herbs gathered under a waning moon hanging to dry, an airy Victoria sponge to welcome me – oh Lordy, sweet pea. It's a mess!'

Rachel winced. Now she really wished she'd put Tim off until everything had been done. To see the dust and mess anew, through someone else's eyes, brought it all into a sharp and cruel relief. She was amazed she'd been able to live alongside it. And a little proud that she'd made steps to conquer her tendency to be anal, in a way her mother never had.

'I'll just put the kettle on, shall I, and then we can have a good old gossip? Or would you rather have a proper drink?'

'Oh whatever, wonderling. Whatever you can rustle up in this pit.'

This hit a nerve.

'I did mention the cottage was a mess and hardly habitable, Tim. You insisted on coming.'

Tim slapped a hand over his mouth and said, in muffled tones, 'Gone too far. My apologies.' He blew a kiss. 'Forgiven?'

'Sit down and stop winding me up.'

He pouted. 'But I'm so good at it!'

Rachel laughed. She could never stay cross with Tim for long. 'We'll have tea, then, and drink it in here. Believe it or not, along with the sitting room, it's one of the least-worst rooms.' She switched the kettle on. 'Go on,' she added, nodding towards the kitchen table, 'sit down. Just mind those gaps along the skirting board.'

Treading gingerly, Tim made his way to the table and settled down. He ran a hand over the old oak. 'I like this,' he said, 'you'd pay a fortune for it in London.'

Rachel looked startled. 'What, even in that state?'

'Oh, yes, my darling. Shabby chic they call it. The good folk of Chelsea are spending all their ill-gotten gains on distressing their furniture and impressing their house designers' bank accounts.'

111

'Well, you'd know all about it,' Rachel said, bringing over the teapot. She sat down. 'You and Justin are far more aware of trends than I'll ever be.'

'He's asked me to move in with him.'

'Tim, that's marvellous news!' Rachel put down the milk bottle and took his hand. 'I'm so pleased for you both.' Then she noticed his expression. 'What's wrong? Are you having doubts?'

Tim nodded.

'Oh, come on, how long have you two been together?'

Tim shrugged. 'Five or six years. More off than on, though.' He blew out a breath and watched as Rachel poured tea.

'I've never met two people better suited.' She pushed his mug over to him.

'Despite the fact we have nothing in common and have completely different sets of friends, you mean?' He arched an elegant eyebrow.

'Well, yes, apart from that.' Rachel smiled and gave his hand a little shake. 'You're going to do it, aren't you? You are going to move in with him?'

Tim grimaced in comic fashion. 'Well, if I can get him to let me take any of my stuff with me, all of which, I hasten to add, he says is only fit for a skip and …' he trailed off and gave Rachel a wicked look. 'Of course I'm bloody going to move in with him. Have you seen his house? It's to die for.'

Rachel laughed and leaned back. She thought of Stan's words, that you never have enough time with the ones you love. She reached forward, making her chair creak ominously and took hold of Tim's hand again. 'Do it! Be with the one you love, before it's too late!'

'God alive, Rachel! Has moving to the country addled your brains? What's all this about?'

'Oh, it's just something Stan said. That there isn't enough time to be with the ones you really love.'

'And Stan is?'

'My gardener.' Rachel said it without thinking.

'Gardener, sweetie? Get you! My, you have gone up in the world. Time was you were scraping by in a one-bed in Camberwell.'

Rachel laughed. 'Oh, it is good to see you, Tim.'

'And you, my darling heart.' He looked at their joined hands. 'And I do love you, you know. If I were only straight!'

Rachel laughed again. They'd had this conversation many times. 'And I love you too, Tim.'

He straightened and released her hand. 'Now, enough of this maudlin stuff. Have you heard about Jyoti?'

'What about Jyoti? Do you know, since I moved here, she's not been in touch nearly enough.' Rachel drank her tea. 'I was wondering if I'd upset her in any way, although I can't think of anything I've done. Maybe –'

'She's getting married,' Tim interrupted.

Rachel slammed her mug down. 'What?' she stared at Tim.

'Don't look so shocked, dearie! It comes to us all in the end.' He pouted campily, 'Well, maybe not moi. Someday someone may even come up to your perilously high standards. Yup. She's getting married. To a very nice young man her family know. He's a doctor, based at UCH.'

'An *arranged* marriage!' Rachel was aghast. Jyoti had always been adamant she would never allow her parents to persuade her into one. 'Why hasn't she told me?' She thought back over the last few phone calls. Jyoti had been her usual jokey self, but Rachel had a sense she was holding something back. At the time she'd thought it was Jyoti's lingering reproach over her move out of London. 'Oh why hasn't she told me? We've been best friends since college!'

'I would imagine she was rather fearing your reaction,' Tim said with a smile. 'And judging from your present expression, she'd be bang on. What's so awful about it? He's a nice-enough bloke, they get on well.'

'Get on well! That's not enough for a marriage!' Rachel shrieked and stared across the table in horror. 'Tim, you know Jyoti's battled

113

with her parents for years. They didn't want her to go to university, didn't want her in student digs, hated her clothes and friends. And now,' Rachel gestured emptily to the kitchen, searching for words, 'she's just given in.'

'Rachel, dear girl, think about it. Jyoti, like you and me, has rattled around London doing the same old same old, ever since she graduated. She's gone out with some real horrors. Remember Frank?'

Rachel shuddered. Frank had been more controlling than her parents. And with a coke habit, to boot.

'Precisely. She's finally seen that she can have a good home, children, companionship, security. The usual things. And with a man she likes, that she feels comfortable with.'

'It's not enough,' Rachel began.

'Not for you, perhaps. You want the hearts and roses, the romance, the passion, the man who would die for you – as well.'

Rachel looked at Tim, askance. 'Do I?'

'Of course you do, darling heart, that's why you're still single. Plus the fact that you freeze the bollocks off most men who come near you.'

She let a twitch of a smile play about her lips at his outrageous remark. This was old territory. 'That's not fair, Tim!'

He poured himself another mug of tea. Stirring sugar into it, he said, 'Really? And who have you been out with in the last few years?'

'Er … well, there was Owen.'

Tim raised his eyes to the ceiling. 'He lasted how long?'

'About three months.'

'And why did he get the Rachel Makepeace vote of no confidence?'

Rachel mumbled something into her now cold mug of tea.

'Sorry, dear, didn't quite catch that. Would you care to repeat it, just a little louder?'

'I said, he never picked the towels up off the bathroom floor.'

'So, you gave a perfectly decent, nice man the heave-ho due to

114

his bathing habits?'

'Oh, come on Tim, he'd leave them all over the wooden flooring! It used to leave stains.' She blushed. She knew she was being pathetic.

Tim shook his head in disgust and tutted. 'A perfectly nice man, with a good sense of humour and hung like a donkey. Who else has there been?'

'Graham?' Rachel said half-heartedly. She knew Tim would never allow Graham.

'First-year university fling. Doesn't count.'

'I went out with him all year.'

Tim simply shook his head again and folded his arms. 'Who else?'

Rachel didn't want to admit to Charles. She'd tried her best to forget all about him. 'Charles,' she whispered. 'I went out with him for the best part of two years.'

'And why did he get the old heave-ho?' Tim raised his eyebrows.

Rachel gave him a sullen look. She was still raw from Charles. She'd really opened up to him and had been badly hurt in return.

'You know why. He was seeing Lorna on the side. Give me a break, Tim, I've hardly been lucky with men.'

Tim was silent for a minute, recognising Rachel's pain and then returned to his theme. 'It's all compromise, darling,' Tim said airily, in the manner of one who knew best.

'Oh yeah, like you're going to compromise by not taking your grotty old furniture to Justin's?'

Tim sniffed. 'I think you'll find that's a completely different matter. Some of that stuff is antique.'

'It's a load of crap, Tim.' Rachel grinned. 'I'm with Justin on that one. Hang on, though, how did this turn into an attack on my love life? We were talking about Jyoti.'

Tim put his mug down and sighed. 'Well, to be honest, darling heart, I understand it as little as you do. I can only assume our little Jyoti is looking for something her current life hasn't provided.

Who knows?' He shrugged. 'But, we're invited to the wedding. I hear Hindu weddings are a feast – for the eyes and the palate.'

'She'd better ring me and explain,' Rachel said, with a mutinous look on her face. 'Where is the wedding, anyway?' She looked around at the dirty cream walls still waiting to be painted. The tins of designer paint were lined up along the wall. She was itching to get started, but there was no point until Mike had finished putting in the heating. 'Might be nice to get away from the cottage for a weekend.'

'Perhaps you ought to ring her, seeing as she sent me as peacemaker, although God knows why she's so scared of you. And it's in Wembley, in some leisure centre or something. You can pitch your tent at Justin's if you want.'

'A leisure centre in Wembley?' Rachel said, horrified. It wasn't her idea of a wedding venue. 'Poor, poor Jyoti.' And it wasn't quite the weekend away she'd envisaged.

Reading her expression Tim tutted again. 'She won't want your sympathy. This is what she wants. Can't fit all the guests in anywhere else, apparently. It's going to be a huge event, apparently. I can't wait. Cheer up, wonderling, she's not being forced into anything. She likes the bloke and she wants to give up work and have lots of little chubby babies.'

'Tim!'

'Sorry, darling heart, not pc enough for you? Now, let's change the subject. What delectation have you planned for me tonight? What's the buzz in Stoke St Mary on a Friday night?'

'Well,' Rachel began, 'I thought I could cook something nice and we could open a bottle or two, catch up on all the gossip, you know.'

'What?' exclaimed Tim, 'and miss out on the village delight that is the pub quiz? I saw the board outside the most gorgeous run-down place as you drove me through the village. It's bound to be all sticky carpets and frantically clashing patterns. I *adore* places like that.' He beamed.

'You've got to be kidding!'

'Why not? We used to be a dab hand at quizzes at uni. We'll miss Jyoti's input on science and politics, I grant you, but we can muddle through. We'll easily beat a few rural-oaf types and an old codger or two. You know how I like to *win*!'

Rachel winced as she recalled Tim's fiercely competitive streak. It had seen him through some major athletic events too, before he'd become, by his own admission, lazy. She wondered who might be in the Plough. There was every chance Gabe and his friends would be there. She looked over at Tim. He was dressed in skin-tight pebble-washed denim over which hung a boldly striped shirt proclaiming 'I'm the Gayest Cowboy in Texas' in sequins. She wondered how the Plough's crowd would take to him.

'No goading, alright?' She pointed a stern finger. 'I've lost track of the times I've had to rescue you from getting beaten up.'

Tim followed her eyes to his clothes. 'Well, people ought to be more tolerant. Far too much queer-bashing going on, if you ask me.'

'Tim, you always start it!'

He pouted. 'Oh, alright, point taken. Now, what would be suitable for an evening in the local? Corduroys and a Barbour? Or overalls and green wellies?' He leaned forward with a grin and patted her hand. 'Would you like me to change, darling heart? Are you worried about me showing you up in your new rural idyll?'

'I'm more worried about their reaction to you.'

'Have no fear! I'll find something a little more conservative to put on. Have I time for a shower? There was this divine blonde who kept giving me the eye in the train on the way down. It made me feel positively filthy, I can tell you.' Tim gave Rachel an amused look and noted her horrified expression. 'Don't worry, darling heart, I'll be on my best, best, bestest behaviour in the pub. Absolutely no flirting of any kind. Nor shall I tease the straights. I will be completely angelic! Any hot water, then?'

Rachel began clearing the table. 'Should be but there's no

shower, only a bath. Loads of hot water, though. One of the first things Gabe fixed was the boiler.'

'Then, whoever the delightfully named Gabe is, he shall get a big juicy kiss from me tonight.' Tim stood up and hoisted his bag over his shoulder. He noted Rachel's tight lips and relented. 'Only kidding, tweedle-dums. I'll only kiss him if he's very, very good-looking.'

'Bathroom!' Rachel shot out. She'd had enough of Tim's teasing. 'First on your right. You've got twenty minutes if you want to eat before going out.' She clattered the crockery together, regardless of possible chips.

'Oo-er Miss Bossy! I simply *can't* imagine why you haven't got a man,' Tim said and made his escape before she threw something at him. He clattered up the uncarpeted stairs, singing out of tune, 'I am what I am, I am my own special creation ...'

Chapter 15

As they sauntered down to the pub, Rachel's stomach was in knots and she wasn't sure why.

Was it because she was entering the hallowed halls of village gossip central and having the temerity to join in the quiz? Was it because she was worried about what Tim might get up to?

She flicked a quick glance sideways and breathed out in quick relief; at least he was more soberly dressed now, in black jeans and a long-sleeved t-shirt. Perhaps it would be that rare occasion when he behaved himself. Immediately she felt thoroughly ashamed of herself. It was Tim's right to act in whatever way he wanted and she'd rarely given it a thought in London – unless he'd provoked someone too much.

Rachel looked around, at the yellow fields already shorn of the first harvest, at the lush hedgerow with the finches shooting out in front of them as she and Tim made their way down the track. It must be difficult to be in any way different around here. Everyone she knew of in the village appeared to be straight, married … conformist. Even in Hereford, the local youth dressed in a uniform of baggy jeans and baseball caps. Not one Goth, punk, or anyone else who attempted to stand out in the crowd. It must be a lonely life for anyone daring to be different, let alone gay.

Why do we struggle to please others at the expense of our

true natures, she wondered. She'd certainly been guilty of that with her mother. Then there was Hetty, battling the expectation that she should marry Edward, when it seemed obvious she was far more drawn to Richard. And Jyoti, compromising to keep her parents happy.

Her thoughts skewered to Gabe. Working for his Dad, living at home, always at the pub on Friday nights. All that ambition and raw talent wasting away, untapped. His grinning brown face swam into her vision. Was the knot of anxiety because she might bump into him in the pub? Now why would that be?

'Penny for them, Rachel?' Tim took her hand.

She smiled back and swung his hand in a playful manner while deciding what to say. She certainly didn't want to discuss Gabriel Llewellyn. Playing it safe, she said, 'I phoned Jyoti while you were in the bath.' Rachel made a wry face. 'Attempted a reconciliation.'

'Oh, darling heart, well done. How was the lovely girl?' Tim bent to pick a buttercup and stuck it behind his ear.

'She actually seems fine, happy. We had quite a chat. Said there was no way she'd do anything if she didn't really want to.'

Maybe not such a big compromise after all?

Tim raised his eyebrows in approval. 'Sounds like our Jyoti. What about the doctor?'

'Met him at a family party, got on like a house on fire. Very talented, tipped for the top. Orthopaedic consultant, apparently. He's called Kamal. She said, once the wedding is over and done with, they'll come to visit.'

'Well, hopefully, we'll meet him at the wedding before then.'

Rachel frowned. 'I'm not sure we'll have a chance to talk to the happy couple at the actual wedding. Jyoti was saying they have to sit on some sort of platform and the guests don't get anywhere near them.' She gave a little sigh, trying to keep the longing out of her voice. 'She said meeting him was like recognising your fate. That being with him was supremely comfortable. Said something about the deep, deep peace of the double bed after the hurly burly of the chaise longue.'

'Think I prefer a bit of the chaise longue.'

'You would,' Rachel said, without rancour.

'Oh well, we'll catch up with them at some point, I suppose.' Tim stopped and leaned against a gate. He rubbed his thighs. 'Hadn't realised that track was so steep.' He grimaced, 'How much further?'

Rachel laughed. 'Townie! Have you got so unfit?'

Tim looked up at her. 'We're not at home to Little Miss Smug, are we?'

'I think we might be.' Then she took pity on him. 'We're nearly there. About another half a mile along the lane.'

They continued in silence, enjoying the sharp green scents of the country air and the birdsong fluting across the clear evening.

With the pub in sight, Tim groaned. 'Thank the Lord.'

Rachel's misgivings about the evening returned. She focused her nerves on the upcoming quiz. 'I hope there won't be any questions on the gestation period of sheep or anything like that.'

'We'll be buggered if there is.' Stopping under the bright light, which illuminated the door to the Plough's lounge bar, Tim raised Rachel's hand to his mouth. He gave her a wicked look. 'For those of us about to die –'

'Idiot,' she said fondly, realising how much she loved him. 'Come on, I bet you a tenner we'll win. Oh, wait a minute,' she reached up and removed the buttercup still lodged behind Tim's ear. She laughed up into his face. 'Very fetching, but maybe not for a quiz night in my local!'

Tim looped a casual arm around her shoulders. Giggling, they opened the door and went in.

Unseen, from the shadows at the far side of the car park, Gabe watched them. He got out of the Toyota and then paused, keys in hand, staring hard at the spot where Rachel and the man had disappeared into the pub. Abruptly changing his mind, he got back into the pickup, slammed the door and drove off, sending up dust clouds as he gunned the engine.

The pub was packed and smoky. It was, as predicted, decorated with a riotous clash of worn patterns and possessed the requisite sticky carpets.

Tim shouldered his way to the bar as Kevin waylaid Rachel. She nearly didn't recognise him without his glasses. She often wondered why Mike employed him as casual labour, as he moaned about him constantly. Rachel wasn't at all sure she liked Kevin; there was certainly something about him she didn't trust.

'Rachel! 'Bout time you got yersen in here! You gonna be on our team? We're a man short, seeing as Gabe ain't bothered to make it. Go on, say you will.'

Kevin came closer, invading her body space; Rachel could smell beer on his breath. He was already quite drunk, even this early in the proceedings.

'We only got Stan and Paul and Paul don't know nothing.'

'Well, I'm actually with a friend,' Rachel began. She tried to back away, but there wasn't enough room to put space between them.

Kevin wasn't in a mood to take a hint. 'Sound!' he slurred. 'That'll make up our team, then, if we can get Dawn to get her arse from out behind the bar.'

Rachel felt hounded. She'd hoped she and Tim could make up a team on their own, not have to join in one. Deaf to her protests, a determined Kevin took hold of her arm and dragged her to a table, where, sure enough, Stan and a fair man she assumed was Paul were sitting.

'You all right, our Rachel?' Stan said mildly, as he pulled on a roll-up. 'Wasn't expecting to see you in yere.' He pulled out a chair. 'Sit yersen down, then.'

Rachel sat next to him. 'Didn't think it was your sort of thing either, Stan.'

'Oh, I don't mind a quiz, every now and then.' Stan pulled a face. 'And gets me out o' the house, like. You met young Paul? Lives in one o' them new places down near the main road.'

'Hello Paul,' Rachel said, feeling ridiculously self-conscious, silly nerves making her use a posh London voice.

Paul nodded.

'Who are you with, then?' Kevin asked, as he collapsed into a chair on the other side of Stan.

'Erm ... him,' Rachel replied, just as Tim shoved himself through the crowd, carrying a large white wine and a lager.

Kevin looked Tim up and down suspiciously and Rachel's heart sank. From the little she knew of Kevin she feared the worst.

'Ah, here you are,' Tim said, without a hint of camp. He put the drinks down on the table, with a wink for only Rachel to see. 'I asked what sort of wine they had and the lovely barmaid said red or white, so I hope it's okay.' Then, becoming aware of the group's eyes on him he added, 'I'm Tim. Nice to meet you all. Now, I can see empty glasses. What can I get you?'

As an icebreaker, it wasn't startlingly original, but it worked. Introductions all round followed. Having been offered a drink, the panacea for all wrongs in life, the men grinned, nodded and gave their orders.

Rachel breathed out. Perhaps it was going to be all right after all. Watching Tim, as once again he made his way through to the bar, she relaxed a little and sipped her wine.

In the end, they couldn't persuade Dawn to join the team; she had to work behind the bar but Stan assured everyone that Rachel had fancy degrees and education and what not and they'd be fine with only five players. Paul was an unknown quantity and Rachel had her doubts about what Kevin would know. She chastised herself for being such a snob.

'What are we going to call ourselves?' asked Tim. 'We ought to have a team name.'

Paul and Kevin exchanged uncomfortable looks.

'Well,' Paul began, 'we're usually called Wankers with Attitude.' He shrugged an apology at Rachel. 'Kev thought it up.'

He seemed nice and was obviously smitten with Dawn. Rachel noticed his eyes kept straying to the bar, where the redhead was hard at work.

'There's usually only the three of us,' he explained further. 'Stan's only just started coming into the pub again.'

'Might as well change the name, seeing as we've never fuckin' won,' muttered Kevin into his beer.

'Well, I'm all for a bit of tradition,' Tim put in, unsuccessfully hiding a grin, 'so, if you're always called Wankers with Attitude then that's what we'll be. Perhaps Rachel and I will change your luck?'

'Ar perraps,' Stan added with a raspy laugh.

Alan, the landlord, settled the unruly crowd with a yell and announced that the quiz was about to begin. 'An easy one to get you all started with on the general knowledge round,' he said. 'What is the gestation period of a pig?'

Tim giggled, elbowed Rachel in the ribs and whispered, 'We're doomed!'

'I knows that,' Stan said. 'Put down three months, three weeks and three days.'

'Are you sure, Stan?' asked Paul.

'No, don't seem right to me,' added Kevin. 'What we need is Gabe; he'd know that sort of shit.'

Tim looked at the others. 'Well, if no one else has any better suggestions, we'd better go with Stan's answer.' Glancing at Rachel, who shrugged her ignorance, he pushed the quiz sheet over to her.

Stan merely sat back, looking smug, his strange eyes half-closed over his cigarette smoke.

'Where's Gabe gone, then?' Paul gestured to Kevin's empty glass. 'You ready for another?'

Kevin nodded. 'Into town to see one of his fancy women, I reckon. You know our Gabe, always disappearing off somewhere.'

Paul snorted, asked if anyone else wanted another drink and sauntered off.

Kevin watched him go. 'Look at him, can't keep his hands off her, sad bastard.'

They all watched as Paul leaned over the bar towards Dawn and made her giggle. 'Trying it on while Gabe's not here.'

'What do you mean?' asked Rachel, feeling another prickle of distaste for Kevin.

'Dawn's got the wet knickers for Gabe, like every other bit of skirt for fifty mile round here and Paul's making the most of the fact that lover boy ain't about.' Kevin leered at her and laughed. His face was flushed with alcohol and Rachel decided she definitely didn't like him.

'Look, we playing this quiz or not?' Stan interrupted, getting impatient with the gossiping. 'Put the answer down, Rachel, you got a pencil there? It's three months, three weeks and three days, I tell yer.'

There were six rounds in the quiz. If possible, it got even hotter and smokier. She managed to concentrate long enough to answer which fruit Persephone ate but couldn't get Kevin's words out of her head. So Gabe was a bit of a lad, was he? He certainly had enough charm for it. But why did it bother her so much?

Tim poked her in the side again. He was straining to see the scoreboard. 'We're joint top, I think,' he said, with mounting excitement. 'How many more rounds are there?'

'Just one more,' Paul answered. While Kevin was happy to drink himself into oblivion, he'd been as competitive as Stan and Tim.

Rachel groaned inwardly. With Tim's love of winning, he'd be unbearable if they lost at this late stage.

'And now, the last round,' Alan announced.

Kevin raised a pint in a wobbly hand and cheered sarcastically. 'Thank fuck!'

'Glad you're enjoying it, Kevin,' Alan said, to a cheer from the crowd. 'It's art and books this time. So, get your pencils and brains sharpened and here we go.'

'Christ, it could all be on this last question,' cried Tim in anguish, fifteen minutes later. 'We're neck and neck with the bloody Women's Institute. Come on, darlings, concentrate that grey matter. We've got to win this!'

'Which Dickens novel is set against the Gordon Riots?' Alan's voice boomed over the increasingly chatty crowd and silenced it.

'Bugger,' said Paul, 'that's one for you two, Tim and Rach. Haven't a bleedin' clue.'

Tim's face screwed up in pain, his fist clenched on a tabletop glossy with spilled beer. 'Come on,' he urged himself, 'come on. *Think!*'

Rachel closed her eyes and racked her brain. Dickens ... Dickens. God, why did it have to be a question on Dickens? Now if it had been Austen or George Elliot she might be in with a chance.

'*Barnaby Rudge,*' said Stan, in a hissed whisper. 'Go on, put it down. Right answer, that is, make no mistake.'

The rest of the team, bar Kevin, who had drifted off into an alcoholic daze, looked blankly at him.

Panicking, Tim peered over to their rivals. 'They're writing something down!' he groaned. 'You got any ideas?' he asked Rachel. She shook her head.

'Well, put it down then, sweet pea,' he urged. 'We haven't anything else to offer and Stan's got a lot of answers right this evening.'

'Yes, but they were all about plants and crows and things,' Rachel whispered back.

'Go on, Rachel love. It's the right answer. I'm certain o' it.' Stan said, sounding supremely confident.

Rachel stared at Stan's face, with its permanent cigarette hanging from a corner of his mouth and the green eyes belying his age. He was the most surprising man. She wrote down the answer: *Barnaby Rudge.*

As the quiz sheets were handed in, a collective sigh of relief rippled around the room. Now the quiz had finished, some real drinking could begin.

'There'll be a short break, as usual,' intoned Alan, 'while we mark the papers. Snacks on the bar everyone. Help yourself.'

As soon as he'd said this, there was a stampede to the bar – and to a very startled-looking Dawn. It was led by their very own Paul.

Stan laughed. 'Folks round 'ere likes summat free and no mistake.'

'How did you know that?' Rachel asked.

'What's that, then?' Stan extinguished his roll-up between thumb and finger and, as was his habit, placed the butt neatly in his tobacco tin.

'About the Dickens novel?'

Stan pursed his lips. 'They drilled it into us at school. Dickens. *Great Expectations, Dombey and Son, Bleak House* and the like. Never lost the love for a bit o' Dickens. You not read any, then?'

Rachel shook her head. 'Not Dickens, no.'

'Don't know everything then, do you girl?'

Rachel shook her head again. Had she been so transparent? Had she fallen back into her habit of pre-judging everyone? True, Kevin had been a waste of space, but both Paul and Stan had answered lots of questions correctly. More, in fact, than her. Looking Stan in the eye, she had new respect for both him and Paul. She was ashamed of herself and vowed to try better at accepting people for who they were – and not loading them with her pre-conceptions. She'd done it with Gabe and she'd done it again tonight.

'Alan's about to announce the winners,' Paul said, as he and Tim came back to their table and sat down. They'd brought back plates laden with sausages, sandwiches and crisps. Paul shovelled a sausage into his mouth and spoke through it. 'It's got to be us. We've got to be in with a chance of winning this time?' His eyes were over-bright and his face flushed and, although drinking at a slower pace than Kevin, he was definitely tipsy.

'Got to be, darling heart,' said Tim in return.

Rachel watched Paul closely. The endearment had gone unnoticed. So, she'd been wrong about how they might react to Tim. He'd been less camp than normal, but not really by much. And, apart from the choking smoky atmosphere and the new knowledge of Gabe, which nagged at the back of her mind, it had actually been a really good night. She took a large slurp of wine. She'd been wrong about lots of things tonight, it seemed. She ate a sausage. It was delicious.

It was time to let people in, to give them a chance. She'd been closed up for years. It was time for a new start, a new her. To discover a zest for life and meet it head on. Be more like Hetty.

'And the winning team is – Wankers with Attitude! Come on up lads and, er, lady and collect your prizes!'

As Alan made his announcement to the raucous crowd, Gabe slipped into the pub. He leaned against the bar and ordered his drink.

'The boys did well tonight, then,' Dawn said, as she pushed over his pint of Stella. 'You missed a treat, Gabe.' She smiled at him and jiggled the neck of her t-shirt a little lower.

Her efforts went unnoticed. Gabe's eyes were on Rachel, as she celebrated with her team. She and Paul leapt up and hugged one another and the tall, thin man he'd seen with Rachel earlier shook Stan by the hand and then grabbed Rachel and kissed her resoundingly on the lips.

'I take it they've won,' he said sourly and took a swig of lager.

'Mate, where've you been? It's been a crackin' night.' Spotting him, Paul made his slightly unsteady way over to the bar and slapped Gabe on the back. 'Another pint, my lovely Dawn, please.'

'Haven't you had enough?' the barmaid said, eyeing his swaying form. 'You been trying to catch up with Kev?'

'I'm drunk on success and besides, Dawnie, I've never had enough from you.'

Dawn raised her eyes to the ceiling. 'Don't know how you put up with those two, Gabe, I really don't.'

'So, where *have* you been, then?' Paul tried and failed to focus on his friend.

'Had some stuff to do,' Gabe said shortly.

'Your Rachel's a bit of all right, mate.'

Gabe watched as the thin man hung an arm round Rachel's

shoulders. 'She's not mine, Paul,' he said and turned to go.

'Gabe,' Paul called. 'You haven't finished your drink!'

Gabe strode to the door. 'You have it. I've gone off the idea.'

Chapter 16

Rachel crept down the stairs, early next morning, so as not to wake Tim.

They'd all carried on the celebrations late into the night at the pub. Last orders had somehow never been called and when Rachel realised the time, it had been three in the morning. She'd dragged a reluctant Tim home.

Now, too few hours later, she was desperate for a cup of tea to dull the headache drumming at her temples. As she waited for the kettle to boil, she hopped from one foot to another; the quarry tiles were cold and the chill struck through, even though she wore her sheepskin slippers.

Leaving Tim to sleep and desperately in need of liquid, she took the teapot into the sitting room. She drank the first mug sitting alone on the sofa, her feet curled up underneath her, enjoying the quiet.

Last night had been fun. She still hadn't taken to Kevin. He'd got even more drunk and had eventually been poured into a car and driven home by Dawn. Paul and some of the others there had been good company. The real revelation of the night, though, had been Stan and Tim bonding, over of all things, the Bauhaus arts and crafts movement!

'Hetty, what else did the social scene offer you, apart from afternoon tea? No pub quizzes, I expect' Rachel glanced at the biscuit tin, lodged in its usual position on the bookshelf. She cocked an ear upstairs, if Tim kept to his usual habits he wouldn't surface until lunchtime. 'Lots of time, then,' she said to herself with glee. 'Lots of lovely time to find out more about you.' Rising, she walked over and took down the Huntley and Palmers tin.

Ignoring the headache still thrumming between her ears, she found the diary and settled on what looked to be a continuation of Hetty's description of that eventful Christmas.

January 1908, Delamere

Richard continues to fluctuate in mood, as do I. We are a volatile pairing and clash continually – that is, when he isn't off riding with the Parkers.
Yesterday he found me in the schoolroom. It was a dark day filled with sleety rain. I was ensconced in a blanket on the window seat, where I could at least have enough light with which to read. I did not want to be disturbed.
Richard was bored. 'Oh come on, Hetty. Let's do something,' he wheedled.
I refused to look up. He was making my body do strange things and filled me with odd emotions. I did not want to be with him. 'I'm happy reading,' was my only reply.
He peered over my shoulder at my Girl's Own Annual. 'God, what rubbish you read.' He was so scornful it made me laugh. 'Come on, Hetty. I have to go back to school next week.'
'And you cannot ride because of the weather.'
He shifted on his feet, guiltily. 'It's not just that. I thought we could have one last adventure. I won't be back until Easter, remember.'
I looked up then, at his blue eyes gleaming from under sooty lashes, and relented. How could I not? I would miss

him terribly until he came home again, despite his trying moods and his teasing me with Flora. Putting my book carefully in my desk, I pulled the blanket more closely around my shoulders and shivered violently; the entire house was freezing.

'Very well,' I said. 'What have you in mind?'

'Good-oh Hetty, you're such a brick. You're more fun than all my school fellows put together.' He kissed me quickly on the cheek and then took hold of me and danced me into the corridor.

'I doubt that very much,' I gasped. 'Oh Richard, let go of me, do. I've got dust all over my sleeve.' He stopped whirling me around and brushed at my arm, where the crumbling lime-washed walls had shared their flakes with me.

'I know,' he said, his face aglow, 'let's go and do some dancing where we have plenty of room.'

I knew that look. It meant trouble. 'Wherever do you mean?'

'The ballroom, ninny.'

'If you call me ninny again, I shall not go anywhere with you,' I said, folding my arms primly over my chest. I blew out a breath and watched it mist in the dull light of the corridor. I shivered again. Maybe dancing would warm me up.

Richard looked abject, but only because he wanted his own way. 'Sorry. Are you coming, then?'

I shrugged and followed.

We ran down the two flights of steps, using the servants' stairs and then crept along the main hallway past the aunts' sitting room. We stood, for a second, in front of the double doors. Beyond here was strictly out of bounds. It was the part of the house that was falling down. Neglected, it had become unstable and therefore

132

dangerous.

Richard turned to me, a grin on his face. 'Do you dare?'
We had, in fact, once or twice before, ventured through.
Each time we visited this part of the house it seemed
more decrepit. There were pigeons roosting and swallows
in the summer. Bats at night and more spiders than I ever
wished to see. But I could never resist Richard and, truth
be told, he was far more exciting than Lucy Maud
Montgomery's latest serial. I nodded my assent and we
slid through.

It was very dark in this corridor. Richard felt for my hand
and I gladly gave it. I was not sure who was comforting
whom. I brushed away a cobweb in disgust and shut my
mouth to prevent anything going in.

We felt our way along before coming to yet more double
doors, which we knew led to the old ballroom. Richard
pushed at them. They gave an almighty creak and one
dropped entirely from its hinges with a crash.

We staggered back, blinded and choked by dust, giggling a
little from fear. Then froze as we listened for a reaction
from the other part of the house. Nothing.

We could now see slightly better and, when we entered the
room, could see why. Part of the roof had collapsed,
taking most of the wall with it. The cold shuddered its
way through, along with what little light the winter day
could provide. Sleet puddled on the floor and daggers of
window glass lay about. I could understand why this part
of the house was out of bounds; it looked to be in imminent danger of collapse.

In its decaying state, it had a kind of Miss Havisham-style
beauty. Stepping over the prone door, I ventured in. Most
of the old chandeliers were still in place but were swathed
with cobwebs and dulled with inches of dust. The wall
sconces had yet more cobwebs stringing down and

drifting in the wind, which was blowing the sleet in from outside.

'It's in an awful state, isn't it?' Richard wandered around, tentatively fingering a rotten chair, its gilt eaten by wood-worm. He went to the grand piano, still holding a regal position in the corner and safe from the dereliction of the east wall. He pressed an ivory, but only a dead plonking sound emanated. Mice must have eaten the strings.

'I hate it seeing it like this!' Richard exploded. He wheeled around, rage filling his face.

I went to him. 'But there's nothing any of us can do.' I put my hand on his arm. He was shaking. 'It would take too much money to make good.' I shrugged. 'And we have none.'

He stared at me for a second, but I could not discern his emotion.

'Do you know why we have no money, Henrietta?'

I shook my head. He was unnerving me.

He brought his face close to mine. He had a smudge of dirt on one cheek. 'We gambled it all away. Every last penny. Be wary about joining the Trenchard-Lewises, Hetty, we've always been a bad lot.'

'Aunt Hester said it was something to do with the farming crisis in the 1880s.' I stuck my chin out. I did not like to think of my adopted family being tainted.

Richard grinned with malice. 'Believe that if you will, innocent little Hetty.'

Sometimes I wondered if he were quite sane, with his delight in untruths and his wild moods. To appease him – and stop my violent shivering, I said, 'I thought we came here to dance?'

His shoulders dropped and the smile he gave was less manic. 'Then, shall we?'

He put me into the correct position and, for a moment,

we were very close. I thought he might kiss me he was staring at me with such intensity, but he simply smiled again and led me in a waltz. We swayed across the floor, stumbling a little over the debris. Neither of us were very good dancers.

After I had trodden on his foot for the third time, Richard strode off in a huff, saying it was no good without the music. He left me to make my own way along the dismal corridor. I would have to make up a story to explain the mess on my skirts.

Rachel frowned. This diary extract made for dismal reading. Richard sounded downright odd. He delighted in taunting Hetty and deliberately played with the truth. She could understand the attraction the girl had for him, but he played games with her. She knew how that felt; Charles had been an expert at it.

'And we don't deserve that, do we, Hetty? No matter how hot the guy is.'

Something in the room rippled around her.

Rachel flicked through the pages for something else to read, something lighter, which didn't test her hangover.

One entry, dated May 1910, summarily dismissed the month as a 'dull time, during which we are all in enforced mourning for the king and cannot do anything, lest we show disrespect. It is terribly dreary!' Another, written earlier in the same year, described a party, a hunt ball, Hetty's first.

Rachel sat up eagerly, wanting to read about a slightly older Hetty. She skimmed the lines, but it wasn't Hetty at her best. The tone was unusually stilted and formal. It turned out to be a fairly dry account of a new dress, of dancing with Edward and of Richard flirting with Flora. Disappointing.

After a while, the effort of reading the spidery writing was too much. Rachel's hangover had begun to make her feel sick and, with a craving for more tea, she rose stiffly and tiptoed into the kitchen.

135

She was sitting at the kitchen table in a daze, trying to summon up enough enthusiasm to take a mug of tea up to Tim, when the kitchen door burst open. The noise shattered any remnants that were left of 1910.

'There's an Adonis on your roof!'

Tim stood, hands on hips, an enormous grin on his face. He was wearing an odd collection of clothes: jeans from last night, the diamante wellies and a huge baggy t-shirt.

'What?' Rachel's brain was befuddled with alcohol and she wanted to linger in the past, with Hetty. She struggled to make sense of the peculiar vision standing in front of her.

'A veritable god, darling heart – ooh is that tea?' Distracted, Tim slid onto a kitchen chair. 'Heaven,' he sighed, as he drank. 'Just what a boy needs. Actually,' he sniggered, 'I think what this boy really needs is the god on the roof. My wonderling, he's gorgeous, I've never seen such beauty.'

Rachel wrinkled up her nose and listened. There were, now she came to think about it, faint sounds coming from the roof at the back of the house. Surely it couldn't be Gabe or Mike here so early on a Saturday morning? Padding back across the hall, carefully avoiding the holes in the floorboards, she drew back the curtains and peered out of the sitting-room window. Sure enough, there was the Toyota pickup parked in its usual position, under the deep early-morning shade of the horse chestnut tree. Mike, although well preserved, would hardly qualify for Tim's fevered description, so she assumed it was Gabe.

When she re-entered the kitchen, Tim was busy adding boiling water to the teapot. He poured another mug, added milk and sugar and drank. 'Nectar!' he exclaimed, with a smack of the lips.

Rachel's hangover wasn't sure it was in the mood for Tim's exuberance this early in the day. 'You seem to be in a very lyrical mood this morning. What's brought this on?'

'Oh, Miss Grouchy Rachel, how I'd forgotten your hangover moodiness!'

Putting his mug down with a bang that was far too loud for Rachel's currently sensitive state, Tim rose and tried to dance her around the kitchen. She shrugged him off, slumped back down at the table and poured herself yet more tea.

'I didn't know you'd got up. It's most unlike you. What are you doing up this early?' Rachel wrapped her hands around her mug and sipped. The aspirin she'd taken first thing was just beginning to work and her headache was gradually easing.

'How could I not be when in Elysium?' Tim clapped his hands together and noticed, with glee, that the noise made Rachel wince. 'You've lost your drinking head, my darling.'

'Last night was the first time I've ventured into the pub since I got here. Mostly, I just have the odd glass of wine here in the evening. But only the one.' She shrugged. 'I think you're right, though, I have lost what little tolerance I had for booze. And anyway, you know I don't like drinking alone.' Rachel frowned. She wasn't at all sure she was making any sense. The image of her mother, drinking alone in her pristine kitchen flashed before her. Paula was at her most venomous when drunk. All the frustrations of her life were tightly bottled, until the pressure cap was released by gin.

Rachel sank into gloom.

Tim was determined the morning shouldn't be spoiled, however. 'I went *walking*,' he said, with the emphasis on the verb. 'A walk! Me!'

Rachel managed a laugh. 'Where to?'

'Oh, just down the track again and through the village to the church.' Tim waved his hands in the air. 'My wonderling, it is so lovely here, I'm almost tempted myself.'

The thought of the very urban Tim in her little village made Rachel chuckle. 'You'd last five minutes. No proper clothes shops, you can't get sun-dried tomatoes for love nor ready money and there's no broadband.'

Tim sat back, his mouth agape. 'What? However do you manage?'

Rachel pulled a face. 'Dial up. Which I use very sparingly. It costs me a fortune otherwise. And I warn you to do the same while you're here.'

'No wonder you haven't been in touch much recently. I thought you'd just found new friends to play with. You should get yourself a mobile phone.'

'Thought of that. The network coverage is crap, though.'

Tim made a face. 'I'm rapidly going off this place.'

'I thought you might.' Feeling stronger, Rachel tackled a chocolate digestive.

'There are, I believe, some compensations,' Tim began, helping himself to several biscuits. 'Talking of new friends, just *who is* that darling man on your roof?' He winked.

'Gabe,' Rachel said expressionlessly. She didn't want him exposed to Tim.

'Oh my God! The same Gabe who created all the lovely, lovely hot water? So he's good with his hands too? As well as being so divinely handsome? I haven't seen lean muscles like that since a certain strip joint in New York. Oh my.' Tim began to fan himself.

'Leave it out, Tim. He's straight.'

'A man can always hope.' Tim treated her to a comic leer and swallowed a biscuit whole. He munched, his cheeks bulging and rolling his eyes.

'You are incorrigible!' Rachel pointed a reproving finger. 'Come on, seeing as we're both up with the lark, what shall we do with the day?' She peered out of the kitchen window – it was sunny again. It was turning out to be one of those long, hot summers when you forgot what it was like to be cold or bothered worrying about the chance of rain.

'Well,' Tim began doubtfully through a mouthful of crumbs and looking around at the dilapidated kitchen. 'I suppose I could always give you a hand with some decorating. It must be driving you absolutely nuts to have to live like this.'

Rachel laughed again. 'Actually, you know, I'm coping far better than I thought I would. I really think, after you've lived with the dust and mess for a while, you forget to see it, if that makes any sense.'

She followed Tim's disbelieving gaze and, while her eyes saw the toolbox left in the corner and the alien-looking pile of brass plumbing bits, her mind saw the finished kitchen. 'It'll be lovely in here, one day.'

Tim reached forward and put his hand on hers. 'You've changed,' he said abruptly. 'For the better. Thank God,' he added, as if it was all getting far too emotionally intense. 'Couldn't have borne a weekend with the anally uptight old maid you were becoming. I saw a spinster and her pussies looming!'

'Thanks a bunch!' Rachel grinned, manfully ignoring the jibe. 'But, back to the subject, what *do* you want to do today? If we're not careful, we'll fritter it away and it's another gorgeous day.'

'I'm in your hands, darling heart, but if you can rustle up a nice stately home and a National Trust luncheon then I'll be ecstatically happy.'

Rachel laughed. 'Around here? There are loads of them.'

'Oh goody. You know how I like to goad those Trusty volunteers. They're so *wonderfully* earnest and sycophantic.'

Rachel groaned. Another one of Tim's hobbies was to fake an intense interest in displays, museum exhibits or art collections and engage any hapless attendant unlucky enough to be on duty in lengthy discussion. His record to date was forty-five minutes in the Museum of London. National Trust volunteers were a special target.

'Oh, I was right all along, this is heaven indeed!' Tim took another noisy slurp of tea.

'You won't be saying that when you have to toil down the track to collect the Sunday papers from Rita in the morning.'

'What, no lusty youth pedalling up the hill to have a glass of homemade lemonade and a ginger biscuit, all ready to have his sweaty brow mopped?'

'You'll have to be content with mopping Rita's sweaty brow instead. She's menopausal. Go on, get back up those stairs and put something half decent on.'

'So bossy,' grumbled Tim. He pulled his lanky frame off the kitchen chair and plonked his mug in the washing-up bowl. 'I'm definitely going off this B&B. Never stayed anywhere like this, where you get bullied so much by the landlady.'

'I'll do worse than bully you, if you don't get out of my kitchen,' Rachel giggled and, grabbing a tea towel, snapped it at Tim's rear.

'Ouch!' he shrieked. Then he bent over, presented his behind to her, and wiggled it.

'Ooh, spank me some more, matron. I love you when you get all dominant.'

Rachel flicked the tea towel again. It met its target with a crack.

'Ow!' Tim put up his hands in surrender. 'All right, I'm going, I'm going!'

On the roof, Gabe paused in the act of fixing on a new tile and listened to the raucous laughter coming from below. He ran a handkerchief around his sweaty neck and shoved it into his back pocket. With a grim expression, he continued to work.

Chapter 17

Coming back on Monday lunchtime to an empty house, having dropped Tim off at the station, Rachel found herself wandering around a silent cottage. There was no sign of Gabe or his father, no familiar red Toyota pickup in its parking space.

She felt so restless she'd even welcome the distraction that was Kevin, even if he was always looking her over. There was something sleazy about him in the way he always talked to her cleavage and never her face. Even so, today, she'd gladly make him his usual coffee, if it gave her something to occupy her. She felt itchy under her skin, had a million things to do, but didn't want to settle to any of them.

She and Tim had had a lazy Sunday, having collected the papers from Rita in a mood so foul it even silenced Tim. They'd taken them to the front garden and had snoozed and read and eaten and drunk far too much. But it had been good to have some catch-up time.

They discussed Jyoti again, going over the same ground, with Tim exhorting a promise from Rachel to ring her again – and soon. Then Rachel had broached the subject of Hetty. She hadn't given the woman much thought since Tim arrived; he'd filled the house so completely there was no room for even a suggestion of a ghost or memory.

'So, you think you're going to put all her notes and things together to make a book?' he asked lazily, as he fanned himself with the Sunday review section. It was a hot day yet again.

'Well maybe, but probably just concentrating on her childhood and teen years. That seems the most detailed part of the journal, from what I can see. It tails off and gets scrappy after about 1910.' Rachel poured more wine and handed a glass to Tim. 'It's almost as if something interrupted her flow and she didn't get to finish her life history. I've just read some bits of diary written in 1910 and they're not that interesting either. It's very frustrating.'

'Well, you might have enough to make it interesting, anyway. You know, the more I think about it, the better an idea it sounds. Shall I ask Justin about it, wonderling?'

Rachel turned to him in gratitude. 'That would be great, Tim.' Justin was one of those people who had contacts in all sorts of worlds. 'I'll discuss it with Freda, too, of course,' she added, referring to her agent, 'but ask Justin to put some feelers out, would you? Ask him if he thinks there might be a market for something like that. And he might know the best person to send it to.' She grinned. 'He's the sort of bloke who knows stuff like that.'

Tim took a sip of his wine. 'Oh, he's certainly that, alright. He amazes me sometimes, the contacts he has.' He wiggled his bare toes pleasurably in the sun. 'Would you put in some of your lovely, lovely drawings?'

Rachel nodded. 'That's the plan. And some of the cottage too.' She gestured to the half-dug beds, 'Maybe some of the plants in the garden, if Stan and I get going on it.'

In fact, Stan had made an impressive start already; there had been just enough room on the cleared front path for she and Tim to put out a couple of kitchen chairs. 'And I'm going to hunt down Delamere House.'

'That was the big house?'

'Yes. It's in a village called Upper Tadshell, not far from here. If it's still in one piece, that is. I get the feeling from Hetty it was in a bit of a state.'

'No rellies left?'

Rachel shook her head. 'Not one, as far as I know. Good, I suppose in a way.'

Tim slid his sunglasses down his nose and looked at her through one opened eye. 'Why, pray?'

'Well, if there were, I'd have to give the journal and letters back. Or ask permission to use the material, at the very least.'

'Ah!' Tim nodded knowingly and pushed his glasses back into place. He changed tack. 'But can you cope with the workload? Can you get your bread-and-butter stuff done *and* a book? And I know it's idyllic out here, but the inside of your new house, my darling heart, is a mess. You've still got a lot to do.'

'The sitting room's fine,' Rachel began defensively.

'Apart from the hole in the skirting board.'

'Okay, apart from the hole in the skirting board,' she admitted but added, 'that won't be there long. Mike and Gabe are doing a great job and it looks as if Gabe might have finished the roof while we were out yesterday.'

Tim curled his lips wickedly. 'While we were out torturing National Trust ladies. Bliss!' he cried. 'Heaven. The one in the grand salon was a hoot.'

'You were very cruel pretending to be an expert on porcelain and claiming that vase was fake. She nearly had a stroke. I don't know why you like to do it.'

Tim lifted a hand and waved it around, languidly. 'She deserved everything she got. She wouldn't let me try out the chaise longue. And, you must admit, purple brocade is very *me*.'

Rachel giggled. 'You nearly got us thrown out.'

Tim did a lazy stretch. 'I did, didn't I?' he said, with satisfaction. 'But you have to admit, however annoying the guides are, the NT do a lovely lunch.' Absentmindedly, he flapped a droning bee away.

'It's only you who find the guides annoying,' Rachel reproved. 'The rest of us don't mind them at all.'

Tim sat up suddenly, making the pile of papers on his lap slide off. 'Do you think this Betty woman –'

'Hetty,' Rachel corrected, hoping that if the ghost of the old woman was around she wouldn't be offended.

'Oh Hetty/Betty whatever. Do you think she lived in a place like that? Can you imagine it?' He looked at Rachel over the top of his Ray-Bans. 'Servants at one's beck and call, stable boys to frolic in the hay with.'

Rachel giggled. 'I don't think it was quite like that at Delamere House. I get the feeling they only lived in part of it, and, as I said, it sounds as if the rest was falling down. And get your mind out of the gutter, Tim.'

'It was in the hayloft, actually.' Tim sat back again, took his sunglasses off and lifted his face to the sky. 'Oh this glorious weather! One never feels the sun in quite the same way in London. Too much pollution, I suppose. Still, can't get goggle face, never hear the last of it from Justin.' In one of his lightning changes of subject, he got back to the topic. 'Why didn't Hetty live in the lap of luxury, then?'

Rachel had wondered about this too. She'd found pages and pages that described the house at length. 'Well, they might have lived in an enormous house but, from reading her journal, it was clear the family didn't have money. From what I've read, it sounds as if they only had a cook, a couple of maids and two gardeners. Oh, and someone to drive the dog cart.'

'Poor things!' Tim said drily, 'however did they manage? And there they were, the poor, living in back-to-backs, fifty million families to a hole in the ground.'

Rachel reached over and poked him in the ribs. 'You know what I mean! It's all relative. It's not a lot of people to run a big house. The family must have been quite impoverished.'

'So, no stable boys, then?' Tim sighed in an overly dramatic fashion.

'There was one, apparently,' Rachel giggled. 'He was called Sam.

Hetty speaks of him with great affection.'

'I'll bet she does.' Tim gave a dirty laugh.

'No,' Rachel answered, suddenly certain of the fact but having no idea why. 'Do you know, I think she was in love with her cousin.'

'Keeping it in the family, that's our aristo families for you. You mean this man she was supposed to marry?'

'Well, he wasn't really a cousin as such. Distant relative, though.' Rachel scrunched up her eyes at the glare of the sun. Was that a movement over by the chestnut tree? She shook her head. The unwise combination of wine and sunshine was making her imagine things. Still, she could have sworn she'd seen a flash of a woman in dusty black. Hetty. Confirming that what she was about to tell Tim was the truth. 'I think she was fond of Edward,' she began slowly, 'but I think it was Richard who she really loved.'

'Richard? Sexy name!'

'He was another cousin, distant cousin, that is. Younger.'

'Oh, you can't beat the allure of a younger man,' Tim said and gave another, even filthier, laugh. 'What was this Richard like, then?'

'Blue-eyed, black-haired. Bit of a dare-devil, liked to hunt.'

'Well, darling heart, she'd be mad not to prefer him over Edward. What was *he* like?'

'Um … academic, bit stuffy. What they'd call a "good egg" I think.' Rachel ears pricked. Was that a girlish giggle she'd heard? Or just birdsong?

'But you think she married Edward and not this delicious-sounding Richard?'

Rachel blanked off her mind from the delirious possibility that Hetty was eavesdropping their conversation. 'I think so,' she answered, distracted. 'Haven't got to that part yet.'

'Didn't you say there are some letters wrapped up in ribbon in that tin of yours? Bound to be love letters, aren't they? Haven't you read them?'

'No.'

'Why ever not, wonderling? Be the first thing I'd dive into.'

'I can't quite bring myself to, somehow. Seems too much of an invasion.' Rachel shifted. The hard wooden chair was getting uncomfortable.

'Well, Hetty left them in the attic for *someone* to find,' Tim pointed out reasonably. 'She must have had half an idea they'd be found and read. Do you want me to look at them?' He began to get up.

'No!'

There was something in Rachel's tone that made him sit back down. 'Okay, darling,' Tim spread his hands, placatingly, 'but I think you're mad not to read them. They'd be the first thing I'd go for. When are we talking about exactly? What period in history? Remind me.'

'The actual journal begins in 1963, but Hetty's living here then. She describes going to the big house in 1903. The last bit I read was a diary entry. It described a hunt ball in 1910. It was one of her first proper social outings.'

'Christ!' A blackbird shot up into the air, cackling, startled into flight by Tim's oath.

'What?' Rachel peered at him.

'They haven't got long to go, have they?'

'Until what?' Rachel asked, puzzled.

Tim tutted. 'Sometimes, dear girl, I despair over your education. The *war*. The Great War. World War One. Millions dead, even more terribly injured. You know, the war to end all wars.' Tim snorted. 'Some hope. You can bet your beautiful Richard and dutiful Edward went. Not to mention Sam the stable boy.'

Rachel sat up, feeling unutterably stupid. She clapped her hands to her face. 'Oh my God! I hadn't thought. I hadn't put it all together. I've been so engrossed in Hetty.'

She glanced at Tim and tried to explain. 'Somehow, the outside world didn't impact much on their lives at Delamere.' She shrugged. 'There was the slightest mention of the king dying, but they seemed to live in their own little bubble.' Rachel gestured to the garden. 'Come to think of it, it's just like that around here even now. People get on with their lives, but London and the rest of the country, let alone the rest of the world may as well not exist! It's peculiarly remote.'

'Very.'

Despite his answer, Rachel was aware that Tim didn't really understand. After all, they were only three hours, by train, from London. There was television, a phone. But she felt it was true. Stan, Paul, Kevin, and even Gabe, went about their lives, not all that much differently to how their ancestors had lived a hundred years ago. Everything focused on the village or nearby Fordham. A trip into Hereford was rare and even then the city had more the feel of a large market town than the county capital. Most knew one another – and one another's business! Strangers struck up conversations and, at the very least, shared a cheery greeting and a comment about the weather. That much Rachel enjoyed and found refreshing after the anonymity of London. But the county could also be unremittingly parochial and it was very male-dominated. Only the other day, she'd had to swallow back a retort when she'd heard Kevin refer to women as 'birds'. She knew it would have been useless to begin an argument with him.

Herefordshire was a county unchanged and unchanging. Almost secretive. The inhabitants stuck to their ways, regardless of what went on in the outside world. It occurred to Rachel for the first time, that for Hetty, a young girl on the cusp of adulthood and possessing such a zest for life, it must have been suffocating. She did not have the luxury of choice that Rachel enjoyed. No vote, no position unless married, no career.

She stared out, beyond the garden, to where she'd seen movement before. Nothing moved, not even the leaves on the tree. It was very still and very warm. The air hanging low and heavy in an impossibly blue sky. But Rachel sensed a rush of gratitude from Hetty and knew she'd got it right. 'And yet, despite all that, you didn't let it defeat you, did you?' she murmured. And got a faint laugh in response, as if to say, 'Certainly not!'

Tim coughed slightly and rustled the paper. His interest had moved on; he'd picked up the Sunday supplement and was now engrossed in what looked like an article on the new Tate Modern opening. She'd let him read and continued to watch the view in silence.

And now, Rachel stood in an echoing house, at the sitting-room window, again staring out at the view but, this time, seeing nothing.

Tim had filled her little cottage with laughter and filthy jokes and, for a while, Hetty, Edward and Richard had faded into the past, probably where they belonged. She shivered. For the first time in three months there was a hint of chill in the air. Even though it was still only June, autumn was giving a premature warning. In contrast to the weekend, the weather was dank and misty. And depressing.

The tin on the shelf behind her was calling again. Crossing the room she took it down, pulled the throw around her and settled on the sofa.

Her fingers trembled as she picked up the little bundle of letters and untied the ribbon. The first one was small, stained brown and, as Rachel sniffed gingerly, a strange odour rose from it. Damp and age she thought, at first, and then ... death.

The letter smelled of death.

Hardly wanting to, she unfolded the thin slip of paper and began to read. Tim had been wrong. They weren't love letters at all.

4th December, 1914

1st Bn The Worcestershire Regiment
BEF

My darling girl,

Can you believe we have been married a year? Not quite the married life we hoped for, alas.

I am glad my last letter reached you and you found it 'topping'! Is that a Richard word? As you can imagine, letters mean so very much to us all out here, so keep yours coming! I may not always have time to pen much more than a scribble, but I always appreciate your news.

Well, we have been in some scrapes, but the men have been marvellous and there is a great team spirit amongst them. We have had one or two casualties, but nothing to the losses in other battalions.

We are not at the sharp end all the time, thank goodness. It can get a bit stiff there and there have been some near things. When we are held back in reserve, it can even be quite a jolly life. I was billeted with a wonderful family recently, complete with its very own Aunt Leonora, can you believe? She was a tiny, wrinkled old thing of near eighty or so but she ruled the roost, I can tell you.

Rations are not half bad and we had the most enjoyable curry last night. Richard might, indeed, have called it 'topping'! It is not too bad a life at all and, for the first time ever, I feel my life has purpose. Whatever the outcome of this thing, I feel I will, at least, have done my bit.

And now, onto practical matters. Dear girl, could I presume to ask you to send me one or two things? Some more writing paper would be most appreciated, of course, but also some tobacco (my favourite if you can get it, but any will do) and socks! It gets so very cold out here unless I am lucky and get put up with the redoubtable Madame Orianne, as mentioned before. She keeps a great fire going. Heaven knows where she finds the wood!

Hetty, old thing, give my best to the aunts and to that young scrap Richard. Tell him not to be in such a tearing hurry to join us out here. He would hate to see what they do to the horses. Can you believe it will soon be Christmas? No

chance of leave, I fear.
I can't say much, but there's rumour of a Big Push coming
up, so wish me luck, old thing!

With happy and fond memories of our wedding day,
Yr loving husband,
Edward

So Edward *had* fought in the war! Rachel refolded the letter into it well-worn creases and laid it tenderly in her lap. Of course he would. He was exactly the type to do so. Where had he been when he wrote to Hetty? How long had they been married? What had happened to Richard? It was all so frustrating! She'd known it was a mistake to read the things out of order. She found another letter, a shorter one this time and in a different, more female, hand. This too had the same stench emanating from it but, unlike its predecessor, was written in ink.

March 14th, 1915
Dear Mrs Trenchard-Lewis,

I am a VAD stationed at Ward Twenty-Four, Etaples. Your
husband is in my care, having been wounded at Neuve
Chapelle. He was most adamant I write to you to say all is
well and not to worry. He has a shoulder wound and a
touch of fever, but is showing good grit. He has been
showing us all his wedding picture of you both and, may I
say, what a handsome couple you make.
Captain Trenchard-Lewis is cheery but cannot use his right
arm due to his injury. He sends his regards to all at home.

Dorothy Turnbull VAD
24 Etaples

Rachel could hardly bring herself to open the third letter in the pathetic little bundle. It was shorter still and she knew its content before even reading it. It was a telegram:

Regret to inform you Captain Trenchard-Lewis died of wounds 25th March, 1915

Rachel let the papers sit in her lap while she stared unseeing into the fireplace. She couldn't believe that the Edward she had begun to know, through Hetty, was already snuffed out. That was ridiculous, of course, he'd died more than eighty years ago but, to her, he had only just begun his life. Had married Hetty, was just beginning his adult life. Rachel shivered again. She felt a wave of desolation wash around the room. Poor Hetty and poor, poor Edward.

She sorted through the papers in the biscuit tin, rifling through Hetty's diary accounts of Richard's childhood misdemeanours, some not inconsiderable bitching about Flora and a description of another party – she'd come back to them later. Then she found it. Just a short few paragraphs dated April 18th, 1915.

Diary: a parcel arrived today. It contains Edward's things
from Etaples. Why they felt it necessary for us to have
them I cannot imagine. There were only a few sad items:
some of our letters to him, our wedding photograph, his
pipe and tobacco wallet. There was also a case of ciga-
rettes, one of which was half-smoked. With trembling
fingers, I put it to my lips. Perhaps this had been the last
thing that touched his? With it all was a letter from a
VAD. She claimed Edward had had a 'peaceful death' and
she was with him at the end. I can only hope so.
But then I unwrapped his tunic. It was stiff with blood
and stinking. The horror of it all lay in my hands. The
mud and blood and stench of death. This unholy mess.

The mess that has ended my short marriage, my hopes and Edward's brave life.

I could not bear for the aunts to see it, so I burned it. I took it to the brazier in the stable yard and burned the whole sorry lot. It was as if I had burned Edward himself. Afterwards I washed and washed my hands. I even scrubbed them with carbolic in the scullery. But I could not rid myself of that stench. I can smell it even now.

We are a sad household, indeed. Cold supper tonight. Cook is too upset to do more.

Rachel read through tears, then shoved the papers back into their tin and closed the lid. It was too much. Too much sadness. A sigh, the softest echo of long-past unhappiness shivered through the room and then the phone rang and tried to steal her back to the twenty-first century.

'Rachel?'

Rachel cleared her throat to answer. 'Mum?' The last person she needed to talk to, at the moment, was her mother. The ghosts of Hetty and Edward still lingered in her head – and in the room.

'Hello, darling, how are you? Just thought I'd ring to see how you're getting on.'

'Okay. Fine ... erm, I'm fine.' Rachel hoped her bafflement wouldn't communicate through the receiver, her mother hardly ever rang.

'Are you sure? You don't sound terribly fine. Is it living in the country?'

'No, I'm enjoying living here. It's very peaceful. I'm getting lots of work done.'

'Good.'

Rachel raised her eyes to the ceiling and then wished she hadn't; there was a spot in the corner she'd missed in her hurry to paint it. Dragging her brain into the conversation, she said, 'Yes, I've got a big commission to draw a series of flower paintings. I'm

152

really pleased, I –'

'Rachel,' her mother interrupted, 'I didn't ring to talk about your job. I wanted to see if you were coming to see Daddy and me before we go.'

Of course, her mother hadn't rung to ask about her work. Rachel had never had a discussion with either parent about work since her decision to swap to an art course halfway through university.

'Go?' asked Rachel stupidly, half her brain was in 1915 with Hetty and Edward. Go where?'

'Rachel!' her mother reproved, in familiar fashion. 'To Portugal, of course.'

'We thought it might be rather wonderful to get a few people from the golf club together before we leave. Tristan and his family will be there.'

Rachel winced. Tristan Wallingford worked at something in the city. Their fathers were golfing partners and both families had been, to the eternal embarrassment of their offspring, trying to get them together since they were teenagers.

'That's nice.'

'Rachel, is that all you can say! Tris is doing so well at the bank, he's been promoted again, you know. Such a lovely boy.'

'Yes.'

'Rachel, are you sure you're alright? You sound very distant.'

Rachel was, very much, not alright. This seemed too jarring a conversation to have, immediately after discovering Edward's death. How had Hetty ever found the courage to deal with that awful package? She was in awe of the girl's unblinking attitude to life – and to tragedy. There was a shifting in the sitting room behind her. She could feel Hetty willing her on.

'Mum,' she began, 'have you ever been proud of what I've achieved?'

'Darling, whatever do you mean?'

'I know you never wanted me to swap courses at uni.'

There was a silence. Rachel could hear her mother thinking

through what to say.

'Whatever's brought this on, Rachel? I only rang to invite you to the party.'

'Have you ever loved me?'

'Rachel, what a thing to ask! Of course your father and I love you.'

'You've never told me.'

'Well one doesn't think one has to.'

Rachel laughed bitterly. 'I might have needed to hear it, especially when you gave me so much grief over changing to a graphics degree.'

Another silence, longer this time. 'I'm not sure this is the conversation to have over the phone, but of course we love you. Daddy and I were worried, of course. It wasn't what we had envisaged for you. I can never see how people make a living from art, but you, well you seem to be doing quite well.'

'Not a hobby any more?'

Paula had the grace to give an embarrassed laugh. 'It doesn't seem so. I think you've proved to us that it's no longer that.' Her voice became stilted. 'And we are proud of you, you know. I was only pointing out that lovely feature you did for the National Trust magazine to Tris's mother the other day. It was quite beautiful.'

Rachel's throat constricted. She couldn't speak.

'Are you still there, Rachel?'

'Yes.'

'Perhaps we don't say these things often enough?'

Not nearly enough.

'You will come to Portugal to see us, won't you, darling? Lovely wild flowers to sketch.'

Was this Paula's way of reaching out, of apologising?

Rachel heard a sigh come down the line. 'And you always were such a sensitive child. Never had enough confidence. I never had much of an idea how to talk to you, if I'm honest. I'm sure half these wrongs are only in your head. Now,' Paula added briskly, as

154

if all was dealt with, 'about the party —'

Rachel smiled. It looked as if that was all she was getting. But it was enough. For the moment. A step forward, maybe. She felt a weight just begin to lift from her shoulders and gave up a little prayer to Hetty.

Her mother continued to chat about the move, about the amount of packing required, the struggle to get things just so for the party and her worry that it was all going to be too much.

It occurred to Rachel for the first time that maybe her mother lacked confidence too. Was that what was behind the iron control?

'Are you there, Rachel? Has the line gone?'

'Yes, Mum,' Rachel answered, wincing as her mother banged the receiver. 'I'm here, I told you. Must be a bad line. When is the party?'

'Two weeks on Saturday. Can you come, darling? It would be so good to get the family together before we go off.'

Maybe it would.

'Rachel?' Her mother's voice was sharp, she was losing patience and had things to do. To organise. To follow a cleaner around.

Rachel took a deep breath. 'Yes, I'll be glad to come.' But she'd need support. They'd only taken a tiny step forward, after all. 'Can I ... erm ... bring someone?'

'Is there something you'd like to tell us, Rachel? Her mother's voice had taken on a knowing quality.

'No,' she answered, deliberately vague. 'Just be nice to have company on the drive, that's all.' Rachel cursed under her breath. Why had she said that? She just hoped Tim was free. He would, at least, make the party fun.

'Of course you can, darling. Must go now. Bye Rachel, see you soon. And, and well, love you!'

Tears stinging, Rachel took a breath and then replied. 'Bye Mum, love you too.'

She put the phone down and stared at the receiver. A boarding-school childhood with nannies and au pairs had left her wanting nothing. But she would have swapped it all in an instant for that phone call. She knew she could be over-sensitive, that her lack of confidence made her think she was unlovable. Maybe she too had a part to play in the rocky relationship with her parents? She tried to see it from their point of view. All they'd ever wanted for her was material success, with a career and a husband providing that. Instead, they'd produced a daughter who wanted to paint. Even she had to admit making a living from art was a precarious business. 'We simply don't understand each other, do we? Or our life choices. Perhaps it's time to begin.'

'Hetty,' she said to the wall, 'I may have crossed a threshold here. Thank you. And I'm so, so sorry about Edward.'

A wave of something, gratitude and sadness maybe, washed through the room. Then the ghosts of the past slipped away.

Chapter 18

Rachel woke with a start.

Boom!

She lay rigid and confused, wondering what the noise was. After a few minutes it came again and then, immediately again. There was no rhythm to it. For a delirious second, she thought she'd been transported to the trenches and could hear gunfire.

Boom! Boom!

Giving up on getting any more sleep, she got up and opened the curtains. It was a peerless day, only spoiled by the mysterious noise in the distance, and it was later than she'd thought. Stifling a yawn, Rachel stretched and looked down on the sight of Stan weeding her front garden. She smiled. Since he'd begun to work there, he'd transformed the place. Along the sunniest side he'd cleared the alarming five-foot-high nettles and had created his vegetable patch. It was part of the deal; he escaped Sharon, his well-meaning but overly fussy daughter-in-law, in order to work on Rachel's garden, but had this space to grow his fruit and vegetables.

He'd already made three raised beds and filled them with enticing-looking topsoil, so different to the fertile but sticky red clay surrounding them. You could make pots out of the stuff Stan had dug out. He'd planted some leeks in one bed, some tomatoes and lettuce plants against the sunny wall of the cottage and had said to Rachel that he'd really get going in the autumn, in readiness for next spring.

Rachel didn't really mind what he did; anything was better than the depressingly overgrown front garden she had inherited. She was looking forward to home-grown strawberries and salads made with Little Gems. She didn't mind waiting. The thought of the permanence of being at the cottage thrilled her.

Boom!

There came that sound again. That, and the rattle of Rachel opening her bedroom window, had Stan looking up. He waved, the ever-present cigarette stuck stubbornly to one corner of his mouth.

'Bloomin' bird scarers.' He nodded over to the rolling fields. 'The Garths always get one goin' this time o' year. Can only hear it when wind's in this direction.'

That explained the noise, then. Rachel nodded, not really much the wiser.

'Looking good ain't she?' Stan went on.

'She' was presumably the garden.

'Hope you don't mind, like, but I got an early start. Going to be hot 'un.'

Rachel laughed and shook her head. 'You carry on, Stan. I overslept. Was working late last night,' she added as explanation. Even though she didn't really need to justify herself to him, somehow she felt she had to. She always felt so guilty sleeping in on these glorious mornings. The myth was true. Country people really did seem to get up earlier than their urban counterparts. 'I'll put the coffee on, shall I?'

Stan's answer was another cheery wave.

Rachel took his instant coffee, milky with three sugars, out to him, along with her usual strong, perked stuff. With it, she carried two fat Danishes, bought from Mervyn's bakery the day before.

They took their breakfast in silence, enjoying the morning. Rachel had picked up a couple of canvas deckchairs from the charity shop in Fordham and she always found Stan's company undemanding. Swifts screamed overhead, making Rachel jump as usual. She looked up and watched house martins swoop to and from the eaves of the cottage and felt supremely content. Thanks to the combined efforts of Gabe and Stan, she was gradually learning to identify the birds that visited. She gave a happy sigh and leaned back in the chair, gazing up at the sky. It had been the right decision to move here. So much of her life seemed to be settling into place – and, despite the interruptions, she was working in a way she'd never done before. Somehow she knew Hetty had been happy living at the cottage too.

'You know,' she began, half to herself, 'I thought it a bit strange having the main bit of the garden at the front. But now I wouldn't have it any other way.' She thought of the back of the cottage, with its small lawn leading up to the steep hill beyond. There was a gate leading out of it to the path, which eventually took you to the gastro pub Neil had taken her to. That night Neil had gallantly paid the bill, but Rachel knew it must have been an expensive meal. She couldn't see herself returning unless for a very special occasion. But it might come in handy if Tim brought Justin to stay and if Jyoti ever visited.

'You want to get yersen a little old shed to go round the back. Come in handy, like.'

Stan's voice startled Rachel out of her reverie. She jumped again as the swifts swooped.

Stan laughed. 'Little beggars,' he said, fondly. 'The birds have allus liked it up here. Old Hetty used to feed 'em. Used to have birdhouses and what-not up here. Used to feed the squirrels as well. Bloody rats with bushy tails, though, them things. You don't want to encourage them varmints to visit.'

Rachel smiled at him. She loved it when he mentioned something about Hetty. The snippets she gleaned from people who knew her all helped to create a picture of Hetty as an older woman. So far, she'd discovered she was fierce, wore black, rode a bicycle and fed the birds. They were more pieces of the jigsaw. Rachel wondered how Hetty had got to be like that when older. What had happened to her in the long years in between beginning her life in the big house and ending up in the cottage? The death of Edward must have affected her terribly.

'I'm sure Hetty would have known what all the wildlife was. Unlike me,' she said to Stan. 'Thanks to you, though, I'm beginning to learn. I can spot a swift and I'm almost certain of the difference between the house martins and the swallows.'

'You want to look at the chests, Rachel. That's how you tell 'em apart. Swallows got those brick-red chests. Bigger an' all.' Stan emptied his mug and wiped coffee from his mouth with the back of his hand. 'What you going to do with rest of the garden, then?'

Rachel screwed up her eyes against the light and scanned the garden. Stan had already made a huge difference, but it was a big space and there was still a lot to be done. 'I'm not really sure.' She bit her lip.

To the left of them, the vegetable beds took up most of the room and Stan had cleared the long grass and weeds to reveal what must have been cottage-garden-style beds at one point. To the right of them, however, it remained a wilderness. There was a part of Rachel that rather liked the towering grass, with a few hardy surviving bluebells poking through the cow parsley, but it hardly looked neat. She sighed. 'I don't know, Stan, any suggestions?'

'Well, you could have a few small beds, mixed in with a bit o' gravel. Don't want anything too difficult to look after, do you? You ain't got the time.'

'True.'

'And what about 'ere? You sit out 'ere a lot, don't you? What about a bit more gravel and some slabs. You could have a proper place to sit out. A bit of owl frisky living, like.'

Rachel looked at him blankly and then understood, but was in too mellow a mood to correct him. And she wouldn't dream of laughing at him. Since the quiz she'd become very fond of Stan, even if he did have a habit of stripping down to his string vest on warmer days.

It *was* her favourite place to sit. The back garden was more private but, as hardly anyone ventured up to the cottage, it didn't really matter. A place for a bit of alfresco living sounded just the ticket. Stretching out her legs in contentment, she agreed, 'That sounds like a marvellous idea, Stan.'

'You needs a clematis as well,' he responded, obviously on a roll now. 'Hetty was proud o' the one she had growing up round the front door. And mebbe a honeysuckle. The scent is good on a summer evening.'

Rachel thought about the day ahead. She ought to get down to some work. The deadline for the flower illustrations was looming and she was behind with a commission for some Christmas cards. But, try as she might, she couldn't block out this glorious June morning and really didn't feel in a mood to conjure up wintry scenes. And, after all, you couldn't call a cottage after a plant it didn't have. Making a snap decision, she turned to her companion, who was now sucking on a roll-up. 'The garden centre's having a sale. Fancy a trip out?'

Stan didn't need asking twice.

The garden centre was, indeed, having a sale and all their terracotta pots were on offer at half price. It was too much to resist. Rachel had been dying to plant something up, but had been waiting until the garden was in a more finished state. She drove home, feeling stupidly excited. The load of three pots of various sizes, two bags of compost and assorted plants weighed down the boot of her ancient Fiat so much it made the nose of the car stick up. The gravel and some slabs were ordered and were due to be delivered later in the week.

Stan coughed noisily. Rachel suspected he was dying for another cigarette but knew he didn't like to smoke in the car or house.

'You got yersen a good little lot 'ere, an' all.' He said and held onto the plant on his lap a little more tightly as she rounded the last bend before their turn off to Stoke St Mary. 'This hosta will want a bit o' shade and that fuschia'll come back next year alright for you.'

Rachel grinned. She'd never really understood why people got the gardening bug – until now. She couldn't wait to get started on planting up the pots. Until now she'd observed plants simply in order to draw and paint them, but she'd never given a thought to how they grew or what they needed. And she could just see herself, sitting on a chair, a little round table in front, balancing a large glass of red. She could enjoy inhaling the scents of the plants and watching the birds. It would be the perfect end to the day. And maybe, just maybe, Gabe might share it with her. It was time to start letting people into her life. It was a risk and they could hurt her, as Charles had, but with Hetty's help, she was learning to embrace life and all its opportunities.

'Can I have some lavender and –' she furrowed her brow to think, 'some rosemary in the little round beds? I like the scent.'

Stan laughed. 'Ar. Them'd be good. Nice cottagey plants, they are. Rosemary's alright with a bit o' lamb too. My old Eunice used to do a bit o' lamb summat special with rosemary.'

With that Stan lapsed into silence. Rachel didn't want to pursue the subject, his grief was obviously still raw.

They were in the village now, driving past the church and the green. There wasn't a soul in sight. It had turned into too hot a day. Rachel turned right and then braked at the bottom of the track leading up to the cottage. She thought about the load in the back and winced on behalf of the car.

'Hold on tight, Stan, I'm not sure I'll get up with this lot in the back.'

'Let me out 'ere then an' I'll walk up.' He already had his hand on the door.

'Are you sure?' Rachel looked at him anxiously. 'It's got very hot.'

It had, without a breeze to ease the building heat of the afternoon.

'You get on, lovely. I'm not all that aged. I could do with a walk.'

'Well look, give me the hosta. You can't carry that all the way up there!'

Stan got out of the car awkwardly, as it was at an angle. Rachel took the plant off him and fixed the seatbelt around the sticky plastic pot. 'There, won't go anywhere now. I'll see you at the top. Okay?'

'Alright.' Stan stood to one side of the track, in the shade of the hawthorn hedge. He waved her off and began to fumble in his pocket for his tobacco tin and matches.

Rachel grinned. She'd been right about his need for a cigarette. She gunned the engine hard, sending up a cloud of dust, but the car wouldn't budge. Its wheels spun uselessly on the loose stones.

'Less gas,' shouted Stan, through the cloud of exhaust fumes. 'She won't go nowhere like that. Ease up on the throttle. If you wants to get her up that track on the stones or mud or snow, be more gentle, like.'

Rachel peered through the passenger window at him and took her foot off the accelerator. She reapplied the power more gently and, to her astonishment, the car began to inch up.

'Don't let me down,' she whispered, through gritted teeth. 'I can't afford another car and I can't do without you.'

It was true. There was no bus service out of the village, the nearest train station was Hereford, a good forty minutes away and Rita sold only the most basic of supplies. And, even then, begrudgingly. Rachel hadn't thought through how vital a car would be to her. She'd gone for days in London without having to use one. Now it was her lifeline.

At the top, as the Fiat groaned to a halt, she heaved a huge sigh of relief and backed the car up as close as she could to the garden gate.

'What you been up to, then?' Gabe said as he leaned in through the open driver's window and watched as she switched off the engine. 'I got here to do the kitchen radiator and there was no one in.'

163

'Buying up the entire contents of Roseberry Garden Centre,' Rachel answered, relief that her old car had made it to the top in one piece making her expression warm.

Gabe quirked an eyebrow and grinned back. He loved it when Rachel smiled – it made her whole face light up. 'What have you bought?' He laughed at the sight of the hosta, still secured with its seatbelt on the front seat. 'Good to know these plants know how to "Clunk Click Every Trip"'.

Rachel rolled her eyes at him. 'It was the only way I could stop getting soil all over the place. Stan was holding it but I had to jettison him at the bottom of the track.' Gabe was disconcertingly close but she ignored her quickening pulse. She could feel waves of heat coming off his body. She got out of the car, pushing him gently out of the way. She needed some distance from him. 'What haven't I bought!' she said, in an overly bright voice. For some reason his nearness was making her nervous. 'Come and see.' Gabe followed as she opened the boot.

He sucked in a breath. 'You should have said. I could've picked up this lot in the van. It would've saved your suspension.'

Rachel pouted. 'It got up here. Just.' Then she had doubts. 'Do you think I've really damaged the suspension?'

Gabe bent to look under the car, his t-shirt rising up to give a tantalising glimpse of smooth brown back as he did so. He gave the suspension a summary look. 'Naw, it looks okay. You want me to unload?'

'Oh Gabe, would you? Don't think Stan's up to it and I'm worried he'll try.'

'Yeah, won't take a mo'. You get that small pot out and I'll shift the rest. Where d'you want it?'

Rachel gave him another grateful smile. He really was a lovely man. 'Thanks so much, Gabe. Put the compost bags by the front door, please. I've got some gravel and slabs on order. They're for my new patio area.'

'Oh right,' Gabe said, as he helped her with one of the planters.

164

He winked. 'And who's going to lay that for you, then?'

'Well, I wouldn't like to take advantage of you,' Rachel began doubtfully and then saw his face. 'Oh would you?'

Gabe grinned again, this time with the air of one who suffered. He wanted to tell Rachel she could take advantage of him any time she liked. 'I suppose I could fit it in, like,' he said, pulling a face. 'Along with the central heating and the roof and the re-pointing.' This was shouted after her as she struggled up the path with her terracotta pot. 'Oh and Rach –'

'I know, I know, put the kettle on!'

Stan, puffing on a foul-smelling roll-up, joined Gabe. He leaned against the car and gave a thoughtful sigh. 'She's got a lovely little figure, that one.'

Gabe watched as Rachel's bottom wiggled with the effort of carrying her load. 'You can say that again, Stan, you can say that again.' He was just glad the thin bloke from the quiz seemed to have disappeared.

Two days later Rachel leaned out of her bedroom window to see Gabe's Toyota parked neatly by her Fiat. Stan had been busy clearing the area marked out for the 'owl frisky' living and it was now a bare patch of solid red clay.

Rachel wondered how anything could grow in such inhospitable-looking soil but she'd been assured by Stan that, once established, plants did really well in it and it was fertile. Considering how many crops were grown in the land around the village, Rachel conceded the point. She couldn't wait for her patio to be ready and be able to enjoy the warm evenings and the spectacular sunsets.

She watched as Gabe carried a slab from the pile at the front gate. She almost called out to him and then stopped. She loved watching him work. She crouched down so she wouldn't be seen and felt very naughty.

Gabe put the slab down on its edge and seemed to be considering where to put it. Rachel held her breath. She hadn't discussed this in detail with either Gabe or Stan and part of her wanted to call down to Gabe and tell him where to begin. But she found it was more fun watching him, so for once relinquished artistic control. It was only a few paving slabs, after all. She could trust him.

Gabe was apparently still thinking. Then he wiped a hand over a brow and snagged a lock of hair behind his ear. He lifted the slab – Rachel held her breath – and placed it, with infinite precision, to the left of the front door. Perfect for the pot of hostas that she'd planted up, Rachel thought and released the breath. They'd get shaded from the worst of the heat by the cottage wall.

Gabe disappeared to get another paving slab. Rachel watched in fascination as the muscles in his shoulders strained with the effort of carrying it and how his biceps bunched as he placed it, with just as much care, next to the first. She almost giggled and called out to him, but then he took off his t-shirt and she stifled a gasp.

Gabe was beautiful. Wide shoulders with pronounced muscles and well-tuned biceps, a chest that was hair-free and finely sculpted by what she supposed would be called a six- pack. And he was very suntanned. He was a golden brown, slightly lighter than where his t-shirt exposed him to the sun, but still smooth-skinned and jewelled with sweat. His wore his jeans low so Rachel could see where his stomach hollowed. Her fingers itched for a pencil; she'd love to draw him.

Time stood still and thickened, like the hot summer air. Hardly daring to breathe, Rachel watched as Gabe stretched his arms up to the sky. He was, maybe, only easing out a kink in a muscle, but he looked as if he was worshipping the sun. He ran a brown hand through his hair, making it loosen from its ponytail. Once again, Rachel admired his fingers; long and lean like the rest of him.

Toffee ice-cream. He looked as if he would taste of toffee ice-cream! She salivated and had a sudden urge to lick him.

All over.

She ducked down and knelt against the wall under the window. She found she was breathing heavily, her breasts straining against her thin shirt. She felt very aware of her nipples and put a hand to each. They pushed against her palms, her breasts weighing heavy and hot. An urgent beat set up between her legs. She collapsed against the wall, feeling at once soporific and strangely tense. Boneless and yet aware of every fibre and nerve of her being. She wondered what the hell had happened. She'd never had such a physical reaction to any man.

She began to giggle helplessly. She'd just been ogling. Letching, as Tim would say. What if she'd been caught? She must be years older than Gabe. It just didn't seem right. And yet, in some way, nothing had felt more right. Levering herself up again, she couldn't resist taking another peek.

'Ah, there you are, Rach. Was wondering if you were around.'

Damn! He'd spotted her.

'Thought I'd get an early start on this, like. Got to go over to the other job later.' Gabe used his t-shirt to wipe the sweat from his brow, flung it over a shoulder and grinned. 'Don't mind, do you?'

'No!' Her voice came out as a squeak. She was still trying not to giggle.

'You alright, Rach? You look a bit flushed.'

'Get yourself under control, woman,' she muttered and then said aloud, 'I'm fine Gabe.' She tried to sound casual. 'You just carry on. You're doing a great job.' She waved down in the vague direction of the two carefully placed slabs. 'That's exactly where I want you. I mean, them.'

'Okay, then, if you're sure.'

'Yeah. Just off for a wash, then I'll make some tea, shall I?'

'Sweet.' Gabe watched, as she gave another frantic wave and slunk from the window. He laughed and shook his head. She hadn't a clue that he'd been perfectly aware she'd been watching him.

He tucked his t-shirt through a loop in the waistband of his jeans. Nor had she a clue that through her white shirt, stretched tight across her breasts where she leaned onto the window ledge, he'd enjoyed the view of her jutting nipples.

He re-tied his hair back into its elastic band and grinned. It was a good way to start the day, he reckoned. 'Beat that lanky city boy,' he muttered to himself. Then, walking a little awkwardly, he went to fetch the remaining slabs.

Chapter 19

Neil took Rachel out again, this time to a new Italian in Hereford. A throwback to the seventies, the restaurant had fake leather banquettes, red velvet drapery and dripping candles stuck into Chianti bottles. It also had the kind of maître d' who revelled in being a professional Italian. Rachel didn't have high hopes of it being a good night.

She tried valiantly to be interested in what Neil said, but she couldn't escape the fact that there was something missing. There was absolutely no spark of attraction between them. He was good-looking and well-mannered; eminently suitable in so many ways. He just wasn't the right man.

It didn't help that images of a t-shirtless Gabe kept flashing into her head.

Neil was unusually quiet; he didn't keep up the steam train of chatter as he had on their last date. The trouble was, it led to great gaps in the conversation. And they weren't of the comfortable kind. It was weird; she and Gabe were often silent, but it had never mattered.

There was quite a wait for their food and, after a particularly embarrassingly long pause, he said, 'So, have you read any more of Hetty's journal?'

Rachel shook her head, relieved that she had something to

talk about. It was one of the few times that Neil had expressed any interest in her. Frustratingly, their pasta arrived at that very moment. The maître d' insisted on doing something showy and embarrassing with an enormous pepper mill, so it was a while before she could answer.

'Only bits and pieces,' she continued, eventually, when the fussing was over. 'I've read a letter Edward sent Hetty from the war and the part where she describes how she received his things from the Front. After he'd died.' Rachel shuddered.

'How awful.' Neil tutted in sympathy.

Rachel warmed to him. She put her fork down and sipped the house red he had ordered. This was good too. It was turning out to be a better evening than expected.

'Yes, it's hard to imagine why they thought sending back his bloodstained tunic would help. But it's obviously something they did sometimes. Oh, I'm sorry,' she added, as she noticed Neil had stopped eating. 'Not really a subject for conservation over dinner.'

'No,' he shook his head and smiled as he agreed. 'But I did ask! It's dreadfully sad. This was Edward, was it? Her first husband?'

Rachel nodded and wound some pasta around her fork. 'Yes,' she said, when she'd swallowed. 'I haven't got to the bit where she marries again, but I've a feeling I know who she married after his death.'

'Who?' Neil raised a beautiful black eyebrow in query and took a gulp of water. 'My, this arrabiatta is warm. How's yours?'

Rachel looked at her salmone al penne. 'Delicious, actually,' she said, in surprise. 'Very creamy.' She'd done it again, pre-judging something. This time she'd judged the restaurant far too quickly and the food had actually turned out to be really good.

Neil touched his mouth with the tip of his napkin in a delicate gesture. 'That's a relief. This restaurant has had excellent reviews, but you never know what it'll be like when a place has only just opened.' Leaving his food untouched, he returned to the subject. 'I'm so sorry, Rachel, I didn't let you answer. Who do you think

Hetty married?'

'I think she may have married Richard. The other brother,' she added as Neil looked blank.

Neil crumbled a chunk of bread on his plate. 'But why are you sure it was Richard she married?'

'Well, she seemed very fond of him, although he comes across as odd. Hot-headed, mercurial. The sort who would attract a young girl, but wouldn't necessarily treat her well. And, of course, she doesn't change her surname. Throughout her life she seemed to be known as a Trenchard-Lewis.' Rachel chewed her pasta thoughtfully. Neil, she noticed, was ignoring his. Too spicy, perhaps.

'And this was when?'

Rachel shrugged. 'I don't know yet. It's all in a bit of a mess. There's a whole load of bits of paper, letters and all sorts of scraps that, for some reason, she didn't get around to sorting out.' Rachel pushed her plate regretfully away. The food had been good, but the portions had been huge and she couldn't eat any more.

Neil grinned over his glass of water. 'It's exciting. Just like a detective puzzle! I can't wait to see it all.'

'Yes, you must sometime,' Rachel strived to sound vague. She wasn't sure how she felt about someone other than herself and Gabe looking over Hetty's papers. Besides, although she liked Neil, she didn't want to encourage him too much. She suspected they were only ever destined to be friends.

It had turned out to be a nice evening, Rachel thought, as Neil drove her home. Grown up, civilised. She settled back into the leather seat of his four-by-four, replete with good food and enjoying the luxury of being driven. She gave a contented sigh.

'Good time?' Neil looked over in the gloom of the car interior and she heard him smile.

'Very, thank you. My mother would thoroughly approve.'

'Of me?'

Rachel giggled. 'Oh, she'd definitely approve of you. But I meant she'd approve of the evening. She never quite got why I liked going clubbing with Tim or going for a girly night with Jyoti. They're my friends in London,' she added.

'Then I'm very glad.'

Once back at the cottage, Neil again came round to open the car door for her. She bit down a giggle at the gesture, realising she wasn't totally sober.

She made coffee and they settled in the sitting room.

Neil looked around him admiringly. 'I have to say, you've made a big difference to this room.'

'Just as well, seeing as the rest of the house is still a tip.' Rachel grinned ruefully.

'One thing I've learned about builders is that it always takes twice as long for them to get anything done. Mike's busy over at the Hallidays, isn't he?'

Rachel looked at Neil startled.

He laughed. 'Another thing about living in a small community is that everyone knows what everyone else is doing! I sold the Hallidays the house some years ago. I like to keep in touch. They're extending the original two-up-two-down thatched cottage. It's a big job. I'm not surprised Mike is falling behind on this one.'

'I'm really pleased with what they've done, actually. Gabe's doing a good job,' Rachel said, wanting to defend them.

'Ah Gabe! His heart's not in it, though, is it? He'd rather be off playing the tortured artist in a garret.'

Rachel wasn't comfortable discussing the Llewellyn family with Neil. It smacked of gossiping. What's more, she didn't like the way in which he was belittling Gabe. 'More coffee, Neil?' she asked, brightly, in an effort to change the subject.

'Well, I wouldn't normally. Too much caffeine in the system plays havoc, but seeing as this is so delicious, I will have another cup. I heard a grinder. Don't tell me that you made it fresh?' He held his cup out for a refill.

'I did.'

'Wherever did you get the beans?'

'I picked them up on my last trip to London. I still have to go back every now and again to see my agent. You're right, though, they're hard to track down around here.'

Neil leaned back on the sofa and looked up at Rachel with a frank appreciation. 'I do so admire you, Rachel. You seem to have everything sorted.' He gestured to the room. 'You're getting the house fixed up, you have your work and you still have that connection with the more exciting places in the world. So in control, so sorted. You know what you want from life.'

Rachel didn't know how to respond. Was that how she was seen? Tim's comment about her becoming far too anal and in danger of ending up alone, with just a cat for company, ghosted into her mind. How could people not see beyond the exterior and into the morass of insecurity and panic that normally existed in her head? Why did no one understand what she was really like?

'I well ...'

'I'm so sorry, Rachel. I've embarrassed you.' Neil gave her a dazzling smile. 'Forgive me.' Draining his espresso he glanced at his watch, his brows shooting up. 'Time for me to go.'

'Well, thank you again for a lovely evening,' Rachel said, itching for him to be gone.

As she showed him out, he paused. 'Let's do this again, shall we? And maybe next time I can have a look in that biscuit tin.'

Rachel smiled and closed the door. Leaning against it, she grimaced. He was getting a bit keen.

A whirl of displeasure scuttered around the hall. 'And you don't seem to approve either, Hetty. Not the right one for me?'

Rachel felt Hetty give a soft laugh.

As she was clearing away the coffee things there was a knock on the door. Irritated, she wondered if it was Neil returning. It wasn't. It was Gabe.

'Was that Neil Fitch's car I saw in the lane?'

She was too taken aback by his suspicious tone to not answer honestly. 'Yes, we've just been out to dinner.'

'Very nice.'

'It was, actually.'

He looked down at the cafetière in her hand. 'And came back for coffee?'

'Yes, Gabe. He came back for coffee.' She frowned up at him and added emphatically, 'just coffee.' Arching an eyebrow, she didn't bother to hide her sarcasm. 'That alright with you?'

Sensing her irritation, Gabe ran an embarrassed hand over his face. 'Sorry. Bad mood. It's been one of those days.'

Exhaustion was etched into his face and it made him look older. Softening, she let him in. 'What did you come up this late for?'

'Left a drill here. Dad needs it first thing in the morning at the Hallidays'. I've only just got back in. He gave me a bit of grief over it.' He followed her into the kitchen.

Rachel switched the kettle back on and made him some tea. Holding it out to him, she noticed he hadn't said where he'd been. It couldn't have been a job as he was dressed in dark jeans and a rugby shirt. He looked disturbingly sexy. 'Come on through to the sitting room, you won't get dust on your nice clothes in there.'

'Thanks, Rach.'

Gabe collapsed onto the sofa, closed his eyes and let out an enormous sigh. 'It's so good to stop.'

Rachel took the biscuit tin down and joined him. As Gabe stretched out his long legs and concentrated on drinking his tea, Rachel idly leafed through the diary. It was peaceful and, with a curl of her lip, she noticed that even Hetty was quiet. Maybe the old woman approved of Gabe more!

After a while, Gabe picked up the journal Rachel had put to one side. He looked through it with interest. 'It's fascinating, isn't it?' he said, eventually. 'The early stuff about her life at Delamere. What a childhood, having a rambling, run-down house as a playground! There's plenty of material here for your book. Are you still going to do it?'

Rachel nodded, slowly. 'I think so. It's getting very sad, though.

I've just found out she married Edward Trenchard-Lewis and he was killed not long after, in the war. The Great War, that is.' It sounded very bald saying it like that.

Gabe looked up, tiredness shadowing his eyes. 'That's awful. Just as her life was starting too.' He blew out a breath. 'A whole generation of men wiped out. And a whole generation of widows created. Awful.' He was silent for a moment. 'Suppose I would have gone. I'm the right age.' He stared into the fireplace, looking so sad that Rachel wanted to reach out and hug him to her. It wasn't just Hetty's tragic wartime story making him so troubled. She wondered what was on his mind.

He blinked several times and came back to her. Flipping through to the back cover of the leather-bound journal, he exclaimed. 'What's this? There's something here, Rachel, there's something underneath the lining.'

Gabe handed the book over to Rachel and she slid her slimmer finger into the camouflaged slit nestling under the hardback cover. She tugged out some sheets of paper, so thin they were almost transparent. Holding her breath, she unfolded them and scanned the first few lines.

'Anything interesting? Must be secrets, hidden like that.'

'Um, maybe,' Rachel said, her eyes still glued to what she held in a slightly shaking hand.

There was a silence as she began reading avidly.

Gabe yawned, hugely. 'I'll leave you to it. Better be off, I suppose.'

Rachel looked at him, saw the sadness and exhaustion hollowing his face. She put a hand on his arm. 'Don't go. Stay a while longer. If you don't mind me reading this?' She held up the fragile pieces of paper. 'I'd like the company, to be honest.'

Gabe gave a tired smile. 'Nowhere else I'd rather be,' he said, softly. Settling back on the sofa, he watched her begin to read the sheets of paper, made soft by age, drooping in her hands.

Chapter 20

June 1963, Clematis Cottage

Hetty sat at the desk in the window and tapped her pen with nervous fingers. When she'd read her diary entry describing the hunt ball she'd laughed a little. She wanted to do more justice to it. To tell the truth. How innocent those days seemed. Full of pretty dresses and show tunes. None of them had any idea of the apocalypse that was to come.

She smoothed out the papers of her old diary. She knew the contents by heart, but the dull text did not mention the breathless thrill of that kiss ... that first kiss. She began to write.

The year 1909 had been horribly blighted by news of
Father's death in Africa. Having succumbed to one
malarial fit too many, he had been buried where he fell
sick, in French Guinea. I did know how to feel for a father
I hardly knew and yet who had been my last remaining
close relative. I had no idea how to grieve without the
evidence of a grave. I had no body to weep over. And yet,
I was expected to mourn.
That Christmas had been a subdued affair with a small
chicken instead of a goose and the only celebration a toast

to the King. However, the aunts had finally allowed the putting off of black crepe and announced that I was to be allowed to attend the hunt ball.

My first proper dance!

And not only was I to be allowed to dance, but I was to have a new dress, a party frock. I hadn't had new clothes since I stopped growing at fifteen. I was now, as Leonora was forever pointing out, rather tall. My family legacy, I supposed. I did not remember dear Papa being overly tall, although that may have been in contrast with my two cousins who, sharing the Trenchard blood, as did I, were uncommonly tall also.

Richard was now sixteen and a strapping youth with a bony frame that promised still further height and strength. He ate us out of house and home when back from school, which this year had been rare. At his pleading, Cook fed him in the kitchen in between meals as he was permanently hungry. Hester made soft, fond comments about Edward being just the same at that age. I hadn't seen much of Edward either as, since leaving university, he had been staying with various friends. He and Richard had spent some time with the Parker family at their London house. I had been madly jealous at being left out. I never seemed to go anywhere remotely exciting.

The aunts tried to hide it, but their relief at not having the expense of feeding two ragingly hungry males was palpable.

Edward and Richard had travelled back, with the Parkers, to attend the dance. Flora was now out and rumour had it she had ignited much excitement in society. Aunt Leonora commented that the excitement would soon die down, once she was exposed as the daughter of new money. For once, I agreed with my caustic relative.

But – back to my dress! As a special treat, Aunt Hester

had hired a dressmaker from Worcester, the material having been found in an old packing case in one of the Delamere attics. It was beautiful – a pale grey, as befitting my state of half mourning, but with a silver thread running through. I had had only one fitting and was desperate to try on the finished gown.

It arrived two days before the ball and Aunt Hester ran upstairs with the package herself. She took me to her dressing room, it having the only long mirror not spotted with a patina and therefore the only one worth using. She was as excited as I when we fumbled, like giggling school-girls, with the brown paper. When she eventually fastened the neat row of buttons at the back and turned me to face the mirror, I gasped. It was utterly beautiful. The colour removed any redness from my complexion and compli-mented my brown hair. She held my hair up so I could see the effect once it was dressed.

I was silent for a moment and then I said, 'Oh, Aunt, I look quite grown up.'

'Of course you do, my dear. You are grown up now. Seventeen.'

'Nearly eighteen. My birthday is later this month.'

'Of course, nearly eighteen. I forget how you are all growing up.' She sighed. 'You truly look like a young woman.' The inference was clear, so I turned and gave her a hug.

'Aunt,' I began, 'Why have you always stayed at Delamere? Why did you never marry?' I felt her body still against mine.

The candle flickered in the January gloom and smoked. It cast shadows on the dressing-room walls and hid the shabby wallpaper. Hester remained silent. I had over-stepped a boundary, but I did not know how.

Aunt Hester turned me back to the mirror and spoke to

my reflection, over my shoulder. 'Hetty,' she reproved, but only lightly. 'You are forever the one asking questions.'

Our eyes met in the mirror. I had not realised how similar we were. Both tall, both with chestnut-lit hair. Hester was the more beautiful, though, with narrower features and those strange, lilac-coloured eyes.

'I was to be married, Hetty. At one time. I lost my betrothed in the War.'

I frowned. 'The Boer Wars?'

'Indeed.' Hester gave my arms a squeeze, tears gathering in her eyes. 'Be happy, child. Be happy.'

And then she was gone. Slipping into the shadows like a wraith.

I would glean no more information from Hester, I knew my aunt too well to hope for more, but I couldn't help but sigh for her lost opportunities. Poor Hester, having to sacrifice her youth and beauty to Delamere and, worse still, to Leonora. It was a wonder she remained so kind and sweet. My love for her deepened.

Then, with the self-absorption of youth, I stared at my reflection again and wondered what everyone would think when they saw me. I would have no formal coming out, the family simply could not afford it and I had not yet come into my money. This would be my one chance to take my place in the world. Hence the aunts' agreement about my early leave from deep mourning. The hunt ball would be their opportunity to declare me an adult and therefore marriage material in the eyes of our small and provincial society. Aunt Hester's revelation had shocked me. I had never before given any thought to her as a person. She had been my darling aunt, whom I had loved from the first. I knew what she wanted from me. How I could make her happy. I had to secure Edward and it was not an entirely unpleasant thought. Edward was kind, clever, thoughtful. Good husband material.

And I owed Hester her happiness.

I wondered how Edward would react when he saw me in my new dress. I was usually dressed in a dull pinafore and blouse. This dress was heavenly; the most glamorous thing I had ever owned. The sleeves were elbow-length and I was to borrow some long gloves from Aunt Hester. There was a deep v-neck at the front, but my neckline was discreetly covered with a placket of fine silver gauzy stuff. As dictated by the new fashion, the waist was high and the skirt narrow. It was the most perfect, most gorgeous, thing I had ever worn.

I attempted a few coquettish poses in the mirror and giggled. I could not wait for the dance – and for everyone to see me.

The evening of the ball was one of those perfect winter nights, silver with hoar frost and shivery with expectation. I stood on the front step, waiting for Sam to bring round the old dog cart. Richard had ridden on ahead and Edward was to drive me to the Parkers'. They were hosting the evening at Breckington. Mr Parker was attempting to secure his family's position as the most eminent in the county. In my head, I could hear Leonora's sniffing out the words, 'There's no substitute for class, not even money made from indigo dye can buy one that,' and giggled a little.

I knew Edward had already arrived at Delamere as I'd heard the aunts exclaiming over him earlier in the day, but I'd kept myself from him. I wanted to astound everyone with my grown-up glamour and wanted Edward to have his first sighting of me in my new gown. I had timed my arrival downstairs with care. I turned as I heard a commotion.

'Edward, my boy, how splendid you look in white tie!'

It was Aunt Hester clucking. The aunts were standing with him at the foot of the staircase. Edward, tall and straight-backed, was indulgently waiting while Hester brushed a non-existent piece of fluff off his shoulder. He had grown a moustache and it made him look older, far older than his twenty-three years but, perhaps, that was what two years in a life away from Delamere did to one.

I had overheard the aunts talk of him joining the army. It would be the sensible thing to do as Delamere could not hope to support him, even with the addition of my inheritance.

Money, it always came back to money! I wished there were a way I could keep him at home, where I suspected he longed to be. Still, he might be the sort to enjoy army life and it would afford the opportunity for him to travel. A thought occurred, how should I like being an army wife? Excitement rising, I realised I would travel! See more of the world than this little corner of a rural, and very dull, county.

'Hetty!'

Edward saw me and came towards me, his hands outstretched. He took mine in a friendly gesture. 'Come into the light, dear girl, you'll freeze out there. Let me look at you.'

He pulled me closer and then stopped. 'Oh I say, Hetty, that's the most marvellous dress.' He dropped my hands abruptly. 'Hetty, you'll be the belle of the ball.'

We stared into one another's eyes, newly aware. No longer children. All I could hear was the gas light in the hall, hissing against the dark of the night. It gave off a strong smell of paraffin, which singed the inside of my nose. My eyes watered, but I tried not to sniff, striving for an adult composure.

I studied him with interest, gratified to have made such an

impact. He hadn't changed a great deal, apart from the moustache. His hair seemed darker, but that could be the brilliantine slicking it down, and he was much broader and muscular than I remembered. He seemed completely foreign to me. Very much a man now and the knowledge gave me a little shiver.

'I say, you are cold, old thing. Come on, let's get you wrapped up warm and to the Parkers.' Hester passed Edward my cape and he put it around my shoulders. It was old and spoiled the effect of my party dress, but was welcome in its warmth. His hands skimmed my arms, bare above their gloves, and I shivered again.

Once at Breckington Hall, we abandoned the dog cart to one of the Parkers' stable boys and followed the maid to the sounds of laughter coming from their drawing room. Nanny Walker, my chaperone for the journey, disappeared to the kitchens.

I looked about me in awe. The newly done drawing room was decorated in the latest creams and whites, with a grand piano in one corner and luxurious yellow drapes closed against the cold. It was crowded with people. For a second, I couldn't fathom why it dazzled my eyes so, then realised; the Parkers had gone ahead and put in electric light. I remembered Flora telling Richard about it – and the new generator was installed in a purpose-built outhouse. The room shone as bright as the new money that had made it happen. It was all so terribly exciting. Leonora's voice sounded in my head again and my lip curled. Although, looking around the room, society didn't seem to care that it was all provided by 'new money'!

Flora greeted us with a surprising enthusiasm. 'Henrietta, darling, how are you?' she gushed. 'It's been simply an age. And dearest Edward too.'

She leaned in for a kiss and Edward complied. I was

rather startled and assumed it was London manners. Flora had taken advantage of the London fashions too. She had on a white skirt so narrow I was frightened she would trip, let alone be able to dance. She wore, in her hair, a matching feather, which rivalled even Edward's height. All pleasure in my own dress fled. I was reminded of her as she was when waiting for the hunt to begin, when she flirted with Richard. She looked to be on the hunt tonight, but I suspected her prey was not the fox. Richard had returned from hunting with her earlier in the day. He had been muddied and glowing with bloodlust, his forehead having been bloodied in the traditional manner for a first kill. I had hated the metallic odour that had lingered on him.

'You don't mind if I borrow Edward for a moment, do you Henrietta?' Flora was now saying. 'Mother and Pa would so like to speak with him.' With that, she ushered Edward to the side of the room, where her parents stood. I was left standing on the expensive Axminster, feeling – and looking – like an ingénue. If I were to secure Edward, I might have to try harder.

'Hello, Hetty,' said Richard, behind me.

I turned, I hadn't heard him enter the room. I gasped at the sight of him. He was wearing white tie too, but wore it in cruel comparison to Edward. Whereas the older brother looked smart and distinguished, Richard looked utterly and devastatingly handsome. I'd seen him rarely since Easter. When not in London with the Parkers, he spent his time here on their estate, riding with David and Lawrie.

Richard's blue eyes shone as he grinned. 'All alone, Cinderella? Let me help you to some punch.' He took my arm and led me to where the punch bowl sat gleaming on a side table.

'Richard,' I exclaimed. 'We cannot have that. Isn't it alcohol?'

He made a face. 'When did you become so unadventurous? That's not the Hetty I know.' He filled two cups so generously that some of the liquid slopped out onto the snowy cloth. He held one out to me, as a challenge.

I looked about. Not one person was giving us any attention. Giving Richard a scowl, I took the cup from him and sipped. 'It's delicious,' I admitted.

He drank his down in one and then poured another. He was a different person tonight. At once much older but still childish in his dares. I took another sip of my punch and felt it warm me. I decided I liked alcohol. At one end of the drawing room I became aware of movement as the Parkers began to escort their guests to the ballroom.

Richard held out his arm, 'May I have the honour? Let me take you, Cinders, to the dance.' Then he reverted to a school boy again as he looked over to where Flora had her arm through Edward's. 'Looks as if Flora has Edward ensnared good and proper!' He gazed at me, with a strange expression. 'Come along, Henrietta, you can be mine tonight instead.'

I took his arm, feeling a little dazed by all his glamour. The punch had made my head feel muzzy, but not unpleasantly so. Smiling up into his wicked blue eyes, I let him take me.

As we entered the ballroom, I remembered Aunt Hester telling me once that the hunt ball used to be the privilege of the Trenchards. The Delamere ballroom had long since fallen into such a state of disrepair as to render it unusable. I had begun to say that Richard and I had once danced in the old ballroom. Aunt Leonora had glared so fiercely at this, it made any further disclosures impossible. The ballroom I now entered, on Richard's arm, couldn't have been more different to the one he and I had played in. It ran the entire length of the west wing of the house and, as a statement of wealth, could not have been bolder. More creams and yellows decorated it, with several electrically lit chandeliers hanging from the ceiling. An orchestra was already playing, situated on a dais at one end. Gossips had it that the Parkers had overstepped the mark in offering to host the ball – the temerity of new money! However, looking about me and seeing many familiar faces, I could see most people had no qualms about accepting their invitation.

It was impossibly elegant and a world away from Delamere.

Richard escorted me to where Flora stood with her parents.

He turned to me and said, 'Regretfully, I am already promised to Flora for the first dance.' He raised my hand to his lips and kissed it, giving me a veiled look. 'I will seek you out later in the evening.'

I murmured something in return to the Parkers' greetings and then Edward claimed my hand for a dance.

'Do you remember, long ago, that afternoon in the summer house?' he said with a smile, as we swirled around the floor. It was a waltz and therefore straightforward. A relief, as I was not very practised.

Edward's dancing, on the other hand, had improved vastly since he had been in London. Obviously he had had much opportunity for socialising. I wondered, as I looked up at him, with whom he had been dancing. The hollow feeling, that I was the one always left behind, returned.

I thought back to that wintry afternoon when I had fled Richard's joke and had been found by Edward, my saviour. I blushed.

'Sorry, old girl, didn't mean to embarrass you.'

'You didn't.' I smiled. 'I was very young then.'

'Not so old now.' He was trying hard to be gallant.

I shook my head. 'Of course not. But older.'

Edward nodded. 'Older. And most beautiful tonight.' He coughed. He really didn't do this sort of chat well. Perhaps London life had not afforded him all that much social opportunity after all?

I felt my blush deepen. I was honest enough to admit that, despite my fine feathers, I was still something of an ugly duckling. I looked over to where Flora Parker was dancing with Richard. In her white dress, she looked truly beautiful. And, judging from the way Richard was holding her, he thought so too. Then he glanced over her shoulder and to me and something odd happened. Our eyes met and held. It made me feel most queer inside.

The dance ended and Edward, having led me to the tables, was gathered in by Flora and her academic uncle, eager to quiz him on university life.

At once, Richard was at my side, helping himself, this time, to champagne. He drank, all the time staring at me. I thought him rude. Then he said, 'Hetty, you are looking rather splendid tonight. That is a most remarkable frock,' which took the sting away from his lack of manners.

He took another flute of champagne and turned to me with a wicked grin. It made his eyes sparkle.

'Thank you,' I said and was quite proud of my grown-up performance. 'May I return the compliment?'

'Of course.' He pursed his lips, bent closer and whispered, 'My suit is Lawrie Parker's cast off. But don't tell Leonora, she'd have forty fits.' He posed, 'A Trenchard-Lewis does not accept charity!'

It was such an accurate impersonation of our waspish aunt I giggled.

I knew he spent a deal of time with the Parkers in

London, along with Edward. The four boys were great pals. I tried to imagine what sort of life it was. The Parker offspring were all rather glamorous. And, as the invitation had not included me, imagination was the only tool I had. Richard had changed. He looked as if some of the Parker worldliness had rubbed off onto him. He was far taller than I, with broad shoulders and the Trenchard long legs. He motioned to the footman, who passed me a glass of champagne.

I sipped it. My first taste of champagne! It was not as sweet as the punch and the bubbles tickled my nose.

'What was it like in London?' I tried to keep the longing out of my voice.

'It was great fun.' He glanced at Flora; she smiled knowingly at him and then returned to her conversation.

I followed the look. Swallowing the rest of the champagne far too quickly, I said, 'Flora is looking very up to the minute.'

'Oh, yes, Flora is up to all sorts. What a bricky girl she is!' He looked over again to where she and her uncle were having an animated discussion with Edward. 'Can't say I thought she'd set her cap at Ed.'

'Has she?' I was startled.

'Poor Hetty. Are you still marked out for him? I thought that idea had been scuppered long ago.'

'As I recall,' I said stiffly, 'you were the one who put the idea into my head.'

Richard took my hand and studied it. 'Well, what was I to think? You arrived with due ceremony, to join us waifs and strays.'

'And you listened to the servants' talk!' I interrupted.

With another, impossibly fiendish wicked grin, he lifted my hand again and kissed it lightly. He bowed. 'I own that I did.'

187

I snatched my hand away. It burned where his mouth had touched it. 'You seem to have learned some interesting manners. Is this the London influence?'

'The Parkers do seem to run with a rather fast crowd, it's true.' He took my empty glass, placed it on the table behind us and began to lead me to the dance floor. 'A dance, Hetty? You will see that it is another thing I learned at the Parkers.'

I let him lead me to the dance floor. There was something hypnotic about him tonight; he seemed older than his years and far more sophisticated than I. Harder. If this was the "London effect" I wasn't at all sure I was sad to have missed it.

Richard placed his hand on my waist and I felt it only too clearly through the thin material of my gown. I had already taken off my gloves and, with my usual careless-ness, had lost them somewhere. I regretted this now as Richard held my hand in his. The skin-on-skin contact was disquieting. As we began the dance he pulled me closer until my breasts rubbed against his jacket and I could feel his breath hot on my cheek. This was so very different to when we danced in the ballroom at Delamere. We were playing at it then. This felt as though it was grown-up stuff. Serious.

We danced wordlessly. I did not nod and smile at acquaintances as we passed them, as I had when dancing with Edward. I was only aware of Richard's body pressed against mine and his mouth so near.

When the band finished and we had duly applauded, Richard once again took my hand but, this time, led me through the French doors and into the darkened garden. It must have been cold but I didn't feel it. I was no longer the tomboyish older cuckoo in the nest and Richard was certainly no longer the mischievous, teasing boy I had grown up with. Something had happened to change him and I was certain it had happened in London. He was the adult and I the raw girl.

The night was frosted silver and the sky was clear and a dense, frozen black. I stumbled and wordlessly he put an arm around me and hugged me close. He took me to the bare branches and thorns of the rose arch. And I let him. I followed, as I had always done. I followed where he led. We had begun this pattern as children and now we continued it. This time, though, it was a more serious game. He drew me nearer, even more tightly against him and I felt his long body hot against mine.

'Hetty,' he said it on a suggestion of a whisper. 'How I've longed to do this.'

He slid a hand across my shoulder, my neck, cupping my head and bringing it closer to his. Our mouths were within inches and then his lips descended.

My first kiss!

It began gently. Richard knew what to do. His lips against mine felt delicious, smooth and sweet. I drank in his kisses, enraptured, curious. Strange excited urgings welled deep within me and instinct led my hands to search under his jacket and across his hot back. I heard him groan as if in pain. His lips left my mouth bereft and began to explore my skin. My head fell back as if my neck were too weak to hold it and I trembled. I felt Richard's hot mouth move – to my ear, my collarbone, to where my breasts swelled. He held me hard against him, his arm strong against my back. His mood changed. I felt teeth nipping. His hand rose to hold my breast and he caressed it. The trembling increased and my knees buckled. My head swam, but from the champagne or Richard's caresses, I could not tell. Did not care. He groaned again and muttered something. His mouth traced a path downwards,

189

nudging aside the flimsy gauze and finding flesh. The shock sent a sharp need through me. I hardly knew what I wanted or how I was to obtain it.

I knew I had to stop.

It wasn't right, it couldn't be. I pushed at him, but at the same time shutting my eyes to better drink in the ecstasy. And yet, I knew I had to put an end to this.

'Hetty,' Richard murmured. 'Please let me.'

His hand was now at my side, gathering the material of my skirt and raising it.

'Richard! No!' I gathered every ounce of strength and all my will power and shoved him away. 'Stop. Please stop!'

He stood apart from me, swaying, his eyes glazed. More drunk than I thought.

I pulled my dress back into place with shaking fingers. 'I … I … we shouldn't have done that.'

He shook his head, as if to gather his senses. 'Why?' he demanded. 'Why shouldn't we have done that? Didn't it feel good, Hetty? Admit it, it's the most marvellous thing.' He began to come closer again. I raised my hands as a barrier. 'No!'

He stopped, a disgusted expression creeping over his face. 'You can't say you didn't enjoy it,' he sneered. 'I felt you, I felt you respond.'

I shook my head. Had I enjoyed it? I was too confused to pick apart exactly how I felt. I took a step forward.

'Richard I –'

'You're just like Edward,' he said in disgust. 'Neither of you willing to step into the unknown, to try things. You'll deny yourself and your feelings, won't you Hetty?' He came to me again, but this time in anger. 'Marry him, then, Hetty.' He took my elbow in his hand, in a vice-like grip. 'Marry him,' he snarled, his eyes hooded in rage. 'You deserve one another.' He turned and strode away, disappearing into the dark.

I stared into the blackness long after he had disappeared and held my arm. I would have bruises later.

The rest of the dance passed in a blur. I danced with Edward again, made small-talk with some of the other guests, drank too much champagne and felt numb inside. Richard had disappeared.

I wondered, for a long time afterwards, whether that had been the beginning of what was to come. That I had somehow been the cause of Richard's decline.

Hetty rubbed some life back into her writing hand. Did she really want anyone to read this? Why would they want to? And yet, she couldn't bring herself to destroy what had just caused her so much pain to write. With trembling fingers, she folded the paper into two, firming down the creases. Rising stiffly, from sitting too long, she fetched a kitchen knife and made a slit in the lining of the book she had bought to make her journal. Sliding the papers into their hiding hole, she closed it and then laid her head on her hands in a sort of prayer for forgiveness.

Chapter 21

Rachel lay back on the sofa, puzzled. Hetty had married Edward, having been kissed so passionately by his brother. It didn't make sense.

'Did you really marry Edward simply to please Hester?'

Hetty's ghost declined to answer.

Richard seemed an odd mix of wilful and disobedient boy and charismatic youth. And certainly remarkably self-assured. Rachel shook her head, it was wrong to force her like that. Hetty had been such an innocent.

She remembered the photograph of a man on horseback. It had to be Richard. Unearthing it from under the pile of letters, she stared at the image. He must have been tall, she decided, looking at the length of his legs, and he was broad-shouldered and athletic-looking. Picking up Hetty and Edward's wedding photograph, she looked from Hetty to Richard. She had a nice face, with the snub nose she so despised. But it was as nothing to Richard's beauty. Dark hair cut short, but with a lock over his forehead giving a rakish look, matched by a wide grin and devilish eyes. Hetty would have been an easy victim to this boy's charms. She hadn't had a chance.

'So Hetty,' she said to the empty room, 'if you were so attracted to your Richard, why did you go and marry Edward?'

The room, again, remained frustratingly silent.

Rachel glanced at Gabe, now sleeping beside her. She hadn't the heart to wake him, so she tucked the rug over him and left him in peace.

Hunting through the morass of papers, Rachel found some more scraps of diary entries. Unfolding them, she began to read, hardly wanting to. It would be awful to see Edward mentioned, knowing he did not survive.

Tuesday, October 13th, 1914

Dull weather. Our beautiful summer seems but a distant memory.

We are in full War Fever! The newspapers are filled with Hun atrocities. Leonora reads them out with horrible relish and they make Hester turn pale and sick. I wish Leonora would not do it, but it seems to be the one thing she holds on to, as if she cannot quite bring herself to think of her boy out there. If it is indeed true that the Germans are bayoneting babies, and worse, then I hope Edward will acquit himself and do his best. Oh, but it is hard to think of my husband being 'At War'. At least he has his Egyptian experience to rely upon; he is certainly not some callow youth.

Sam has also 'gone to be a soldier', in the words of Dorcas. As has Robert. Recruiting sergeants were in Hereford and they took the King's shilling on Saturday, along with Sidney Knight and Gerald Trainor from the Parker estate. Glorious boys, doing service for King and country! It is all very thrilling.

I admit to being selfish in praying Albert will not go, for who, then, will look after Snowy? I am to help out as best I can. Elsie is back with us at last; it has been impossible to manage without her. She seems recovered from her illness, but it has taken a time and Hester will insist on being vague with the details. As if I cared when my husband is at the Front!

Hester and I give our thanks, daily, that Richard stays up at Oxford. It will not be long before he goes, however, as he so loves an adventure. I am piqued that he does not return my letters. He has still not forgiven me, although I continue to write. I cannot bear the thought of him going to war angry with me. Silly boy.

Meals have become dreary. Cook complains it is already difficult to get supplies. She says there is much talk in the Butter Market of hoarding.

Thank goodness Delamere has always been used to providing for its own. We should be able to manage as long as we keep the chickens. They are to be my responsibility. In Elsie's absence, I learned how to make bread. I enjoyed this immensely, despite Cook's disapproval of my appearance in the kitchen. Hester is talking about acquiring a goat, although I am not sure I should enjoy milk from a goat.

I am feeling Very Useful and Busy!

Thursday, 22nd October, 1914

Awful, awful news. David Parker has been killed in action at the Battle of Marne. He was twenty-six. Albert drove me and Hester to Breckington today.

His parents are devastated, but holding up well. Flora is full of a fierce anger and energy. She will become a VAD, she says. Her poor parents! One son dead, another on active service and a daughter resolute in her decision to go away from them.

'I need to do something,' she whispered to me as I was leaving this sad household. 'I cannot bear to sit and sit

and wait and wait for another telegram. I cannot bear to
see Mother and Pa's face. You think I am selfish, but if I
stay here I will go mad, Hetty.'
I need to decide what, if anything, to tell Edward.

Monday, 2nd November, 1914

I have decided. I am to help teach at the village school.
The headmaster met Aunt Hester in Fordham on Friday.
He is short of teachers as several have volunteered.
I am to report on Monday next and will assist a Mr
Innisford. I am so looking forward to it. After the argu-
ment with the aunts about becoming a nurse I am glad I
can do something to help the war effort. I shall have
Flora's bicycle, as she says she won't need it in London.
How I have misjudged dear Flora! She has become such a
friend since Richard went up. We have promised to write.
I shall enjoy her adventures vicariously. It is some
comfort. My role as army wife in Egypt is denied, now
Edward's battalion is in France. Shall I ever see the pyramids? Perhaps the Worcesters will return after the war,
with Edward and myself at the helm. On camels! What
fun that would be.
 Leonora disapproves of my bicycling mode of transport,
but there is simply no other way to get there. We cannot
spare Albert and Snowy, alas, is getting ever-more weary.
To work. I am going to work. I know it is wrong to be so
excited, but at last I feel I have something to do!

Rachel shook her head in confusion. So much had happened!
Hetty married, Edward having been in Egypt, presumably with
his regiment. One of the Parker boys dead so soon into the war ...
 Her head swam with unanswered questions, but it was too late
to do anything about them now. Glancing at the clock, she saw it

was getting on for two in the morning. She tucked the rug more firmly around Gabe. There seemed little point in waking him up to make him go home. She went with instinct and kissed his cheek. It was smooth and warm. Vital. Rachel gazed at him for a moment. She'd hate to see him go off to war.

Trying to be as quiet as possible, so as not to disturb him, she put Hetty's life back into its biscuit tin and tiptoed upstairs.

Chapter 22

After a fitful night's sleep, Rachel woke to the telephone ringing. Staggering downstairs, shaking sleep out of her brain, she picked up the receiver.

'Hello?'

'Rachel, hello!'

It was Neil.

'Oh hello.' Rachel yawned, glancing around and, noting the folded rug on an empty sofa. Gabe must have gone very early.

I'm sorry, have I woken you? I was out for a morning run and I sometimes forget that not everyone likes early starts as much as I do!'

'No, not at all,' Rachel lied, trying to clear her fuzzy head. 'What is the time exactly?'

'Eight-thirty! And a lovely day! But as it's Sunday, I'll let you off a lie-in.'

'Thank you,' Rachel said, not bothering to disguise the sarcasm. 'I was wondering –'

'Yes?' Rachel hopped from foot to foot. As usual she'd forgotten to put on her slippers and there was a draught cutting under the door.

'Well, I was just wondering if you were doing anything next weekend? There's a film on at the new arts centre in Hereford and one likes to support these things. Took ages to raise enough funds for the building. I hear the food's good and they have jazz playing at lunchtimes. I don't suppose it compares with sophisticated outings in London, but I thought ...' he tailed off, obviously embarrassed by her silence.

'Oh, Neil, I'm sorry, I'm seeing my parents. They're moving abroad soon and it's the last chance I'll have of seeing them for a bit.'

'Oh, that's too bad.'

There was another silence.

'Look, Rachel, have I done something wrong? I thought we had a good evening together, but then I wondered if I'd done something wrong?'

Guilt flooded through her. Neil was a nice man and didn't deserve to be treated as she had treated him last night. 'I'm so sorry, Neil,' she began, 'living and working on my own, as I do, means I forget my manners sometimes. I think I'm getting a little eccentric!' Tim's words that she'd end up a lonely old spinster with only cats for company came back to haunt her.

'Just as long as I haven't done anything to upset you. I really wouldn't like to do that.'

'No, you haven't.' Ooh, it was too early in the morning for a conversation like this. Rachel shifted her brain up a gear.

'Really?'

'Yes, really.' Rachel was getting impatient now. She began to hop again; this time because of a combined need for caffeine and the loo. She wanted to get Neil off the phone. Something about his neediness irritated her and guilt about how she was treating him nagged.

'Look, Neil, would you like to come with me?' She said, without thinking. 'Don't read anything into it,' she added hastily. 'Mum and Dad have a big house and there'll be shedloads of people there for the party. One more won't be a problem.' And you can keep Mum from foisting Tristan on me, she added silently.

'I'd be delighted. Are you sure, though? Won't you want to be

198

on your own with your parents, if they're moving away?'

'Oh no. We're not like that as a family.'

'Well, if you're sure. Shall I drive?'

Relief relaxed Rachel's shoulders. Neil really was the ultimate gentleman. She hadn't been looking forward to the long drive in her unreliable Fiat. Being driven by Neil, in his more luxurious car, would be bliss.

'That would be marvellous, I'd be so grateful. It's quite a way, though, they live near London, I'm afraid.'

'No problem, I'd be happy to,' Neil replied, stoutly. 'Anything for you.'

Another warning bell went off in Rachel's head. She was going to have to sort this out. And soon. It simply wasn't fair on a nice man like Neil Fitch to let him think they could be anything other than friends. But maybe she should try harder with him? He really was ... nice. That word again. She suppressed a sigh. Nice was so damning. And not sexy.

As there was yet another silence, Neil went on. 'I'll say goodbye until Saturday, then. I'll give you a call later in the week, shall I? To finalise arrangements?'

Rachel smiled. He made it sound as if it were a major expedition. Then immediately felt guilty again. Going in her little rust-bucket of a car *would* have been a major effort and possibly abortive.

'Yes, give me a call on Friday. Must go now, Neil.'

'Will do! And if you're ever in Fordham, don't forget that Roger and I would love to see you in the office.'

'I'll see what I can do,' Rachel said faintly, with the feeling that this was all moving far too quickly for her liking and knowing it was her own fault. ''Bye, Neil,' she said and replaced the receiver, wondering exactly what she'd just done.

Rachel took her coffee outside, to enjoy the glorious morning. The swallows and house martins swooped and chattered high above her and she could hear the church bells revving up for the Sunday service. Everything had greened up in spectacular fashion; the countryside was almost rude in its display of life. In the distance, in the Garths' fields, the half-grown calves grazed, interspersed with white bundles of cotton wool, now no longer lambs. Rachel took a deep breath in. The air was clean and pure and made her feel alive. She was so lucky living here. It had been the right decision.

Returning her mug to the kitchen, she knew she ought to get on with some work. She was behind with the twelve flower illustrations. She was only up to the month of May and halfway through a painting of some bluebells shot through with some red campions. Painted against green, they looked stunning. But she couldn't resist. Going into the sitting room and wrapping herself in the rug, which smelled of Gabe's soap, she dived back into Hetty's life.

Going with a hunch, she slid a craft knife further under the back cover of the book. Holding her breath, she peeled back the leather binding and found what she was looking for: another hidden piece of paper, flattened by an age of being hidden and transparently fragile. Rachel unfolded it and began to read once more. It was another journal entry.

June 1963, Clematis Cottage

I am determined to finally write the truth about my first marriage. And so, I need to continue, whatever pain the memories may bring. I need to tell of the petty squabbling with Richard and my headless rush into marriage with Edward.

Was it Edward's promise of travel that decided me? His regiment was stationed at the British garrison in Egypt and I had had little opportunity to see anything of the world. Or had I given in and complied with what everyone seemed to expect? To please Hester, as I longed so to do. Or did I think myself unable to take Richard on?

200

I had little hope he still liked me, after all. Not after our dreadful quarrel at the ball. Maybe I simply married Edward to spite his brother.

Friday, 5th December, 1913 was my wedding day. It was to be my wedding night.

I remember clearly waiting in the bedroom for my husband to come to me. Hester had helped me out of my dress, brushed my hair and then, after a quick hug, left me alone.

I sat facing the dressing-table mirror in Edward's room. From somewhere money had been found to have it painted and prettified in my honour, but it remained Edward's bedroom and stultifyingly masculine.

I stared at my face, at the lines of tension and at the expression in my eyes. I was nervous and, if I admitted the truth, afraid. My only knowledge of the marriage act was based on the pictures Richard took such glee in showing me all those years ago from which I had fled and which had made me feel sick. I was feeling a little sick now – too much champagne at the wedding breakfast, no doubt. It had been a sedate affair, just the aunts, the Parkers, the vicar and staff. And Richard. A tiny group celebrating with meagre fayre; the minimum the family could provide without losing face.

And now what was in store for me? What was it actually going to be like? Would I have a child? I had very little idea of what to expect.

The door behind me opened and Edward peered in cautiously. 'All right, old girl?'

I turned and watched as he made his way rather unsteadily over to me. His face was flushed and I remembered he had been drinking throughout the day – most unlike him. It occurred to me that he might be nervous too.

'Edward? What shall I do? Shall I get into bed?'

He nodded and waved to the bed. 'Best thing, little Hetty. Pop yourself into bed and I'll be back in a moment.'

As I obeyed him I wondered where he had gone and then remembered the little dressing room next door. I was relieved he was not undressing in front of me. The bed was cold and I shivered as I slid in and pulled the bedclothes up to my chin. Really, this all felt remarkably awkward. For a second, I wondered what Richard and the aunts were doing. Were they still carousing with the remaining guests or had they too retired? I felt detached from everything and it reminded me of the first time I had come to the house, bewildered and terribly lonely. I started as Edward came back into the room.

'That's the thing, in bed, good-oh.' His voice was over-loud and it had a forced jollity to it. He was nervous. He took off his maroon dressing gown to reveal a nightshirt and folded it meticulously over the small chair by the bed. Then he pulled back the bedclothes and got in beside me. The bed sagged alarmingly under his weight. A very strong smell of alcohol wafted over, underpinned by the acrid stench of male sweat. Or maybe it was fear I could smell.

'Shall we have the lamps off then, old thing?'

Glad to turn away from him, I nodded and turned out the bedside lamp. It was too cold to sit up, so I slid under the clothes again and lay frozen with tension, flat on my back. Darkness enveloped the room as Edward reached for his lamp and then he too slid into bed properly. We both lay rigid, with Edward breathing heavily, listening to the house shifting and sighing as it settled for the night. Then Edward rolled over to me and laid a heavy arm on my middle. I felt his moustache tickle my ear as he whispered, 'It'll be all right, Hetty. I'll make it all right for you, little one.'

I felt somewhat reassured, but was still unprepared for what happened next.

Edward lurched to lie half on top of me, propping part of his weight up on one arm. But he was still heavy and it made me feel trapped.

'May I?' he asked, his breath heavy with the smell of whisky.

I nodded, not knowing to what I was acceding. He searched for the buttons on the front of my nightgown, bumping into my chin and apologising as he did so. His breathing became ever more laboured as he found the topmost button and undid it. Then he unbuttoned another and another until it was open and I was bared to my ribs. I felt cold again and shivered.

'Oh Hetty, my little Hetty,' Edward groaned and covered my mouth with his. I tried not to recoil with shock, but I really did not like the feel of his moustache against my lips. I liked it even less when his tongue forced my lips to part and entered my mouth. The wet, hot thing flapped about inside my mouth and saliva dribbled onto my chin. I jerked away.

'Sorry, sorry,' mumbled Edward. 'In too much of a hurry, old girl. Been thinking about this all week, you know. Longer really. Looking forward to it.'

I would have looked forward to it too, had it not been for his constant calling me 'old girl'. It made me feel like one of the Parkers' prize heifers. A bubble of hysteria threatened, which I bit down. It ceased abruptly as I realised Edward was hunting over my nightgown. I'd never realised what big hands he had until one captured its prey. I stifled a yelp as my left breast was squeezed painfully. A great shudder went through Edward's body and, thankfully, he loosened his grip and then began to rub. This was nicer, I thought, and I relaxed a fraction. Whenever his palm made contact with my nipple it actually felt quite good. A warmth began to spread within me and trailed downwards. I wriggled and Edward grunted a little.

Then to my dismay, just as I was beginning to enjoy his touch, his hand left my breast to grab a handful of my nightgown and ruck it up. It was difficult as I was lying on it and the material became stuck at my hip.

Edward rolled right on top of me and lay heavily on me. With one of his knees he nudged aside my thigh and shuffled in between my legs. I tensed again, but Edward took no notice, he was breathing very heavily by now and his hand was fumbling at the join of my legs. He touched me there and I shot upwards on the bed, so great was the shock. He let out a great groan and put his other hand atop my head to pull me down again.

I became aware of a hard, hot thing bumping against where his hand was and became confused as to quite what he planned. I could feel his fingers around something and then the hard, hot thing nudged more insistently at me. Edward muttered something and pushed and the thing actually came inside me a little way. I felt it drag at my skin inside. It was a most peculiar feeling.

Edward was shaking. I could feel the tension in his legs lying against mine. He seemed to be making the most tremendous effort at something. I did not know what to do to help, so lay there, feeling invaded and helpless. Then he gave one more push and entered me completely.

It hurt.

No one had told me it would hurt. They had hinted at what was involved, had said it was my duty and that I would soon have a bouncing baby to care for. But they hadn't mentioned the pain.

Again, I shot away from him, but this time Edward was

prepared and held me in place. His thighs tugged at my skin and stretched it, pulling it painfully tight. I felt horribly dry and sore inside. The skin dragged inside me as he thrust once, twice and then for one impossibly violent push, once more. He gave a great shout and then collapsed on top of me.

I lay, too shocked to move or speak, simply wanting his weight off me, his thing back outside me, where it belonged. The rucked-up material of our nightclothes was pressing as a hard wedge into my hips and Edward's coarse moustache prickled through the thin cotton covering my breasts. I was desperate to move, to get away, but I was trapped. Too dry-eyed with shock to cry.

After some time, Edward's breathing steadied.

'My little love,' he said, with a gratitude I had never heard from him before. 'Oh my little wife.'

I had no response to this, so remained silent. My throat ached with unshed tears. I had never wanted the peace of my own bed more. I sensed Edward had fallen asleep, suddenly, like a puppy worn out from play. I lay like that, pinned down, unable to move for a long time and then, at last, I too drifted off to sleep.

I came to with Edward still lying heavily over me. His moustache still prickled through the front of my unbuttoned nightgown and irritated my skin. I was bone-weary but could not get back to sleep.

Half-awakened impulses still fired through me, an itch irritated somewhere I did not know and did not have the knowledge to assuage. I lay for some time, stiff and sore and confused. I had known Edward would be gentle with me, as indeed I supposed he had been, but the mechanics of it all had appalled me. A great lump of unshed tears and exhaustion lodged in my chest. Was this it? Was this married life? Was this what I must endure for the rest of my life?

I pushed at the inert body, causing Edward to grunt once and then, to my relief, to shift to his side of the bed. I did not want to wake him and risk enduring a repeat of the humiliating process. As quietly as I could, I slid to the edge of the bed. Edward mumbled something and then turned over. He'd drunk throughout the day and I hoped it would be enough to keep him asleep. I had to get away from him. From this bed.

Wrapping my shawl tightly around me, I padded barefoot and silent to the door. Then I paused and turned back to watch Edward sleep, and thought back over the events that had brought this night about.

After our argument at the hunt ball, Richard had barely been at Delamere, preferring the fast life in London with the Parker boys and, I suspected, Flora. The aunts shrugged off their responsibility for him with relief.

When he went up to Oxford we saw even less of him. Our friendship had been severed in a way I still did not really understand. I had written many times and his rejection of me ate away at me. So I turned to gentler Edward, always my protector.

Edward, as predicted, had joined the army. He left, with the First Battalion of the Worcestershire Regiment, for Egypt. I had been pleased for him. It was somewhere he had always longed to go.

He wrote. They were long, entertaining letters. He enthused about the pyramids at Giza and complained of the Australian soldiers, who, if he were to be believed, were more trouble than all the Arabs combined.

Then, quite unexpectedly, he sent me his proposal. Should I like to be married to him? The married quarters were quite adequate, he explained, and he thought he and I would make a good fist of the job of marriage. Had he mentioned my money, then I believe I should have refused. But he didn't, neither was love mentioned. I think, possibly, Edward was lonely. Perhaps army life was not quite as he had envisaged. And he was far from home. From Delamere. And I was lonely too. I had nothing to look forward to except an existence as dreary as my aunts'. Daily, I saw Hester grow ever-more faded, the flower of her life strangled before it had a chance to bloom. I never knew much more of Hester's story. I assumed, after the death of her fiancé, she had returned to Delamere to raise other people's children and look after a vinegary, embittered sister.

I did not want to be like either of them. I wanted a life, to travel, to experience a little of the glamour I had glimpsed through Flora Parker. The unthinking, rash selfishness of youth!

Mostly, I was bored, and I have never dealt with boredom well. Richard seemed lost to me. Hester was quietly encouraging, so I said yes. I agreed to marry a man who I knew little of and did not love, certainly not as a woman ought to love the man she was to marry. But I did not fully understand that type of love. It came to me too late. As soon as I accepted him, I regretted it. Edward had already written to the aunts, who were ecstatic. Richard remained at university – and silent. He gave no voice of approval or otherwise. The great marriage machine trundled into motion. An old dress of Hester's was adapted for me, money scraped together for a breakfast of a sort and, before I knew it, Edward and I were married.

Memories of the day are a little blurred, but I remember Flora holding onto Richard's arm with a possessiveness I thought distasteful. Richard, himself, said nothing to me at all, despite being Edward's best man. I was a foolish girl to marry to get out of a life she did not want. But I wasn't the first and wouldn't be the last.

So, I suppose I deserved what had been imposed on me on my wedding night. That was the deal. I exchanged my dignity for a life that might be a little more thrilling than the one I had.

With one last look at my husband – my husband! – sleeping contentedly and snoring a little now, I closed the door behind me – and the awful scene and memory. I made my way upstairs. Without really realising where I was going, or where I wanted to be, I found myself in the old nursery corridor. I had no idea why I wanted to be there or what I would do, but it symbolised a sort of refuge, a bygone memory of simpler days. Going into the schoolroom, I stopped short.

A man was standing smoking by the window, one knee up on the window seat. He was silhouetted against the steely moonlight, but from the shape of his head and his stance I knew him immediately. It was Richard. At the sound of the door closing he turned. Even in the gloom of the half-lit room, there was just his night candle alight on the old desk, I could tell his eyes were focused on me.

'What the hell. Hetty?'

I forgot we were enemies. I forgot we had quarrelled. I forgot we had had months of silence. I stumbled towards him. 'Oh Richard!'

'What is it, Hetty? Are you alright? What's the matter?' His voice was harsh, but I didn't care, he was the only one I felt would understand.

'Oh Richard, it was awful. I feel awful. Edward –'

'Edward what, Hetty?'

His tone checked me. I stood before him, feeling foolish and chilled. 'It … we …' I had no words. My breath misted out in a frigid cloud.

'You have done what married people do on their wedding

night, I trust?' He still had not moved. The cruelty, always simmering near the surface, barbed.

Why was he being like this? I had felt sure, with all his knowledge, he would understand, but he was angry. Angrier than I'd ever seen him. Now he took a step closer and I could see how white his face was. In contrast to Edward, Richard had hardly drunk all day, but now I could smell port on his breath. I felt suddenly alive all over.

'Richard I —' My words were snapped off as he reached out and snaked a hand around the back of my neck.

'I see you've been bloodied good and proper. How does it feel, Hetty? How does it feel to be a real woman?'

His hand was hurting the back of my neck. His fingers were pressing into my flesh. But I didn't care. To be near him was intoxicating.

'Bloodied? I don't understand.'

Richard lifted a handful of my nightdress and, looking down, I gasped. There was a smear, dark-reddy brown and, unmistakably, blood on the front of my gown.

'Oh God!' I said, with a kind of numb horror as I remembered the process by which it had got there. The whole thing was disgusting.

'So how does it feel, little Hetty, to be married off for your money, to be a real woman at last? Does it feel good? To have your devoted Edward enslaved at last?'

His grip hardened around my neck. 'Please, Richard, you're hurting me.'

'I can smell him on you,' he sneered. 'I can smell him … oh God, Hetty.'

His mouth crushed mine. I felt his moustache graze my already sensitised mouth and I tasted port and cigars on his breath. His tongue forced my lips open and invaded my mouth. He pulled me to him so my breasts were seared against the buttons of his dress shirt. I felt my nipples harden with the roughness and it sent a shooting arousal to my belly. His hand left my neck and searched downwards, gripping my rear through the thin cotton of my nightgown. He pressed me against him and I could feel him, hard and demanding.

'You're my Hetty, you're …' His mouth left mine and raked a trail down my neck. He pushed aside the neck of my nightgown and traced a hot tongue down to my collarbone.

I lifted my arms to entwine around his neck, to fist in his hair and bring him nearer. Was this what it was supposed to be like?

Richard released his hold on me and snaked a hand under the thin cotton. I felt hot flesh mould hot flesh. He pressed me against him harder and I returned the force with equal pressure. I was out of my mind, obeying the leaping instinct which my body craved. Acting with natural feeling, listening to the age-old rhythm, seeking the physical comfort denied to me by my husband.

My husband. Richard's brother.

I stilled. Richard sensed the change in me and stopped too. His mouth nestled in the curve between shoulder and neck and I could hear his harsh breathing and feel his moustache scratch. His chest heaved and I could still feel his hardness against me.

So this was how it was supposed to feel. This wild cry from the very heart and soul, this leaving behind of all rational thought. This surrender to heat, to the power. Yes, there was a kind of violence in it, an overwhelming terrible blackness that was beautiful and desperate.

We stood for a moment, bodies meshed until sanity returned.

Richard's shoulders began to shake. I felt a hot wetness on

my neck. He was sobbing into my shoulder. In all the years I'd known him, I had never witnessed him cry. Even when caned on the legs by Leonora for stealing sixpence, even when the rotten apple tree branch gave way under his weight and he fell six feet. Even when forced to visit his mother's grave. Richard never cried. We held each other still, but with a different kind of need.

'Oh my darling. My darling boy.' I clutched him to me and tears of my own began to fall.

'It was always you, Hetty.' His voice came out, thin and ragged and despairing. 'But you never realised. It was always you. I've loved you for so long, but I knew you were destined to be Edward's. And now you have married him.'

'Hush.' I stroked his hair, not knowing what else to do, struggling with the tumult of emotion. Richard, who alternately drove me mad with anger or hysterical with laughter. Richard, with whom I had shared my dreams and hopes. Richard, who had given my life its flavour and excitement. Why had I not realised, until now, that it was Richard who I loved?

And now it was too late.

He released me and moved away. I began to shiver; it was penetratingly cold in the school room. In the gloom I saw him light another cigarette with shaking hands. He took in a deep drag and ran a hand over his face in a weary gesture.

'Richard, my love.'

He held up a hand to fend me off. 'Don't,' he pointed a wavering finger at me. 'Don't ever call me that.' Anger lit his words. 'You have made your choice, Hetty. This never happened tonight. Never, you understand. Now go. Go to your husband. Go to my brother's bed.'

'Richard?' I moved towards him, but saw a stranger's eyes.

With a sob, I turned and fled.

The following morning I breakfasted alone. My new husband was sleeping off his hangover and Richard, it seemed, had gone riding with the Parkers.

I had married the wrong brother and Richard would never forgive me.

Rachel sat on the sofa stunned at what she had just read. She'd understood that girls of Hetty's generation had known very little of what to expect on their wedding night, but this was almost legalised rape. Edward wasn't to be blamed. From the sound of it, he knew little more than Hetty.

Rachel did a hazy calculation. Edward must be in his twenties by now, maybe the same age as Gabe. But inexperienced. Unlike Gabe. And then there was Richard. She hadn't guessed, as Hetty hadn't, that Richard truly loved her. And she'd married his brother!

Poor Hetty. Poor doomed Edward. And poor Richard. Rachel gave up a foolish little prayer that Richard survived the war.

Chapter 23

A sharp rapping at the door startled her.

Rachel rose to let in a familiar, and very modern, figure. Dressed in his usual faded jeans and scruffy t-shirt, he was instantly recognisable. What really took her by surprise was how pleased she was to see him.

'Gabe, it's Sunday!'

'Just come to start the wiring,' he said cheerfully. 'Seeing as the place is ripped apart for the radiators, I might as well do a bit more damage.'

She followed him into the kitchen. 'Are you an electrician as well as everything else?' Rachel automatically flicked the kettle on. She knew what was expected. She turned and smiled at him, pleasure at seeing him washing over her. 'You're a man of many talents.'

Gabe grinned at her warm tone. 'I have, as you say, many talents.' He winked. 'No but seriously, I've got enough sense to stick to the chippying. Dad's mate Brian will come over and do the tricky stuff once I've got it all prepped.'

'You must've left early this morning.' Rachel handed him his tea.

'Yes, sorry about that.' Gabe looked embarrassed. 'Didn't mean to fall asleep on you. You should have woken me up.'

Rachel cocked her head on one side and pouted. 'But you looked so peaceful all wrapped up in the rug. And snoring.'

'I do not snore.'

'How do you know?' She raised her eyes to the ceiling, enjoying teasing him. 'It was like a steam train in there.'

Gabe concentrated on his tea. 'Yeah, well. Never had any complaints before.' As Rachel didn't answer, he asked, 'Did you find out anything interesting – from those hidden papers?'

'Mmm.' Rachel poured herself some tea, not liking the idea of anyone knowing about whether Gabe snored. 'Hetty married Edward. She's endured her wedding night. And found out she's really in love with Richard.' She turned to face him. 'Her now brother-in-law.'

'God! It's better than Coronation Street.' He chuckled and then stopped. 'What do you mean, "endured"?'

Rachel pulled a face. 'Hardly any sex ed in those days. Let's just say Edward didn't know a great deal about foreplay.'

To her surprise, instead of saying something laddish, Gabe winced. 'Poor Hetty. Do you think it'll be a happy ending?'

'I hope so.' Rachel sighed. 'It's not looking promising at the moment, though.'

Gabe drained his mug. 'Well, I hope so too. She's a game girl is Hetty. I'm getting quite fond of her.' He swilled his mug and put it in the sink. 'Better get on.'

'How long do you think you'll be? Not that it matters.'

'Can only do this morning. Got to be somewhere later.'

He always seemed to be going somewhere. Rachel wondered what he'd been doing the evening before to so exhaust him.

'Well, at least it's not Kev doing it,' she said, more sharply than she intended.

Gabe gave her a glance. 'Is he bothering you?'

'No, not really. What do you mean, exactly?' She frowned.

'He's a bit … has trouble keeping it in his trousers, if you see what I mean,' Gabe said, looking down at his feet, obviously embarrassed. 'That's why we don't let him be here on his own. Does a good job, but he can't always be trusted. Not round women.'

Rachel felt sick. She'd always kept clear of Kev and disliked the greasy looks he gave her sometimes; they made her feel grubby, but she hadn't suspected this.

'Oh, he's not a bad lad,' Gabe added hurriedly. 'He had a spot of bother a few years ago but he did his stint in Borstal and he's been clean ever since. It's just he can't get a job, though, not with his record, so Dad helps him out every now and again. Not a great deal round here, you might have noticed, except for a bit of fruit-picking and that's seasonal. Dad's trying to give him a chance to get going in a trade.'

'Right,' Rachel said faintly, all thoughts of Hetty and Richard fleeing, 'I don't suppose there is much work going. Not for someone with his background. Well, thank you for looking out for me.'

'No worries.'

She turned to make more tea. She found she had a strong desire for it – and to mull over this new information about Kev.

'Rachel?'

'Yes?'

'That bloke, the one who came to stay. Is he a boyfriend, then?'

'Tim? Oh no, he's just a friend. From London.' From somewhere, deep inside, anger was uncurling.

'Oh right,' Gabe nodded vigorously. 'Just wondered. Kev thought he was okay.'

'Did he?' Rachel took a deep breath and blew her fringe out of her eyes. She concentrated hard on pouring boiling water into the teapot. 'Well,' she said, through thinned lips, 'you might like to tell Kev that Tim liked him too.'

'Yeah, okay.'

She turned on him. 'Only, you might add that Tim is gay and, that along with Kev, he has a little trouble keeping it in his trousers too.'

Relief then shock flickered across Gabe's face.

She couldn't hold the anger back any longer. 'Thank you for foisting an ex-criminal on me in my own home and only just

215

thinking of telling me,' she began. 'And thank you *so* much for protecting me from him.'

'Rach, I didn't mean –'

'And thank you, too, for your interest in my private life.' She realised too late she'd gone too far. She saw Gabe's expression cloud. 'Gabe, I'm sorry, I didn't mean –'

'No, no need to apologise,' he said, an unusual sarcasm edging his voice. 'After all, you can't blame folks round here for being curious when they see you with one bloke one day and you out with Neil Fitch another.'

Any concern about hurting Gabe's feelings fled. 'Neil Fitch! What's he got to do with anything?'

Gabe examined his hand. 'Hasn't escaped notice that he and you have been going out.'

'And?'

'Well, people talk.'

'Do they?' Rachel's voice was acid.

'They do in a small village like this.'

'Well, you can tell this small village that what I do in my private life, in my private time, is my own private business.'

Gabe watched, through narrowed eyes, as she turned on her heel, marched to the sitting room and slammed the door shut. The cottage shuddered with the impact.

Rachel leaned against the door and didn't know whether to laugh or cry.

Her simple country life was turning out to be anything but. She had a known criminal lurking around, the entire village gossiping about her supposedly wanton behaviour and now Gabe was going to rip holes in the walls to match those in the floor.

She put her head in her hands. How had it all come to this?

'All I wanted was somewhere quiet to work!' she moaned, managing to laugh at the absurdity of it all.

An escape of a sort beckoned, though, and she really needed it.

'If the village thinks I'm going out with Neil, then I may as well.'

The room hummed with something. More disapproval? But Rachel was in no mood to listen to ghosts from the past. She would take Neil to her parents' party after all. Sod the lot of them. Gabriel Llewellyn included.

Gabe winced. He knew he should have kept his mouth shut, but he'd had to know. He'd had to push at it.

'Good going, Gabriel boy,' he muttered, running a hand through his hair in exasperation. Jeez! Jealousy was a terrible thing. The knowledge that Tim had been staying with Rachel had been like having an itchy scab – and picking at it. And he was still no nearer knowing the truth about Rachel and that smooth bastard Neil Fitch. At least he'd cleared up one mystery: Tim was no threat. Best keep the knowledge that he was gay from Kev. Although he'd admitted to liking him, Kev wasn't known for his liberal views.

Last night here was the only place he'd felt like being. He thought he and Rachel were getting on better. Getting closer. It had felt right being on the sofa. Peaceful. And he'd needed a sanctuary. His father accusing him of not being committed to the family firm still rankled. If he ever had the chance to discuss it with Rachel, he knew she would understand. Would know about the need to create something overriding anything else. And that included putting in a kitchen at the Hallidays'.

He looked to the resolutely closed door of the sitting room and made himself promise to tell Rachel, as soon as possible, that Kev had only been in Borstal for a bit of joy-riding. 'Might put her mind at ease,' he said to his toolbox and, picking it up, made his way upstairs.

Chapter 24

Rachel knew she'd made a huge mistake as soon as Neil collected her in his car.

'We'll stop on the way, shall we, for a spot of lunch? I've researched a good place,' he said, with an important grin.

Poor man. He was condemned by that opening statement. It made Rachel realise just what it was that irritated her most about him. He was prematurely middle-aged. All his fussing over not drinking too much, getting an early night, making sure he trained properly. It made him so dull. Rachel knew she was being completely unfair; he was probably some girl's ideal man. Just not hers.

She bit her lip and handed him her overnight bag. He made a great fuss of stashing it in the boot and then came round to open the passenger door for her. His good manners just made Rachel feel even worse.

The weekend went as Rachel expected. When she and Neil arrived, there was already a crowd of tipsy golf-club types milling around the half-packed-up house. Paula gave her daughter an unusually warm hug, but there was no time to talk. Inevitably, though, she made a huge fuss over Neil. Then there was a crushingly embarrassing moment when Neil and Rachel were shown to the double-bedded guest room, only resolved when Rachel said she'd camp out in her old bedroom.

As the afternoon wore on, even more people arrived and spilled out into the garden. Too many people and too much alcohol. The party became ever more drunken and Rachel, never easy with the social scene her parents enjoyed, slunk out into the garden, leaving Neil discussing property prices with her father.

Her mother had made it abundantly clear he was earmarked for a son-in-law. 'So suitable, darling,' she whispered into Rachel's ear, as she clung on to her daughter's arm. 'You know we just want to see you happy, settled. And I think he could be the man for you!' Rachel didn't bother to protest. It didn't seem the right time.

Dodging around a giggling couple who were heading for the hot tub, she made her way to the far end of the garden and her long-forgotten childhood swing. Sitting on it and sipping wine, she watched the partying from a safe distance.

She missed the inky blackness above Herefordshire. Here, the sky was a light-polluted dirty orange. She couldn't see a single star. The soundtrack to everything was the relentless hum of the M25. No owls hooting, no screech of a hunting vixen. Even the air smelled different. She was glad she'd come, though. To do something which made her parents happy.

Neil made his way through to her. She admired his side-step from an over-amorous friend of her mother's. He seemed to be taking everything in his stride and was accepting the situation with his normal good grace and faultless manners. Rachel felt a surge of gratitude towards him.

'I'm so sorry about all this,' she said, when he reached her and gestured to the drunken middle-aged golfers who were playing a rowdy game of 'pass the keys'. Rachel winced as one of the women shrieked and tried to fish the keys out of her cleavage.

Neil perched himself gingerly on an upturned wheelbarrow and looked about him. He raised one black brow. 'They certainly know how to have a good time.' Then, just as Rachel thought he might be about to say something pompous again, he produced a bottle of white from under his jacket. He clinked glasses with her and grinned. 'Might as well join in!'

Rachel smiled back. He was making it all so easy for her. He'd batted off her mother, had a long conversation with Tristan, giving Rachel the chance to talk to her father before he got too drunk to make sense and had been, in every way possible, the perfect guest.

She tried to picture Gabe in the same situation and couldn't. Gabriel Llewellyn simply didn't fit into this middle-class, middle-aged suburban revelry. But then, neither did she. She never had. She was confident the relationship with her parents would improve at some point in the future. She just had to grit her teeth and get through now.

Rachel counted the hours; it was eleven-thirty. Possibly they could escape by ten in the morning. Any earlier and her parents wouldn't be up. With any luck, she could say goodbye over their first coffee and cigarette of the day.

Portugal wasn't a million miles away and she promised herself she'd visit. And build more bridges.

She bit down on a sudden giggle. Bringing Neil, who was so eminently suitable and good-looking, was the most conformist thing she'd ever done. If her parents went off to their new life thinking their daughter was settling down, she was glad. She just hoped Neil didn't have the same impression.

'And I'm so sorry for all the fuss my mother made about the rooms,' she said to him, as he poured her another glass of wine.

'Oh, please, don't worry about that. It was an easy mistake to make, putting us in the same bedroom. Now we've found somewhere a little quieter to sit,' Neil said, 'you can tell me what you found that was so fascinating in Hetty's journal.'

Rachel's gratitude burgeoned. 'I'd really like that,' she said and, looking into his handsome face, realised it was true. She launched into a summary of the latest instalment of Hetty's story.

On their return to Clematis Cottage, on yet another sublime day, Rachel saw Gabe's Toyota parked under the chestnut tree. Her heart sank. She'd hoped to say a polite goodbye to Neil and slip back into some work. She needed to catch up with a deadline.

Last night Neil had listened to her ramblings about Hetty, Edward and Richard in a polite and attentive silence, but she was sure he wasn't particularly interested. It was just another manifestation of his good manners. Rachel was frustrated. Apart from Gabe, no one seemed as enthralled as she was in the journal and she was beginning to have doubts as to whether an illustrated version would find a market.

And now, on this gloriously sunny Sunday afternoon, the last thing she needed was a standoff between Neil and Gabe.

She opened the car door as soon as Neil had switched off the ignition. Before getting out, she turned to him. 'Thanks so much for coming with me. I really appreciated the company. And thanks so much for driving, Neil, I don't think my Fiat would have survived that journey!'

'No problem, Rachel. I enjoyed it.'

She gave him a querying look. 'It surely can't have been much fun having to put up with drunken strangers all weekend?'

He grinned. 'Yes, truly. I like being with you, Rachel. You must have realised that by now.' He reached out a hand and took hers. 'I'd like to ... I'd like to see more of you.'

Rachel panicked. She should have known, should have realised Neil would read more into the weekend than was meant. And it was hardly unexpected. He'd given off enough signals. She'd just been selfish and ignored them.

'Look, I've really got to go,' she began. 'I've got a deadline to meet and I ought to check on Gabe. Not sure what he's working on.'

Without giving him the chance to respond, she slid out of the car, wrenched open the boot door and grabbed her overnight bag. 'Thanks again, Neil. See you!'

Racing up the path and finding the front door open, she hurried inside. She shut the door behind her and leaned against it. The house welcomed her with its calm and cool and she felt it settle around her. She closed her eyes. Peace.

'Back then?' Gabe was standing in the doorway of the kitchen, the inevitable length of wiring in his hand.

'Yes.'

'Had a good time?'

Rachel nodded warily. 'You know, there's nothing between Neil and me,' she blurted out, not knowing why it was so important that Gabe should understand.

'Oh, right,' he said, 'that why everyone is talking about you two?'

'The village can gossip all it likes, but it's the truth. He gave me a lift, that's all.'

'And spent the weekend? Met your parents?' Gabe raised an eyebrow in disbelief. 'You know how that looks.'

'Well, go on then and book the bloody church.' Rachel snapped and picked up her bag. 'Yes,' she said wildly, 'we're violently in love and planning a spring wedding!' She stomped to the bottom of the stairs. 'And Stan's going to be bridesmaid. He'll wear his string vest. So tell that to the village gossip machine as well. See what they can make of that!'

She ran upstairs, her shoes making an impossible racket on the uncarpeted wood. Slamming shut the bedroom door, she flung herself on the bed. This would never happen in London. She could have slept with nineteen men on one night and no one would have given a monkey's. No one cared enough. She sat up and pushed the hair from her eyes. That was the difference. Here people cared.

She looked towards the door. Did Gabe care? And how did she feel about him? He was younger than she was – by some way. He was so different to her in many ways: hadn't travelled, hadn't made the most of all the potential she knew he had. He could even be called 'unsophisticated'. But he was kind and generous, sensitive and loyal. And hot. A memory of him shirtless made lust curl within her. He was as unsuitable as Neil was suitable. So why did Gabe make her heart race when Neil sent her to sleep? Guilt crowded in. She'd been so unfair to Neil and needed to explain to him that they'd never be more than friends. And she needed to do it soon.

There was a knock on the door.

'Come in.' She looked up as Gabe entered. His hair was as untidy as ever. There was a rip across one of the legs of his jeans, exposing a length of smooth, brown skin and he had dust smeared liberally across his jaw. He couldn't have been a greater contrast to the man who had just dropped her off. But he was utterly gorgeous.

'Tea?' He held out a steaming mug to her.

'Thank you.' She sipped. 'I don't have to explain anything to you,' she muttered, keeping her eyes on the mug.

'Nothing at all,' Gabe replied, his voice expressionless.

She met his eyes. 'So why do I feel I have to?'

Gabe shrugged. 'Beats me,' he said and, after giving her a shuttered look, left.

Chapter 25

In the dying embers of her thirtieth birthday, Rachel caught the last train from Paddington. It had been a good day. A meeting with Freda had resulted in a new commission and it had been followed by a boozy late lunch with Tim and Jyoti.

Catching up with Jyoti had been a joy. She'd radiated happiness and had been full of news about the upcoming wedding. Rachel made a valiant effort to understand her friend's motives for marrying and had given up in the face of Jyoti's newly found contentment. Kamal met them at the end of the meal and he was charming. Rachel saw them onto a number thirty-eight bus with tears in her eyes. She couldn't believe her best friend was getting married without the magical spark she'd need herself, but it seemed to be working for Jyoti.

Tim had been his usual self and had flirted outrageously with all the waiters. His present, a blow-up 'perfect boyfriend' was stowed (now deflated) in her bag. She'd let him off as he'd also bought her a digital camera.

By the time she got out at Hereford station, it was dark. She stood on the platform for a moment, enjoying the cool July night air. The city had made her feel clammy, with a sweaty grime lodged under her nails and in her skin. It would be good to get home. It was the first time she'd thought of her little dusty, half-finished cottage as home. She felt her shoulders sink back down to their more normal position and, closing her eyes, raised her face to the indigo sky and breathed. There was a hint of rain in the air and she felt cleaner, refreshed.

The train behind her geared up and heaved itself out of the station and she made her way to the exit. Finding her car marooned in a deserted car park, she drove into the city in search of a shop. She was out of milk and, strangely, instead of her normal coffee, she craved tea.

Cruising through the shuttered centre she realised it was a faint hope – nothing seemed open apart from the pubs. Stamping on the memory of the 'Eight 'Til Late' that had been just around the corner from her London flat, she concentrated on driving through her tiredness.

Knots of teenagers gathered around each brightly lit oasis of alcoholic promise. At ten o'clock, the youth of Hereford were just beginning their night out and made Rachel feel old in her longing for her bed and a mug of tea. She slowed for the traffic lights on the Commercial Road and locked her door from the inside as she saw a particularly large and raucous group pushing and shoving good-naturedly in the queue for the nightclub. The lights turned red, so Rachel stopped and looked over at the crowd. Then she saw him.

Gabe.

He was more formally dressed than she'd ever seen him, in a white shirt and black trousers. She watched him curiously. He was laughing and joking, slightly apart from the rougher elements of the crowd. Then Rachel caught her breath. A girl detached herself from the queue. Her flame-coloured hair marked her out instantly as Dawn, the barmaid from the Plough. She gazed adoringly at Gabe, hanging onto his arm, making her feelings obvious.

If Rachel was in any doubt about her own feelings for Gabe, the reaction she had now made it abundantly clear. The pain of the jealousy shooting through her was primeval.

This just wouldn't do, couldn't happen. She couldn't let herself fall for a man barely into his twenties – and who was her *handyman*! What would Tim say? Rachel forced herself to grin; she knew precisely what Tim would say. The car behind Rachel's hooted and she jumped. The lights had gone green. Flustered, she stalled the engine and the car behind hooted again. Looking in her rear-view mirror she saw the driver make an obscene gesture. In her panic to move off she couldn't see if Gabe had responded to the girl.

Miserable and milk-less she turned for home, refusing to dwell on the dull ache setting up residence inside her.

Mike and his friend Brian turned up the following day, to begin the rewiring in earnest, but without Gabe. Rachel longed to ask where he was, but managed to restrain herself. His private life was his own business, after all, and, after what she'd said to him, she could hardly pry into his. She busied herself with preparation for her next commission: a series of watercolour illustrations for a new edition of fairy tales. She wouldn't begin it before finishing the flower pictures, but needed to get some notes down while ideas were fresh in her head. It was a big job and she was grateful to get it; the house was drinking money. And besides, it was all she could concentrate on. Gabe insisted on occupying her thoughts. Relentlessly.

'How could I have fallen for him?' she muttered to herself, wincing at sounds of the drill coming from upstairs. A frisson of something like laughter rippled around the sitting room. 'You may well laugh,' Rachel said to Hetty, 'but he's not at all the right man.' The laughter dulled to a feeling of sympathy. Rachel leaned back in her work chair and stared blankly out of the window, for once the view forgotten.

Gabe had been brilliant, she admitted. He'd turned up on evenings and weekends, had gone well beyond what was expected of him. He was very easy company; sometimes they'd sat on the front step without talking for hours. She found him peaceful to be around and missed him when he wasn't. She liked his sense of humour, his quiet ability to get on with the job in hand. She heard a chuckle. 'And alright, yes, Hetty, he's pretty hot in those tight jeans.' She felt Hetty approve.

'But he's younger.' The lasciviousness toned down into sympathy. 'And we have nothing in common.' Rachel pursed her lips. 'He drives me mad with his constant tea-drinking, I don't think he's ever been further than Hereford and he reads a tabloid!' A wave of uncertainty washed over her. 'Okay, I know that makes me a snob, but don't you need some things in common to make a relationship with?' Rachel rubbed at her temples. 'Am I really having a conversation with a ghost?' She felt laughter in the room again. 'And what do I mean by having a relationship with Gabe? I don't even know how he feels about me!' There was a thud of a door shutting above her. 'I know what Tim would say. Shag him and get it out of your system.'

At the sound of Mike clattering down the stairs, any ghost or spirit or remnant of Hetty fled, leaving a cold emptiness behind.

Rachel saw Mike and Brian out at six and went upstairs to run a bath. She needed to unknot the tension in her shoulders caused by a long and fruitless stint at the drawing board. Frowning at the idea of Gabe's possible relationship with Dawn, she swirled a dollop of Jo Malone bath oil into the water. As the sandalwood and ginger aroma rose in the steam, she inhaled greedily. It was her birthday present from Jyoti. Rachel muttered a prayer. She hoped her friend would be happy.

Turning on the radio, she found Radio Three. Whatever workmen she had in her house always seemed obsessed with Radio Two and she was forever re-tuning it. Getting into the hot water, she lay back and sighed with pleasure. Closing her eyes she let herself drift off with Sibelius.

Something, some sixth sense, made her open her eyes. Squinting through the steam, she saw, on the taps and just above her toes, a dark blob. Focusing harder she made out the biggest, hairiest spider she had ever seen.

She froze.

Rationally she knew the spider was harmless and that it would go on its way without bothering her. But phobias aren't rational and Rachel had a phobia about spiders. She loathed them, and as if sensing this, the spider froze too. The idea that the spider was possibly staring back at her was the final straw. Rachel screamed and launched herself out of the bath. Grabbing her wrap, she fled out of the bathroom.

There was a furious hammering at the front door. Snatching the silk around her wet body she tripped downstairs and wrenched open the door to find Gabe standing there with a tool box.

'Rachel, you all right?' I thought I heard a scream. 'Dad asked me to drop this off,' he began and then, taking note of her ashen complexion, stopped. 'There *is* something wrong.' He backed her into the hall, dropped the box and kicked shut the door behind him. 'Rachel?' He took her by the arms to find her shaking uncontrollably.

'I'm f-fine. Spider. In the bath.'

Gabe relaxed. 'Oh is that all? I thought it was something serious.'

'It is! To me!'

Gabe took another look at Rachel's face and nodded. 'Okay, I'll go and slay the beast, shall I?' He made his way along the hall.

'Gabe?'

'Don't kill it.'

He waved a hand as he ran up the stairs, taking them two at a time.

After a few minutes, when she thought it might be safe, Rachel followed him. She met him coming out of the bathroom, an enormous smile on his good-looking face. 'You were right, it was a big one.'

Rachel paled again.

Gabe came to her. 'All sorted now. I put it out of the window. You really don't like them, do you?' Going with the moment, he took her in his arms and inhaled more of the intoxicating scent from the bath. She smelled expensive and female. She burrowed into his chest and shook her head against his shirt.

'Poor lovely.' Stroking her hair, damp from her bath, he couldn't quite believe it was the usually remote, strung-up Rachel he had in his arms. She nestled in closer and the trembling lessened. 'Just as well you've got Big Bad Gabe to get rid of the nasties for you.' He felt her giggle vibrate against his chest. It made him harden. He stroked a hand across Rachel's narrow waist and felt her still in response. The clinging silk robe made every curve of her body beg to be caressed.

'Gabe?' She gazed up at him, eyes huge in a white face.

He couldn't resist. Didn't want to. Risking everything, he threaded a hand through her cool hair, pulled her to him and kissed her. She tasted of toothpaste and desire. He was painfully aware of her naked body beneath the flimsy robe and he could feel her breasts pressing against his shirt and making it damp. Need pulsated through him.

For the second time in her life Rachel did something truly impulsive, possibly even a little mad.

She kissed him back.

She arched into him so she could sense every sinew of his lean, strong body against hers. He felt so good. It felt so right kissing him. Rachel opened her mouth and deepened the kiss. It was heaven – or as close to it as she'd ever been. She inched her hands under his linen shirt and stroked the smooth skin beneath. She'd never met a man who was so sexy, who she wanted so urgently.

Stepping out of his embrace and smiling at his expression, she took his hand and led him to her bed.

It was like being immersed in liquid, was Rachel's last coherent thought. Warm, slow-moving liquid, with heat at the edges taking control and sweeping them up into fire.

She came to with Gabe lying half across her. She stroked a hand over his hair and discovered it was something she'd always longed to do. No wonder it was always escaping the ponytail, she giggled, it was cut in layers. It felt as silky as it looked. Golden brown with lighter highlights from all the sun they'd been having.

Rachel felt as if she had the sun inside her, she was so warm and replete. Relaxed. Satiated. Gabe was breathing quietly and regularly so he must be asleep. Resting her hand on his smooth, brown shoulder, Rachel followed.

It was almost dark when they woke. The last of the evening shadows lengthened in the room and brought with them a breathing, pulsing intimacy.

Gabe gave a cat-like stretch. 'Sorry, did I crash out?' he murmured and pulled her close again. 'Busy day.'

Rachel smiled. 'Have you been working hard today?'

'Not as hard as I just did.'

She giggled and he kissed her.

'I was right,' he said, his mouth inches from hers.

'What about?'

'You *are* like a glass of water. Long and cool. To be sipped slowly.'

Rachel raised her brows quizzically. 'I haven't the faintest idea what you're on about.'

'That's what I thought when I first saw you. Outside the cottage. Long and cool.'

'Not a stuck up in-comer?' She asked on a sigh as his kisses travelled along her jaw, to where she was most sensitive.

Gabe grinned and nipped her ear. 'More sort of aloof.'

'So, I'm an aloof, cool drink to be sipped slowly? I still have no idea what you mean.'

Gabe traced a lazy tongue around the areole of a breast, making Rachel suck in a breath and then trailed leisurely kisses over her stomach to her sex. Cupping her with gentle hands, he parted her thighs. As he lowered his head, his hair slipped forward and tickled deliciously. 'To be sipped again and again,' he whispered. And did.

The cool, early-morning air sliding over their naked skin, and the dawn chorus woke them. Indignant, the sparrow was in overdrive.

Rachel rolled onto her side to peer at the clock. Neither of them had got much sleep, but she'd never felt more alive, more revitalised. She looked across at Gabe, who was rubbing a hand across his face. What a beautiful man I've just bedded, she thought, gazing at his wide, suntanned shoulders and strong hands, with their square-tipped capable fingers.

'Morning,' he said, scrubbing at his eyes and yawning hugely. 'What's the time?'

'Just after five.'

He grimaced. 'Better go home. Got to get over to the Hallidays and I need to get changed first.'

The image of Gabe standing at the door flashed into Rachel's memory. He'd been dressed smartly, in a linen shirt and the black trousers she'd seen him in outside the nightclub. Jealousy gnawed again. 'Where were you going last night?'

He glanced at her. 'Only off out to see a film with Dawn and Paul and the gang.' He flung himself onto his back and stretched, making the bed shudder with his weight.

Rachel admired the length of his side, slightly paler than the rest of him, ribs showing through the thin skin as he raised his arms above his head. She even liked the look of the soft brown hair growing in his armpits and the trail of it leading towards his groin. He was very *male, masculine*. Nothing metrosexual about Gabe.

'It'll be okay, they're used to me not turning up sometimes.' He gave Rachel a wicked look. 'They'll put it down to a woman. Only this time they'd be right.' He rolled over to her and kissed her shoulder, looking up from under dark lashes, the sherry-brown eyes impish.

'Had many women, have you Gabe?'

'A few. Not as many as folk say. They like to think of me being some kind of stud round here.' He shrugged. 'You know how they like to gossip.'

'Only too well,' Rachel said drily.

'Well, don't believe everything they say.' Lifting the duvet, he slid his warm body against hers. Instantly, she wanted him again.

She bit down on her lust. 'How old are you, by the way?'

Gabe slid a hand under the duvet and across Rachel's flat stomach, into the dip between her hip bones. He kissed her shoulder again and nuzzled at her arm so he could kiss the delicate skin at the side of her breast. 'Twenty-six. Twenty-seven in November.' He gave a muffled laugh. 'I'm legal, if that's what you're worried about.'

Rachel tried hard to concentrate, but was distracted by her desire for this man. 'You're older than I thought.'

With strong hands, Gabe slid her under him. 'Good genes,' he said and took her nipple into his mouth, 'and all the clean living. And you're thirty.' He grinned at her startled expression and moved downwards. 'I saw the birthday cards. Kind of turns me on, the older woman thing.' He settled in closer and kissed her hard.

'I thought you had to go,' she gasped, as he slid into her.

'I do,' he said on a groan of pleasure. 'And Rach?'

'Yes, Gabe?' Rachel managed, on a breath, the waves of ecstasy already building.

'I'll need a cup of tea afterwards ...'

Chapter 26

Fordham was looking chocolate-box pretty in the mid-summer sunshine. Bright-pink petunias spilled in profusion from hanging baskets fixed to the timbers of the black-and-white market hall and everyone seemed to have a smile on their faces. Or so it seemed to Rachel. She returned their cheery 'good mornings' as if she was a native.

She hesitated, with her hand on the door of Foster, Grant and Fitch Estate Agents, before pushing it open. This wasn't going to be easy.

Neil was alone in the office and rose to greet her. 'Rachel, what a lovely surprise!' He took her hands and kissed her on the cheek. 'What a shame you didn't come in a little earlier, I have to go out to an appointment in a moment.'

He was as well-mannered and dapper as ever. Rachel felt her guilt lie heavily.

'Neil, have you got a minute to talk first?'

'With you? But of course! I'll just make a phone call and say I'll be delayed.'

Rachel put a hand on his arm to stay him. 'Please don't, I'd hate to interrupt your working day. This won't take long.' Was it imagination or wishful thinking, or was there a glimmer of understanding in Neil's beautiful blue eyes?

'I'm not sure how to say this.' she began. Neil raised his brows in query and indicated a chair. He perched on the edge of his desk, one long leg swinging. Rachel sat down. Flicking her hair nervously, she launched into her carefully prepared speech.

Driving back afterwards, Rachel couldn't believe how gracious Neil had been. Without mentioning Gabe, she'd simply explained the wish that she and Neil would stay just friends. When she said she hoped he hadn't got the wrong impression about the weekend at her parents, he'd given a shrug.

'Do you know, Rachel, I sort of knew you didn't feel about me as I was beginning to feel about you.'

Rachel blushed. 'You are a lovely, decent man, Neil.'

'Just not right for you.'

'Just not right for me. I'm so sorry.'

Neil put his head on one side. 'I admit to hoping, but after I dropped you off after our weekend away, I suspected it wasn't to be.' He smiled. 'I'll just have to chalk it up as one of those things.' He got to his feet.

Rachel took it as a hint that she should go. She jumped up. 'I can't believe you're still single,' she said impulsively and kissed him on the cheek. 'You're such a lovely man.'

'Yes, well,' he replied, embarrassed. He gave her a hard hug. 'Friends it is, then.'

They broke apart as Roger crashed into the office. He was bearing the inevitable box from Mervyn's.

After exchanging pleasantries and assuring him she wouldn't be a stranger and would return soon for coffee and cakes, Rachel had made good her escape.

She just hoped the village gossip machine wouldn't catch up with Neil too soon. He was a nice man and didn't deserve to be a victim of malicious tittle-tattle.

As she gunned the Fiat's noisy engine along the main road, back to Stoke St Mary, she turned up the radio. Radio One unexpectedly blasted out, but she didn't bother retuning. She hummed along instead.

Neil might well be the more suitable man, but it was Gabe who floated her boat. And Gabe floated her boat very nicely. Rachel grinned even more widely and turned up the radio further. 'Who let the dogs out,' she yelled, along with the inane pop song playing. Winding the window down, to let the hot summer wind blow through her hair, she put her foot down. She was happy.

Lying in bed with Gabe a few nights later, Rachel explained she'd spoken to Neil.

Gabe grunted. 'Thought you said there wasn't anything between you two?'

'There never was,' Rachel said indignantly.

'Good.'

'What about you, then? Rachel asked. 'Any other women on the scene?'

Gabe rolled her over onto her front, so she couldn't see his expression. He feathered a light finger down her spine and relished how it made her shiver. He loved the feel of her skin, he loved how she was so self-contained, so cool – and then exploded into passion with him. Letting his mouth follow where his finger had led, he delayed answering.

He'd never had a woman quite like Rachel. He loved her. Everything about her. The way she stroked a pencil lovingly across the page to create beauty, the way she worried over her friends, even her obsession with Hetty. But he wasn't about to tell her. He'd never felt like this about anyone and he wasn't sure how to handle it. One thing he was sure of, though, the time to tell her wasn't now.

'One or two,' he said airily, 'but not one compares with you.'

Distracted by his kisses, Rachel had to be content with that.

Chapter 27

Rachel and Gabe settled into a sort of routine. Gabe continued to work on the house, with Brian continuing the rewiring and Kev working alongside him, but didn't go home at night now. Instead he and Rachel would share a simple meal – a steak or some pasta – and then he would settle down to an evening in front of the television while Rachel worked at her drawing board in front of the window.

It amazed Rachel how she could get so much done, with the noise of Big Brother blaring out from the small portable, accompanied by Gabe's comments as he read the local newspaper from cover to cover. When she'd had enough of work and her back was aching, she'd slide onto the sofa beside him, open a bottle of wine and the kissing would take over.

It was remarkably companionable and easy having Gabe around, even if he did insist on watching trashy television and preferred a can of Stella to any wine she might offer.

They didn't talk much. Often Rachel was engrossed in Hetty's journal and Gabe in the football results, but it suited them.

Mike came over, when he could, in between tasks on the Hallidays' cottage. Rachel often felt his eyes on her, but couldn't tell how he felt about the situation.

She wasn't all that sure how she felt about it herself. It had all happened so fast.

I have just seen off the district nurse. She got into her
Mini and disappeared down the track at speed. The
woman is as irritating as that damn fool curate at St
Mary's. Always telling me what is best. As if I don't know.
Yesterday, Duncan Wilson had the temerity to lecture me
on the Great War and he not dry behind the ears! He is
still very interested in what he insists on calling My Life,
but refuses to accede to the request I made last November.
So be it. This journal will become Richard's memorial
instead.

And motor vehicles for nurses? What is wrong with
walking, or a bicycle? How I loved my first bicycle. It
brought me freedom, work and a deep friendship when I
had given up on finding it.

I learned how to ride Flora's bicycle on the carriage drive
in front of Delamere. It was some months after the hunt
ball. I think it may have been April. I remember the swallows swooping low over us. A wonderfully sunny spring
day. Before the war. Before it took Sam, David Parker and
Edward from us. Richard too, in a way.

It was one of the few days Richard spent at Delamere. I
wondered if he was avoiding me. I no longer understood
or trusted him, but I was still, in some mysteriously physical way, deeply attracted. I had come to consider his
behaviour at the ball had been, at the very least,
un-gentlemanlike.

Learning to ride a bicycle had been difficult; I had never
been blessed with much physical coordination. Flora and
Richard held me upright, shouting to mind the ruts in the

unkempt drive. How I'd wobbled about! I thought I would never master the thing, that it would be consigned to the same scorn I kept for horses. I had been flying over the rough gravel screaming and screeching to Richard not to push me so hard, that this was quite fast enough, when I'd looked around to see Richard and Flora tiny on the horizon, standing by the crumbling portico of the great house and waving. And I'd screamed again, this time with laughter and joy that I'd done it! I could ride a bike – just like Flora!

And had promptly fallen off.

Flora came rushing to me, a look of concern on her pretty face. 'Hetty! Darling Hetty, are you alright?'

'Of course she's alright,' Richard drawled as he strolled over. There was something cruel in his face that I did not like. He reached a hand down and pulled me to my feet. 'Made of solid stuff is our Hetty.' There was a nasty streak of sarcasm in his voice. 'One bloodied knee isn't going to put her off. Get back on, old girl. Straight back on the horse, as Flora's father always says.' They exchanged a look which excluded me. My old dislike of Flora resurrected itself.

Richard hoisted me, none too gently, back onto the saddle and pushed me, wobbling precariously, back to the house. And I did have a bloody knee and an enormous hole in my stocking. But, as Cook tutted over it and cleaned out the gravel, I could only feel Richard's arms around me as he gripped the handlebars to steady my hold and feel the cold vacuum left when he released me.

I had made a mistake with him, that evening at the hunt ball. I could see that now. But, how was I supposed to have conducted myself? I was no sophisticate. I'd had no opportunity to practise flirting and risqué small talk with men, as I'd seen Flora do. I didn't know what men wanted and, more importantly, how to rebuff them without injury to their pride.

Before he left for the Parkers' London house that weekend, I argued with Richard once again. This time it was the death knell.

Superficially, it was about Flora. But our enmity went deeper than that and was darker in hue. All the old petty jealousies had come back to haunt me. I'd seen how Flora and Richard had looked at one another as we had trundled back to the house, with me on the bicycle between them. I had sensed their lust for one another burning through me. They had knowledge of something unknown to me and I detested them both for it. Oh, and how I envied them!

The memory twists in my gut as surely as if it happened yesterday. There were times in my youth when I thought I would never escape Delamere and would never have the chance to be someone other than the cuckoo child.

Edward was about to join the Worcestershires, Richard was to spend Easter in London with the Parkers and I was to be left behind once again. My frustration, combined with the old jealousy of Flora, ignited a fury within me that I'd rarely experienced before or since.

Richard and I were in the old library. Leonora had tasked us to find Papa's old atlas to map Edward's route to Egypt. 'You and Flora seem awfully close,' I began.

'Yes we are. At least she knows what's what,' Richard sneered.

I had obviously not been forgiven. I wasn't sure what he referred to, but could hazard a guess. I rounded on him. 'She's ... she's immoral. Fast!'

Richard roared with laughter. 'Oh yes, pettish little Hetty, she might well be, but Flora's more fun than you'll ever be.'

I thought back to the hunt ball and flushed. I'd never felt more gauche or ignorant. Everyone, Edward, Richard even Flora and her brothers were doing things, going to places that were more exciting than Delamere. And I was doomed to be stuck here, preserved in aspic like the aunts. I puffed myself up. 'I come into my money soon and then we'll see who is more fun. I'll ... I'll –' I cast around wildly for something to say to fight back. 'I'll marry Edward!' As soon as the words came out I regretted them. I watched as Richard's face paled.

'I'll marry Edward and be an army wife and travel the world. As soon as his commission comes through he's off to Egypt. I'll marry him and go as well. So you can keep London and the Parkers' parties. I'm going to Egypt!' I stopped, having run out of breath.

Richard's face closed, his lips tight. 'Has he asked you?'

'Of course,' I lied airily. 'He asks me constantly.'

Richard laughed, in a peculiar way. 'Of course you'll marry him,' he sneered. 'Isn't that why your father dumped you with us?' And, at this, he came nearer and I could smell the tobacco on his breath. 'Why else would anyone marry you, Hetty? You're not the greatest catch, you know.'

I gasped. His teasing of my freckles, of my snub nose, all came flooding back. Only this time it was no longer a tease. Richard said the words with venom.

'You are vile,' I managed. 'At least I'll have a husband. At least I'll get away from here and the aunts. What's going to happen to you, Richard? Do you think your precious Flora will want to marry you? How would you pay for her horses and dresses? You haven't got any money at all! You'll end up being louche!' I said the word without any idea of its meaning. And, as soon as I had uttered it, knew I had gone far too far.

Richard took a step towards me, one fist raised, his face

puce with rage.

'Don't you dare put a hand on me Richard Trenchard-Lewis! Don't forget I'm to marry the heir to Delamere.' I said, in desperation. 'I can decide your fate!' I tipped my chin up in false bravery.

Richard's hand raised an inch more and I tried not to flinch. There was a beat pulsing wildly at his neck. Then he grinned, lowered his fist and laughed; a cold harsh sound.

'If you marry Edward, you might have money and this joke of a house, but you'll never have me. Admit it, Hetty, you love me – just as I love you.'

I was so shocked that, for a second, I could not speak.

'Love!' I gasped. 'Love? You call hitting a woman love? What do you know of it, Richard? You, a mere boy!' I spat out the last words. I pulled myself to my full height and glared at him.

He seemed, at that moment, to be nothing more than a wilful, indulged child. As, indeed, was I.

My parting shot was, 'Edward is a man. More of a man than you'll ever be.' I turned and stomped to the door. Pausing before I went through and mindful of servants' ears I hissed, 'You Richard Lewis, are a boy!'

That had been the last I'd seen of Richard until my wedding day.

What a foolish, reckless girl I had been. Any misunder-standing at the ball had been cemented with that argu-ment. Would I have acted differently had I known what the future would hold? Marry Richard not Edward? Had it been that which had tipped Richard over the edge?

Hetty put her head in her hands and felt very old, very weary. She no longer wanted to delve into her past, to reread her diaries. There were too many bad memories. Too much death. A time black-fringed with loss and misery. Enough. No more. No good could come of it.

She looked out into the gathering June evening and took a deep breath. A bat flitted quicksilver against the sunset. Something about it lifted her mood a little. She must remember the good times. There had been many, even if she had continued as a cuckoo in other people's families, caring for their children, travelling their world.

And she had been lucky; many women of her generation had no husband at all. And then there had been Peter. Dear Peter.

As her eyes became accustomed to the gloom, she stiffened. There was a man striding up the track. Was it that young whipper-snapper Stanley again? He and his young lady thought Hetty didn't see them, courting in the shadows. But she did. And left them alone. Most of the time. She had learned, through experience, that you had to grab at love's chances whenever you could.

This man was taller than Stanley, with a more familiar, gangling gait. It couldn't be. Could it?

Chapter 28

Gabe rolled over and slid a lazy hand along Rachel's thigh.

'Morning.'

It was Saturday and his day off. He planned on staying in bed as long as he could get away with it, preferably in Rachel's company.

Rachel giggled, Gabe's touch tickled. She twisted to look at the clock and then sighed with pleasure. Seven o'clock. One good thing about summer, the light always tricked you into waking earlier. She began ticking off a list of things to do in her head. Washing, plant up the geraniums Stan had bequeathed, go into Fordham for a coffee, maybe, pick up the papers, have a leisurely lunch. Then she got distracted by Gabe's fingers. Evidently he had rather different plans.

Later, Gabe tried to sleep but couldn't. Rachel, despite his vigorous attempts to keep her in bed, had got up, claiming it was far too nice a day to laze in bed all morning. Gabe, anticipating a lazy lie-in, couldn't persuade Rachel otherwise.

Turning the pillow over to the cool side, he flipped onto his back and spread out across the double bed. Cool white cotton sheets – no duvet as it was far too hot.

The whole room was evidence of Rachel's innate good taste. Cream, pale blue and white. Decorated, now most of the new electrics and the radiator pipes had been installed upstairs. Most of the work was nearing completion. Just one or two snagging issues to sort and it would be finished. Gabe wondered if Rachel would carry on seeing him. The wicked fairy on his left shoulder whispered that she was only sleeping with him as it was so convenient. Get two jobs done in one, so to speak.

He hadn't a clue why she was with him. Take today; they had very different ideas of how to spend the time. Had even had a slight post-coital tiff about it, until Gabe relented and let Rachel get up to do whatever imaginary chores she had lined up. She'd warned him she was going to change the bedding this morning and he'd got until eleven.

Gabe gave a gusty sigh and stared at the ceiling. The sex was great, no denying that, but he wanted more. He suspected Rachel was happy with what they had. So what did that make him? A stud? A toy boy? Her bit of rough on the side? Flicking back the sheet, he gave in and headed for a bath.

Rachel, halfway through potting up the geraniums, heard the water gurgling and smiled. Great! Gabe was getting up and now they could go into town. She hoped Gabe wouldn't put wet feet all over the newly sanded and painted bathroom floor. It looked so nice when Kev had finished it the other day. She was about to go up and remind Gabe to borrow her towelling mules when she spotted Stan making his way up the track.

Straightening and wincing at the stiffness in her shoulders from a long stint at the drawing board yesterday, she smiled and waved. 'What brings you here today?'

'Mornin', Rachel.' Stan paused to get his breath back and felt in his pocket for the inevitable roll-up.

As he lit up, Rachel had it on the tip of her tongue to suggest he gave up, but kept quiet.

Stan noticed her look and waggled his baccy tin at her. 'Don't start! I've got enough with our Sharon going on at me. 'Specially now.'

Rachel smiled. 'Coffee?'

'Ar and then I can tell you why I'm yere.'

When Rachel returned with their mugs, having taken Gabe some tea – he seemed to live on the stuff – she saw that Stan had settled himself on one of the charity-shop deckchairs. He'd worked hard on the front garden, fuelled by a desire to avoid his nagging daughter-in-law. The cottage now looked out on neatly planted raised beds and a gravelled space dotted with small lavenders and other fragrant herbs. It was exactly as Rachel had suggested to Stan all those weeks ago. Even the hostas had thrived, despite the hot, dry weather, with her tender care.

She passed over Stan's coffee, trying not to shudder. It was instant and extremely sweet and milky, just as he always drank it. Sliding into the other chair, she handed over the biscuit tin. Stan was partial to a custard cream, or three, with his coffee.

He dunked one in silence and then said, without preamble, 'I'm going to be a granddad.'

Rachel turned to him. 'Oh Stan, that's fabulous!' He didn't look thrilled.

'You reckon so? I suppose.' He drank his coffee, thoughtfully. 'Won't be a lot of room in that house, what with the four of us. Get in the way as it is.'

Ah. So that was it.

'I'm sure they wouldn't have asked you to move in if they hadn't really wanted to.' Poor Stan, he looked really worried.

Stan shifted uncomfortably. 'No, but there ain't nothing like putting your own slippers to warm by your own fire.'

Rachel, now unable to see herself living anywhere else but the cottage, couldn't help but agree. 'Do you know, somehow I think Hetty felt like that about here. That she'd found somewhere she could finally call her own. I know I certainly do.'

They lapsed into silence.

'What did you do, Stan, for a living?'

Stan laughed. 'Job got a bit interrupted like, what with the war.'

'Oh, I'm sorry, I hadn't realised you were in the war.'

Stan gave an indignant snort. 'I'll have you know I was too young. I'd only just started at my training at the Water Board, but had to go and do my National Service, didn't I?' He flicked a biscuit crumb off his shirt. A beady-eyed robin, hovering near by, spotted it, swooped down and it was gone. Stan laughed. 'That one comes and sits on me spade when I've finished digging.' He stared up at the sky. 'Making the most of us keeping the swallows away. Territorial little beggars, swallows.'

Rachel's thoughts weren't on robins and swallows. She was confused. 'You did National Service during the war?'

'No, I had to go in '48, that were when I was eighteen. Joined the Worcestershire Regiment.'

'That's who Edward Trenchard-Lewis served with.'

Stan finished his coffee in one gulp. 'Who's that, then?'

'Hetty's husband.'

'Oh, Hetty.' Stan put his mug down. 'He'd be an officer, then.' He began to roll another cigarette.

'Yes. He died in the First World War.'

Stan nodded and, lighting his cigarette, took a deep drag. 'Good many men from round yere lost their souls that way. My Uncle Reg, he went. Died at Passchendaele. Drowned in the mud, they said. His horse an' all. God sent hell to earth that day.' He coughed and pinched a bit of cigarette paper off his tongue.

Rachel couldn't imagine the horror. Didn't want to. The images of the First World War, the symbolism, the poetry and the poppies were so familiar, but it was another thing to hear about the squalid reality. Poor Reg. Poor Edward. The lost generation. How could she have coped with the thought of Gabe fighting – or dying? She shivered. Hetty was a stoic, bearing all with an astonishing bravery.

Rachel and Stan resumed their companionable silence, each lost in their own thoughts. They watched, as the robin returned, one eye focused hopefully on the biscuit tin.

Rachel opened it and crushed a biscuit into minute pieces. She threw them towards the bird. Brushing off her jeans, she asked,

'Do you know anything about two brothers?'

'You got any names?'

'David and Lawrence Parker. They lived at Breckington Hall, somewhere near here. Hetty mentions them once or twice. One brother died quite early on in the war.'

'Breckington's out Worcester way, just off the main road. You had a look on the War Memorial on the village green? No?' Stan shrugged. Their names might be on there, but it's not likely if they lived at Breckington.' Seeing Rachel's lack of comprehension he added, 'There'd be summat in their estate church, I expect.'

Rachel frowned. 'I suppose,' she began, 'but I get the impression from Hetty it was a new house, for the time, that is.'

'New money, eh?' Stan nodded. 'Mebbe no church built then.'

'So worth having a look at the village war memorial?'

'Oh ar.' Stan rubbed his chin thoughtfully. 'Parker you say? Breckington Hall? Think that family paid for a bit of the school. The one on the Downs. It's where our Sharon wants the little 'un to go.'

'Bit early to be thinking of schools, isn't it? Rachel laughed.

Stan pulled a doleful face. 'According to our Sharon, it's never too early to get put down for a good school. Me and Eunice went there, an' all. Remember a roll of honour in the hall.'

'I'll check it out if I can,'

'Toffs were they, these brothers?'

Rachel shrugged. 'Hetty suggests they had money, so I suppose so.'

'Ar, well, they might be in the church as well. There's some plaques in there. Rich folk paid to put them up. Death don't recognise money, though, do it? Our Reg just got his name engraved on the memorial. Not much to show for his sacrifice.'

Rachel made a mental note to check out the church. She hadn't yet ventured down that end of the village, where the squat building with its fat tower lay, nestled alongside the stream.

She looked at her watch. Gabe was taking his time in the bath.

She was itching to get into town; there was a good market on Saturdays. Stan, obviously in no hurry to go anywhere either, had settled into his deckchair, with yet another roll-up dangling from the corner of his mouth. Still, it was a beautiful morning. Perhaps she should succumb to the pace of country life too? To ease her impatience, she went inside to make fresh coffee.

As she gave Stan his mug, she asked, 'So, you were being trained up as a water board official, then you did your National Service?'

Stan squinted against the bright sunshine and nodded. 'Got sent to Aldershot. Right 'ole that place was. Then they sent us lads to do the Berlin Airlift.'

'The what?'

'You don't know your history, do you?'

Rachel smiled. 'My friend Tim, the one who was at the quiz night, says the same thing.' She laughed. 'I think I've learned more about history since living here than I ever did at school. Tell me what the Berlin Airlift was all about, then.'

'We had to airlift food and stuff into Berlin. The city was being starved to death by the communists, the Russians.' He tutted. 'Was the start of the Cold War, but we didn't know it, then.'

Rachel was intrigued. It was strange how you were tempted to write off old people as, well, simply *old*. You forgot they'd had a past – and an exciting one in many cases. She leaned forward, 'Did you fly planes?'

'No, lovely,' Stan looked gratified at her sudden enthusiasm. 'I just carted the stuff into the hold. Exciting, though. To think you'd been in a bit of history, like. Allus thought I'd like to go back, to see the city, but I never did.'

'You could always go now.'

'What, at my age?'

'Stan, you're fitter and more active than most people of my age. Of course you could go!'

'No, don't want to go on my own,' he said, childishly. 'No fun that way.' He squished his butt end between nicotine-stained fingers and pursed his lips. He ferreted out his tin and, putting the stub in, took out another. Then, seeing Rachel's face, changed his mind. Snapping the lid shut, he shoved it into his flannels.

'Then, what about the Social Club in Fordham?' Rachel was wracking her brain, trying to think of ways to get Stan out of the house. He obviously felt uncomfortable being there and would be even more so when the baby arrived.

Stan snorted. 'What, that place? Full of crotchety old women on the lookout for hubby number two to kill off. Bus don't go at the right time, neither.'

Rachel giggled; she couldn't help herself. It seemed that Stan was not in the mood to be helped. Then she had an idea. 'What about a shed? Remember, you suggested a shed to go at the back? We could get a biggish one and you could have a chair and a radio and my old electric heater. I won't need it once Mike and Gabe have finished putting the central heating in. You could be in there as long as you like. I won't mind.'

'Ar Rachel, love —'

'No honestly, Stan. In fact you'd be doing me a favour. When I first moved in, I thought I'd like the quiet, the isolation. I thought I'd get loads of work done. But sometimes,' she paused and thought of Hetty's presence felt only too clearly in the house, 'I miss having people around me. In London I had neighbours all around me, above and below. I didn't know them, really, but I knew they were there.' She trailed off. She wasn't sure how much truth there was in that statement. She wasn't feeling lonely in the cottage, especially with Gabe becoming a more or less permanent fixture, but it would be good to have Stan around more. She'd buy him a nice new kettle too.

'I don't know, Rachel.' Stan, for some reason, was obviously feeling uncomfortable. 'Don't want to intrude, like.'

'You never intrude, Stan!' Rachel put her hand on the old man's roughened one and patted it. 'You could have a kettle in there, too, so you could have a coffee whenever you like.'

'Well that'd be good. You never make it sweet enough.'
Rachel laughed.

He harrumphed. 'And could I, you know, have a –'

'Yes, Stan, you could smoke in there. Deal?'

'Go on with you, then. Deal.' Stan laughed throatily. 'You know, our Rachel, I've got very fond of you, like.'

Rachel's throat tightened. She'd become fond of Stan too. Then she wondered how much sheds cost. She'd find the money from somewhere – maybe the latest commission would fund it. Somehow, she knew a mutual declaration of affection wasn't what was called for. Changing the subject, she said, briskly, 'Can we grow some pumpkins for the autumn? I'd like to carve them out and put candles inside for Hallowe'en.'

Stan cleared his throat. They were back on safer ground. 'Ar, squashes an' all. Nothing like a bit o' soup made with one of them boys. I'll get 'em planted up. It's a bit on the late side to be putting 'em in, but we'll give it a go. Might have some fine 'ole specimens come October.' He stood up and adjusted his braces, shiny with age and, without looking back, strode off to his vegetable patch.

Rachel watched him go. When she'd first moved here, she'd had a romantic vision of a creative solitude, of having just herself to look after and to look out for. She thought of the people who had entwined themselves around her: Stan; the kind but abrupt and permanently cross Mike; Kev with his sleazy ways; Roger and his cream-cake addiction; boring, good-looking Neil.

And Gabe. Gabe with his wide smile full of white teeth, with his strong body and willing hands. Gabe. Young and energetic and straightforward. She still wasn't sure how she truly felt about Gabe or where their relationship was heading.

Then the thought of damp footprints on her new bathroom floor had her exclaiming and hurrying upstairs.

Chapter 29

Monday 9th November, 1914

It has been the most exciting day!

I was shown into the main room of the school by a Miss Fletcher, also a teacher at the school and a surprise. I thought they had only men teaching there. She presented me to a tall, thin man, who was standing in front of a very large group of children.

'This is Mr Innisford,' she said, 'he will explain what our expectations are.' And with that, she swept out, swishing her rusty black skirts with an imperious air.

I stood, self-consciously waiting for my next instructions.

'You have come rather late, Mrs Trenchard-Lewis,' were his first words. 'I have been waiting for you.'

My heart sank. I had the distinct impression I was not approved of.

'Please take a seat and observe. I will be able to discuss things more fully at lunch time.'

Feeling chastened, I scanned around for a chair and found one next to an ancient and very blackened stove, protected by an equally filthy guard. How Dorcas would love to get her hands on that! I sat, as primly as I could manage, on

251

the edge of a hard wooden chair. I was determined to show this Mr Innisford that I could be useful and hard-working.

I saw fifty or so children, ranging in age, I imagined, from about six to eleven. In this, I later found out I had been wrong. The class was Standard IV, the older pupils in the school. Unaccustomed to ordinary country children, I had forgotten that poverty and poor food did not strong bones and tall youth make.

I thought the room dismal. The direful warning: 'All liars shall have their part in the lake that burneth with fire and brimstone' was inscribed on the wall. With the windows being so high, there was little natural light and it was very chilly. There was the distinct aroma of damp, a smell I was only too familiar with from Delamere. Underlying it, the odour of poverty and unwashed bodies.

Not one child looked at me; they were held in rapt attention by their master. I think, even then, I recognised the respect they had for him. He had a rich, deep voice and I found myself enraptured too. I could not take my eyes off him. Here was a man dedicated to bettering these children's lives through education – and his devotion was obvious. And although stern, he was not unkind. The task could have been a dull one: copying a poem from the board. Peter Innisford, however, read the poem aloud first with such dramatic flourish it made the pupils laugh and eager to practise their copperplate.

I thought him wonderful.

An hour passed. After the recitation of times tables, the girls were set to their sewing while the boys undertook some kind of technical drawing. I looked at the pupils in front of me. One or two of the nearest risked a glance at me and I smiled back. One boy giggled, which earned him a gentle rebuke from his master.

At the end of the lesson, the children trooped out to the playground past me, each saying a polite good morning. Mr Innisford gave me the hurried directive that I should follow them, where after scrubbing their hands, they would line up and I was to inspect their hands and nails to see if they were fit to eat lunch. I was to inspect the girls. This I did, for the few girls who remained at school for their meal. Most, it seemed, walked home and returned for the afternoon session afterwards.

'That is,' explained Mr Innisford, as we oversaw the pupils eating their meal whilst eating our own, 'if they bother to return at all. Most get called upon to do chores at home and do not manage the afternoon.' He sighed. 'We try very hard to improve our attendance. We have awards and give out certificates, but we're fighting against what these children have to cope with at home.'

'And what is this, Mr Innisford?' I was trying hard to sound grown up and intelligent. I wanted to prove worthy of my new role. Here was a man of principle and good intentions. Excepting Hester, he was the first person I had met who genuinely wanted to improve the lives of others. I wanted to impress this man.

'Mrs Trenchard-Lewis,' he began heavily, flicking his hair back. 'I am sure you cannot contemplate the difficulties these young people have to face on a daily basis. Sent out to pick up stones from the field so as not to blunt the plough, having to care for five or six younger siblings, gathering apples and berries, slopping out the household buckets.' He stopped abruptly, as if sensing he had gone too far. He put a hand to his forehead. 'I apologise, please forgive me. It has been a long morning. The headmaster is at a management meeting in Fordham and I have already had to deal with three cases of suspected chicken-pox and broken the news of the death of an ex-pupil to the school.

One who met his end in France. I am sure you have not had to face this kind of situation and neither should a woman of your class have to.'

I stiffened. It was obvious he was under a deal of strain and seemed to be battling an instinctive antipathy to me, based on what he perceived as my privileged position. If only he knew how many times, like the children around us, I had had to eat slabs of bread and cheese for lunch! Despite his misconceptions, I sensed a decent man labouring under some great weight of worry. My heart softened to him. Too much so, for a married woman.

I tried for dignity. 'I can assure you, Mr Innisford, I would not volunteer for this role had I thought myself incapable of giving service to the children and the school. I understand you are a teacher short, with one enlisting. I may be inexperienced, but I am a hard worker and a useful one.'

'But what can you do?'

Forgetting that sewing made me even more fingers and thumbs, I answered rashly. 'I am sure the sewing in Standard IV is not beyond a woman of my class. With a husband at the Front I wish to do whatever I can to help.'

Mr Innisford looked down at his meagre lunch of some sort of cold pie and gave a tight smile. His shoulders relaxed a little. After a pause, during which he seemed deep in thought, he said, 'I apologise again, Mrs Trenchard-Lewis. These are difficult times – for us all.' He straightened and said, in friendlier tones, 'if you are of a mind to do so, it is gardening this afternoon. With food in short supply, we are endeavouring to grow our own.' He smiled. It transformed his thin face into a very appealing one. 'And with some success, I might add. You look a capable sort. I'm sure we'll be able to find a use for you.'

June 1963, Clematis Cottage

Hetty watched as the old man made his way along her garden path. He walked with a stick, but she knew who he was. She flexed her stiff shoulders and leaned back on the chair, amazed it was him.

How she had struggled with Peter Innisford! He was as stubborn as she, but a warm and respectful friendship had evolved. There might have been more had circumstances been different. The War! It always came back to that. It destroyed lives – and not just those who had died.

Her role at the school had settled into a pattern. For three days a week she undertook whatever was asked of her. When the weather was dry, she helped the children with their cottage garden; a rather fine effort, Hetty remembered with a smile. She even began a knitting circle to knit socks for the brave boys at the Front and coached some of the girls for the concert they were to give at the workhouse.

Hetty grew misty-eyed at the memory, she had loved every minute. Then Peter Innisford's sensitive, intelligent, beloved face crept into the edge of her memories. She'd found out later why he was so distracted that morning. In his pigeon hole in the school office he had found a single, solitary, accusing white feather.

The old man knocked at the front door. Hetty rose and went to answer it. She was done with waiting.

August 2000, Clematis Cottage

'You still reading Hetty's journal?'

Gabe's voice brought Rachel back to the present with a jolt. So disorientated was she that, for a moment, she could not answer him. They were sitting on the sofa, she engrossed in Hetty's diary, Gabe watching television. It was a chilly evening and he'd lit a fire. The flames crackled and glowed, adding a warming third presence

255

to the sitting room.

'What's she getting up to now?'

'Who?'

'Rach,' Gabe's voice was impatient, 'Hetty. What's she doing now?'

'Well, she's had an awful argument with Richard and is volunteering at the local school. The one on the Worcester road.'

'That'd be St Mary's, then. My old school.'

Rachel turned to Gabe, face alive with enthusiasm. 'Do you think they'd mind me popping in?'

'Shouldn't think so. What are you hoping to find out?'

Rachel was silent for a moment. 'I don't really know.' she began, 'I'm trying to understand it all myself. I think I'd just like to get a feel for the place. She's working with this man – a Peter Innisford – and I think he's going to be important to her.'

'Go Hetty! She doesn't hang about, does she? One husband dead, his brother after her and now this Peter bloke.' He stretched and yawned, running a tired hand over his face.

Rachel laughed. 'No, you've got it wrong. Edward's still alive at this point, he's away at war.'

Gabe pulled himself up. 'What did she look like?' He flicked channels and found a football match. 'I don't think you've ever shown me a photo.'

Rachel hunted through the mess of papers and found the wedding photograph. It was the only one she had of Hetty.

Gabe glanced at it, half an eye on the game. 'Well, I'm not sure I can see the attraction. She's only about a seven, as Kev would say.'

'You score women?' Rachel was horrified. 'You give them marks out of ten?' Her voice rose.

'I said *Kev* did.' Gabe reached a good-natured hand to the back of Rachel's neck and caressed it. 'It amuses him. Doesn't get him anywhere, but it amuses him.'

Rachel shrugged off his hand, too cross to respond. She wished Gabe would ditch Kev, he was a bad influence.

Gabe nuzzled her earlobe. 'You coming to bed?' he murmured.

Rachel batted him off. 'No,' she said, without looking at him. 'I want to read on. This bit's absolutely fascinating.' As he got up, she added, 'Gabe, I keep meaning to ask, have you thought about doing some more sculptures?' She looked up at him, missing his sudden rigidity. 'You're really good, you know. Bags of potential.' She waved the old photograph at him. 'You found Hetty's tin for me and it was you who suggested I make a book out of it. I can't tell you how grateful I am.' Smiling, she added, 'I'd love to do the same for your career. You know, get you going on a project somehow.'

Gabe was silent for a moment. 'Not the right time for that now.' His tone was dismissive. He turned and went upstairs alone.

Rachel returned to Hetty's journal.

How I wanted to curse Peter Innisford that cold December morning!

He had tasked me with taking a small group of girls and teaching them 'Onward Christian Soldiers'. Miss Fletcher was supposed to accompany us at the piano. Except Miss Fletcher disappeared. How those girls fidgeted, fiddled about – and their voices! I doubted anyone would be uplifted by the sound.

I argued my case at the end of the day when I found him in the main hall. To my surprise he roared with laughter. 'I'm sorry,' he said, as he wiped his eyes. 'I had thought you safe with Miss Fletcher. She really shouldn't have left you alone.'

'They were a handful,' I hadn't wanted to disappoint him and it made me snippy. 'I had not thought teaching would be so hard. It will not be a pleasant sound for the work-house concert.'

'Perhaps not, but I'm sure the sad folk there will appreciate it anyway. I'll speak to Miss Fletcher about it.'

'Thank you, Mr Innisford.'

'Please, when it is just us, call me Peter. I cannot abide formality.'

I was taken aback, but demurred. 'Then you ought to call me Henrietta, or rather Hetty, as most do.'

Peter gave me that beguiling smile. 'I should be honoured to do so. Are you on your way home, Hetty? If so, I should like to walk with you.'

And so it began, that deep, deep friendship. I never said a word to the aunts about Peter escorting me part of the way home, pushing Flora's bicycle for me. If they had known, all would have crashed about me.

Peter was a gentle soul. Intelligent, with a curiosity that even matched my own. We talked, as we walked along, our eyes adjusting to the gloom of the winter afternoons. We discussed many things: how much more we admired this king than the last, the lack of coal to keep the pupils warm – and the dreadful, endless casualty lists. I told him of Sam, once our stable boy and now missing in action, and of David Parker, cut down just the month before. In return, Peter explained how angry and ashamed he had been on finding the white feather and his confusion over what to do. He abhorred killing, he explained, but if the war continued he could have no choice but to go.

Peter *listened* to me. He did not constantly dare me into frantic escapades as Richard had done. He wasn't the unknown quantity of my husband. He accepted me for what I was and asked nothing in return. If Richard had been my affair of the body and Edward my affair of expectation, then Peter was the affair of my soul.

It should have been a time of great fear and anxiety – and, of course, it was – but it was also one of quiet, guilty joy.

For far too short a time.

After Edward's death, Leonora made it clear I was
required at home, now more than ever. She had plans, she
said, for my money. Hester, destroyed with grief, needed
me desperately. Of the staff, only Cook and Dorcas
remained and they were getting old.

As with Papa, I had no body to bury, no graveside on
which to place flowers. And, again, I had no idea how to
feel. Edward had been in my life both forever and hardly
at all. And for too brief a time as husband. Had I loved
him? I wasn't sure. I certainly hadn't loved him as a wife
should love her husband. I'd never been given the chance.
I grieved, instead, for the loss of a fine young man.
Another who had had all hope ripped apart in the squalid
mire of industrial warfare.

In the spring of 1915, when the war should have been
over long before, I took my news to school. It was the last
time I saw Peter.

It was very early, far too early for anyone but he to be in
school. I found him in the main hall.

'The aunts have told me I cannot come here any more,' I
burst out, through tears. 'I am needed more at home.
How I shall miss you all. You, most of all.'

He took one look, crossed the room in swift, long-legged
strides and embraced me. His arms felt warm and solid
and he held me for a long time, letting me sob, saying
nothing, simply being Peter. I cried for Edward, for the
thin rag that was now Hester, for all those lost boys.
I wept for a world robbed of its innocence.

'I heard about Edward. I'm so terribly sorry, Hetty,' he
whispered, eventually.

At length, I broke away from him and turned to tidy
myself, reverting to convention, as emotions were again
threatening to engulf. 'Hester cannot be left. I have to be
with her,' I said, my back to him.

259

'Of course. I understand.'

I asked the question, but dreaded its answer. 'Will you have to go?' It came out on a strangled whisper. I heard him move away, heard his footsteps on the wooden floor. 'I fear there is no alternative.' He gave a strange laugh. 'And I find I cannot bear my parents' disapproval any more. Or that of those around me.'

Turning, I saw he stood against the window, one arm on the high sill, his head resting on his hand.

'I never disapproved, Peter.'

'I know.' He straightened. 'And I love you for it.'

We gazed at one another from either end of the hall. Love and understanding humming between us, only strengthened more by our distance. I wanted to run to him, to clutch him to me, to feel the solidity of his arms around me once again. Instead I simply said, 'Write to me.'

He nodded. 'I promise. Hetty, I will write.' He added in a kind of urgent despair. 'I will write.'

He never did.

Chapter 30

Rachel stood outside St Mary's Primary School with her fingers itching for her pencils. She had half a mind to sit down and sketch the place right now, but thought it might look suspicious. Better to go straight in.

It was ridiculously pretty. Victorian, with the date 1880 proudly displayed in coloured tiles over the main entrance and its bell tower on top of the roof. Behind her, another view of the county spread itself in all its glory, with the Malvern Hills blue in the Worcestershire distance.

The school was halfway up the main hill out of the village, on the road towards Worcester and reached by a narrow B road pitted with potholes. It would be lethal in winter, but on a day like today, in the last-gasp days of a hot August, it was breathtaking. What a place to come to school!

She'd come here on another impulse. From being a woman with the strong habit of caution, her impulses were getting alarmingly regular; they'd get her into trouble one day. She had forgotten it was still the long summer break and unlikely that anyone would be here. In this, it seemed she was wrong. There were three cars parked outside: one swanky little red convertible, a more humble people carrier and a VW Polo, which looked vaguely familiar. They could belong to people walking, she supposed, but it was worth a try, now she'd come, to see if anyone was in.

The main entrance did not bear any resemblance to Hetty's description of separate doors for boys and girls. It was an enormous sheet of green glass, with an oak door set into it. Carved onto that was the name of the school and an accompanying crest. It showed a lion and a lamb nestled together, with the school motto underneath, *So Shall the Strong Aid the Meek. Together We Triumph.* Rachel rang the bell and stepped back to admire the craftsmanship. She liked its message.

'Good afternoon. I'm afraid we have no school places at present.' A slim blonde, in her mid-forties or so, opened the door and looked enquiringly at Rachel. She had a slight accent, which Rachel couldn't place.

'I'm so sorry, perhaps that's not why you came?'

Rachel smiled. 'It isn't actually.' She hesitated. 'I'm not sure why I've come, really. I wanted to see the school where Hetty volunteered.'

'I see,' the woman said, with impeccable politeness, though she plainly didn't.

Rachel began to feel foolish.

'Was this Hetty a friend?' The r rolled. A Scottish burr.

'No, not really. I live in her house. Well, what was her house. One of them. She's dead now. Died a few years back. She worked here a long time ago. During World War One.'

A light-brown plucked eyebrow rose. 'How very intriguing. Then perhaps you'd better come away in.' The woman smiled broadly and gestured for Rachel to go in. 'I'm Shona Cameron, the head teacher. How nice to meet you.'

'Rachel Makepeace,' Rachel said and shook the proffered hand. It was, as expected, cool and assured. She relaxed a little. Her primary head teacher had been nothing like this smooth, stylish creature.

'Come along here, Rachel, we're just having tea. And you'll not say no to a scone? Bridget makes them especially for these days when we sneak in to work when everyone else is at play.'

'Thank you, I'd love to, that's if it's not taking up too much of your time. I'm pleased to find someone here. I expected the school to be closed up for the summer.'

'Well, it is mostly. Bridget is my school administrator and we like to get together in the weeks before we go back proper just to catch up on one or two things.' Shona winked. 'I like to steal a march on my teachers. Keeps them on their toes, poor wee things.'

She led Rachel into the staff room. 'Bridget, we have a visitor. Can we make the cream and jam stretch?'

A large woman, with a florid expression and untidy gunmetal hair, stood up. She was in direct contrast to the cool Ms Cameron. She smiled at Rachel and nodded wordlessly. Rachel wouldn't have been surprised if she'd curtseyed. 'One more for tea, Sheila,' she called to a woman in the adjoining kitchenette.

'Oh hello, Rachel, fancy seeing you here!' Sheila Llewellyn bustled through, carrying a large brown betty teapot.

Rachel blushed. It was embarrassing enough having to face Mike on a regular basis, but far worse to face her younger lover's mother. 'Sheila, how lovely,' she managed.

Shona glanced from one to the other curiously. 'Sheila is a governor, Rachel. Perhaps she can give you the grand tour later on? Shall we sit down and enjoy our feast, ladies? Then Bridget and I can enjoy our break and we can hear all about Rachel and her friend Hetty.'

Sheila settled a cosy on top of the teapot and sat down. She began to hand out plates and knives. 'Ah, so you're still finding out about Hetty, are you, Rachel?' She looked around to the other women. 'Rachel is going out with Gabriel. He's told me all about Hetty.'

'He did smashing work on my kitchen, Gabe did,' Bridget spoke up. 'Lovely cabinets, oak veneer they are. Proper job.'

'Och yes, and he was wonderful with Key Stage Two that time, with the Senses Garden project. The sculpture he created with them is marvellous. You must see it before you go, Rachel. He made our magnificent front door too. A talented man.' Shona beamed at them all. 'Now isn't this blissful? Tea?'

Rachel was bemused. Gabe had never mentioned the work he'd done here. Her heart blossomed with pride. And she knew he could do so much more with his talents, if only he was a little more ambitious.

Over tea and scones, Rachel explained about the box of documents found in the cottage and the latest information about Hetty volunteering at the school during the war.

'How completely fascinating.' Shona clapped her hands together. 'And are you planning to do anything with the information, Rachel?' She looked discreetly at her watch.

'Well, I'm not sure at the moment. I'm an artist. I draw illustrations for books and magazines. I had thought about writing a book about her life and creating some drawings to go with it, but I'm not so sure now.'

'Gabriel says Rachel does some beautiful stuff,' Sheila interjected.

'And why are you not sure about the book, Rachel?' Shona asked.

Rachel hesitated. 'I'm not sure there's a market for it,' she began, 'actually, the real reason is it seems too much of an intrusion, somehow. Some of the things I've found out about her later life are very personal and I don't have all that much information about her childhood.' She shrugged. 'I'm no writer. I don't know what form the book might take.'

'I know I'd buy it,' Bridget said. 'I love that kind of thing.' She began to clatter together the tea things. Break time was obviously over. 'You know what might help,' she looked to Shona, who caught on immediately.

'The Log Book!' Shona rose in one smooth movement and groaned. 'I'd love to chat with you a wee while longer, but the dreaded paperwork beckons. Bridget, can you find the copy of the Log Book, do you think?' She turned to Rachel, 'The original is in the County Museum. We're one of the oldest schools in the area, you know. Much as I'd love to hear more, I must away.' She headed to the door. 'Could I ask a favour?'

Rachel had the feeling no one said no to Shona and lived. 'Yes?'

'Would you be prepared to come in and talk to the children about what you do? Perhaps help out with an art lesson or two? We're always looking for helpers. That much hasn't changed in a hundred years!' She grinned and then issued orders, 'Bridget, find the Log Book and Sheila, could I impose on you to give Rachel a tour?'

'I'd be happy to come into school, I think,' Rachel said, aware of more people entwining their lives around hers. Of becoming rooted in a place. It would be fun, though, to work with the children. 'Just before you go, Shona, can I ask you a question?'

The head teacher turned, obviously impatient to get on, but too well-mannered to hurry off. 'Of course.'

'Do you know anything about a Peter Innisford? He taught here about the same time as Hetty volunteered.'

'Mr Innisford?' Shona twinkled. 'Have a look at the board in the hall and you'll find him.'

With that, she vanished into the corridor, followed by a bustling Bridget.

'Quite a woman, isn't she?' Sheila said and loaded a tray with crockery.

Rachel laughed. 'She's that alright.'

'She's worked miracles since she came here. I love being a governor, although I'm not too sure how much longer I can do it.'

Rachel took the tray off her, thinking Sheila looked tired. The women went into the kitchenette and washed up the tea things in a companionable way.

'How long have you been one?' Rachel asked as she dried and then stacked the cups and plates in a tidy pile.

'Oh, since Gabriel was a pupil here. I sort of carried on after that, although Mike kept on at me to give it up. I nearly did and then Shona came along and it's such a joy to work with her, I wanted to keep doing it.' Sheila paused to scratch her chin, leaving a bubble of washing-up liquid on it. 'It's a bit thankless at times, but I love coming in and hearing readers, that sort of thing. Makes up for all the bureaucracy.' She emptied the bowl and dried her hands on Rachel's tea towel. 'Leave the rest. I'll do it later. Come on, then. If it's a tour you're after we'd best get started. Hall first, I think.'

Rachel followed Sheila down the corridor, dull and bare without its term-time displays. 'I didn't like to show my ignorance, but just what is the Log Book?'

Sheila laughed. 'It's a record of daily life in the school. Every head teacher had to keep one. A sort of diary, I suppose. I suppose Bridget meant that it might give you some more information to flesh out your book. It's an idea. I'm sure the entries for the Great War will be fascinating. Speaking of which, there he is, there's your Mr Innisford.'

Rachel looked up. They were in the assembly hall. On one wall was a wooden board. It was the roll of honour Stan had mentioned.

Please let him have survived the war, she prayed. It was ridiculous, she had never known the man. The board was divided into two, with one entitled In Memoriam, written in gilt copperplate. Steeling herself, Rachel scanned the names of those staff and pupils who had given their lives in service in two world wars. No Peter Innisford. She allowed herself to breathe. There it was, his name under Roll of Honour, head teacher from 1927 to 1952. Thank goodness, he was alright. And had returned and risen to head teacher!

Sheila looked at her curiously. 'Is Peter Innisford anything to do with Hetty?

'Well, they were certainly close friends. In fact, I'd go as far as saying they loved one another.'

'Mmm, funny pairing, though. She all hoity toity war wife and he a school teacher.'

Rachel laughed. 'I'm not sure Hetty was all that hoity toity. Stubborn and wilful maybe, with a destructive temper, but not stuck-up. But I suppose they were from different classes, so yes, a funny pairing,' she admitted. She turned to Sheila, realising how much she liked her. 'I'm not sure they even got on to begin with.'

'Still, you can't always choose who you fall for, can you?' Sheila said, meaningfully.

'Isn't that the truth?'

The two women smiled at one another in understanding.

Rachel realised she'd made an ally. Whatever Sheila's feelings about her relationship with Gabe, it wasn't going to get in the way of their friendship. She warmed to Sheila even more.

'So, come on then,' she said, 'where's this tour you promised me?'

Rachel rattled up the track to her home feeling happy. She'd enjoyed seeing round the school and had spent the rest of the afternoon sketching it. She'd loved trying to see it through Hetty's eyes, although there was scant left of the original Victorian interior. She'd loved, even more, seeing the school Gabe had gone to as a child. Sheila had fished out some old school photos and there he was, in the football team, a mop of unruly blonde hair and a familiar cheeky expression.

What had been even more thrilling was Sheila knowing about Delamere House, the Trenchard-Lewis home. To Rachel's joy, the house still existed and they'd planned to visit sometime. Rachel hoped it would be soon. She couldn't wait to see where Hetty had grown up. She was also looking forward to spending more time with Sheila. She'd liked her immensely.

Parking the Fiat next to the Toyota, Rachel paused for a moment to admire, yet again, the view from her cottage. She leaned on the steering wheel and grinned to herself. Life was good.

Trailing inside and finding Gabe sprawled on the sofa, fast asleep, she put the precious school Log Book on her desk and made her way upstairs. There, any contentment fled. Gabe had obviously had a bath. Not a problem. However, the grime ring around the rim and the heap of dusty clothes littering her new bathroom floor definitely was. Then Rachel sniffed. The familiar scent of Jo Malone hung in the air. The evidence, an empty bottle on its side in the sink. Gabe had helped himself to her bath oil and, what's more, had used the lot.

Horrified, Rachel gathered up the mess he'd left and stormed into the bedroom. There was worse. Gabe had left all his sopping-wet bath towels on the throw at the foot of the bed. It was pale-blue silk. Rachel gave a little scream of terror and snatched off the offending towels. Too late. The colour from the darker-blue embroidered pattern had bled. It would never be the same again.

'Gabe!' she roared, turning to find him leaning lazily on the door jamb.

'Hi, Rach. You've been a long time. We finished over at the Hallidays' early for once. Came home and crashed.' He scrubbed a weary hand over his hair, oblivious to the woman's anger.

'Look at this!' Rachel pointed to the ruined throw.

Gabe yawned and stretched. 'What's the matter with it?' Blinking, he sensed he was in trouble – again. He looked closer at the throw. 'Oh, I'm sorry, babe. It'll come out, though, won't it?' He looked at Rachel warily. They'd had arguments like this before and he always trod carefully. He didn't understand Rachel's obsession with having everything just so, but he knew when he'd upset her and hated it. He came towards her. 'I'm really sorry, Rach.' He put his hands on her arms and caressed them.

She shrugged him away, she wasn't letting him off that easily. 'And your work clothes were all over the bathroom *and* you've used the last of my Jo Malone.'

Gabe frowned, 'Your what?'

Rachel exploded, 'My bath oil!'

He tried to gather her to him. 'Oh babe, I'm really sorry. I'm a pig. I'll buy you some more. And a new bed thingy.'

Rachel stepped out of his embrace. 'One, I am not your *babe*,' she said, through clenched teeth, 'and two, I doubt that you could afford it.'

Gabe's face closed. He ran a hand through his hair again. 'Yup, you're probably right. I'm just a working bloke. One who has to have a bath to get the stink of honest graft off his body. One who is so knackered by the fourteen-hour days he's been putting in that he forgets to stuff his clothes in a bag and drops the towels all over the place, goes downstairs and falls asleep before he can tidy up before Miss Anal Retentive comes home.'

Rachel flinched. That last barb hit home. It was too close to the warning Tim had given her. Too close to the truth. What she'd said to Gabe had been unforgivable. 'I'm sorry.' She took a breath. 'I am, really. You're probably right. I am a bit anal.'

'A bit?' He looked at her from under his lashes, still wary.

It had been too nice a day to spoil it by ending with an argument. 'Alright. Very,' she conceded.

He came to her, relieved. He couldn't understand this side of her. The jibe about money had got to him, but he wanted her too much to let it rankle and he'd never been the sort to sulk. 'I'm sorry too,' he repeated as he put his arms around her and nuzzled her hair. 'I am a pig and a lout and I don't deserve you.' He backed off a little and met her eyes. 'Perhaps this is all going a bit too fast? Maybe I should go home tonight and leave you to your own space for a bit?'

Fear flickered through her. She didn't want to lose him. 'No, don't do that. It's me, Gabe. I need to relax, to chill a bit more. I like you being here. Don't go.' She reached up and kissed him. He smelled wonderful, as well he might, she thought, and her lips curled. 'I'm a buffoon,' she said, through her kiss. 'I don't deserve you.'

'So, I'm a pig and you're a baboon?' He put a warm hand on the side of her breast. 'Sounds like a match made in heaven.'

'A buffoon,' she began, but was silenced by his kisses.

269

Chapter 31

'Right, that's sorted, then.' It was Sheila on the phone. 'Pick me up on Thursday. I don't believe in putting things off any more.'

Rachel, just as keen to see Hetty's old home, was thrilled to have Sheila as a fellow enthusiast. She was looking forward to a girly day. Making small talk with Kev, Brian and the team got a bit wearing.

Rachel stole a glance at her passenger as she put the car into third and eased down the narrow lane Sheila dictated was the route to Delamere House. Sheila had mentioned, without going into the reason, why she felt better on some days than others. Today, she was glowing.

'Looking forward to seeing the house, then?' Sheila now asked.

'I can't wait. Hetty sort of described it, but I haven't got a clear picture of what it's like.'

Sheila nodded. 'It's one of those houses that's tucked away. Half the folk round here don't know it even exists, even if they can afford it.'

Rachel dropped down into second. She'd never get used to the one-track roads in the county. This one had grass growing along the middle of it, 'What do mean?'

'It's one of those snooty health spa places now.'

Rachel giggled. Whatever its fate, she hadn't imagined that. 'I wonder what Hetty would have thought of that? Or the aunts?'

'The aunts?'

'They looked after Hetty when she moved to the house. One was a bit stern. Leonora.'

'I think the spa is called Leonora,' Sheila added, drily.

Rachel laughed out loud. She'd been right. It was going to be a good day. She wondered gleefully what Hetty's crusty old aunt would have made of having a spa named after her.

'Do you know, although Gabe's told me a bit about your Hetty's journal and I've always known the house, I really don't know anything about the family. I asked Gabe, but he's such a man, he never wants to talk about anything.'

Rachel laughed again. It was an accurate picture of Gabe. He was interested in Hetty, but only up to a point. He certainly didn't want to discuss her endlessly, as Rachel wanted to. She found herself telling Sheila all about Hetty and Edward and Richard. It was a relief to have an avid audience, as curious as she was.

After another ten minutes of excruciatingly narrow lanes, Rachel pulled up on an elegant, gravelled carriage drive in front of a compact stately home.

'Oh,' she breathed, leaning forward on the steering wheel, 'it's so pretty. I hadn't thought it would be pretty.'

Sheila nodded. 'It's a bit lopsided nowadays, can you see? When the new people took it on, the right side was in so much disrepair it had to come down, so it's lost its Regency symmetry.'

Rachel stared at the house. Mellowed red sandstone had turned pink in the August light and, despite its truncated exterior, it was still attractive. A portico rose above a grand set of steps designed to impress – or intimidate the visitor. On three sides, the house was sheltered by beech trees, giving it a secretive air, but on its western side, the grounds fell away to the sky. A slew of discreetly expensive cars were parked up, but there was no one in sight.

'Doesn't seem to be anyone around,' Sheila said, 'shall we go in?'

Rachel looked at her, excitement levels rising. 'Do you think we could?'

'I don't see why not. It's open to the public. We can always pretend we're interested in one of those spa days. Actually,' Sheila said with resolve, 'I *do* fancy one of those spa days. I'm going to treat myself!'

'Today?' Rachel asked faintly. She hadn't brought anything appropriate and was fairly sure she couldn't afford even a neck massage in this place. The day was taking an interesting turn.

'No, not today. But sometime soon. Would you like to come with me?'

'I'm not sure.'

'Well,' Sheila said kindly, 'we'll see what it's like, shall we? You can make up your mind afterwards. No hurry, for you that is.'

Rachel locked the car and, with her new camera, took a few pictures. It was a beautiful house, but she was struggling to see it as Hetty had. Then she hurried off after the suddenly dynamic figure of Gabe's mother, who was marching up the vast steps. One of the double doors opened just as Sheila's hand rose to knock and a young blonde woman smiled at them.

'Good morning, ladies. Welcome to Delamere Hotel and Spa,' she said in what was definitely not a local accent. 'My name is Ingrid. Have you come for treatments?'

'We –' Rachel began.

'We're thinking about it,' Sheila took over. 'We'd like to see the facilities, if we may. To see what sort of thing you do.'

'Of course,' Ingrid said smoothly. 'Come to the drawing room and I'll take some details. Would you like coffee?'

'Coffee would be good,' Rachel answered as she and Sheila followed Ingrid through a marble hall and into a gold-and-cream sitting room. Rachel looked around in wonder. Was this the same room Hetty had been shepherded into on her very first visit? It could be; she remembered a description of some French doors opening onto a terrace. She felt excitement kick in as, directed by their efficient hostess, they sat on the sofa.

It might well be the same room, but it had definitely changed since that first tea with the aunts. No sign of the genteel poverty suffered by the household. The only shabbiness was of the carefully constructed, chic, kind. The interior was as delicately pretty as the outside. 'What a marvellous house!' she burst out.

Ingrid gave a smug smile. 'We think so. Please make yourselves comfortable, ladies. I'll ring for coffee. We can discuss your needs and then perhaps you'd like a look around?'

Rachel and Sheila caught one another's eyes and stifled a giggle. This was going to be fun.

And it was. After taking endless details and providing them with a pot of excellent coffee, Ingrid finally allowed them to look around the house and, even better, she claimed a prior engagement and left them to their own devices. As long as they didn't enter any rooms marked Private or go into rooms with a red light on above, meaning that a treatment was in progress, they could wander anywhere.

'And do try the dining room for lunch or afternoon tea on the terraces,' Ingrid trilled. 'The salmon parfait is divine and we do a wonderful range of low-calorie cakes. I do hope we'll be able to meet your needs.' And, wafting a cloud of a delicious-smelling something, she skittered off.

'Thank you so much, Ingrid,' Sheila called back in a reasonable impersonation. Then she turned to Rachel. 'Rita from the post office could learn a thing or two about customer service from her.'

Rachel laughed. 'Do you know, I think I rather prefer Rita's brand of charm. I think Ingrid might get a bit –'

'Sickly?' Sheila supplied.

'Precisely! Can you imagine running in to get the papers, with a Sunday-morning hangover, and facing that?' Then Rachel clapped her hands together and focused her mind. 'I can hardly believe I'm here. Where shall we start?'

Sheila looked at the floor plan Ingrid had given them. 'What about the library? It's just down this corridor on the left, I think.'

The library. The place where an adolescent Richard had shown Hetty those drawings. The room where they'd had that terrible argument, after which she'd stampeded into marriage with Edward.

She nodded at Sheila. 'The library it is, then.'

The door was open, so the women walked straight in, trying not to feel self-conscious. Rachel's first thought was that it was smaller than she had imagined but, even so, it was a large room by an ordinary house's standards. Sheila went to leaf through some magazines on a vast oak table by the fireplace and began chatting to the only other occupant – a woman in a tracksuit.

Rachel hugged herself as she looked around. The room couldn't have changed all that much since Hetty's time, although the furniture had that carefully eclectic look that spoke of an expensive design consultant. It had luxurious rugs partly covering a wooden floor and she couldn't stop a thrill running through her as she realised she was walking on the very same floor that Hetty and Hester and Richard and Edward had troddon on all those years before. 'Get a grip,' she whispered to herself and studied the books on the endless shelves. 'I wonder if any of these came with the house?' she murmured, as she ran her hand along the spines. The titles were dull; agricultural catalogues or breed indexes. No Victorian porn, as far as she could see.

The room was lovely, though, with its dark wood furniture, softly lit lamps and heavy brocaded curtains. A huge bowl of roses on a circular table in the middle of the room drenched everything in a subtle scent.

They were always her favourite rooms, libraries. In all the big houses she and Tim toured, in his endless quest to wind up volunteers, the libraries were the rooms that drew her back. There was something about being surrounded by polished wood and old books that was infinitely soothing.

'Hello, Hetty,' Rachel whispered to the carefully manicured gloom. 'You must have found this all so overwhelming after the villa in Kent.'

'Rachel,' Sheila called out suddenly. It broke the spell. 'Come and look at this.' She held up a photograph frame. 'Could this be Hetty, do you think?'

Rachel went to where Sheila was standing, by a whatnot stand in the corner of the room. 'Oh, Sheila,' she breathed, as she took the photograph from her. 'I think it is!'

It was a typical Edwardian photograph. Several people were grouped on what she recognised as the steps at the front of the house. They were stiffly posed and dressed in formal high-necked clothes. Hetty was in the front row next to Edward. 'It can't have been taken long after the wedding.'

Sheila took another look. 'Or an engagement photograph?' She peered at Hetty's left hand. 'No, not clear enough to see if she's wearing a ring. How frustrating. But the two in the middle, your Hetty and the man, they're definitely posed as a couple.'

It was true. Hetty and Edward had been placed right in front and a space had been left around them.

Rachel eagerly scoured the rest of the group. A tall woman in an old-fashioned dress and hairstyle must surely be Hester; the frowning, dried-up woman hanging onto her arm could only be Leonora. She wondered if it was the cook, wearing an apron – she looked kind. And that must be the elderly groom who looked after Snowy; he stood with his hand on the shoulder of a youth – Sam the stable boy! It was as if the members of the house were coming alive to her, she felt she knew them so well. She'd love a copy of it, to show Gabe. Sneaking a quick look round, she got out her camera, held it as close as she could and took a picture.

And then Rachel caught her breath. The impossibly handsome man, standing a little distant from the group, was Richard. An older, taller and broader Richard. He had changed. He had a modern-looking face, somehow, with smooth good looks.

He had changed in more ways than just physically. Gone was the devil-may-care expression of the photograph taken of him on horseback. Here, he looked pinched and wary. Withdrawn into himself. Without hope. And now Rachel knew why. She shivered. She wasn't sure she liked the look of him.

'It's so hard to look at photos taken at this time in history and not think of what they've got to come,' Sheila murmured. She glanced at Rachel. 'The war.'

Rachel frowned and ran a finger lightly over Edward and Hetty posed, not so very happily, as the happy couple. The image of them about to launch into their married life, not knowing what was to come, was heart-breaking.

Sheila nudged Rachel's arm, kindly. 'Let's look at the rest of the house and get some lunch. We've been in this gloom long enough.'

Rachel replaced the photograph reluctantly and followed Sheila out. She was right, the room had become suffocating. She was in danger of drowning in the tragedies of the past.

The rest of the house was as lovely, but it was harder to find whispers of Hetty and the others in the clinical-looking Leonora Spa treatment rooms and series of sitting rooms.

Feeling very grand, they ate lunch on the terrace, overlooking a vast expanse of manicured lawn and a Spanish chestnut-tree avenue. Although Rachel looked hard, she could see no sign of the rundown little summer house.

'Do you know?' Sheila said after they'd eaten. 'I haven't had such a nice day for ages.' She rolled her eyes, 'It gets a bit too macho at home, with my two. Thank you so much for bringing me. I think I'm getting nearly as fascinated as you about the Trenchard-Lewis family.'

Rachel looked over and smiled. 'It's nice to have someone to share my enthusiasm with. The Log Book will be a great help. Please pass on my thanks to Shona and Bridget. It fills in some detail about school life back then. Apparently, the boys were sent out to chop wood in the winter, when coal became scarce, and boys and girls were taught different subjects!' Rachel raised her eyebrows. 'Can you imagine that happening now? She leaned back on her chair and lifted her face to the sun. 'Roger and Neil, at the estate agents where I bought the house, were sort of interested for a while, but not as obsessed about it all as me.' She closed her eyes, drinking in the warmth and peace.

'Ah, Neil Fitch. Nice man.'

Whoops.

Rachel sat up with a jolt. 'He's a very nice man,' Rachel answered finally. 'And such a keen sportsman.' She caught Sheila's eye and they laughed.

'It's just such a shame he's so boring. So handsome too. Quite a catch for someone.'

'Not me.'

'I'm very glad Gabe has found someone like you, Rachel.' Sheila reached over and patted her hand. 'For a while, I thought he'd rattle around from one conquest to the next, never settling down.'

'Well, he's very young,' Rachel began defensively.

Whoops again.

'Not that young. Mike and I were married when we were twenty-one.'

'And so were my parents,' Rachel admitted. 'And Hetty was only about twenty. I think it's slightly different nowadays.'

'I suppose. Tell me about your parents, Rachel. Gabe tells me they've gone to live abroad. How lovely.'

Yes, Dad's a keen golfer, so they've got a place on the Algarve,' Rachel answered, relieved to have the subject changed. They carried on chatting over coffee and petit fours. Sheila was a good listener and seemed genuinely interested in hearing about how Rachel had changed courses at college.

'Must be lovely to have a talent like yours.' Sheila sat back and put a hand to her eyes. 'Oh, I'm sorry. Think I've overdone it.'

Rachel looked at her companion. She looked drawn and pale. 'Are you okay, Sheila?'

'I'm fine. I just forget sometimes.'

'Is there anything wrong?'

'Oh, it's just something and nothing.' Sheila gave a smile. 'It's being treated. Just makes me tired, that's all. Nothing to worry about.'

Rachel looked at her friend, concerned. 'We'll go when we've got the bill, shall we?'

'You don't mind not looking around any more? I'm happy to sit here while you wander the grounds.'

Rachel shook her head. 'No, let's get back. I've got work to do anyway. Time to say goodbye to Hetty for today.'

After she'd dropped Gabe's mum off Rachel drove thoughtfully through the village. She was anxious about her; Sheila hadn't looked at all well.

She'd seen Sheila into the kitchen and had made her a cup of tea. Before she'd left, they'd made arrangements to visit a nearby garden centre that specialised in clematis. Rachel had been dying to visit it but other things had got in the way. Another girly afternoon out, with an afternoon tea thrown in sounded wonderful. But she was worried. Worried about what was wrong with her new friend and worried even more that Sheila seemed to think her son was happily settled at last. It was evident Sheila was happy about it. It was just that Rachel wasn't sure if Gabe was really the right man for *her*.

Chapter 32

It was Peter!

Age hadn't changed him much. He was still thin and upright, he still had that shock of unruly hair, maybe a little thinner and grey, but still untidy, still flopping over his forehead to be impatiently pushed back. How she remembered that gesture.

Hetty rose, stiff from sitting at the window for too long and went to the front door. Her hands shook as she opened it before Peter had chance to lift the knocker.

All she could manage was, 'Oh Peter!'

In response he took her hand and raised it to his lips. 'Hetty, my Hetty.' When he stood upright again, there were tears in his eyes. Their embrace was tender, memories of each other's bodies fierce.

She took him into the kitchen and sat him at the scarred oak table – one of the few things she'd rescued from Delamere. After she'd bustled about making tea and searching for the old Huntley and Palmers biscuit tin, with a few soft ginger-nuts lurking within, she finally sat opposite him. She expelled a long breath.

'You haven't changed one bit.'

'Neither have you, Hetty.'

She grimaced. 'I think we both know that that's not true.'

He shrugged his thin shoulders and gestured towards the stick. 'Picked up a leg wound at Verdun. Maybe we have changed?' He gave a short laugh. 'It's been a good few years. Time has smoothed a few corners, perhaps.' He looked directly at her. 'In essence, though, I think we're both the same.'

Hetty poured tea, in an attempt to quieten the tumult of emotion she was feeling. She pushed a cup over to him and gestured towards the milk jug. As Peter stirred in milk and sugar, she gazed at him.

The feelings that had begun, so tentatively, illicitly, so very long ago, had never really disappeared. But Peter had.

'You went to war?'

He took a sip of tea. 'I went into the army.'

'I remember that horrible, vile white feather.'

He nodded. 'It wasn't only thing which decided me, but I couldn't not go, not after that.'

'You were so angry that morning when I came into the school for the first time.'

He sat back, shoulders relaxed. 'First, I find a white feather in my locker and then I'm told I'm to have a young lady from the big house foisted upon me.'

'Was I really foisted upon you?'

Peter grinned. 'You were and I didn't know what to do with you. For all I knew, you'd be useless at everything.'

Hetty laughed at that. 'I was very nearly brought up to be so.' She leaned forward. 'But I proved useful, helpful, didn't I?'

He took her hand. 'You did. You were a solace and a comfort. A sparring partner and a great friend. For too short a time, though.'

'We were, weren't we? Great friends. I think both of us had need of friendship at that time. I know I needed one when Edward died.' Hetty warmed at the memory of Peter's consolation at a time when she hadn't comprehended what was happening. He hadn't said much, had done even less, but she knew he *understood*.

Peter nodded. 'It was partly his death which made me join up.

280

There was so much sacrifice. I couldn't bear the guilt. Everywhere I looked, from dratted Miss Fletcher's white feathers to my parents' bewilderment at my lack of willingness to enlist.' At Hetty's shock he nodded. 'Oh, yes, it was our delightful colleague who was so generous with her hat feathers! She went to be a nurse, did you know?'

'Those poor soldiers,' Hetty said, with feeling.

They laughed.

'You went so abruptly.'

Peter sighed. 'I couldn't say good bye, Hetty, knowing I might not come back to you.' He smiled bitterly. 'And I so wanted to come back to you.' He rubbed a hand over his face. 'Once a coward, always a coward, eh? I'm so sorry.'

Hetty shook her head. 'You were never a coward!' she said, stoutly. 'And there is nothing, *nothing* to apologise for.' She shrugged. 'It was the war. We were all so terribly affected, at sixes and sevens.'

'At least you had Edward for a little while?'

'He was a good man, but we were never really suited.' She caught Peter's look. 'Have I shocked you? I think I did him, rather. I was too wild, too unfulfilled for him. I don't think he really knew what to do with me either.'

'And you were too young.'

'Too unworldly. But it was what was expected of me. And I so very nearly had the chance to see some of the world with him. As an army wife,' she added. 'But it was cut short, like so many other marriages. Blighted lives.'

Peter frowned. 'Has it always been blighted?'

'Oh no,' Hetty said, too briskly. She poured more tea. 'Far from it. I went to London. Flora Parker, of all people, helped find me a nannying position.'

'A nanny? I can't imagine you as a nanny!'

Hetty stiffened. 'I was rather good at it, don't you know! And I finally got to see some of those places I dreamed about. The ones

I thought were only for others to see.'

'The pyramids?' Peter asked impishly.

'You remembered!'

'Of course I remembered. You talked about little else.'

Hetty swirled tea around her cup. 'No,' she admitted, regret staining her voice, 'I never got to visit Egypt. The family with whom I travelled the most enjoyed the Riviera and the States. But I enjoyed it, nonetheless. I still hear from the children.' She smiled warmly at him. She might be unused to having guests in her little cottage, but she was enjoying the company of this one so very much.

'You were always good with children, as I recall.' Peter grinned.

'As were you. Did you go back to it? Teaching?'

Peter nodded. 'I did. I came back to the school after the war. Ended up as head teacher. Married eventually. Had a life.' He took Hetty's hand again. 'I asked about you, but no one seemed to know anything about you or what had happened to the family.'

'The Parkers bought the house after the aunts died, but it needed too much work. They didn't keep it very long, their hearts weren't in it. I don't think they ever really got over the death of their son. And then ... well, there was very little to keep me here, so I went to London.'

'But you came back.'

'I did. I've been living here for ten years. I love it. I enjoy my garden, I love the birds that visit, the squirrels and the view too, of course. And it's not too far from the places where I was happiest. Delamere. The school. I finally have a place to call my own after all these years. What could be better after travelling the world than to come home and put my own slippers in front of my own fire.' She looked at him, the young girl emerging from its mask of age. 'Did you never think to look me up, if you were still in the area?'

'Hetty, are you flirting with me?'

She laughed. 'Maybe.' She removed her hand from his and sat back in reproof. 'I haven't decided whether to forgive you for not writing, never letting me know you'd survived. I wondered, you know.'

Peter was silent. 'I regret that deeply, Hetty,' he said, eventually. 'You have no idea how much.' He took a breath. 'I wasn't well … afterwards. Maybe I wasn't well throughout the war. How could I explain the horror of it?' He shook his head. 'I had no words. I still don't.'

'Was it your leg wound?' Hetty asked, knowing it was so much more than that.

He nodded. 'And … other things.' He looked up at her. 'Another life blighted, eh?'

'Oh, my dear. I'm so sorry.' This time it was Hetty who reached across the table. 'But you recovered? You married?'

'I did. To a wonderful woman called Naomi.' Peter gave Hetty an embarrassed look. 'She was my nurse in the field hospital.' He shrugged at the cliché.

'Oh, Peter!'

They laughed again.

'She helped me through some very black times. She was a saint. I owe her my sanity.' He sobered abruptly. 'She died some years ago.'

This time Hetty's 'Oh Peter' had a very different tone.

'Don't be sorry. She had a long illness. In a way it was a release when she went.'

'And children?' Hetty couldn't quite keep the envy from her voice. How she would have loved having Peter's children.

'No. We were never blessed.' A sigh. 'But I dedicated my life to the children of others. It was nearly as fulfilling.'

'Of course.' Hetty understood that only too well. 'And where are you living now?'

'Worcester. I have a house with a view of the river.'

Hetty leaned back, making her chair creak. 'So here we are. Two people at the end of two busy lives.'

'The end? Rubbish, woman, you've got years to go yet.'

Hetty giggled, young again. 'I'm seventy-one next year.'

'As I said,' he drained his teacup and put it back on its saucer, with a decisive chink, 'a mere youngster. We've got lots of time to catch up with one another.'

Hetty looked at him. Her beloved, long-lost Peter. 'Friends again, then?' She took hold of his hands. She remembered them well. Thin-fingered but warm and capable.

Peter returned her gaze. 'Oh, I think it's time for more than friendship, don't you? I think we've both waited long enough.'

'I do, Peter, my darling,' she said, on a sigh full of longing. 'But I'm not sure I deserve it. I have something to say first. It's something I've spent a long time feeling guilty about. I'm worried you may not feel quite the same about me when I've told you.'

'You can talk to me about anything, Hetty, you know that.' Peter smiled. 'Just take your time and tell me.'

So she did.

Chapter 33

They ended up going to the pub.

Again.

They always ended up going to the pub. It wasn't that Rachel really minded, it was just she would have liked to have gone somewhere different occasionally. Gabe didn't see it that way. The last thing he wanted to do, he reasoned, was get all dolled up and drive miles after a long day at work. And Rachel had to concede he had a point. He was working harder than ever and trying to get as much outside work done while the weather held.

So Rachel stifled her resentment, shrugged on a thin jacket and took his hand.

A dry, gusty wind blew as they strolled down the track. It blew the orange clay dust into their hair and eyes and irritated Rachel further. It seemed even the wind hadn't the energy to get going properly, as if it too had had enough of the endless hot weather.

The summer heat was continuing into September and the papers were hysterical with the promise of an Indian summer reaching well into October. Tucking a lock of hair behind her ear, Rachel longed for a cool breeze and some crisp air. As if to echo her thoughts, a sparrow cheeped dejectedly from the hedge, no energy to do any more. Rachel wondered if it was a descendant of Indignant, now absent from her windowsill.

'You alright?' Gabe looked down at her.

'Fine. Why?'

'You're a bit quiet.'

'No, I'm fine.'

'It wasn't the mess I left in the kitchen, then?'

Gabe had made himself fish-finger sandwiches when getting in late the night before. He'd left crumbs and tomato ketchup all over the table. He hadn't told her where he had been, either. She was pretty sure it hadn't been work. Charles had been like this, when he'd begun seeing Lorna.

'No,' Rachel lied. 'It didn't bother me.'

Now Gabe knew there was something wrong. Rachel always blew up at him about such things. And his liking for tea at all times of day and night. And his preference for white bread. And cold lager instead of red wine. Rachel ate wholemeal brown, red wine and sought out organic vegetables. Such differences didn't bother Gabe, but they seemed to increasingly irritate Rachel. Then there was the paper he chose to read and the television programmes he liked to watch. It was just as well they were so good in bed, Gabe grinned to himself, because they were dangerously incompatible out of it.

'Why are you smiling?'

'I was just thinking, that's a good old table, that one you've got in the kitchen. Solid oak. I could maybe have a look at it, rub it down, re-stain it. I reckon it'd come up a treat.'

Well, anything would look better than tomato ketchup stains.'

'Aw, Rach, I'm really sorry. I meant to tidy up, I really did. It's just that I didn't get in 'til gone eleven and I didn't want to wake you with all my clattering around.'

That his lack of cleaning up stemmed from consideration for her further irritated Rachel. She bit her lip. What was it with her lately? Every move he made, everything he said or did made her nerves stand on end. She really liked him, she did. She *loved* the things they did in bed. She had let him into her life, into her heart. Was he going to trample all over it as Charles had?

It's just that you're too used to doing things your own way; that's all it is, she admonished herself silently. Compromise, that's what's needed in a relationship. But she was no good at compromise. And Gabe *was* wonderful. Kind helpful, considerate. Mostly. It shouldn't matter that he was untidy and uncultured; that he didn't know best Colombian from milky Nescafé, that he ate chocolate digestives in bed, that he sometimes forgot to take off his muddy boots before coming into the house.

That he often disappeared without explanation.

He was loving, gentle, fiercely passionate in bed – at this, Rachel felt the familiar sexual tug pull at her. The sex was amazing. Mind-blowing. Exhilarating. Even now, simply walking alongside him, the image of his lean, brown, eager body came to her. She wanted to leap on him, push him into the nearest hedge and take him there and then. She yearned for him. Craved him. But could you base a whole relationship on sex? Tim, when she'd discussed it with him, had said an adamant yes and what was she whining about? And that had been said in between the accusations that she didn't recognise a good thing when she saw it. His vocabulary had been slightly more Anglo-Saxon, but that had been the general gist.

Rachel stole a glance at Gabe. At his well-defined cheekbones and strong nose. At the lips which could drive her crazy with desire and had done things to her which made her blush.

But she needed to trust him too.

'Sorry,' she said and lifted his hand to kiss it. 'In a foul mood. Work didn't go well today.' A little white lie.

Gabe kissed her temple. 'You're too hard on yourself. Ease up a bit. Another day tomorrow.'

'I suppose, although I'm behind with the fairy tales illustrations. Gabe?'

'Yes, Rach?'

'The idea about the table, it sounds great. If you have time to do it, that is.'

'For you? Anything.' He held the pub door open for her. 'Here we are, then. What are you having?'

'Wine, what else?'

'What else, indeed?' He grinned at her and kissed her full on the lips. The kiss deepened. Intensified. The dance of love, of desire, practised well but one that was never tired of.

For a moment, they stood in a heated embrace and then Kev's wolf whistle, as he barged past them, broke them apart.

Two weeks later, the scene was set. Candles on the kitchen table, spaghetti bolognese wafting garlic and herb scents, garlic bread warming in the oven and a bottle of Chianti open and ready.

Rachel went outside to cool down a little. It had got hot in the kitchen while she cooked. She leaned against the front door and enjoyed the evening. The nights were drawing in and there was a bite of autumn in the air. Her garden seemed strangely still and quiet, blanketed around her. Looking up she realised the chestnut tree, where the swallows had gathered, was empty. Hetty had gone too. Although Rachel had a strong sense Hetty approved of Gabe, she wondered if she didn't like them living together?

'I'm not sure he's actually moved in, Hetty,' she said to the emptiness. 'Not properly. He comes and goes when he wants. You wouldn't approve of that at all, would you?' With a sigh, she added, 'I just hope you both agree with what I've got planned for this evening.' Shivering, she retraced her steps.

Back in the kitchen, Rachel adjusted a fork to an infinite degree and smiled. She wanted this night to be perfect. She'd pulled in all her contacts in the art world and it had worked – she'd got Gabe a stand at the prestigious arts and crafts fayre in Olympia in November. She couldn't wait to see his reaction.

This might be the push in the right direction that Gabe needed. He had far more talent than his current occupation merited. With his skills and the feel he had for wood, he could go places. And the fayre was the ideal stepping stone. She braced herself as she heard his footsteps in the hall.

'Rach? You around? There's that French film you wanted to

see. It's on at the Courtyard.' Gabe stopped abruptly. 'Woo hoo,' he said in appreciation. 'What's going on here?' He sniffed. 'Spag bog? My all-time favourite.' He came to her and threw his arms around her waist, half lifting her to his lips. 'And don't tell me you've done that garlicky bread stuff again?'

Rachel nodded against his kiss.

'Died and gone to heaven.' He began to sit down, saw Rachel's frown and retreated into the hall to take off his work boots. 'Don't worry,' he called back, 'I'm not too muddy. Bit dusty, but no mud.' He poked his head around the kitchen door. 'Can I come in now, miss?'

Rachel laughed. 'Sit down, I'll get it served.'

Gabe loped across the kitchen and tore off great strips of kitchen towel. Rachel squashed her irritation, but he caught her look. 'Aw lovely, you know how messy I can get with spag bog.'

'There are napkins,' Rachel said primly, she couldn't help herself. She put the bowl of sauce on the pot stand.

'Wouldn't want to ruin your white napkins,' Gabe said. 'This'll do fine.' And with that, he shoved a corner of the square of kitchen roll down his t-shirt.

Rachel tried not to wince and passed over Gabe's bowl of pasta. 'Help yourself to sauce, but be careful, the casserole dish is hot.'

'Yes, ma'am,' Gabe said cheerfully and began to eat with gusto. 'Wine?'

'Rather have a can of Stella, but don't worry, I'll start with wine.'

She watched him as he took a great gulp. He looked exhausted. 'Hard day?'

Gabe put his glass down and nodded wearily. 'The Hallidays are quibbling about the bill and still haven't paid and Mrs Sutherland-Harvey doesn't like the layout for the conservatory.'

'I can't believe you're still doing work for that woman.'

Gabe gave a short laugh and crunched his strong white teeth into the garlic bread. 'She's never happy with anything, which means she wants to change everything all the time, which means more work for us. But at least she pays her bills on time. Never had any problem getting money out of Mrs S-H.' Gabe waved the piece of bread in defence of his argument and scattered crumbs over the table.

Rachel pushed aside her bowl of pasta. 'Wouldn't you like to do something else?'

Gabe stiffened. They'd had this conversation many times over. He knew Rachel wanted him to pursue a more artistic career. What she didn't seem to realise was he needed to eat as well. And there was no market for his fancy bits and pieces of wood around here. What folk wanted was craftsmen-built kitchen units or oak staircases. And he couldn't leave the family firm. Not now.

'Some day,' he said, guardedly.

Rachel fished a letter out of her handbag. 'I've got something for you.' She unfolded it, smoothed it out with nervous fingers and slid it across the table.

Gabe frowned. 'What's this?' He scanned the contents and the frown deepened.

'I've pulled all the strings I have. Tim helped; his partner has a few contacts and I've got you a stand at the British Exhibition of Arts and Crafts at Olympia. London,' she added, as Gabe looked blank.

'I know where Olympia is. Funnily enough.' He looked at her. 'What have you done, Rachel?'

'I thought you'd be pleased.'

'And what am I supposed to put on this stand. In Olympia. In London?'

'Well, that oak piece you've been working on ... and ...' Rachel faltered. She was beginning to realise she might have made a mistake.

'That's right, what else?'

'But you're always working on something. Other smaller things.'

'Oh yes, odds and sods, nothing I'd want to show anyone. Nothing I'd care to exhibit in Olympia. In ruddy London.'

'Don't shout, Gabe.'

'Well, how the fuck did you think I'd react? Didn't you once think to discuss this with me first? Didn't it occur to you that I might not have anything to show?'

'No, I ... but there's time.' Rachel stabbed a finger at the letter. 'The show isn't until November.'

Gabe jumped up, making his chair screech across the quarry tiles. 'Christ, Rachel, I can't just drop everything and ... and ... *create* things. I've got a living to earn.' He shook his wrist at her, pointing to his watch and making her flinch. 'It's gone nine now and I've only just come back from the Sutherland-Harvey job. When the hell do you think I've got time to fit in anything else?'

Rachel's temper rose to meet Gabe's. 'Well, you could stop hanging out in that dingy pub with your no-hoper friends,' she blurted out.

Gabe went very still. 'Just why do you tolerate me, Rachel?'

She looked up at him in shock. She'd never seen him like this. 'What do you mean?'

'Well, let's see.' He began ticking things off on his fingers. 'My job obviously doesn't meet with your approval, you hate me drinking beer, you wince every time I speak – no I see you, I've seen you do it. You don't want to get to know my friends, I've never even met any of yours and now you want to make me into some kind of poncey artist.'

'Gabe, I never meant any such thing. I just think you've got so much more to offer,' she added, lamely.

'Let me tell you this. When I decide to change direction, it'll be my decision and I'll do it in my own time, when the moment's right.'

'Then you'll never do it because you've got no ambition!' The instant she said it, Rachel realised how cruel she sounded.

Gabe's lips thinned. 'That's what you think, is it?'

Rachel nodded, she didn't trust herself to speak. She had the terrible, dreadful feeling she'd gone too far with this. Much too far.

'I see.' Gabe was calm now. Horribly calm. He picked up his jacket off the kitchen chair. 'Well, I'll be off, then. Nice knowing you,' He nodded.

'Gabe?' Rachel couldn't believe what was happening. Was he leaving? Was he leaving *her*? 'Gabe you're not going? Come back and finish your supper.'

He laughed. It was a horrible sound. 'Don't worry about me, I'll get something down at that dingy pub.'

'With Dawn, I suppose,' she spat out before she could stop herself. The age-old jealousy and insecurity rose in her like bile. She was sure of it now. He'd been playing her like a fool, just as Charles had done. It could be the only explanation for his constant disappearances.

Gabe gave her a hard stare, began to speak and then thought better of it. He shook his head and scrubbed an exasperated hand through his hair. A pulse leapt at his throat.

She followed him into the hall. He picked up his boots from where he kicked them off in the hallway, then straightened. Rachel saw his expression and knew.

'You know, Rachel, there can't be anything worth having without trust; it goes a long way in a relationship. So now I know what it is I've done wrong, what it is that makes you so fucking irritable.' His face was tight with a kind of quiet fury. 'It's been like walking on fucking eggshells with you.' He paused, his expression hardening. 'And now you think I'm not good enough for you. Well, perhaps I never was.' He came closer. 'Or maybe, just maybe, you're not good enough for me. Think about that.'

He shoved his feet into his boots and, without waiting to tie the laces, wrenched open the front door and disappeared into the night.

Chapter 34

For days all Rachel did was wander the house as if Gabe was playing a joke and hiding somewhere.

But he wasn't.

He was nowhere to be seen. Nor did he ring. Hetty ignored her too; all she was aware of was a cold and accusing silence sliding round the walls of the sitting room. On the third day after he'd gone she finally slumped at the desk, staring blankly at the view. She'd lost him and it was all her own stupid fault.

She laid her head on her arms and wept.

The autumn wreaked revenge on what had been an Indian summer by bringing a premature winter, with howling gales and rain, which lashed at the windows of the cottage, exposed as it was, high on the ridge.

Rachel's life closed in on itself. She hunkered down, with her work and with Hetty's journal. She read a few more of Edward's letters, with their brittle attempt at making the best of what must have been a truly dreadful situation. They included yet more requests for socks, as the winter cold set in, and writing paper. Then Rachel found one that mentioned Richard. It must have been one of the last letters Edward had written before being wounded at Neuve Chapelle.

26th February, 1915

1st Bn The Worcestershire Regiment
BEF

Darling girl,

*No, of course I did not mean anything by my comment
about Flora. I do think she is brave, however and especially
so after David's death. From what little I have seen of the
work they do, VADs are doing all they can to help us win
this filthy war. Redoubtable ladies, all of them. But I did not
mean any criticism of your actions. I know you are doing
your bit at home and the aunts cannot be left, especially
now Richard has joined up.*

*Your work at the school is tremendously useful – and suit-
able. Your Mr Innisford sounds an interesting man and I am
pleased you have found a new friend. You sound as if you
are loving it all, although I simply cannot imagine you knitting! Tell me more about it. It is pleasant to be reminded of
home. I long to see Delamere.*

*Oh, but foolish Richard, what was he thinking? He hasn't
even graduated! And why enlist as a 'gentleman soldier'? He
will regret his impulsive action soon enough, once he is out
here. Why does the boy never think? I send prayers to keep
him safe and urge you to do the same.*

*You asked for more detail about the goings on out here. Well,
my darling, forgive me if I do not tell you too much. There
is little time to write and I would prefer not to linger on
what has been done. Suffice to say I got back at about 10pm
last night, after a stint and had the most splendid night's
sleep. We had been conducting the rations party to the front
trenches and had a narrow escape. Fritz's guns were going
like billy-oh. Sadly couldn't take the boots off, when we got*

here, but it mattered not. Just glad to get my head down. The trenches beggar belief; we are often knee deep in mud. Although, now the colder weather is upon us, it has hardened and we have a different problem; one or two of the men have gone down with frostbite. France and the Hun conspire to get us one way or another!

Thankfully, last night, some of the men organised a singsong, which has lifted spirits no end. Some of the sergeants sang in parts beautifully, although the guns made the windows of HQ rattle a bit as an accompaniment. It was very pleasant and I know we all gave our grateful thanks to those who thought to do it. There is talk of a concert later in the year but none of us likes to tempt fate by thinking too far ahead. On the same subject, there is little hope of me obtaining leave at present, dear girl. It is a little too lively in these parts for any officer to be granted leave. We've seen one or two exciting doings. The Hun make life interesting, I can tell you!

Do let me have any news about Richard. My love, as always, to you and the aunts.

Edward

Even lost in her own misery, Rachel empathised with Edward. Head of the family, stuck at the Front and worrying over his wife and brother. Was there a hint of jealousy there too? And it was typical of Hetty to get indignant about Edward praising Flora!

She continued to leaf through more of Hetty's papers. There were one or two more letters from Edward and some diary entries describing her work at the school. She seemed to relish volunteering at the school and wrote, in glowing terms, about her friendship with Peter Innisford. Good for Hetty, thought Rachel. She must have felt she was actually doing something useful at last.

There was one more letter, reeking of the familiar stench of war. But this one wasn't from Edward. It was signed Richard.

27th April, 1915

8th Bn Devonshires

Hetty,

I am saddened beyond belief to hear news of Edward's death. Of course, you were quite right to tell me – never think of holding any news back, no matter how distressing. It may be my turn soon. The Devonshires are soon to go to France. I had imagined I would ride fearless into battle. It will not be like that, I'm told. Still, it will be an adventure and I am determined to do my best for king and country, but most of all for Edward and you, dear Hetty. Please write – and don't forget me, Hetty.

I remain, as ever, yours in heart and soul and blood, Richard

So Richard had gone to France, leaving Hetty, once again on the fringes of life – and death. A widow to one brother, fretting over another and Peter at war too.

Scanning through some brief diary entries, Richard's name caught her eye again:

Wednesday 15th December, 1915

What will 1916 bring? It surely cannot bring us any worse news.
The letter from Richard has not been followed by others. I write often but hear nothing. I fear he will almost

certainly try something headstrong, something he thinks is
heroic. I call him selfish and then sob and beg his forgiveness. We are forever linked, in heart and soul and blood.
Whatever happened before the war is forgotten. Against
this slaughter it is less than trivial. Will you survive,
Richard? I am willing it so. But – why do you not write?
The newspapers are our lifeline but we dread them also.
None of us can bear the lists of names. Gerald Trainor,
from the Parker estate, was reported killed in action last
week. The misery, the slaughter, is unending. Is there to be
no man left, no home untouched? Sometimes I cannot
bear the pain. Anxiety and love for Richard and Peter
overwhelm me. I have to absent myself from the aunts
and weep over what our lives have become.
Leonora becomes ever more demanding and fractious. I
fear for Hester's health too. She tries to do too much. We
all do. Elsie has gone to be a munitions girl and, with
Cook ill, Dorcas and I run the household. Such that it is.
The house is falling down about our ears and we live in a
few unheated rooms. We lead a claustrophobic life, three
women dressed like crows, hunched over and waiting to
hear news we do not want.
It is a miserable existence.

Friday 18th December, 1915

Richard is home! What a Christmas present for us!
After such excitement, our greeting was subdued. Richard
is changed. He is too thin and terribly sallow, with a
cough that doubles him up. He has been in hospital since
Loos. We are told it was gas.
We are determined to keep our boy safe and to make him
well again!

Friday 31st December, 1915

A quiet Christmas and New Year. I killed one of the older chickens and it made for a pleasant meal.

Richard worries us all. I endeavour to keep the papers from him. If he catches sight of one, he will take it to the sitting room and pore over it like a man possessed. And the papers have such horrors in them. Line upon line of names. It is too much to bear. Only last week there was a report the Bosch had crucified a Canadian soldier. A crucifixion! Is there any horror to which our enemy will not stoop? The stories from Belgium in fourteen were bad enough but this!

Friday 14th January, 1916

I look at Richard sometimes when we are reading in the evening. I look at his hands, which he tries so hard to quieten but which jump and twitch with a life-force quite alien. It is as if all the energy of the old Richard, the pre-war Richard, has concentrated in his hands, for he has no energy for himself. The war has bled that. I take hold of his hand sometimes and it trembles underneath mine, but he will not meet my eyes and soon rejects any contact. He is one living apart from all of us. If one can call this living. I fear the war is one adventure too many for him. I fear for his mind and mourn the lively, impulsive, wild-eyed Richard I used to know.

I look at those hands and wonder if, he too, had committed acts of horror. Has he killed with them? Did he bayonet and shoot? The answer is, of course, yes. That is war. But he will not talk, not even when woken from his nightmares. He suffered one last night – I could hear his screams echoing along the corridor.

Richard is showing signs of improvement. His cough is improving. There is talk of him rejoining his regiment. Could this happen? Hasn't he done enough? The thought of him going back to the Front fills me with horror.

I tried to talk to him today. I am afraid I asked him what it was like. I confess I had a selfish motive; I am yet to hear from Peter and fear the worst.

Richard and I were sitting in the kitchen. He was studying Papa's old atlas, I was huddled near the range, knitting yet more socks for yet more soldiers to die in.

'You never wrote, Richard.' I looked up and saw his shoulders stiffen.

He straightened and gave a curious smile. 'What did you want to know?'

'Just that you were well. Nothing more. We heard nothing from you for so long and we were desperate for news.'

'Desperate to know what it was like?' He leaned back against the kitchen chair, one arm swung carelessly over its back. His eyes were shuttered.

'No. Just that you were alright. Not injured. Still –'

'Alive?' He shoved the atlas across the table, making me jump. 'What if I told it was a living death? That I died a hundred, a thousand, times. That I trod on bloated corpses, which were eyeless, eaten by rats. That the phantom of gas came over us and we blessed it as it silenced the screaming of the dying in No Man's Land. Is that what you needed to hear?'

I flinched, trying not to let him see my tears. Was this what Edward, with his bracing, brave letters had shielded us from? Had he suffered like that? Was Peter, even at this moment, going through this hell? Not for the first time since he had been back, I wondered if Richard were quite sane. He was certainly being cruel. Then I cursed myself. Had I not asked, not probed, these nightmarish thoughts may not have resurfaced.

'We only wanted to know if you needed anything.' I said the first thing that came into my head and, because I was trying not to cry, it came out sounding prim.

Richard roared with laughter. He came to me, snatched my knitting away and, taking my hands, lifted me to my feet. 'Hetty! That's why I love you.' He kissed me soundly on the lips. 'You are the one thing that kept me going. You and Delamere. And now, with your money, we can re-build it together. After you've married me, of course.' He had a maniacal look.

'I do not –' I began, 'I am not sure I can marry you.'

'Yes you can,' he said, misunderstanding. 'There is a new law. You can marry your husband's brother. As long as he's dead, of course.'

I pushed him away. 'Don't say things like that, Richard.'

'There's no one else, is there?' It was a voice filled with cold menace.

Concentrating on gathering my wool and needles, I said, 'There is no one.'

There was a long moment when I could feel Richard staring at me. The back of my neck prickled with his gaze. He knew. Heat filled my face. I heard the kitchen door slam.

I found out later he had gone to Breckington, to ride. With no one left to exercise them, the horses had become out of condition.

Rachel clipped the lid back on the biscuit tin. She hoped Hetty and Richard hadn't married; he was a cruel and unstable man and had been even before the war. Yet, they must have done. She remembered Gabe saying Hetty had had two husbands. She pressed

300

the lid more firmly on and, in the process, sliced open her finger. The memory of Gabe's concern when she'd cut herself the last time, all those months ago, flooded through her.

Going to the kitchen to find a sticking plaster, she wept over it. There was no plaster to help heal the pain in her heart.

Chapter 35

Rachel's frozen heart refused to thaw. She had spent the Christmas holiday with Tim and Justin and had even managed to get together with Jyoti, but she mumbled her way through things, in a dream, in a numbed state, only eating and drinking when she needed to and doing very little else. She lost weight, her hair lost its lustre and she didn't have the energy to work. Tim and Jyoti expressed their concern, but she refused to listen. She spent days listlessly watching the clouds obscure the view from her desk. Hetty remained silent, but shadows of sympathy sometimes flitted across the room.

The weather refused to help. Rachel had never known it so cold and dark. And when it wasn't icy, it rained – a heavy, sleety rain, which left the roads and fields a monotonous and depressing mud-brown.

Salvation arrived, one frosty February morning, in the shape of a wriggling black-and-white bundle.

'A puppy!' she exclaimed at Stan.

'Thought you might like him. Runt of the litter, see. No one wants him, 'specially now after Christmas, like.' He stood, on the doorstep of the cottage, his breath misting in the cold air and a hopeful expression on his face.

'What the hell am I going to do with a puppy?'

'They don't need much. Just a bit o' love and food and suchlike.'

'But I haven't got time to walk him,' Rachel lied.

'Won't need no walks for a bit. Too little and needs to have his jabs. He can't go out for a while longer.'

Rachel was overwhelmed. A million problems crowded in. 'Oh, Stan, it's a lovely thought, but I don't know the first thing about looking after dogs or puppies. I've never had one. Mum always said they'd make too much mess.'

'That's as maybe. Thought he'd be company for you. I got the feeling you were a bit lonely, like.'

Don't go there, thought Rachel. The village gossip hotline was the last thing she could cope with. She looked down at the warm, surprisingly heavy, bundle in her arms and saw two mournful eyes gazing back at her. 'He's lovely,' she faltered, as the puppy nestled into the crook of her elbow, 'but I just can't have him.' She held the puppy out for Stan to take back and, as she did so, the puppy reached out a long tongue and licked her ear.

'See, he likes you,' Stan said, with some satisfaction.

Rachel and the puppy stared eye to eye. 'What will happen to him if I don't take him?' She wasn't sure she wanted to know the answer. The puppy whined and struggled a little, so she put him back against her body and he settled.

'He's too runty for gun work and they don't know what's gone into him.' Stan shrugged. 'Reckon he'll get taken to that rescue place in Hereford and mebbe someone'll take him in. Otherwise,' Stan drew a finger across his neck. Rachel hugged the puppy to her, horrified.

'The Garths' springer bitch was got at a while ago, so he's got some springer in him, but don't know what else.' Stan ruffled the puppy's ears with affection. 'I'll take him when you have to go to London,' he said, pre-empting Rachel's next objection. 'No better company than a dog and I reckon he'll be so grateful to be saved that he won't leave your side.'

As if in agreement, the puppy snickered, so Rachel tucked her other hand around his scrawny little body and felt the thin ribs under the warm fur. The puppy burrowed its nose into her arm and her heart softened – just a little.

And that's how the thaw began, with a tiny puppy.

Stan had named him Patch because of the large black mark on his rump, but he soon had another. Maybe it was because he was the runt, or perhaps he was just plain greedy, but Patch ate everything put in front of him – and more. Rachel nicknamed him Piglet and, to her embarrassment, the dog answered to no other name. The name stuck.

For the first time in her life, Rachel allowed herself to be needed. And relished it. Maybe she could learn to accept being needed by Stan, Sheila even? Was it too late for Gabe? She should have paid more attention to Hetty. For all her faults, the one thing Hetty always did was let people *in*.

So, to Rachel's surprise she coped when Piglet peed on the kitchen floor, or got her up in the middle of the night, when he was crying for his litter mates. After three sleepless nights in a row, Rachel took him up to her bedroom. She laid copious wads of newspaper on the carpet and snuggled him up in a blanket. But it wasn't good enough for Piglet. He cried piteously, so Rachel gave in and tucked him against her in bed. There, the puppy snuffled and wriggled against her and they eventually slept.

To Rachel's amazement, Piglet succeeded where countless men had failed; he unlocked her obsession with cleanliness. She found it impossible to be cross with the dog, even when – horror of horrors – she trod in a puppy poo in the hall. Piglet looked at her with those imploring eyes and she accepted defeat and went to get the mop and bucket.

Stan, when he wasn't accusing Rachel of spoiling Piglet, helped train him. Soon, the puppy was sitting to command and became, more or less, house-trained.

Rachel gradually began to pick up her work and even found she got more done, as she had to grab her chance when Piglet was asleep. As such, she concentrated more and procrastinated less. And she loved her evenings now, with the puppy's soft head on her lap, warm against her.

Her walks had new purpose now. She had to go out, whatever the weather, and found she even enjoyed walking in the rain, although she wasn't sure about the wet-dog smell on their return. She found countless narrow lanes to walk along.

Then disaster struck.

She'd heard on the news that an outbreak of foot and mouth had broken out in the south-east but hadn't given it much thought.

Driving back from the station one afternoon in the frozen gloom, she came upon the sign. Her client had loved the work she'd done on the wild flowers and had commissioned some more. What's more, Freda had green-lighted the Hetty project and had a publisher in mind. Apart from the constant aching loneliness left by Gabe's departure and the utterly miserable weather, Rachel was in a good mood.

As she turned off the main road, the sign loomed into view. It shocked her. Huge and sinister and bright red, it stated she was now entering a FOOT AND MOUTH-AFFECTED AREA. She slowed the Fiat, her heart hammering in her mouth. What should she do? Was she allowed to drive through? Did she need to drive through some kind of disinfectant? She edged the car on. There was no one else in sight. Come to think of it, she'd seen no other car since leaving Hereford. The village was peculiarly quiet – and eerie. Rachel put her foot down and drove home.

When she got there, she found Stan entombed in his shed, a mug of coffee in his hand and the local radio station on.

'It's a bad business,' he said and shook his head.

Rachel fended off Piglet's ecstatic welcome and collapsed onto the other chair. 'What does it mean?'

'Ruin for folks round here,' was Stan's only reply. He slumped in his chair and stared silently out into the dismal afternoon.

Rachel left him to his radio and, with Piglet at her heels, let herself into the house.

It was a black few weeks that followed. People moved about as little as possible, pubs remained empty, supermarkets lost trade. Rita threatened to close down as trade was so bad. Bridle tracks and footpaths were closed, meaning that Rachel had few options for walking Piglet and the dog became stir-crazy, chewing anything to hand. It wasn't as if she *couldn't* go out, it was just that she felt it looked insensitive to do so, when all around her farmers were barricaded into their homes. When she did venture out, every shop and business had revolting-smelling disinfect mats to walk through, reminding everyone that it was the biggest disaster to hit the countryside since 1967.

Eventually, even Rachel became bored with her own company and she and Stan took Piglet to the Plough. It was empty. Alan greeted them with a desperate joviality.

'Thank the good Lord,' he said, as he pulled Stan's pint. 'Punters. First round on the house. Been quieter in here than Pugh's,' he shook his head, referring to Fordham's funeral directors.

Rachel gave Stan a sideways glance. 'I don't know about anyone else, but I didn't feel I was helping by coming out unnecessarily.'

Alan shrugged. 'Folks round here still got to make a living. It spreads like wildfire. For all you know, could be spread by the car you park next to at the Co-op and I don't see folk not buying bread,' he said, in misery. 'Don't think those disinfectant mats help neither. So you're not helping any by staying in and depriving *me* of *my* livelihood.'

Stan nodded, acknowledging the man's anger. 'No, but you do what you can, don't you?' There was a gloomy silence.

'How's that baby of your Sharon's then, Stan?' Having poured Rachel's wine, Alan reached for a glass and began polishing it. He was obviously in need of company and making an effort, now the subject of foot and mouth was closed.

Stan shook his head and concentrated on his beer. 'Bouncing little boy,' he said with a grin. 'Takes after me,' according to Sharon. 'She's mighty vexed about that. No peace and quiet, though.'

'Never much of that around with babies.' Alan peered over the bar, to where Piglet was scratching vigorously. 'Or dogs, come to that. Reckon that collie at the Cross Farm got to the Garth's springer, by the looks of things.'

'Ar. Reckon so, he's clever enough to have collie in him.' Stan got some money out. 'Another round and this time we pay. One for yourself?'

Alan nodded. 'Might as well,' he gave a short laugh, 'it's not going to busy tonight. Again.' He took Stan's pint pot and began to pull another beer. 'Speaking of the Garths, did you hear?'

Stan pursed his lips. 'Saw the sign up on the fence. Man's lost his livelihood overnight. Had a slaughterman's licence, so he's shot 'em himself.'

Rachel looked at them both, an ominous feeling rising in her gut. 'What's happened?'

Stan took a long gulp of beer and wiped his mouth before answering. 'Foot and mouth notice gone up at the Garth's. He's had to shoot five hundred sheep and over two hundred cows.' Stan took another long draught of beer, emptying the glass.

Alan gave a heartfelt sigh. 'They've been farming in the village for over two hundred years. Terry Garth's been put on suicide watch, I hear.' He tutted. 'Bad, bad business.'

Rachel reached down and tugged gently on Piglet's ears. She needed some physical comfort. She'd only glimpsed the Garth family around the village, but knew they were one of the longest-established in the area. The views of their land and its livestock were one of the joys of living up on the ridge. It was shocking to think that their whole farm was gone and that a man would be so afflicted by the crisis he was considered vulnerable to suicide.

She thought back to her day in London. Although foot and mouth had been in the newspapers, the city functioned as usual, impervious to the unfolding rural disaster.

Alan refilled Stan's glass. 'Fancy a sandwich? Was just going to make myself one. No meat,' he added, as unspoken comment on their topic of conversation. 'I've got a bit of Hereford Hop and some of Rita's homemade pickle.'

Neither Rachel nor Stan were in the mood to eat, but sensed Alan wanted to keep busy.

When he'd disappeared into the kitchen, Stan said, 'The countryside's showing you another side of its skirt, isn't it? The grubby side. It ain't all wild flowers and pretty views.'

Rachel nodded. With the long dark days, the endless mud and now this, the reality of living in the countryside was beginning to hit hard. 'What will the Garths do?' She knew they had a teenage daughter and a son at college.

Stan shook his head and replied, through thin lips, 'There's talk of compensation, but money don't fill the gap the animals left. Terry's spent his life building up his herd of Herefords.' He shrugged and sank into gloom.

Alan bustled back, carrying heavily laden plates. 'On top of everything else, I'm going to be a barmaid short. Did you hear Dawn's got herself in the family way?'

Rachel felt herself stiffen.

'No,' Stan said in a non-committal tone. 'Wenches these days, eh? Don't wait to get a ring on their finger, do they?'

'That they don't. But she's getting wed. To young Gabe, I reckon. When all this is over with.' Alan waved his hand at the empty pub meaning the foot and mouth crisis.

With a heavy heart, Rachel led Piglet to a table by the fire. Stan followed and they spent the rest of the evening sat in silence, each deep in their own thoughts.

So Dawn had ensnared Gabe; there was no chance of him returning to her now. Staring into the fire, Rachel wished she'd stayed at home. At least she could have pretended, for a while longer, that she and Gabe had a chance. She cursed herself for letting him go, for driving him away – and tried to hold back the tears. Her romantic rural idyll was turning out to be anything but; her beloved village was drowning in a life-changing crisis. Even the weather conspired to depress. And now she'd lost Gabe forever.

'At least,' she whispered to Piglet, his nose resting devotedly on her knee but really edging closer to her half-eaten sandwich, 'I haven't ended up a lonely old woman surrounded by cats.'

But this was little comfort when she didn't have Gabe.

She couldn't bear it any longer and left Stan in the pub.

As she walked up the track, she became aware of a smell. It was all-pervading and oddly familiar but sickly – like a burnt Sunday roast. Rounding the last bend, she could see the sky glowing orange. She ran the last half mile or so, Piglet bounding in front. Something was wrong. Deeply wrong. Now burning invaded her nostrils, acrid with an underlying oily accelerant. She had put the fireguard around the open fire, hadn't she? Ignoring her protesting thighs and gasping lungs, she got to the top of the track and stopped. Her cottage was intact. Not on fire. Leaning on the chestnut tree, to catch her breath and ignoring a barking Piglet, she looked towards the burning horizon.

The pyres ran the entire length of the Garth's biggest field. Flames, peculiar, unnatural bluey-red flames shot thirty or forty feet into the uncaring night sky. Terry Garth was having to burn his stock. His life's work. His family's future.

Standing against the tree, her legs shaking from the shock and her face heated by the fires, even at this distance, Rachel's eyes and nose stung with the drifting pall of smoke. It was apocalyptic.

It looked as though the end of the world had come.

Chapter 36

April 2001, London

'I haven't a bloody clue what's going on, have you?' Tim squinted at the service sheet they'd been given on entry to the leisure centre.

'None at all,' Rachel replied.

They were at Jyoti's wedding. The sports hall in Wembley was packed. Some sort of ceremony was going on, on a platform at the far end, but from where Tim and Rachel were sitting, they could hardly make out what was happening. The only contact made with Jyoti was a swift smile as she processed to the wedding platform on the arms of her brother and father. Then she resumed a shy, solemn expression.

She looked completely unfamiliar. Heavily made up, dressed in sumptuous red, white and gold, with bangles weighing down both arms and a heavy gold nose ring and chain linked to enormous hooped earrings. Despite her doll-like appearance, Rachel thought she looked content, serene. Radiant. Maybe this marriage wasn't such a mistake after all.

Tim and Rachel were surround by women in a gorgeous array of vividly hued saris, gossiping and minding babies. The men stood at the back, chatting animatedly, apparently ignoring the wedding rites being performed, and children ran about the badminton

310

court, playing.

'They look right together,' Rachel whispered, nodding towards the elaborate red-and-gold canopied altar, which housed the happy couple.

'They do, don't they?' Tim squeezed Rachel's hand and she was glad of the physical comfort. So much life and colour was bewildering after coming from a muddy and depressed Herefordshire.

'Less of a compromise, maybe, made on behalf of our best friend, than we expected?' He looked insufferably smug.

Rachel pursed her lips and stayed silent. She hated it when Tim was right.

'Oh come on, sweetness. The man's a consultant surgeon at UCH. Jyoti's made for life.'

'And that's the main thing, is it? To have a new Mercedes every three years and holiday in the Caribbean?'

Tim laughed. 'Sounds peachy to me.'

'Oh, I forgot, I'm talking to a kept man.' Misery was making Rachel bitchy.

'Meow said the pussy.' Tim turned to her. 'You know, ever since you got to town, you've had your cat's arse face on. It's been months since your bust up with the Love God.'

Rachel's face crumpled.

Instantly stricken, Tim said, 'Oh, babe, what is it?'

'He's got another girl pregnant and I think they're going to get married,' she wailed. 'I don't think he's ever going to come back to me.'

'Oh, darling, shush now.' Tim put an arm around her, but Rachel shook him off.

Rachel stifled her sobs with a tissue, appalled at her display of emotion. 'Don't be nice to me. I won't be able to keep going. Got to put my happy face on for Jyoti and Kam.'

Tim looked around at the mass of people surrounding them. 'Darling heart, shall we go? Find somewhere for a ruddy great big drink and a chinwag? I don't think we'll be missed and we haven't the fairy faintest of ideas what's going on anyhow.'

'We can't leave,' Rachel said, scandalised, 'in the middle of a wedding!'

'We'll hardly be disrupting the ceremony,' Tim said and he pointed towards the networking men at the back. 'Don't think they've stopped talking since the whole shebang began.'

'I quite like it,' Rachel replied, dabbing her eyes and fighting for control. She watched two little boys play tag in the space behind some chairs. They were giggling and slamming into the plastic chairs, making them screech along the floor. No one rebuked or hushed them. In fact the women keeping an eye on them watched with tender pride.

'Let's stay – until the bitter end.'

'What – tomorrow?'

Rachel looked at him startled.

'Oh, yes,' Tim nodded, 'this has been going on for two days already and there's another day of it tomorrow. Family only. This is the public bit.'

'What did they do yesterday, then?' Rachel asked, momentarily forgetting her misery.

Tim shrugged. 'Don't know the details, but it was more an intimate family thing, you know, they had to do the official stuff too, at the registry office. They just invited the odd two or three hundred guests to that do.'

Rachel giggled and then her breath caught and ended as a sob. She was jealous. Jealous of Jyoti finding her man, getting married, being happy, no matter what the compromise. Compromise in relationships was what it was all about. You were never going to find someone absolutely perfect. Look at poor old Hetty. Married and widowed in a few short months and not very happy while it lasted. Loving Richard, only for it to end in misunderstanding, maybe loving the mysterious Peter. And then there was Tim. Living with Justin, permanently arguing, always threatening to walk out.

She bit her lip. Why had she been so horrible to Gabe? What

had he done, after all, that was so bad? Forgotten to do the washing up once or twice, left his copies of newspapers mounting up in an untidy heap in the sitting room, trailed mud in. She remembered how kind he was, how ready to help. She missed the feel of him holding her in the night, his gentle hands caressing her as if she were something very precious. She'd been awful to him. So presumptive. Always trying to boss him about, make him better himself when he was actually perfect as he was. She'd turned into her mother. She was ashamed of herself. No wonder he'd run to Dawn. Her lips trembled and she felt Tim take her hand again.

'Courage ma petite,' he whispered. 'If you insist we stay, we shall. But you're going to have to locate that happy face if we do.'

Rachel didn't know how she got through the wedding. There was food at some point, served refectory-style from vast aluminium tanks. Tim said the curries were to die for and tucked in with gusto, but she hardly ate a thing.

As he ate, an usher explained that the sacred fire was being prepared. The *Agni Parikama* – walking around the fire – would soon take place. It was the central act of the ceremony, he explained. The couple would be tied together and walk around it seven times. They must promise to tend to each other's needs and be true companions for life.

For once, the crowd silenced and watched as Jyoti and Kam pledged their lives to one another. It was very moving and more than Rachel could bear. She needed to escape. She realised, whatever the compromise, she wanted to tend to Gabe's needs and be his true companion for life. How could she have been so selfish? God, she *missed* him.

When the usher tactfully suggested it was time to go; that this part of the day was over and that the evening party was for family only, Rachel was only too thankful to leave. There hadn't been a chance to say hello to Jyoti or wish her well, but they'd all catch up soon.

They took a taxi to Justin's house. It seemed very quiet after the noise and buzz of the wedding.

'Wine?' At her assent, Tim poured two enormous glasses of Chablis and directed her to the cream leather sofa. 'Sit,' he commanded. 'Drink and tell Uncle Timmy everything.'

Rachel was swept with an overwhelming sadness and more than a little self-pity. She sniffed a little. 'I don't think I do that compromise thing enough,' she began. 'Well, not at all, really.'

'You never did, wonderling,' Tim replied, only just hiding a grin. 'You never did. But maybe, just maybe, now you've realised, perhaps you can start working on it.'

'I think I might need some tips, Tim.'

He raised his eyes heavenwards. 'A road to Damascus moment. Halleluiah!' He slid on the sofa beside her. 'Twelve-step plan?' he said and Rachel managed an attempt at a smile.

Chapter 37

She shouldn't be here, but Neil had caught her at a weak moment and she'd said yes. And, after all, why shouldn't she spend an evening with a friend? She stifled the nagging feeling that she was in danger of leading Neil on.

Again.

The film had been good. It had been kicking around the West End for a few months now and, had she still been in London, she would have seen it ages ago. It had turned up at the Courtyard, as part of a rural film initiative and it seemed churlish not to support what the arts centre was trying to do.

Oh and it was so good to be out again doing something fun. When the horrible signs had appeared, with their stark letters proclaiming the village and its surroundings a foot and mouth zone, it had seemed indecent, certainly insensitive, to go out just to enjoy yourself. After shutting themselves away, like the plague victims of Eyam, people were daring to relax a little, straining for normality. Even so, they went about with blank faces, as if working their way through a nightmare. And it didn't look as if the end was in sight any time soon.

A nagging feeling remained – and not just because of the foot and mouth crisis. Rachel hoped Neil would take it as it was – two friends on a casual outing.

Rachel enjoyed the film, although Neil fidgeted for the last half hour or so. She tried for charitable thoughts and wondered if the seat had failed to give him enough legroom.

Neil was subdued as they made their way to the bar for a post-film drink. He shook his head, 'Can't say I understood much of that, Rachel. Maybe I'm more of a blockbuster type of a guy –'

Then she saw him.

Gabe.

He was leaning against the bar with Dawn. Pregnant Dawn.

As if sensing her presence, Gabe turned as they approached. 'Hello, Rachel.'

Her world revolved and disappeared in on itself. The chatter from the room hurt her ears. The lights dazzled and blurred her eyes. She felt dizzy.

'Gabe.' Rachel nodded, coolly. 'Hello, Dawn. You both know Neil?' She wanted to rush into Gabe's arms. She wanted to bind him to her, as Jyoti and Kam had been bound. She simply wanted.

The silence was awkward.

Neil's immaculate manners rescued the situation. 'Gabriel, Dawn.' He smiled, in a not-unfriendly way. Then he took Dawn to one side. 'Excuse us,' he said, as he took her further down the bar. 'Dawn, I hear your mother is looking for a bungalow,' they heard him say. 'Might have just the thing for her. Just going on the market.'

'Drink?' Gabe gestured towards his pint of lager.

Rachel nodded. 'Thank you.'

'Wine?' That he'd remembered what she drank almost brought her to tears. Striving for control, she said, 'Just a small one please. I think Neil's keen to go soon.'

Gabe gave her a neutral look and then glanced at Neil and Dawn, still deep in conversation. 'We're off to try that new club in a minute.'

'Oh.' Rachel didn't know what to say. Couldn't bring herself to say the thing she most wanted to. Come back to me, Gabe, she pleaded with her eyes, but he had already turned away and was busy ordering her drink.

Taking her wine from him, their fingers touched. The brief contact nearly undid her. But, instead of reaching up and kissing his dear face, she muttered, 'Did you enjoy the film?'

Gabe grinned. 'It was okay. I liked that cherry wood table. At the beginning. The one they made love on. Nice dovetail joints.'

Rachel spluttered into her wine. 'Gabe,' she reproached, 'don't make me laugh when I'm drinking!' God, how had she forgotten the way his eyes crinkled up when he smiled. She felt as if she were seeing him for the first time. She must have been crazy to let this man slip through her fingers. She loved him so much. Her fingers, itching to touch him, gripped too hard around the stem of her wine glass.

'Well, that sort of film was never my thing, we both know that.' He shrugged, unabashed. 'It was Dawn's idea, she's going off to do a fine arts degree in September.'

Fine Art? Dawn? And pregnant? 'Good for her,' Rachel said. 'Where?'

Gabe finished his pint. Rachel found herself mesmerised by the sight of his long, strong throat muscles working as he drank. He put the empty glass down, frowning. 'Manchester, I think.'

Manchester was a satisfyingly long way from Hereford. She gazed at Gabe, drinking him in. Ripped from the sun and warmth he was paler, his hair a shade darker. He was thinner in the face too. Less glamorous, but more real somehow. And definitely putting up a guard.

'How's your mum?'

He smiled and she saw a little of the old Gabe return. 'Good.' He fiddled with the edge of a bar towel. 'She misses you, you know. Just because you and me ... well, it didn't work out, doesn't mean you have to avoid her.'

317

'No.' Rachel was ashamed. 'Tell her I'll pop round. We'll do a day at a garden centre or a big house and afternoon tea, maybe.'

'She'd like that.'

They stared into each other's eyes. 'Gabe –'

Then, the moment broke. Neil, having secured another possible sale, returned to them. 'Time to go Rachel,' he said, briskly. 'I've got a training session in the morning.'

'You still doing those triathlons, Neil?'

'Certainly am. Any time you want to join the training, Gabe, you just come along.'

Rachel winced. Neil was pompous sometimes.

Gabe grinned. 'Bit too busy, mate.' As they turned to go, he added, 'See you both.'

Neil opened the door for Rachel and she couldn't help glancing back. Dawn and Gabe's heads were close together and they were laughing about something. The black mood descended again. She allowed Neil to take her arm and lead her to the car park, into the thin, blue April evening.

Rachel decided to celebrate a year in her cottage with a roaring fire, a quick cuddle with Piglet and time with Hetty's embryonic book. It was coming along slowly. As it had been difficult to travel around freely, she'd used aeons of dial-up time researching the local area and had some great images of Delamere House to work from.

Her plans went awry. Although Piglet was happy to snore on the sofa (she'd given up trying to stop him) the fire, no matter how much she tried, refused to light. Remembering Mike telling her to call anytime there was a problem, she picked up the phone. Twenty minutes later there was a knock on the door.

'Oh, hello, it's you. I was expecting your Dad.'

Gabe stood on her doorstep.

He gave an uncharacteristically weary grin. 'He's busy,' he said, shortly. 'You got me instead. What's the problem?'

His abruptness flustered Rachel. 'I tried to light a fire earlier, like Mike showed me, only it won't take. It keeps going out,' she

318

added feeling foolish. 'I'm really sorry to bother you, only Mike said I should get in touch. He said there might be a few teething problems as it hasn't been lit for a long time.' She trailed off.

'No worries, it's okay, I'll take a look.' Gabe passed by her to go to the sitting room and Rachel caught the familiar scent of him: soap and the expensive hair conditioner he liked.

'Tea?' she called, in a desperate attempt to distract her thoughts.

'No, I'm good,' came the muffled reply.

Rachel heard him being greeted by a rapturous puppy. Some guard dog Piglet was turning out to be.

It didn't take Gabe long. All he did was rake out Rachel's ineptly laid fire, poke around the chimney, relay it and it was soon catching the newspaper again.

'You might want to get some firelighters and a bit of coal,' he said, as he played with Piglet. 'Firelighters will get the thing going a bit more easily and coal keeps it in.' He picked the puppy up and held him like a baby, cooing. 'Nice dog.' Piglet's tongue lolled out and his eyes rolled in ecstasy. Gabe looked at Rachel with a curious expression on his face. 'Thought you'd be more of a cat person.'

Rachel pulled a wry face. 'So people like to tell me.'

'You've got a fireguard?'

She nodded, trying not to feel jealous of Piglet.

'Well, don't forget to put it in front before you go up tonight.' He smiled and made Rachel feel about five. 'Don't want the Llewellyn building work going up in flames. All sorted now, probably the wind in the wrong direction or the cold air lying low or something. Not like switching on a radiator. Heating's working alright, though?'

'Oh yes,' she nodded hastily, wanting to reassure him that the Llewellyn's reputation on that front was secure. 'It's just that, well with just me here, it's seems a bit extravagant to put it on this late in the year.' Again she trailed off, the unspoken lying heavily between them, like the cold air outside.

Gabe handed Piglet back to her. The puppy whined disloyally.

'Right, I'll be off, then. Better get back. Mum's not had a good day.'

'Sheila's been ill?'

Gabe looked away and took a deep breath. 'Bit worse than that, Rach. She's got cancer. You might as well know. Everyone else seems to.'

The heavy air fragmented and shattered.

A million images crowded into Rachel's memory. The envelope on the Llewellyns' kitchen table – the one with the hospital logo. The way Sheila had laughingly dismissed her tiredness that day at Delamere Hall. Mike's unpredictable moods.

'Oh, Gabe, I'm so sorry. I had no idea.' She clutched onto Piglet, making the puppy whimper at her tight hold.

He thrust his hands into his jeans pockets, but not before Rachel noticed how much they trembled. 'Mum doesn't ... didn't want anyone to know.'

Another memory flashed into Rachel's head. Something Neil had said, ages ago, about it being a shame about Sheila. 'But you said everyone does know.'

Gabe looked at her then. 'I reckon everyone does and all. But Mum doesn't want to know they know. And folks keep up the pretence.'

'But why?'

'You like everyone knowing your business, Rachel?' Gabe gave a short laugh. 'No, well neither does my mum. She doesn't like it when dad has to take her all the way to Cheltenham and misses a day's work, either.'

Rachel was confused. 'Cheltenham? Why Cheltenham?'

Gabe sighed. 'Because that's where you have to go to get the treatment. Hereford doesn't have the right equipment.'

'Gabe, that's miles away! It must take an hour easily.' Piglet wriggled and Rachel put him down. The puppy made a beeline for the sofa.

'Too right it does.' Gabe ran a hand through his hair in

exasperation. 'And by the time you've waited for the chemo and seen the consultant, it takes up the best part of the day.' He gave her another odd look. 'Another corner knocked off your rural idyll, Rachel? It's pretty round here and I don't think I could live anywhere else, but sometimes,' he bit his lip, 'sometimes it isn't easy.'

He made for the hall and Rachel, still taking in his news about Sheila, didn't realise he was going until he'd opened the front door and let in a blast of cold and wet air. 'Gabe, if there's anything I can do, please let me know.

He didn't look back, but answered, on another bitter laugh, 'We'll let you know.' And then was gone.

Rachel returned to the sitting room and curled up in front of the fire, now crackling merrily. She hugged a warm and sleepy Piglet to her.

All those months of knowing Gabe and never knowing about his mother. All those weeks of sleeping with him but never sharing his worries, his fears. She stared into the flames and despite the heat being generated, shivered. She'd never really known him at all.

Then she sat bolt upright. All the grief she'd given him about not being more ambitious, not taking his work further afield, not branching out away from his family. Of course he couldn't. He'd had to stay to help look after his mother, to help out in the business.

It must be killing Gabe to stifle his creativity and spend his time putting expensive kitchens into rich people's homes. And it explained the absences, of course. If Mike couldn't get away to take Sheila, then Gabe would have to do it. And all the time she'd worried he was playing away. How could she get a person so wrong? How stupid and unseeing she'd been. Too much self-absorption and too much Hetty! Rachel shot a guilty look at the biscuit tin, still in its place on the shelf. She had been going to get it down again tonight to hunt through for another mention of Peter Innisford, but now she hadn't the heart.

Walking to the drawing board, she stared, unseeing, into the growing dusk. She hugged her arms to herself and pondered on just how much she'd misjudged Gabriel Llewellyn.

Chapter 38

'So, do you think Hetty lived on her own in this cottage for all those years?' Rachel adjusted her deckchair and lifted her face to the sun.

She and Stan were sitting out on the first hot day of the spring. It had been a long, cold winter. And a difficult one. For some, life changing. Stan had just told her the Garths were selling up.

Rachel put a hand out to Piglet. He snuffled and wriggled to make himself comfortable on her lap, his long legs made for less room nowadays.

Stan grunted. He disapproved of how Piglet ruled the roost. 'We'll never know, will we? Although me and Eunice sometimes saw a man here.'

Rachel sat up, causing a disgruntled Piglet to slip off. 'A man? Who?'

Stan shook his head. 'Dunno.'

'Well, what did he look like? Tall, short, young, old?'

Stan laughed. 'Don't get impatient with me. I don't remember. Just that Hetty was less ornery after one of his visits.'

Ornery. A real Stan word. Rachel smiled. 'He made her happy, then?'

'Mebbe.'

'I wish I knew. I wish I could fill in the gaps.' She gave a heartfelt sigh.

'Rach, don't you think it's time to let it go? Chances are, Hetty married this Richard of 'ers and lived a long, happy life.' Stan got his tobacco tin out and began the ritual of rolling a cigarette.

Rachel pouted. She knew she ought to move on, she certainly had enough material now to fill the short volume on Hetty's younger years – the school log book had helped – but she needed to *know* the end. 'Somehow, I just don't think that's what happened.'

'Now, why do you think that, then?'

This time it was Rachel who shook her head. 'I just know.' She glanced back at the cottage, at a possible shadow at the window. Was it Hetty, waiting? Waiting for the right man? Just as she had done – and had lost him in the process.

'Tried the church yet?'

'The church? Why?' Rachel looked up from where she was gently tugging the puppy's soft ears.

Stan puffed on his roll-up. 'Remember, I told you, there's a memorial stone outside it. Got all the boys' names on it, like. The ones that lost their lives. Mebbe this Richard died in the war?'

'Maybe,' Rachel frowned, but it didn't feel right. 'But Hetty wrote quite a lot in her diary during the war. You'd think she'd write about that?' She pursed her lips, thoughtfully, 'I haven't found any mention of Richard's death. He was gassed, I think, and came home, but Hetty said he recovered.'

Stan looked over his cigarette smoke towards the cottage door, his mind obviously drifting off-topic. 'That ole clematis I put in is looking good.'

It was. The delicate blue flowers framed the front door and nodded in the spring breeze; Hetty would approve. Stan had been a godsend, working as hard as he could to get the garden into shape. This morning he'd been planting up potatoes and staking the tomato plants. He was an expert spider-catcher too. She glanced at him, resplendent in a new pair of shiny brown trousers, exactly the same as his old pair, grey chest hair springing through the gaps in his string vest. Rachel didn't think she'd have got through the lonely winter without him.

Thinking about his suggestion, she decided it was about time she got to see the other end of the village. Going to see the church couldn't hurt. 'That's a good idea, Stan. I'll take Piglet down that way for his walk later.'

'Well, make sure you ties him up proper. Can't take him into the church itself, or the graveyard.'

'I promise.'

Rachel hummed with excitement all day, until it was time for Piglet's second walk of the day. With the puppy in tow, she marched down the track, trying to reign in her impatience when he wanted to stop and do a close inspection of every fascinating smell along the hedge. Still, the hours of daylight were stretching out, so Rachel figured she had plenty of time and forced herself to slow down to the puppy's pace.

It was getting on for six before she eventually reached the church. It sat, fat and somehow complacent, in the middle of a graveyard littered with yew trees and mossy headstones. On the little green opposite was the memorial stone. Rachel went closer. Although small and quite simple, she found it profoundly moving, covered as it was with the names of those who had died in two world wars.

Winding Piglet's lead in shorter, to keep him close by, Rachel stood in awe of how many names were etched into the stone. She counted at least twelve for World War Two and there were many, many more from the Great War.

'Too many dead,' she muttered to the uninterested puppy. Peering closer, she saw a Captain Edward Trenchard-Lewis listed, along with a Private Samuel Jones, who must surely be Sam, the stable boy from Delamere House.

It was nonsense. She had never known these men. They had died nearly a hundred years before and yet, here she stood, a hard lump of sadness forming in her throat, trying not to cry.

She brushed an impatient hand over her eyes and told herself off.

Looking closer, hope flared when she failed to find the name she was searching for. There were several sets of brothers listed but no Richard to accompany his sibling.

'Did he survive? Maybe they did marry after all,' she murmured to Piglet, who pulled restlessly at the lead and gave a bark.

'Are you looking for a relative?'

The voice, deep and resonant, made Rachel jump. She turned to face a middle-aged man in a dog collar. He bent and fussed the puppy, heedless of the mud, which was deposited on his trousers.

'Oh, hello.' Rachel felt awkward. How did one address a vicar? It was way outside her experience.

The man solved the dilemma by extending a hand and saying, 'Hello there. Kim Mansell.'

'Rachel Makepeace.' She took his hand and shook it. Kim's was warm and firm – and friendly. 'And no, I'm not looking for a relative. At least not really.'

'Ah, our illustrator from Clematis Cottage. How lovely to meet you. "At least not really," sounds a promising beginning to a mystery and I love a mystery.' He shivered. 'Getting chilly out here. I was just about to make myself a coffee. Want one?'

'Oh,' Rachel was at a loss. She gestured towards the dog.

'Oh, don't mind him. We've one of our own. They can play together.' As if sensing her hesitancy, he added, 'If you're looking for information, I may be able to help.' He winked. 'I promise I won't convert you.'

Rachel blushed. 'I wasn't thinking that at all,' she lied. At Kim's grin she added, 'And a coffee would be great.'

'Come on, then. The vicarage is just over there.' He nodded towards the line of modern houses fringing the green. 'I can promise a decent cup of Italian and we even have Hobnobs, I believe.' He patted his stomach. 'As long as you only let me have two.' He pulled a face. 'On. A. Diet.'

Rachel laughed. 'You're on.'

The house was large and modern. 'Gone are the days of the grand rectory manor house,' Kim explained. They were met by a gentle retriever, who took Piglet under her paw. Kim let them out into the garden, assuring Rachel that it was securely fenced and that Goldie wouldn't do the puppy any harm.

The vicarage kitchen reminded Rachel of the Llewellyn's. It was untidy and homely, with children's artwork and church notices stuck on the wall and was obviously the heart of the home – and the parish. Sat at the kitchen table and nursing a cup of excellent coffee she watched as Kim settled opposite.

'Enjoying the cottage?' He opened the packet of Hobnobs and put them on a plate. He groaned. 'Oh, they're chocolate ones. Get thee behind me, temptation.'

Rachel laughed, deciding she liked him. 'I am enjoying living there, thank you. How did you know who I was?'

Kim answered, his hand hovering over the biscuits, 'Stan Penry. He's a church regular. Village gossip too.' He shrugged an apology. 'The jungle drums ensure not a great deal goes on without everybody knowing about it.' He smiled. 'I would have called, but with the crisis I've been rather tied up. Besides, not everyone welcomes a dog collar on the doorstep.'

Rachel hid her blushes behind her cup.

'And I believe you know Sheila Llewellyn? She's a regular too.'

'I do know Sheila a little. I haven't seen her for a while, though. How is she?'

Kim gave her a close look. 'Coping, I think. And now, my dear, what is it you are looking for?'

'Do you want the short or the long answer?' Rachel said, with a smile.

The vicar rubbed a hand over his stubble. 'Wife and children at swimming club.' He nodded to the nearly full cafetière. 'Lots of coffee left. Fire away.'

Lulled by the warmth in the kitchen – and in Kim's eyes, Rachel found herself telling him the entire story.

'How completely and utterly fascinating,' he said, when she'd finally come to a halt. 'Oh, sorry, look, there are the dogs.' He rose to let them in from the garden and they collapsed in an untidy heap together in the wicker basket in the corner, bringing chilly air in with them.

'And the name you were looking for on the memorial?'

'Richard Trenchard-Lewis. Although it's not clear what happened to him. Hetty is rather vague on the subject.' Rachel couldn't quite keep the disappointment out of her voice.

Kim shook his head. 'I don't recollect any mention of him. There's a roll of honour in the church as well as the memorial stone and he's not mentioned. His brother is on both, of course.'

'Oh.' Rachel sat back, exhausted suddenly. She'd so hoped to find the final piece of the jigsaw here.

'Of course, I've only been vicar here for three years. The cottage was empty when I came. I assume Hetty had died by then?'

Rachel nodded. 'Or was in the care home.' She bit her lip. 'There are so many missing bits of information. Oh, it's all so frustrating,' she burst out. She caught Kim looking at her. 'I've become rather interested in her story. Obsessed, even.'

'Well,' he said mildly, 'if you're writing a book about her, it's understandable.'

'Village grapevine again?'

'I'm afraid so.' Kim grinned boyishly. 'It's awfully efficient.' He poured out the dregs of the coffee. 'You know, though, I may be able to help you, after all. I can check the parish records.' He added, pulling a face, 'Births, marriages, deaths, it's all in there. And, of course, it's possible my previous incumbent may have some knowledge. Certainly of Hetty. He was vicar for over thirty years in the parish before he retired.'

'Oh, could you ask him for me? Or maybe I could visit him?'

'He's living in France nowadays, but I'll certainly give him a call. Ah, our peace is shattered,' Kim said, at the sound of the front door slamming open. Twin girls burst into the room. 'Meet my angels.'

328

Rachel greeted the chlorine-scented pair and their mother, who followed them in. Piglet was petted and it was only when an offer of dinner was extended that Rachel realised how late it had got. Reluctantly refusing the offer of chicken casserole and a lift, she insisted she needed to get home to feed the puppy and could walk.

'I've got my torch,' she said and brandished it.

'Adapting to country living, I see,' Kim said, as he showed her out. 'Good girl. I'll be in touch with any information.'

The light had nearly gone, but it was pleasant walking through the village. Halfway home, however, Piglet protested his weariness by squatting down and refusing to budge.

'Oh, come on, we're nearly there now. Only the track to conquer.' Flashing the torch in the puppy's direction, she was met with two mournful but determined brown eyes. 'I suppose I'll have to carry you.'

She was in the process of lifting Piglet, who seemed a dead weight and all legs, when the Toyota pick-up cruised by. It passed her, but then stopped and reversed.

'Having trouble?' said a familiar voice.

'Oh, Gabe, it's so lovely to see you.' Relief flooded through Rachel. 'The little bugger is refusing to go any further and he's got so heavy.'

Gabe laughed. 'Get in. I'll give you a lift.'

Rachel grappled Piglet round to the passenger door and put him on the seat. Squeezing in beside him, she gave a sigh. 'Oh, thank you!'

'So, Piglet, you been causing problems?' He ruffled the dog's ears. 'What a mutt!'

'One-hundred-percent bundle of trouble,' Rachel said. She put on her seat belt and gathered the dog onto her lap, not noticing the muddy footprints on her jeans. 'And proud of it.' Piglet licked her ear.

Gabe gave her a penetrating look. 'He's really not the sort of dog I imagined you having. If any at all.'

'I know, I know, I'm supposed to be a cat person.' Rachel laughed.

There was a beat of silence. 'You've changed.' He put the truck into gear and moved off.

'I've changed a lot, Gabe. More than you could ever imagine.'

'What brings you out in the dark? I only just caught sight of your torch.'

Rachel explained.

'Ah, Hetty again?'

'Yes, Hetty again,' she answered defensively. 'Only found Edward's name on the memorial, though. No sign of Richard.'

'The brothers, right?'

'Yes.'

'Maybe Richard didn't die in the war? You sure he joined up?'

'Oh yes, it's mentioned in a letter and, anyway, he was exactly the sort of man who would've rushed off to war. I just want to know what happened to them all.'

Gabe changed gear. 'You didn't know these people, Rachel.'

'I know but –'

'But what?' He glanced over.

'It feels as if I do. Some of the stuff Hetty wrote is so vivid, I can picture completely what they were like.'

They were at the bottom of the track and Gabe made the truck pause before attempting the ascent. He turned to her. 'Do you think – do you think this is all healthy, Rachel? It's bordering on obsession.'

Obsession. There was that word again. It echoed so closely her own feelings that it made her angry. She rounded on him. 'You never really understood, did you?'

He reached out for her hand. 'I tried, you know I did. But even the last of them died at least five years ago.'

Rachel flopped back into her seat, the temper leaving her. She was too weary to fight. 'I know. I just want to find out what happened to Hetty, if she really was happy married to Richard.

330

What happened to *them*? And I know I'm close to that last piece of information.'

Gabe didn't respond, but gunned the Toyota's engine as it climbed the track. He parked up, put the hand brake on, but kept the engine running.

Not coming in, then, Rachel thought, morosely.

'You reckon Hetty got married to Richard, then?' he said, finally.

'I think so, yes. It's the logical explanation.'

'Church records?'

'I told you, that's where I've just been. Sipping coffee with the Reverend Kim and his family.'

'No, not the Stoke St Mary church. This was when Hetty lived at Delamere House, right?'

Rachel stared at him. 'Yes,' she said, slowly.

'The big house probably had its own church. Any records will be in there, I reckon.'

'Oh, Gabe, you're a genius!' Rachel cried. She clasped his face between both hands and kissed him full on the lips. Piglet, squashed between them, gave a whine.

They gazed at one another for a second. It was a moment charged with expectation.

Rachel shrivelled back against the car door. 'Sorry.'

'Don't be,' he said quietly. 'It was never a hardship being kissed by you.'

'Just living with me,' Rachel bit out.

'Oh Rach – Rachel.' Gabe pushed a frustrated hand through his hair. 'We just rushed into something, I think.' He looked at her. 'Good while it lasted, though.'

'Yes, Gabe. It was lovely.'

Another moment that teetered on something unspoken, some possibility. Then it was broken.

'Mum would love to see you. She misses you.'

'I miss her too. How is she?'

Gabe shrugged. 'Okay, you know.'

'I'll pop in. Does she like dogs? I could bring this little rascal.'

Gabe laughed. 'Mum loves dogs. He'll be lucky to go back home with you. Just make sure you keep him away from Ned, he gets very jealous.' He put the car into first, obviously impatient to go. 'Let me know when you'll be round. I'll make myself scarce.'

Disappointment flooded through her. 'You don't have to do that, Gabe.'

'No, I know. It'll be easier, though, and I've always got loads to do. Busy bloke nowadays, you know.'

Rachel managed a smile, thinking of Dawn. 'I'm sure. She opened the passenger door and twisted to get out. And Gabe?'

'Yes?'

'Don't be a stranger, will you?'

'I won't, I promise.'

'And Gabe?'

'Yes?'

'Thank you.'

He put his hand up as an answer and, as soon as she and Piglet were clear of the car, swung the vehicle round and disappeared into the night.

Rachel found herself waving. 'Oh God,' she said to the exhausted puppy slumped at her feet, 'I've got a horrible feeling it's not just Ned who might be jealous.'

Chapter 39

She didn't put off visiting Sheila. As promised, she rang Gabe and he arranged to be out. Mike was absent too. Once Sheila had shut an indignant and spitting Ned out of the kitchen and fussed over Piglet, she settled at the kitchen table and took Rachel's hands.

'It's so good to see you again. Looking too skinny, though!'

Rachel could say the same thing, but didn't. Sheila looked thin and pale. 'How are you?'

Sheila batted away Rachel's concern. 'I'm fine.' She looked the younger woman directly in the eye. 'I'm fine, really.'

There was a moment of understanding of what wasn't to be mentioned, then Sheila changed the subject. 'Gabe tells me you've progressed with the Hetty story. Are you still going ahead with the book?'

Rachel nodded. 'I think so, yes. It got pitched to an editor the other week and she was keen.'

'You'll have to fit it in around your other work, I suppose.' Sheila released Rachel's hands and began to pour tea. 'I've been longing to ask you how you've been getting on but, well, it felt a little awkward with you and Gabe splitting up.' She caught Rachel's eye and grimaced. 'Split loyalties, you know.'

Rachel smiled and shook her head. 'I've been meaning to come to see you for ages, but felt the same, really. And then I got talking to Reverend Mansell.'

'Ah, Kim! Lovely man.'

'He thinks he may know someone who can tell me what happened to Hetty after the war.'

'Doesn't the journal cover that bit?' Sheila pushed over a mug. 'Cake? I've got lemon drizzle or coffee and walnut.'

Rachel grinned. 'Would it be too much to have a little of each? I've walked Piglet this morning and the fresh air's given me an appetite.'

'Ah, I thought he looked tired.' Sheila nodded to where Piglet had made himself completely at home in the cat's basket. 'The little love.' She cut slices of cake, put them on a plate and put it in front of Rachel. 'So, this journal only goes up to the end of the war. How frustrating.'

'It's worse than that. The last thing I can find is a diary entry written in 1916. It's as if something happened that was so traumatic it silenced her.'

'Death of her husband, maybe?'

Rachel shook her head and mumbled through cake crumbs, 'No, Hetty writes about that. The first one, that is.'

'But Kim may be some help?'

'Well, he promised to get in touch with the previous vicar.'

'Oh yes. Duncan Wilson.' Sheila nodded. 'He was here for years.'

Rachel started. 'Hetty mentions him!'

Sheila grinned. 'He was the most terrible gossip. If there's information to be had, I imagine Duncan will have it. He lives in Provence now. No idea why, he hadn't a word of French.'

Rachel giggled. Until now, she hadn't realised how much she'd missed Sheila. 'We never did that garden centre and afternoon tea, did we?'

'No we didn't.'

'How are you fixed for next week?'

'Oh, Rachel,' Sheila clasped her hand again. 'That would be marvellous. My two men just can't see the attraction of either,

I'm afraid.'

They laughed. The idea of Gabe and Mike sipping tea from china cups and eating delicate cucumber sandwiches was hilarious.

'Oh, Rachel,' Sheila said, as she wiped tears of mirth from her eyes. 'You have no idea what a tonic you are. Now, tell me the rest of your news. What's this about Stan going to Berlin?'

'He's going with two friends of mine, Tim and Justin. I feel sorry for him, actually.'

'Who, Stan?' Sheila nodded. 'Well, it might all be a bit much for him.'

'Stan will be fine,' Rachel answered, stoutly. 'It's Tim I feel sorry for. I don't think he knows just what he's taken on!'

More laughter.

'And what about you, Rachel,' Sheila asked, once she'd sobered up, 'still with Neil?'

Rachel frowned at Sheila. 'Oh, I was never *with* him, we just meet for a drink or a meal occasionally. We're just friends.'

'Really? Gabe will be pleased,' his mother said gnomically. 'Do tell me more.'

Rachel pulled a face. 'Let me fill you in.'

When she'd finished Sheila looked very smug. 'I told Gabriel there was nothing between you two,' she said, pouring more tea. Without looking up, she said, 'You did know Paul and Dawn have got together, didn't you?' Seeing Rachel's startled expression, she said, 'No? Well, let *me* fill *you* in ...'

Kim's phone call came a few days later, just as Rachel and Sheila were getting back in the car at the garden centre. Clematis bought (a gift for the cottage, Sheila insisted) and an extremely nice tea eaten, they were about to head home.

Sheila sat in silence while Rachel took the call. She'd given in and bought a new mobile. When she clicked off the phone, she turned to the older woman, her face aglow.

'Well?' Sheila demanded. 'Come on, I can't stand this tension a minute longer.'

'Your Duncan Wilson's come up trumps. He's spoken to Kim and we may just be about to solve the last riddle of Hetty's life.'

'What are you waiting for, then? Drive!' Sheila softened. 'Do you mind me tagging along?'

'Mind? I'm not sure I'll manage without you!'

Kim's kitchen was as warm and welcoming as Rachel remembered it.

'Come in, come in,' he cried, taking their coats. 'Coffee's on. Kids are at school and May has made herself scarce. You've got me all to yourselves.' He kissed Sheila on the cheek. 'Ah, how lovely to see you. How are you?'

'All the better for seeing you, Kim.' She settled herself at the table. 'Now, come on, spill the beans.'

Rachel laughed. 'I thought it was me who was obsessed.' She sat next to Sheila and held her hand. It felt right.

Kim frowned and busied himself with the cafetière. Putting the coffee things on a tray, he set it down on the table and joined them.

'I'm not sure you're going to like what I've got to say. It's not good news, or maybe not the news you're expecting,' he began.

'Kim, if you don't get a shifty on, I'll resort to the thumb screws,' Sheila warned. Rachel gave a nervous giggle.

Kim spread his hands. 'Very well, dear lady, I'll tell all. I must explain first that Duncan and I spoke on the phone and he's going to write later in greater detail. This is the brief version.' He looked to Rachel. 'Your Richard Trenchard-Lewis did indeed fight in the Great War.'

'We know that,' Rachel interrupted. 'And was gassed.'

Kim nodded. 'Hetty and Duncan had a conversation at the memorial stone after an Armistice service one November. She became a nanny, you know, after the war. Highly thought of, apparently. Anyway, when Duncan found her, she was angry as Richard's name still hadn't been added to the stone.'

Rachel frowned. She couldn't see Hetty as a nanny, somehow. Then she leaned forward. 'Tell me about Richard. So he died in the war, then?'

Kim gave a wry smile. 'In a manner of speaking. It seems Richard fought at Loos, where there was, indeed, a terrible gas attack, with many men affected. Not by enemy gas, apparently. It was allied gas, which was carried back on the wind.'

'The men were gassed by their own side?' Rachel said in horror.

Kim raised his eyebrows. 'One of the many ironies of that war. Richard came back to be nursed by Hetty and his aunts.'

'Hester and Leonora.'

'Yes, they were both still alive then?'

Rachel nodded.

'I'm afraid not for much longer. Hester died in the flu epidemic after the war and Leonora soon after.'

'Oh, poor Hester,' said Rachel, stricken. She was glad of Sheila's hand in hers.

'Hetty nursed them both, with help from the few remaining staff at Delamere House and all the time was mourning Richard.'

Rachel looked at Kim, beseeching him to tell her what had happened.

'Hetty told Duncan that Richard's nerves had been shattered by what he'd gone through. He was in the habit of riding their friends' horses, I believe?'

Rachel nodded. 'The Parkers'. Neighbours. He loved riding. I think Richard took to exercising the horses. There was no one else to do it.'

'Well, it seemed Richard went out to ride one morning and never came back.' Kim's voice was low and sympathetic. He'd done this many times before, Rachel thought – broached bad news.

'An accident?' Sheila asked.

Kim shook his head. 'That's the problem. No one really knows. The horse returned, riderless and they eventually found Richard. He'd broken his neck.'

'So it was an accident,' Rachel said. She could believe that. From what Hetty had written, Richard was a dare-devil rider.

'The problem is where they found him,' Kim continued. 'It was at a notorious spot, where it was considered far too risky to jump a horse. Too dangerous, for both rider and horse. Richard would have known not to attempt it. He was a skilled rider, wasn't he?'

'Yes,' Rachel said, emphatically. 'Very, and from an early age.'

'So,' said Kim slowly, 'the obvious conclusion is –'

'He committed suicide,' Sheila finished. 'How awful.'

They were silent for a moment. They only sound, the ticking clock on the wall.

Kim blew out a breath. 'No one really knows,' he said, eventually. 'There was some scandal associated and Hetty had to fight to get him buried in the graveyard at Delamere. The assumption was he had ended his life while suffering from the effects of the war. Shell-shock. Post-Traumatic Shock, we'd call it. Apparently she fought Duncan to get Richard's name put on the memorial stone as she claimed he was as much a victim of the war as those who died actually fighting.'

'Oh my God,' Rachel breathed and then remembered where she was. 'Sorry, Kim.'

'I think, in the light of what you've just been told, the phrase is perfectly acceptable.' He smiled. It lightened the atmosphere just a little.

Rachel frowned. 'The thing is, something doesn't add up.'

'What doesn't?' Sheila asked. She poured them all more coffee. They needed it.

'Richard loved horses. Adored them. He wouldn't have done anything to hurt one.'

Kim shrugged. 'The war did terrible things to men's minds, Rachel. He wasn't a regular soldier like his brother. He wouldn't have been prepared for what he had to go through.'

'I suppose,' she began slowly, then added, 'at least he had time with Hetty, though, as husband and wife.'

'Ah, that's the other thing,' said Kim and then dropped his bombshell. 'They never married.'

Chapter 40

A volley of barks alerted Rachel to someone at the front door. It was late in the afternoon and she wasn't expecting anyone.

'Gabe,' she said in surprise, when she opened the door. 'Oh!' she put her hand to her mouth in shock. 'You've cut your hair.' She stared at him, looking unfamiliar with a buzz cut. It made him look older, more serious.

Gabe shrugged in embarrassment. 'Yeah, I had to – well, I'll tell you about that in a minute. Can I come in?'

Rachel opened the door wider and stood back. 'Of course you can. Piglet, come in, boy,' she called to the dog, as he ran out and sped around the garden. He returned, panting, and nosed at Gabe with interest. Rachel laughed. 'If he jumps up, please push him off. I've been trying to teach him how to greet strangers.'

'Am I a stranger, Rachel?'

She smiled up at him. 'Of course not. Can I get you something? Wine, coffee? Tea? I'm afraid I'm out of lager.'

'Tea would be good.' He followed her into the kitchen and sat at the table. 'I never did get around to renovating this,' he said ruefully.

'Well, there's time yet.' Rachel opened a packet of digestives and pushed them towards him. 'Don't let Piglet have any,' she warned. 'He's the most terrible scrounger.'

The dog sat at Gabe's knee, an imploring expression on his face.

Gabe laughed. 'I see what you mean.' Privately, he was amazed at Rachel's new laissez-faire attitude. She didn't seem to mind the drool dripping from the dog's grinning mouth. Looking around, he saw a dog bed generously endowed with hair in the corner, a bowl with a puddle of water surrounding it and a pile of dirty dishes in the sink.

Rachel saw him looking. 'I'm sorry the place is in a mess. I was working. I was so engrossed I didn't even hear your car come up the track.'

'It looks fine. Homely.'

She laughed. 'Well, I told you I'd changed.'

'You did. And you have.'

'All down to this mutt here,' she said and reached down to fondle the dog's ears. Then, filling the teapot, she brought it to the table. 'The first few weeks with him were awful. The mess,' she pulled a scandalised face at Gabe. 'The hair all over the place. I really thought he'd have to go.' She gazed softly at Piglet, 'But every time I'd reach breaking point, he'd flop at my feet and would give me this heart-breaking stare as if he knew exactly what I was planning.' She broke a biscuit into small pieces and gave the dog some. 'I've never had a dog before, never had any sort of pet. I was never allowed. It's been a revelation.' She shrugged and looked around at the kitchen. 'And what with the mess of the building work, I suppose it's eroded some of my worst habits.' She pushed a filled mug over to him.

Gabe blinked. 'Sweet. And Piglet is a wonderful dog. I couldn't part with him either.'

'It's lovely to see you, Gabe. Really, it is.' She gave him a warm smile.

He reached into his pocket and brought out a sheet of paper. 'I've brought you this.' Putting it on the table in between them, it lay there, faintly accusing.

'What is it?'

Gabe smiled. 'Have a look.' He watched her expression change

340

as she read through the document and took in its implication.

'Oh, Gabe!' she gasped, 'wherever did you find this?'

'I went to the church at Delamere. Mum told me what happened the other day. Kim pointed me in the direction of the warden at the estate church there and he helped me find what I was looking for. Well, what you were looking for. I thought it might interest you.'

'Interest me? *Interest* me? Gabe! She married Peter Innisford. Hetty married the man she met at the school during the war. So, *he* was her second husband, not Richard at all!'

'Looks that way. I don't think they had all that long together, though. The parish records show he died in the 1980s.'

Rachel read down to where the details of Peter Innisford's burial were recorded. '1982,' she said, 'they had about twenty years.' She clasped the paper to her breast, her face alight. 'Hetty had twenty years of happiness with the man she loved. It's wonderful.' Tears shone in her eyes.

'So, she really loved this Peter bloke and not Richard after all?' Gabe asked, puzzled. 'I don't think I'll ever understand women.'

'Oh, Gabe, I think she loved all three men but in different ways. With Peter I think, no I *know*, she found some happiness. Thank you, thank you so much. You've gone to such a lot of trouble.'

He shook his head. 'Well, Mum told me how shocked you all were about what Kim Mansell had found out. I thought this might just add that last missing detail.'

Rachel nodded, too emotional to speak more.

Gabe frowned. 'She never changed her name, though? Bit odd. And they continued to use the estate church instead of St Mary's. Why?'

'That's Hetty for you. A puzzle until the last.' Rachel sensed a ripple of amusement shiver around the kitchen. 'Yes, Hetty, you're still keeping us guessing.' She put the paper down on the table and flattened it out carefully. It was a precious thing. 'I'm just so glad she found some peace, some contentment, at last, after all she'd been through.'

341

'And you, Rachel? Have you found some contentment? You look happy.'

'I am,' she replied, but with a wistful note in her voice.

'No Neil Fitch?'

Rachel smiled. 'There was never any Neil Fitch.'

Gabe returned the smile. 'I know. Mum told me.'

'And you?' Rachel asked, carefully. 'Dawn is off to university, with a baby on the way.'

'Yeah. It'll be hard going, but she'll manage. Tough as old boots, is Dawn.'

'But the baby's not yours?'

Gabe's eyes widened. 'Mine? Of course not. Is that what you thought?'

'It's what I was told. By Alan.'

'Don't believe anything Alan says,' Gabe said, without rancour. 'But honestly, Rach. *Dawn*?'

'Well, she was awfully keen on you.' Rachel could feel her pulse miss a beat.

Gabe scrubbed a hand through his shorn hair. He looked, for a moment, like the Gabe of old. 'Yeah, but I'd make sure I put something on the end of it.'

'Gabriel!'

He grinned. 'The baby is definitely not mine. Haven't you heard? Paul is going up north with her. The kid's his.'

'I was having you on, actually. Your mum told me Dawn and Paul had got together.'

'Tease.' There was a wicked glint in Gabe's eyes. 'Just like she told me about Neil.'

Rachel put her head on one side, coquettishly. 'Has your mother been trying to match-make?'

'Well, she's very fond of you,' Gabe said. He pushed his chair back. Coming to stand near her, he took Rachel's hands and lifted her to her feet. 'And so am I.'

Rachel stared into his sherry-brown eyes. 'Only fond, Gabriel?'

342

'More than fond, as well you know.'

'I don't, actually. Tell me.'

'Oh God, Rach, you know I love you. Always have. Even when you were – we were – driving each other nuts.'

'Gabe,' she said, on a shiver of excitement, as her arms slid around his sweetly familiar shoulders. 'Oh Gabe, how I've missed this. How I've missed you. I love you too. So much.'

They kissed. Not just with passion but with understanding and tenderness and love.

'Do you think we could start again,' he said, hoarsely. 'I can't bear not being with you.'

'Oh please. I promise I'll be more tolerant. And I'm so, so sorry about what I said to you.'

Gabe grinned against her mouth. 'And I promise to be more considerate,' he said through his kiss.

More seconds ticked by, the only sound a snuffling Piglet as he watched the humans avidly.

Then, as Rachel ran her fingers over his haircut, she asked, 'Why ever did you cut your lovely hair?'

'Ah.' He disentangled from her and reached into his jeans pocket again. This time he produced a card. It was an invitation.

'"To an exhibition of Gabriel Llewellyn's sculptures in wood,"' Rachel read, with growing amazement. 'You did it! Oh, Gabe, you did it!'

'Well, I had a bit of time on my hands this winter,' he said, embarrassed, 'what with the farming crisis and everything, so I got a few bits and pieces ready.'

Rachel danced around the kitchen, flapping the piece of card. 'And this is only the premier exhibition space in the Midlands. Oh you clever, clever man!'

Piglet, infected by her excitement, barked and joined in.

'Come here.' Gabe pulled Rachel to him. 'I think we need to celebrate, don't you?'

Rachel threw her arms around his neck and kissed him with

abandon. 'I thought you'd never ask!'

For Piglet this was all too much. He launched up at the couple, barking and squealing.

'Down Piglet,' giggled Rachel, to no avail.

Laughing, Gabe swept her into his arms, away from the over-wrought dog. He carried her to the stairs, with difficulty, as Piglet was still leaping up. 'I think there might be three of us in this marriage.'

Rachel froze in his arms. 'You mean it? Are you asking me to marry you?'

'Oh, most definitely! And, if I can stop this ruddy dog from nipping my ankles, I intend to seal the deal.'

'Piglet,' Rachel said, with withering authority. 'Basket. Now!'

The dog slunk away.

She looked at Gabe, lovingly. 'Bed. Now!'

'Oh boy, I love it when you nag,' Gabe said, with a grin. 'Come on, I think we've waited long enough,' and he carried her up the stairs.

Epilogue

A few years later, Clematis Cottage

Piglet is dozing in the shade. A spaniel puppy bounds across the newly laid lawn in front of the cottage. A little girl follows. She is tall for her age and has long, dark hair. In the distance her parents call her but she ignores them.

She chases white rose petals carried by the hot summer breeze. They lead her to the edge of the garden, where she stands under the shade of the chestnut tree. Peering up, against the sunlight flickering through its leaves, her sherry-brown eyes see the figure invisible to all but her.

'Hello, lovely Hetty.'

Acknowledgements

I could not have written this book without help. Thank you to John Lowles and the other volunteer researchers at The Worcestershire and Sherwood Foresters' Regiment Museum who provided information about The Worcestershire Regiment during World War One. Thanks go to the National Trust's Berrington Hall Herefordshire and its 'Experience Room' where I learned about the tragic fate of the three Cawley brothers and which inspired some of this story. Grateful thanks must also go to Brockhampton Primary School Bromyard, whose log book supplied many details of school life during the early twentieth century. I had a happy time teaching there – thank you staff and pupils! Any mistakes in historical research are mine and mine alone. Huge thanks to Charlotte Ledger, Kimberley Young and the team at Harper Impulse. To Nell Dixon: you're a genius at thinking up titles! Lastly, big kisses to those of you who have encouraged me along this journey. You know who you are.